Soot

Andrew Martin

First published in Great Britain 2017
by
Corsair
an imprint of Little, Brown Book Group

First Isis Edition
published 2018
by arrangement with
Little, Brown Book Group
An Hachette UK Company

All characters and events in this publication, other than those clearly in the public domain, are fictitious and any resemblance to real persons, living or dead, is purely coincidental.

A catalogue record for this book is available from the British Library.

ISBN 978–1–78541–473–2 (hb)
ISBN 978–1–78541–479–4 (pb)

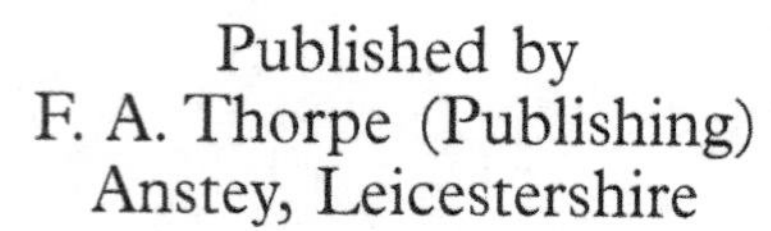

Set by Words & Graphics Ltd.
Anstey, Leicestershire
Printed and bound in Great Britain by
T. J. International Ltd., Padstow, Cornwall

This book is printed on acid-free paper

For Lisa, who bought me a silhouette.

Prologue: September 2012

Sometime after six the train stopped at Vologda. The smokers got up. Diana Maricheva stood too, clutching her school rucksack. She edged past the compartments, their little tables overflowing with tea mugs, beer bottles and abandoned playing cards. Outside on the platform, hawkers were selling herbal teas and packets of dried noodles. Her stomach tightened when she walked past them.

Diana found the toilets and handed over a twenty-rouble coin to the attendant. She wanted to freshen up without inviting any searching questions from the women in her carriage. Inside, she took off her T-shirt to wash her armpits, cleaned her underwear using soap from a dispenser, and then pushed everything back into her rucksack: school uniform, phone and charger, toothbrush and toothpaste. On the platform, she waited for the *provodnitsa* – a conductor of about her mother's age – to check her ticket, before re-boarding the train.

They set off again, and Diana stared out of her dirty window watching the never-ending columns of larch trees roll by. The autumn sun caught her carriage and she turned away, seeing children half her age clamber over the bags and coats spilling into the corridor as they raced each other. In the next four-bunk compartment she saw pink-faced women fanning themselves while listless, bare-chested men spoke in low voices. She tucked her rucksack under her head and went to sleep.

After the train left Tyumen, the carriage filled with the smells of eggs, garlic *kolbasa*, and smoked ham. The two Chinese girls sitting on the opposite bunk opened plastic containers full of rice and fish. One of them gestured to her, making an imaginary bowl with a palm and scooping the contents with chopstick fingers. Diana shook her head, although the two *piroshki* rolls she'd bought for the journey were long gone.

Yesterday her stomach had growled from lack of food. Now it cramped tight as a fist. There was comfort in the pain, the muscles squeezing the shrimp inside her. That's what it had looked like on the internet: a pink, curved creature with a tail, not the start of a baby. Now it was a simple equation. The less she ate, the more the shrimp would disappear. And she was bigger. It would be gone long before her.

The hunger and heat made her drowsy. For much of the three-day journey a dull half-sleep had overtaken her. She yawned, rubbing a hand over her face.

The train jolted to a halt. The two Chinese girls were sitting on the bottom bunk, each with a packed suitcase pressed between their knees. The one watching her turned away sharply as the *platskartny* passengers fought to leave. She waited for them to go, then twisted her arms into the straps of her rucksack. She stood. Her limbs went slack and she felt herself fall back onto her bunk.

When her head cleared, the two Chinese girls were gone, along with most of the carriage. Only two flabby men in sailor's *telnyashka* blue-and-white-striped vests remained. Their suitcases scraped as they dragged them along. They stank of vodka and sweat. She followed them out – at a distance.

Until now, she hadn't thought about where she was going. St Petersburg, with its canals and palaces, was more like Hollywood or Hogwarts than a real city. When her papa was alive they used to sit and watch *The Adventures of Sherlock Holmes and Dr Watson* together. The one starring Vasily Livanov. He told her the station they used in the series was in St Petersburg, not England, but this station didn't look old. Outside, the sky was full of cranes and half-finished buildings; it was hard to believe she was in the same city.

Still – she forced a grin – she had twelve hundred roubles, enough for a night or two in a hostel, and it was sunny, and she was in the most beautiful city in the world, even if the train hadn't stopped in the district she'd expected. She squinted in the daylight. The knotted fist of her stomach gripped tighter as it found something fresh to strangle – she prayed it was the shrimp. Her eyes rolled in her head.

She was sitting on the dusty pavement. The *provodnitsa* from her carriage was leaning over, a hand on her forehead, the mid-blue blouse of the woman's uniform in her face.

Her voice was soothing. 'Are you OK?'

'I felt dizzy.' Diana sat up on the pavement and brushed dust off her jeans. 'I'll be fine.'

'Are you waiting for someone?'

'My mother,' she replied drily. She had been waiting for her ever since her darling *mamachka* had decided to marry the pervert.

She waved the conductor away. 'I'll be fine. I really will. She won't be long.'

After the *provodnitsa* left, Diana thought about accepting help, for a change. The woman had been kind – she might have found her somewhere to stay.

She inhaled warm pastries at a Teremok stall. Her stomach knotted in protest when she kept moving. At the edge of a highway she found a strip of grass and sat down. It was cold. She wanted to wear the jersey in her bag, but it had her school crest on the front. People would ask questions. It was safer to wait. In an hour or two she would be warm.

She found a bench and cleaned her teeth without water. The hunger had made her senses sharp as a dog's. Despite the mint taste in her mouth she could still smell the butter pastries from the Teremok stall. No, it wasn't the stall. A man in a tracksuit was standing three metres away. He was clutching a paper bag with the Teremok logo of a babushka with a fork and spoon. He seemed to be focused on something to her right. She followed his line of sight but there was nothing to see.

He turned slowly, as if he had just noticed her.

Was he even going to eat the pastry? A deep cramp tore at her insides. She wrapped her arms around her stomach and bent forward.

'Excuse me, miss. I saw you at the kiosk.'

She ignored him.

He kept talking. 'The train from the East always arrives too early for breakfast.'

The cramp subsided and she straightened up.

'You look hungry. I bought *syrniki*. I can't eat them all… too rich for me.'

He patted his flat stomach and then laid the fritters down on her bench. He stepped back as if she was a nervous animal he had to take care not to frighten. The *syrniki* smelled better than anything she could remember. 'A kiss of farmers' cheese and sugar,' her grandmother used to say.

'They always give you a little pot of strawberry jam,' he added.

Diana leaned forward as if her stomach was cramping again. The paper bag was twisted at one corner, exposing golden, thick fritters. She imagined dipping a *syrnik* in the jam. It would taste like heaven.

She snatched at the bag and ate the fritter whole while her fingers tore at a second. She ripped the lid off the pot and poured the jam into her mouth. It was super-sweet – the best she had ever tasted. She wiped the pot clean with the pieces of broken fritter.

The man waited for her to finish. 'My wife makes *syrniki,*' he said. 'I can take you to her… if you are on your own?'

Diana Maricheva nodded quickly.

1

July 2017

Elizaveta Kalinina had wanted to do something ever since watching the Bolotnaya protests on television. Facing a long summer at home with Artem and her mother, she finally decided to act. She found the Decembrists on a website hosted in Latvia and followed their instructions to buy a burner phone before calling them. A recorded message told her to leave the new number. Five minutes later her phone rang. The woman on the line was curt to the point of rudeness. "Who are you? What do you do?" And finally, "What can you do for us?"

Almost two weeks after that strange call, she had a text on the phone telling her to go to Moscow Victory Park at noon on the Saturday. She was to wait next to the cross built on the remains of the old brick factory. It was like being in a Stierlitz novel or a Bond film.

Max was half an hour late. He invited her on a trip to the outskirts of the city. He told her it was to check out an eighteenth-century mansion owned by a relative of the Governor. She guessed the real reason was to check her out.

The group's cameraman, Gregor, was in the front passenger seat, and next to her in the back was his drone, carefully packed in Styrofoam. Gregor was bearded and potbellied, and he didn't speak to her for the entire duration of the trip. She wondered if he was paranoid. Later, she would realise paranoia was healthy.

For the journey, Max brought along a ring-binder stuffed with hundreds of pages and penned annotations. On the cover was a handmade label: "Property Register – 2015".

He noticed her interest. 'I'm making a film about the estates belonging to Putin's cronies.'

'A film?' she asked, looking away from eyes the same shade as his faded blue shirt.

'An online one,' he said.

'Don't you have better data?' she asked. '2015 is ancient.'

He shook his head. 'It's all I have. Last year the bastards scrubbed their details from the national database. When I checked, all I found were codes for the owners' names – if the places appeared at all.'

She was quiet for a moment. 'Is it dangerous?'

'A little,' he smiled. 'No more than smoking.'

The trip had been a disappointment. The mansion was closed, and Max and Gregor had kept to themselves while the drone hovered over the property. That evening, she went online and discovered Gregor was Gregor Nikolayevich Bortsov. He was wanted by the police for setting fire to a riot truck parked outside the OMON office on the Griboyedov Canal. He'd also been in *Voina*, the group famous for painting a sixty-five metre penis on Liteyny Bridge. Before the fire brigade could wash it off, the bridge had been raised, erecting a giant *khui* in front of Bolshoy Dom, the city's secret police headquarters. She downloaded an image of it and used it as a screensaver, despite her mother's disapproval.

To avoid choking from Gregor's cigarettes, she opened her window, straining to hear Max.

'We decided to call ourselves the Decembrists last year,' he said. 'They were soldiers who kicked Napoleon's arse all the way to France, then came back with these crazy French ideas of equality and freedom.'

It was a poor choice, she thought. At school, she'd been taught the Decembrists had tried to start a revolution only to be forced over the half-frozen Neva while the Tsar's forces shattered the river ice with cannonballs.

'Didn't they drown?'

'Not all of them… they hung the survivors. Their fate is a reminder for us to be wary.'

Max kept talking, killing her positive mood. 'Last month, two activists were beaten to death. We don't use surnames or share phone numbers. We don't socialise, and we never connect on social media… it's a matter of survival.'

It was a blow. After her first favourable impressions of Max, she had hoped to get to know him better.

He saw her disappointment and misread it: 'If we use social networks and one of us is compromised, the FSB will pass on our details to the street thugs they use to do their dirty work. If you have children they use another trick – social services get a call from them and suddenly you're an unfit mother.'

She felt a cold terror at the thought of losing Artem, but he was also the reason she was sitting in the car with two strange men – it was her responsibility to make sure he had a future. Besides, she would take Artem out of the country sooner than giving him up.

'Do you still want to do it?'

She already knew the answer: 'Yes.'

Max ran a hand through his dirty blond hair. 'Then welcome, Elizaveta.'

October 2017

A group of old women – all headscarves, furs and sunglasses – shuffled past Elizaveta and into the Charlie Chaplin-themed restaurant on her left. She tucked her hands under her armpits. It wasn't a cold day, but after standing still for an hour she was freezing. She checked the time on her phone: 11.48.

From her vantage point, she watched the four Decembrists on the pavement where the Sampsonievsky Bridge rose to cross the grey Neva. A stream of traffic disappeared below their feet into an underpass along the embankment. Max and a beautiful girl with dark hair joined the four. He was wearing his yellow Puffa jacket that was reversible to black. He'd bragged to her about the time he avoided a stupid policeman by turning the jacket inside-out seconds before the *musor* chasing him ran right past.

He pulled a turquoise balaclava over his face, before folding up the bottom half so it resembled a woollen hat.

Liza let out a slow breath.

She tried to distract herself by imagining being in bed with Max. Without a doubt, he would be an improvement on the last time – a drunken fuck six months ago while her mother snored next door. Max had never flirted with her, but she was sure they were compatible. He was only a little older, and unlike those waif-like students who worshipped every word he spoke, he seemed genuinely interested in what she had to say.

She stamped her feet to stop the creeping numbness. A waiter was eyeing her from the Chaplin Hall. She couldn't tell if he was enticing her to go inside the restaurant or curious to know why she had been loitering. She jerked in surprise as her mobile rang. The waiter laughed at her embarrassment. She turned away from him and took off her gloves.

Liza looked towards the group above the underpass. Max had a phone pressed to his ear.

'I can barely hear you,' she shouted.

'They'll be here in two minutes.'

CHAPTER 1

He hung up.

She started walking, turning up the collar of her wool coat. Max was making another call. She saw him raise a hand to Tima in his parked van on the other side of Finlyandsky Prospekt. Seconds later, the van pulled out.

She supposed Tima, the grumpy *mudak*, had been accepted because of his van. In her case, it was her profession. She told Adelina – the woman on the phone – that she was a buildings surveyor, and before that she had studied physics. Adelina put her in charge of logistics for this operation. She took the job seriously, counting the seconds it would take to empty the barrel, calculating the time for the Mercedes to cover the underpass at different speeds. One night she even dropped pebbles from the pavement and measured the intervals before they hit the tarmac below.

For a while she'd had an ominous feeling that everything would go wrong. Before contacting the Decembrists, the worst she'd imagined was a humiliating arrest in front of Artem, and her career ruined by an invisible mark. Now she knew there was far more at stake. She had every reason to be terrified – and yet she wasn't. Her heart was pounding, but her nerves had vanished.

Liza steadied her steps, following the pavement as it rose to meet Sampsonievsky Bridge. By the time she reached the other activists, Tima had blocked one of the lanes with his van. She was close enough to see the black tape fixed to his number plate: it was crudely done, and she doubted it would fool the police. Disgruntled drivers manoeuvred around the van. She heard a creak as the back doors were flung open. Two men wearing surgical masks climbed inside and untied the ropes holding the drum in place.

She caught up with Tima in the driver's seat. He wore a balaclava: an enormous red beanie hat out of which he had cut rough eye and mouth holes.

'What the hell are you doing? You need to be on the other side,' he said, all facial expression hidden.

Liza turned away from him. The adrenaline overriding her fear was making her careless. Max pulled down his turquoise balaclava to hide his face. He was an arm's length from her, with his back to a low concrete wall. Above the noise of the traffic she heard him making a speech into a phone held by one of his students – a young woman with a purple scarf. The remaining two women were wearing colourful balaclavas. They held up a banner with just two words, one above the other:

Retirement
Present

Max's voice was solemn: a priest delivering a sermon.

'Mr Putin, today you will be sixty-five,' he said, 'but instead of retiring, you will cheat your way to the presidency again. We urge you, for the sake of Mother Russia, go now.'

Behind the balaclava, she could sense Max smile. 'I hope your secret police lapdogs in the FSB pass on our present to you.'

A tipper truck went past, drowning out his voice and belching diesel fumes. Liza was distracted by the twinkling of an object above the river – it was the camera drone hovering over the Bolshaya Neva like an oversized insect. She looked for Gregor and found him working its controls from the bridge, a safe distance from the action.

Tima was out of the car now. 'Liza, you can't be here with us. They'll see your face.'

'Don't worry, I'm going.'

She crossed the bridge, her feet seeming to float above it. Her heart was pounding. Nothing was real. She barely noticed the traffic.

CHAPTER 1

Between the four lanes was a dangerous no-man's land for the trams that the cars used as a chicken lane. She stopped there to watch the two men in their surgical masks grappling with the barrel. It slipped from their grasp and fell to the ground. They manoeuvred it into position and removed the metal strip securing its lid. Red liquid slopped out onto the pavement.

By now, drivers were slowing to gawp. She weaved between the crawling traffic, passing a man recording them on his mobile with his elbow extended from his lowered window. She was close enough to rip the phone from his hand but passed his bonnet unnoticed. If the FSB agents in the convoy looked up and saw a masked face, they would react. As it was, they would see her and do nothing.

Gregor sent the drone under the bridge to capture the convoy emerging from the underpass. She feigned interest in the Cruiser Aurora on the far bank of the Bolshaya Neva, holding up her phone to take a picture of the ship that launched the revolution. The blue lights of the motorcade grew brighter. The first of the cars approached, a bulky black jeep bristling with aerials. Behind it was the black Mercedes.

Motorcycle outriders had cleared the way and the convoy was travelling faster than she had expected. For all her efforts, it had come down to guesswork. When the jeep was twenty metres from the entrance, she turned abruptly. At her signal, the two with surgical masks tipped the barrel. Forty litres of fake blood – glycerine, oil, red dye, and God only knows what else – slopped onto the underpass below.

She caught a cheer and saw them lower the barrel to the pavement. Max raised a thumb to her: a direct hit. Below her feet, a reversing engine whined, and she heard a crunch of metal and glass as one car crashed into another.

Everything was still for half a minute. She heard men in the underpass. The plan had been for the Decembrists to disperse, but they were drawn by the new, unexpected drama. She looked to Max, who raised his hands, palms up – he was as unsure as the rest of them. Only Gregor, with his hypersensitivity to risk, was moving. He was walking away from the action, crossing the bridge to Petrogradsky Island. The drone, an exotic pet, trailed after him across the water.

Four FSB bodyguards emerged from the entrance to the underpass. They were crouching low, using the high walls and shadows for cover, each with a pistol in a two-handed grip. They sealed off one side of the bridge. The barrel was smeared in fake blood; it slipped between the hands of the two in surgical masks. On the second attempt they thrust it into the back of the van. Tima wasn't waiting. He drove off before the doors were shut. As he accelerated away, the doors flew open and the barrel bounced on the road, rolling down the slope towards Finlyandsky Prospekt.

Like the old Decembrists, she watched them escaping across the Bolshaya Neva. This time there was a bridge, but it was over two hundred metres long. Panic broke out. Most started running, some yanking off their masks and balaclavas to blend in; others kept them on, fearing identification by the bridge cameras. She spotted Max; he had reversed his Puffa jacket and was jogging purposefully across the bridge, his turquoise balaclava replaced by a baseball cap. Soon they were all out of sight.

One of the FSB bodyguards jogged past her, then stopped and turned. He wasn't any older than her, but he had the swagger that came with power.

'*Ksiva.*'

His voice hadn't been as harsh as she'd expected. If he'd shouted, it might have snapped her out of her fear. She didn't speak. She couldn't take her eyes off his gun. Her *ksiva* – her internal passport – was in her purse and once it was out, the world would stop. He would know she had a child and had never been married. More importantly, it would give him her name, and the address of her mother's apartment.

She had to get away, but it was too late. Her fingers were trembling as she reached into her coat pocket for her purse.

He snatched it out of her hand and drew out her passport, turning to the page with her photograph and name.

'I saw you watching us, Elizaveta Dmitrievna Kalinina.'

She shook her head feebly, unable to put her voice to a lie.

Her non-answer was enough. He grabbed her coat collar and kicked her feet from beneath her, dropping her to the ground. She cried out as her knees caught the pavement. The bodyguard squatted over her, pressing her cheek to the rough concrete with a hand. Across the street, she saw the barrel gathering momentum, leaving a thin red streak behind.

2

January 2018

Natalya Ivanova winced as the police jeep's brilliant headlights reflected off a snow bank, stabbing at her retinas. She straightened the steering wheel of the UAZ-Hunter, then gazed up at the black sky for relief. Barely ten seconds later, she twisted the wheel again to take another bend. It was tight. She jabbed the gear stick into second. The engine screamed with disapproval. The Hunter's military-grade tyres held the road better than she'd anticipated. She took the corner hard, staining the snow bank blue with her emergency lights, and accelerated out of the bend. Chunks of ice thudded on the bonnet from an overhead tree. She flicked on the wipers to clear the debris and kept going. Next to her, Sergeant Stepan Rogov burrowed his head into the fur-lined hood of his parka.

She didn't believe in ghosts – the physical world was fascinating enough – but this part of the city's north-west unnerved her. In these forests, an hour's drive from her sleeping husband, was the largest killing field in the country. From the late 1920s, Stalin's NKVD agents had spent a decade killing thirty thousand of the city's men, women and children. Rounding them up in one purge or another, they delivered the customary bullet to the back of the head at a nearby firing range or else murdered them in *Bolshoy Dom*, the 'Big House' – still the city's secret police headquarters. Nobody knew where the bodies were buried – nobody except the FSB, and their predecessors did the killing, so who were they to say? Thirty thousand people, enough to populate a town. If Stalin's dead could speak, would they be outraged by her concern for one body among so many?

CHAPTER 2

Natalya saw the frosted sign for Kuzmolovsky Cemetery ahead, and eased off the accelerator. A hundred metres ahead, she caught sight of two dazzling white lines on the arm of a Traffic Safety Inspectorate officer. The reflective bands oscillated as he signalled her to stop. She revved the engine to downshift, then gingerly pressed the brake pedal. She needn't have bothered – there was a satisfying crunch as the tyres bit into the snow-covered tarmac. The jeep's four-wheel-drive brought the Hunter to a sharp halt without skidding.

For once, she was grateful for the understaffing during the holiday week – it was the only time she was offered the choice of the department's vehicles.

While Sergeant Rogov remained immobile, she fixed her Makarov in its holster and patted her jacket pockets to make sure she had her torch and latex gloves.

'Rogov, wake up you arsehole.' She punched him on the shoulder.

He swatted at strands of greasy-looking hair stuck to his cheek. She left the engine running to power the emergency lights and lifted the handset to summon assistance. No one answered, and after thirty seconds she abandoned the call. For many reasons she preferred to work alone – efficiency being one, disdain for her colleagues' attitudes another – but a doctor was essential, as well as an expert criminalist to take photographs and catalogue evidence. There was no point thinking about it: with the police budget as tight as it was, she doubted anyone would come two days before Orthodox Christmas.

As the traffic *ment* approached, Natalya observed his squat physique and scowling expression – the stereotypical Traffic Safety Inspectorate officer. In one insulated glove he gripped a regulation black-and-white striped baton as if wielding a club, and in his other he held a cigarette as if it was an intrinsic part of his equipment. She lowered her window; instantly her ears and nose tingled with the cold.

'Sergeant Taniashvili?' she called out.

He strolled casually to her window.

'Captain Ivanova, Criminal Investigations Directorate. You found the body?'

He spoke with the cigarette hanging from his mouth. 'Aren't you too important for this?'

She returned his impertinence with a deadpan expression.

'All right.' Taniashvili's fur-lined hat bobbed. He removed the cigarette with deliberate leisureliness. She caught a mist of sweet alcohol vapour as he replied, 'Two hours ago.'

That explained his sour expression. 'No one relieved you?'

Taniashvili shrugged with his mouth, 'The *menti* told me to wait.'

She cursed the local police. Unless the death was suspicious there was no reason to refer the call to her unit – unless they wanted to preserve their statistics and avoid freezing to death by a forest road in the early hours of Christmas Eve. Still, it wouldn't escape mention in her report.

'I'm here now. Sorry we took so long.'

Taniashvili brought his head to the open window, wafting smoke inside. Natalya fought the urge to bum a cigarette.

'Where's your car?' she asked.

He jerked a thumb behind them. 'I moved it to the cemetery – Kuzmolovsky – after I saw the body. No sense letting some drunk smash into it. Hey, what's with him?' Taniashvili tilted his head in the direction of Rogov.

'Forgot he was on call.'

'Where did you find him?'

'On Sovetskaya Ulitsa… outside Saint Patrick's.'

Rogov had been ignoring her messages. She had found him by persuading her husband, Mikhail, to call and pretend to be interested in a late-night drink.

CHAPTER 2

Rogov grinned in his sleep, revealing nicotine-stained teeth.

Taniashvili said, 'Looks like he's enjoying himself.'

Natalya jabbed Rogov in the ribs. No reaction. She cupped a hand over his ear and yelled, 'Oksana's coming!'

Rogov forced his eyes open. He stared ahead, unfocused, then slowly wiped his mouth with a palm. His hands were shaking as he zipped up his parka. She wasn't entirely convinced the tremor was from the cold. 'Fuck, Boss, what happened to the heater?'

'We're here, that's what happened.'

Rogov was, for some inconceivable reason, Mikhail's closest friend, which made it difficult to reprimand him. To complicate matters, they all worked in the Serious Crimes Unit, where Mikhail was a major, though it was against regulations for a husband and wife to supervise each other. She could only wish the same regulation applied to her and Rogov.

'Who's Oksana?' Taniashvili asked.

'His wife. I hear the Patriarch is considering having her canonised.'

'Mine too,' Taniashvili grunted. He stepped back to let her climb out.

She slammed the Hunter's door for Rogov's benefit. 'Let's look at this woman you found.'

Taniashvili stuffed the cigarette back in his mouth and tethered his baton. She followed him, hearing the clunk of the passenger door followed by Rogov's light footsteps. For a big man, he was surprisingly nimble on his feet. Remarkable, considering an hour ago he was incapable of standing.

Taniashvili stopped at the edge of the road, facing the snow bank, and removed his cigarette. 'She's behind that. There's a drainage ditch on the other side… I only saw her when I stopped for a piss.'

Natalya pointed out an area of broken snow a few metres below them. 'Someone forced their way through there.'

'That wasn't me. I stopped when I saw it, though… I thought I'd stand in there out of the way so I didn't get hit by a car with my *khui* out – that's when I saw her.'

'Did you check her pulse?'

'No need.'

Natalya flicked on her torch and swept its beam over the bank to find a fully clothed woman lying on her back. Mid-twenties, the face could have been sculpted from Moskovsky marble, except for the agonised grimace.

'Did you see her mouth?' asked Taniashvili.

She'd seen it before – or hoped she had. '*Rigor mortis*.'

'Thank Christ.' Taniashvili stuffed the cigarette back between his lips.

She lowered the beam to take in the woman's mid-blue, three-quarter-length coat. All the buttons were intact and secured.

'No obvious signs of injury,' she called out to Rogov.

'I thought maybe she was an *alkash*,' Taniashvili said.

'She took care of herself,' Natalya said. 'Could be a suicide or an aneurism. Maybe a car swiped her or she slipped on the ice.'

Rogov appeared at her elbow, his breath billowing as he spoke. 'Boss, it's fucking freezing out here. Maybe she had hypothermia and got confused. Are we even sure she's dead?'

'I didn't check.' Taniashvili mouth-shrugged again. 'I mean, look at her.'

Rogov wrapped his arms around his waist. 'I heard of this woman a few years ago – she woke up after three days in a mortuary freezer.'

'Tomsk,' he added, as if that explained everything.

'I don't know,' she said. 'I'm not a damned doctor.'

Rogov's tone was conciliatory. 'We should do something… you know, to make sure.'

She felt a prick of guilt at being irritable with him. 'All right.'

Swapping her padded gloves for a latex pair, she leant over the bank. The snow crunched under her weight and she came perilously close to touching the woman's deathly pale face with her own. She ran her fingers along the edge of the windpipe to locate the carotid artery. A murmur of conversation broke out between the two men.

'Keep quiet a second,' she said.

The cold was gnawing at her fingers as she felt for a pulse. Christ, it wasn't her responsibility to do this.

'I can't feel anything,' she said.

She picked up her torch from the bank and shone it into the woman's eyes. The irises were a beautiful shade that matched the mid-blue coat.

'No reaction in the pupils,' she called out. 'Clouding on the corneas… unless that's frost.'

There was a strong smell of cigarettes as Taniashvili leant over. 'You want me to try them again?'

She twisted over the snow bank to look at him. 'Please… see if you can get an ambulance.'

He removed his phone from its pocket on the fluorescent chest-covering of his uniform.

'It's engaged,' he called out after half a minute.

'Of course it is,' she said. 'Don't worry, I've got an idea.'

She stuffed the torch in her jacket pocket then felt for her iPhone. She removed her gloves and stretched over the bank. From ten centimetres away, she could see a filigree of frost coating the skin like a spider's web. Cyanosis had turned the lips blue; the face was as white as a river corpse. Even in Tomsk, she had her doubts this woman could be revived.

There was a waft of perfume and Natalya was struck forcibly by the fact that she had been alive until very recently.

After setting the flash on the phone's camera, Natalya positioned it directly over the woman's left eye. Keeping perfectly still, she touched the white circle at the bottom of her iPhone screen. There was a pause, then a burst of flashes that fought against the Hunter's emergency lights. She stopped, adjusted the iPhone's position to the right eye and pressed the button again.

She pushed herself off the bank and blew on her freezing fingertips.

'Anything, Boss?'

She opened each image. The two men were silent until she had finished.

'Dead.'

'You sure, Boss?' asked Rogov. Without her noticing, he had produced a packet of Winstons and was tapping out a cigarette.

'There's no red eye in the pictures.'

'What's that?' asked Taniashvili.

'Red eye,' she said. 'It's oxygenated blood behind the retina. You don't see it on corpses.'

She caught Rogov tapping the side of his head – a signal to Taniashvili that she was either smart or a lunatic. Whichever it was, she didn't deserve the credit; the red-eye trick had been on a DVD of an American crime series that Leo Primakov, one of the department's expert criminalists, had lent her. She wasn't about to say that out loud, though. It was hard enough being taken seriously.

She returned to the bank and took more photographs of the victim's face, then the body.

'What was she doing out here, Boss?' Rogov called out. 'It's the middle of fucking nowhere.'

She stood, feeling her back crunch as she straightened. 'A Christmas party in the afternoon? Maybe she drank too much and froze to death walking home.'

'A waste,' he said, lighting the Winston.

'With any luck there won't be children,' she said. A thought occurred to her. 'Rogov?'

CHAPTER 2

She stuffed her phone in the back pocket of her jacket, then took out the torch again. Her fingers were stiff as she swept the beam over the body. The snow wall half-collapsed as Rogov joined her.

'Do you see what's missing?' she said.

'No,' said Rogov.

She turned the torch in her hand to angle the beam behind her to the snow-dusted road.

'Do you see now?'

Their eyes met. 'Yeah, Boss,' Rogov said, with a new enthusiasm.

3

Natalya pulled on her insulated gloves. The relief from the cold was immediate. 'You didn't touch anything… or her?' she asked Taniashvili, her expression blank.

The traffic *ment*'s face flashed blue in the beam of the Hunter's emergency lights. 'No. I called you as soon as I found her. I was looking for a place to piss.'

Sergeant Rogov stepped in. 'And did you… piss?'

'Over there.' Taniashvili flicked a finger to the left side of the road, then tossed his cigarette across the snow-covered tarmac.

Natalya studied the traffic cop with curiosity. 'When did your shift finish?'

Taniashvili looked up. 'Six.'

'And you work in the centre?'

'No, Toksovo. I was sent to Piter to cover the holiday week.'

Rogov said, 'If you don't mind me speaking, Captain?'

'Go ahead.'

Rogov sucked on his Winston then wheezed as he exhaled, 'The captain here is making sure you didn't kill the girl.'

Natalya raised her eyebrows, surprised by his bluntness.

Taniashvili's hands were on his hips, his baton jutting out by the movement. 'How dare you. I spent two fucking hours waiting for you… I found her.'

Natalya spoke in a matter-of-fact voice: 'Sometimes killers pretend to discover a body. That way, they can explain away their DNA and clothes fibres. Sergeant, did it snow this evening?'

CHAPTER 3

Rogov took the cue and pursed his lips. 'It snowed from seven until nine in Piter. Looking at the road, I'd say around the same time here.' He swept his arm in an arc over the highway where tyre tracks had blemished a fresh snowfall.

'But there is no snow on her clothes,' Natalya added, taking up her role in the double act. 'She didn't get here until nine.'

Rogov puffed thoughtfully on his Winston, 'You've been waiting for two hours. That means you found the girl around ten. Is that right?'

'So?'

'Answer the question.'

'The news bulletin on Radio Rossii had just started when I stopped for a piss.'

'Then you found her only an hour after she got here?'

'If you say so.'

'It's probably nothing more than chance,' Rogov said, eyeing Taniashvili with suspicion.

The traffic officer read the implied accusation. 'This isn't right… you can't do this to me.'

Rogov held out the flat of his palm towards Taniashvili. 'Don't be offended, my friend, we have to ask these questions, and we have to do it in a certain way.'

Taniashvili scowled at them both. 'Didn't you say she had hypothermia?'

'We've changed our minds. It takes more than an hour to get hypothermia… Besides, she was well dressed.'

Rogov signalled Natalya to step away from Taniashvili. They walked a few paces away for privacy. Above them, pine branches rustled against the glittering black sky illuminated by a half-moon. Rogov stopped to zip up the hood of his parka and she brought her face close to his to catch what he was saying.

'Boss, how long has she been dead, do you reckon?'

'A while. There's stiffness in her face. If I had to guess: this morning or afternoon.'

'What about Taniashvili?' Rogov asked.

'If he killed her, he's not too bright. She'd have been there until the spring thaw if he'd kept his mouth shut.'

Rogov punched out his cigarette. 'Where is his car, Boss?'

'Kuzmolovsky Cemetery.'

'Why?'

She said, 'He told me it was to stop a drunk crashing into it.'

'Or maybe he hit her earlier today and didn't want us to see the damage?'

'Take a look at it, Rogov. Take him along… be gentle.'

'Sure, Boss.'

'Hey, I didn't touch the girl,' Taniashvili called out.

Rogov returned to the traffic officer. 'See, you've been drinking, and so have I. Drinking isn't a sin.' He pulled out a hip flask from his parka pocket and held it out. Taniashvili hesitated, then took it. 'Now let's go for a walk, my friend, and you can show me your car.'

Taniashvili nodded meekly.

'Good man.'

Natalya watched Taniashvili swig from the flask. A moment later, Rogov took out a packet of Winstons and tapped out a cigarette for him. For all his apparent matiness, Rogov was keeping a discreet distance between himself and the traffic *ment*'s baton.

The insides of Natalya's nostrils pinched and she zipped up her collar to bury her nose inside the jacket's fleece interior. The two men were barely visible now, taking the smell of their cigarettes with them. Another ten seconds and they disappeared altogether. Now there was just her, this woman, and thirty thousand of Stalin's corpses.

CHAPTER 3

She presumed the victim had entered the ditch from the roadside. To avoid contaminating the scene, she walked five metres beyond the body, then kicked away at the crystallised ice on the bank until it was low enough to breach. She climbed over to reach the concave ditch with its concrete base. Ahead, the body had been transformed by the Hunter's billowing exhaust into a ghastly apparition. Running beside the drainage ditch was a steep slope to the forest floor. She scrambled up it.

'Ow. Fuck!'

She slipped, scraping her shins on the frozen mud before sliding back into the ditch. The searing pain made her gasp; tears blurred her vision. A stone in the slope was loose, and she prised it out with her fingers to make a foothold. She stabbed the toe of her boot into the hole and leaned out to grab a pine branch with both hands. Her grip held and she heaved herself onto the forest's edge.

The highway was deserted now and she was relieved that Rogov and Taniashvili hadn't witnessed her fall. She crossed the forest floor to the body, trading her insulated gloves for the latex pair. She lay down, the contours of the cold earth stone-hard against her body, and reached for the woman's hand a metre below.

The wrist joint rotated easily enough, but just as cold hid the signs of life, it did the same for death, slowing *rigor mortis*. She looked at the awful grimace again. Perhaps the victim had experienced terrible pain after all. At times like this she fought to keep an emotional distance, convincing herself it was the best way to help the victim. Except she wasn't doing her best, not without a full investigation team. All she could do was log the evidence before it was lost, and hope the pathologist didn't disapprove of her methods.

She shuffled along the forest edge to reach the woman's head. There was no hat – a cause for suspicion, since no one was foolish enough to venture outside in winter without one. She felt the skull for indentations, catching the perfume again. After a while she lowered the head and inspected her own hands for blood, finding none.

She tapped the voice recorder app on her phone and spoke into it.

'Friday, fifth of January, 11:53 p.m. Deceased adult female, aged twenty to thirty, discovered at approximately ten o'clock this evening by Sergeant Taniashvili of Toksovo Traffic Safety Inspectorate. No snow observed on body suggests victim was dumped by the highway around nine. Possible *rigor mortis* in facial muscles, none in wrist. No signs of injury to the head… no hat.'

She checked the coat pockets. Inside one, she removed a grey purse containing two hundred roubles in notes and coins. A compartment in the purse held a number of cards including one for a Sberbank account in the name of "E.D. Kalinina". Another had a picture of the dead woman in a trench coat on a lapsed membership card for the Union of Russian Surveyors.

Natalya undid the buttons on the coat.

She tapped on the recorder. 'No obvious wounds on torso.'

An inside pocket held an internal passport. She flicked through the pages then pressed the button on her phone. '*Ksiva* in the name of Elizaveta Dmitrievna Kalinina.'

The place of birth was St Petersburg and she was twenty-five years old. The photograph, although unsmiling, showed that she had been pretty – not that it mattered.

She felt a sinking in her stomach. There was another photograph in the *ksiva*: Elizaveta Kalinina had a child. She stared at the image of the unsmiling toddler, feeling instant pity for the boy. She took a photograph of his mother's picture and another of the registered address before pushing the internal passport back into the pocket.

Underneath Elizaveta's coat was a knitted pullover with a snowflake pattern that had rucked, exposing white skin. She placed a hand on the underside of the waist and lifted the flesh. It was white: there was none of the bruising she had expected.

She shuffled along the forest's edge to Elizaveta's calf-length boots. She unzipped one, letting the flaps fall open. She rolled up the blue legging underneath to examine the exposed skin. It was purple. She shuffled forwards to peel off one of Elizaveta's mittens – the skin was purple too. She stabbed a finger into the fleshy part of Elizaveta's thumb. The purple flesh turned white. She waited a moment but the area remained pale.

The trouser belt wasn't too tight or loose for the waist. Each button on the fly of the jeans was fastened. She held up the fingers and checked them for abrasions. There was no evidence of violence that she could see. It was as if Elizaveta had laid down in the ditch and died.

She tapped the voice recorder button on her phone. 'Evidence of *livor mortis* from sitting or standing position indicates transportation after death. No signs of sexual assault.'

She heard murmured conversation, then soft, crunching footsteps as Rogov and Taniashvili appeared through the mist of the Hunter's exhaust fumes. They were both smoking and seemed relaxed in each other's company.

'Rogov, can I speak to you a moment?' she called across the ditch.

He took a few seconds to locate her voice. 'Sure, Boss.'

She lowered herself into the drainage ditch and crossed over at the break in the snow bank.

'Did you take a look?' she asked, dusting snow off her clothes.

'Yes, Boss. No dents or scratches – a miracle for a traffic *ment's* car.'

'You all right?' Rogov asked, pointing at the red blotches on the shin of her jeans.

'I slipped. There's something I found,' she said, keen to change the subject. 'The victim has *livor mortis*.'

Rogov's luminous breath expanded as he exhaled. 'You mean the type we see on every stiff?'

She ignored his sarcasm. 'It's on her hands and shins but not her body.'

'Sorry, Boss, I was off the day they gave us medical certificates.'

Was it a gibe? She couldn't tell. 'If a body is left sitting after death, the blood drains into the abdomen, legs and hands. They turn purple while the rest of the body goes white.'

'Yeah, I knew that,' he said.

'After a few hours the blood clots, so the colours remain in the same place even if the body is moved.'

'So this girl?'

She thought of correcting him, and telling him Elizaveta Kalinina had been a woman, a real woman who had reached physical maturity, who suited the colour blue, and wore perfume and childish pullovers, but there really was no use. She might as well recite an Anna Akhmatova poem to him.

'It means this *girl* wasn't lying down when she died. She was in a standing or sitting position for several hours after her death – most likely sitting.'

'So Taniashvili didn't kill her?' Rogov puffed on his Winston nonchalantly, as if he was discussing football.

'No,' she said. 'Not unless he spent the evening driving around Piter with her corpse in the passenger seat for company.'

'Then she was murdered?' Rogov asked.

'Or perhaps she overdosed in a chair and was dumped here. We'll know more after the post-mortem.'

She addressed the traffic officer, 'Sergeant, I apologise for keeping you from your home. We'll be in contact if we need you.'

Taniashvili made a gesture with his arm that was hard to determine against the strobing blue light. She watched him walk back to the cemetery.

CHAPTER 3

'So, what now, Boss?'

'Keep trying dispatch. Ask them to send a forensic team and a doctor as soon as they can.'

'Anything else?'

'That's all. I'll look for blankets in the jeep. We'll stay here until they arrive.'

4

Natalya awoke in darkness. The cartilage crunched in her neck as she twisted to check the time on her phone – 6.05am. The air was stale and stank of Rogov's rank odours. She stretched out her legs on the back seat and pulled the blanket over the exposed skin on her face. With every breath her eyes watered with relief.

She remained in her cocoon for a few more minutes, then lowered the side window to knock away the powdery snow covering the Hunter. It was a pre-dawn black outside and she drew sweet, bitterly cold air into her lungs. In the darkness, sirens were building to a crescendo of wails.

She leant between the front seats, careful to avoid waking Rogov. Her fingers groped for the steering column. She turned the ignition key to the first position to activate the car's electronics. An interior bulb came on and she used it to find the switch on the dashboard for the emergency lights and siren. She flicked the switch and retreated to the back seats.

Brilliant blue lights lit up the interior; the Hunter's siren screamed. Rogov jerked upright. She watched him stare uncomprehendingly at the windscreen. After a few seconds he stabbed a finger at the switch, killing the noise and lights.

In the mirror she caught his scowl. 'Boss, that wasn't necessary.'

'Good morning,' she said. 'I hope you slept well.'

She left him to wake up. Outside, the moisture on her lips tingled as it began to freeze. She grabbed the blanket and draped it over her before slamming the door. Her face creased as she yawned noisily. Trees rustled in the darkness. The sirens were loud now. Beyond the cemetery she caught glimpses of blue lights speeding along the Toksovo highway.

A three-vehicle convoy came into view: a marked police car, followed by a lemon-coloured ambulance and a white van. The police car put on its hazard warning lights to signal to the others and the convoy halted behind her jeep. She parted with the blanket reluctantly, tossing it inside the Hunter.

Inside the police car she saw two male uniformed *menti* in their grey winter uniforms, still wearing their fleece-lined hats. The driver had a pasty face, jowly cheeks, and looked as unhealthy as Rogov. She wondered how men like them ever passed their physicals.

'Captain Ivanova,' she said to him. 'Criminal Investigations Directorate. Tape off this side of the road.' She extended her arm to a point on the strobing snow bank ahead of her Hunter. 'The victim is behind there on a concrete drainage ditch. You see a break in the snow?'

The driver nodded.

'Cordon off a ten-metre strip above and below it. Is that understood?'

'Yes, Captain.' His head bobbed, his jowls wobbling.

She checked the epaulettes on his jacket to make sure he was the senior of the two. 'Notify your command you'll be here all morning.'

'Yes, Captain,' he repeated.

She turned to the other *ment*, a younger recruit sipping an energy drink. 'You get traffic duty. We don't need any drunken idiots crashing into us. Ask someone to relieve you every hour, then take a ten-minute break to keep warm.'

Light glowed where the rear doors of the ambulance had been opened by the driver, a well-built woman in blue overalls. She removed a stretcher with extendable legs and fiddled with the folded plastic sheet on top. A doctor appeared behind Natalya; greying, moustachioed, and in his forties.

His eyes twinkled as he spoke: a ladies' man. 'Happy Holidays!' he called out, seemingly without irony. 'Is she dead?'

'Happy Holidays,' she replied, injecting the right amount of sarcasm. 'There's *livor mortis* and her pupils don't respond to light.'

'That's dead enough.' He shook his head slightly at the driver and she began unfolding the plastic sheet – a body bag.

'It's a crime scene too.'

'Then we'll wait inside if you don't mind.'

The small white van was parked behind the ambulance. From the rear doors, its occupant was extracting a silver case which matched the grey-silver parka he was wearing. He left the case on the van's roof and returned to the cab for a white, nylon over-suit. He performed an exaggerated shudder after taking off his warm parka. She was glad they had sent Expert Criminalist Primakov; he was quietly efficient and honest.

'Leo.'

He glanced up. 'You look tired, Captain.'

'Thanks.'

'I didn't mean…'

'Don't worry, and you're right, I spent the night trapped in a sealed jeep with Rogov… you can imagine.'

Primakov wrinkled his nose in disgust. 'What do you want me to do?'

'You can talk to me. The victim's name is Elizaveta Kalinina. She was dumped here after the snowfall yesterday evening.'

She ran a hand across her eyes. 'Jesus, Leo, I'm so tired I can't think.'

Primakov sat on the edge of the driver's seat and fed his legs into the over-suit. His trousers were padded and he was struggling to thread them. 'I thought that might be the case. I brought you something, Captain.'

'You don't have to.'

Maybe he was just being friendly, but she was sure it was guilt. On a previous case, State Security had forced him to work against her. There was no need for him to worry, though, she really hadn't taken it personally; the FSB usually got what they wanted, one way or another.

'There is… have a look in the back.'

'All right, but you don't owe me anything.'

She opened one of the van's rear doors. Inside, the walls were lined with stainless steel shelving. One area held a number of containers resembling safety deposit boxes. On the floor was a portable generator chained to the far wall next to plastic crates full of aerosols, tools and bottles of chemicals.

He met her at the door. His legs were inside the over-suit and he was threading his arms through with more success. He zipped it up the front, then picked up a thermos secured by a bungee cord to a shelf. He detached the cup from the flask and poured some of the contents into it.

'Monsoon Malabar,' he said, offering it to her. 'I have a friend in Amsterdam who sends some every now and again.'

'I hope it's just coffee he sends.' She tapped the cup with a varnished fingernail. 'Thanks. I needed this.'

He followed as she walked to the site. There was an interior light on in the ambulance's cab where the doctor dealt out playing cards to the driver. Ahead, the two uniformed policemen were threading tape between traffic cones to form a makeshift barrier. Rogov was standing over them, a Winston in his hand, undoubtedly administering words of wisdom. His jaw slipped open when he saw her coffee.

She held up the cup, took a sip and swilled it around her mouth, twisting her face in delight as if it was the finest coffee she'd ever known.

'You got more of that?' he called out.

She pretended not to hear him and turned to Primakov. 'You see that gap?'

'Yes, Captain.'

'That's where I think the person who dumped the victim broke through.'

'Why here?'

She shrugged. 'It's away from the city, and if a traffic *ment* hadn't found her before last night's snowfall she'd have been hidden until spring.'

'There are hundreds of *dachas* out here,' said Primakov. 'This area is full during the holidays.'

'I've been wondering that myself. Perhaps she was partying at one and overdosed. Someone didn't want any trouble, so they brought her here.'

Rogov joined them. 'Or murdered her and dumped her here because he heard this place is full of stiffs.'

'He?' she said.

'Well… you have to admit it's more likely.' Rogov jerked his cigarette in the direction of the ambulance driver in her cab. 'She could do it, I reckon, but not many others.'

'OK, we'll say it's a man for now.' She took another sip of the coffee.

'So the victim was visiting a *dacha* nearby, or else she was dumped here because it's quiet' – she acknowledged Rogov's sensible, if callous, suggestion – 'and he'd heard this place used to be a killing field. Then what?'

'He broke through the snow wall and then went back for her,' Rogov said.

'So two trips?'

'Unless he's built like a T-34.'

'What about tyre prints and footprints?' asked Primakov. 'When he kicked the wall or parked here – there must be traces.'

'Not now. Everything is under five centimetres of snow. I had no way to protect the site last night.'

Primakov bent down and picked up a handful of icing-sugar snow in a gloved hand; he examined it, then blew it away. The particles of snow ballooned as they mixed with his frozen breath, before drifting slowly to the ground. 'There's always a way, Captain.'

She shivered and took another sip of the coffee – it had already turned cold. Primakov was returning to his van and she found an excuse to accompany him in the hope of getting more.

'What are you looking for?' she asked.

'A stove.'

If Primakov had been in the least part heterosexual, she might have contemplated divorcing Mikhail for that answer alone. With his blond curls and tight body, he could also double as an Apollo or Adonis, or some other Ancient Greek who required a certain amount of idolatry. If nothing else, he was a reminder she needed to visit her gym. The last time she had taken out her membership card, it had been to scrape the ice off her windscreen.

She emptied the cup onto the road while Primakov sat hunched inside the van.

'You brought food too?'

Primakov looked up and frowned. 'Food?'

'The stove?'

'Oh… not for food.'

He crawled out clutching a Primus and a silver hairdryer. 'I didn't think…'

She changed the conversation quickly. 'What are you using that for?'

'For the tyre print.'

'To take a mould between two layers of snow?' she said.

'Yes,' he replied, as if it was obvious. 'Can I borrow Rogov?'

'Only if you keep him.' She put her hands to her mouth and yelled into the gloom, 'Sergeant!'

A minute later he came into view. He ostentatiously wiped grease from his mouth with a palm. The lucky bastard had blagged food from the uniformed *menti*.

'Primakov needs a hand,' she said, trying to keep the raw envy out of her voice.

She watched the expert criminalist drag a small generator to the lip of the van. Rogov took it from him and lugged it to the edge of the taped area. Primakov meanwhile had stuffed the hairdryer and stove into a holdall along with one of his chemical bottles. As he left for the crime scene she helped herself to another cup of the Monsoon Malabar. She stayed by the van drinking it until it was all gone.

By the time she returned, the generator was running. Primakov had connected it to a hairdryer he was using to blow the top layer of snow from any promising areas. A few metres away, Rogov squatted by the stove, staring into a stainless-steel jug containing yellow powder. He was wearing a pair of blue overshoes and she imagined the squabbling that must have occurred before Rogov relented and put them on.

'It's melting,' Rogov said. He began stirring the contents with a glass rod.

'Good.' Primakov turned away from the snow bank. 'Now turn the heat down. Be gentle.'

The senior of the two uniformed *menti* was wearing blue overshoes and latex gloves. Primakov had him looking for depressions that might indicate footprints hidden by the last snowfall. The next job would be to lift the snow off the concrete drainage ditch to check for any clues underneath. That, and several other tasks, would normally be done with at least a dozen officers scouring the whole area. Still, there was no point working herself up over the lack of manpower.

'Here, Captain.' Primakov's voice was hurried, full of contained excitement.

He waited for her to join him.

'What's up, Leo?'

CHAPTER 4

'Yesterday evening it wasn't so cold,' he said. 'When the snow fell, it was heavier… more moisture.' He picked up a handful and let it fall to the ground. 'Then overnight the temperature dropped to minus ten. That snow was powder, like you see at a ski resort.'

She bent over a thirty-centimetre strip he had cleared with the hairdryer. Below it was the earlier layer with a tyre mark.

'Shit, it's gone orange.' Rogov called, 'And it smells like rotten eggs.'

'Just take it off the heat and keep stirring. Try not to inhale, the gases are poisonous.'

Knowing Primakov's understated manner, the fumes were probably deadly and she hoped Rogov would take the warning seriously.

She looked at the tyre mark again. It had no distinguishing features and she couldn't understand Primakov's sudden enthusiasm. Not only that: Taniashvili, the traffic cop, had been standing in the road, waving his baton and forcing cars to drive around him. It was reasonable to expect tyre prints from other vehicles.

'It's unlikely to be the car we want,' she said.

'That's why I started close to the break in the snow bank. Whoever dumped her pulled his car in close: less distance to carry the body and more space for cars to overtake.'

'And you found this?' She peered at the print; there were none of the ridges and grooves characteristic of a tyre. 'Leo, there are no markings on it.'

'Yes,' he said, the excitement back in his voice. 'Don't you see what it is, Captain?'

'A bald tyre?'

Primakov shook his head. 'They would have crashed long before leaving the city.'

She grinned. 'It's a skid mark, isn't it?'

Primakov nodded.

She said, 'What are the chances someone would brake on this exact part of the road unless they were stopping?'

'Exactly, Captain. I'll find the actual tyre print at the end of the skid. I'll see if I can get some boot prints for you too.'

Rogov let out a hacking cough. 'It's ready,' he called out. 'What is this stuff? It's evil.'

'Sulphur,' Primakov said. 'Are you sure it's ready?'

'Yeah, it's thin with tiny lumps in – just like you said. Oksana has her oatmeal porridge the same way. Except hers doesn't smell like the devil took a shit in it.'

Primakov inspected the stainless-steel container. 'Thanks, Stepan.'

Rogov lit another Winston, and wrinkled his nose.

5

More staff had arrived at nine, along with her boss, Lieutenant Colonel Dostoynov – a well-built man of the type who reduced their hair to stubble at the earliest hint of baldness. He ordered the road to be closed, forcing the well-heeled traffic from the *dacha* communities to detour via the Sortavala Highway. By then a weak sun was up, casting a silvery light through the trees. Despite a suggestion from Dostoynov that she go home to rest, Natalya found herself making excuses to loiter. For a while she watched four uniforms lift the snow from the drainage ditch and place anything of interest into evidence bags.

'Captain, have you seen the boot?' Primakov called out.

She tried to shake off her exhaustion. 'Where?'

'In the van. Be careful it hasn't set.'

Dostoynov's BMW had taken the place vacated by the ambulance after it left for the morgue with Elizaveta's body. She walked behind it, the snow now flattened and dirtied by dozens of police-issue winter boots. At Primakov's van, she opened the doors to find a container the size of a shoe box. On its lid was a plastic bag containing a pair of Polaroid photographs to indicate the print's location on the snow wall. Inside, nestled in tissue paper, was an orange sulphur cast. At fifteen centimetres, she was disappointed to see it was only a partial print covering the toe to instep.

She felt Dostoynov's presence next to her.

'What do you think, Captain?'

She could only envy the way Dostoynov commanded the Serious Crimes Unit. His decisions were never questioned, nobody sought out another officer for a second opinion; subordinates simply got on with the job without a voice being raised in anger. The only way *she* was taken seriously was by adopting the tone of a humourless bitch who snapped at the slightest infraction.

She glanced at Dostoynov's boots; they were shiny enough to make a cavalry officer proud. 'A man, Colonel. With feet narrower than yours.'

'Murder?'

'I didn't see any wounds, but she didn't get here on her own.'

Dostoynov rubbed the top of his head through his *ushanka* and she wondered if the lambswool lining was irritating his scalp. 'Was it a spontaneous act… her being dumped here?'

'Hard to tell. There aren't many places to hide a body in winter, planned or not.'

'A capercaillie?'

So he was learning police jargon too. A capercaillie was a large grouse favoured by hunters, though in *menti* slang it was an unsolved crime that would eat into Dostoynov's statistics. As much as he exuded natural authority, Dostoynov had used his FSB connections to skip the two decades' experience of serious crimes that normally marked a senior officer in the Criminal Investigations Directorate.

'Too early to say, Colonel. Whoever put her here didn't bother to cover his tracks… that gives us hope.'

He tapped the side of the box with a gloved hand. 'Half a boot-print or even a tyre mark isn't much… we'll soon hit a dead end.'

'Yes, Colonel, but if we find a suspect, we can link them to the crime scene… also there may be more clues. We got lucky here, her body should have been hidden until April.'

CHAPTER 5

'Who was she? A *prostitutka*?'

'A surveyor.'

Dostoynov's face was an impression of neutrality, but his day had just got worse. Elizaveta was a citizen, not someone whose death could be written off as an occupational hazard: a *prostitutka* was a regular-sized grouse, not a capercaillie.

He stamped his feet and the plume from his breath was thick as he exhaled into the morning air. 'You spent all night here?'

'I'll take a medal if you're offering one, Colonel.'

He glared at her for a split second. 'I'll put you in charge of the case, that's the best I can do. Will you see the woman's family this morning… after you've freshened up?'

'Yes, Colonel.'

'She lived in the Ozerki area. Not a bad place.'

'No,' she agreed. Elizaveta was a middle-class woman, not a prostitute.

'Tomorrow is Christmas, you should be with your family,' he said somewhat elliptically.

'Yes, Colonel.'

'Are you cooking?' Dostoynov asked.

'I'm hoping Mikhail will this year.'

She smiled to make it clear it had been a joke, though his reminder was making her feel stressed at the amount of work she needed to do at home.

'Well, whatever you do,' he patted her lightly on the shoulder, 'get some rest. And try to have a happy holiday,' he added cryptically.

6

There was a festival atmosphere as she drove the Hunter into the heart of the city. Well-dressed shoppers shuffled along Nevsky Prospekt, their arms weighed down by shopping bags. Strings of bulbs and decorations had been fixed between buildings and trees to be illuminated at dusk. Even the Troitsky Bridge had a coating of hoar frost that made it look more beautiful than she could remember.

Next to her, Rogov was on his phone, hatching a plan to meet up with Mikhail for drinks.

'Saint Patrick's,' he said out loud, as if he was issuing directions to a taxi driver.

She bristled, then changed direction. Saint Patrick's – the bar where she had found Rogov – was on the way home from police headquarters on Suvorovsky Prospekt and they often used it as a stopping point.

Rogov hung up.

'You don't mind?'

'Mind? You're doing me a favour. The last thing I need is Mikhail moping around the apartment. Promise me you won't get him drunk. Anton's mother is coming tomorrow.'

'Misha told me. I can't believe you're letting Dinara have dinner at yours?' He chuckled. 'Isn't she bipolar?'

'Something like that,' she said, feeling oddly protective of Mikhail's ex. 'But still.'

'It wasn't my idea. We wanted Anton to be with us for Christmas, Dinara wanted him too. Misha suggested a compromise.'

CHAPTER 6

'Shit, some compromise. You'd better make sure he locks up his Makarov.'

'Dinara's not that bad,' she said. Her flat tone did little to disguise her feeling that it was going to be awful.

'Hey, wait.' She stopped the Hunter by a pavement where a *babushka* wearing at least five layers of clothing had her hand extended for alms. The woman shrank from the sight of the police jeep, then relented when she saw Natalya passing a one-hundred-rouble note to Rogov. The *babushka* murmured a blessing as Rogov pressed the note in her hand.

She drove on.

Rogov frowned. 'I hear Misha's in the soup?'

'Who knows? Maybe.'

'It's just that…'

'He shouldn't have been such an arsehole to Dostoynov?'

'Yeah…'

Colonel Vasiliev, their old boss, had let Mikhail believe he would be the obvious choice to take over the Serious Crimes Unit on his retirement. Then with a month to go, Dostoynov had been parachuted in. For the brief period when they were rivals for the top job, Mikhail had been petulant, relentlessly needling the ex-FSB man. Now Dostoynov would most likely force Mikhail to quit. It only remained to be seen how he would go about humiliating him. For Dostoynov to do anything else was to show weakness. As a wife, she ought to be more sympathetic, but Mikhail had brought it upon himself.

'Rogov, can we change the subject?'

He rubbed the stubble on his chin. 'Sure.'

They slowed at a crossing. The sky was grey, but it was nothing compared to the conditions in the south. Despite the centuries-old rivalry between the inhabitants of St Petersburg and Moscow, she could only feel sorry for those in the capital, where a great cloud had hung over the city and they had seen just six minutes of sunshine in the whole of December.

'Do you ever wonder why you bother?' she said.

'What do you mean?'

'Everyone knows the country is run by crooks. What does that make us?'

'While you're being treasonous, Boss, mind if I smoke?'

'Yes, I mind.'

She turned onto 3rd Sovetskaya Ulitsa. He pushed a Winston into his mouth in anticipation of lighting it the moment he left the Hunter.

'My point is,' she said, 'why do we pretend everything's fine when it's not?'

'If I may say so, Boss, you think too much. The law catches flies and lets hornets go free. Well, it's a good day for me if we find the fly who dumped that girl and put him in one of our nice hotels with shitty room service. I'm happy being a fly-catcher. When you start chasing hornets let me know so I can go away with Oksana… far away.'

'Thanks for your support.'

'I'm serious, Boss. All those people who say you have to stand up to make a difference…well, they are selfish arseholes.'

After dropping off Rogov at Saint Patrick's, she parked the Hunter outside her apartment block. She sidled round a heap of traffic-tainted slush to reach the metal door to her building. Usually it took weeks for street cleaners to clear the pavements but in the Moscow suburbs they had worked out a solution. There, the residents spray-painted the mounds with the name of President Putin's nemesis Alexei Navalny, the anti-corruption campaigner. Then, by some miracle, the snow vanished overnight. She was tempted to do the same, but she would face an instant dismissal if caught.

CHAPTER 6

Her pre-revolution block with its high ceilings and elaborate cornices was in the historic district of St Petersburg, and it wasn't modest for two married police officers. In headquarters, most had reasons of their own not to question another *ment*'s wealth, and the few who did were told the same story: Mikhail had inherited the money from his mother, Violka. She had believed it too, until last year when a query over an unpaid bill led her to an offshore account. Then, when she threatened to divorce him, Mikhail admitted that he'd pocketed a bribe for getting a mafia bull off a manslaughter charge. Since his admission, there had been an uneasy truce between them. Once he got rid of his dirty money, she would drop her threat to leave him – but it wasn't so easy when some had gone towards buying their apartment.

The journey home in the Hunter had thawed her but she was still exhausted. Once inside she took off her clothes, climbed into the shower cubicle, and stayed there until the water ran cold. In her wardrobe she found a dark-blue trouser suit and a butter-coloured blouse that was serviceable provided she kept her jacket on to hide the creases.

The journey to the Ozerki district of the city had taken little time and she pulled up outside a new five-storey block with a sandstone façade and modernist curves.

She pressed the buzzer.

'Yes?' The voice came through the speaker almost immediately.

'Is this the residence for Elizaveta Dmitrievna Kalinina?'

There was no reply. She held up her police identification card to a small camera lens. 'My name is Captain Ivanova of the Criminal Investigations Directorate. May I come in?'

The block door opened with a click. Inside, she took the elevator, smoothing her blouse on the way. On the fourth floor a woman was waiting outside an apartment. She was fifty or so, with round features and blonde hair with steel-grey roots. The eyes were swollen but there were no tears in them. Natalya recognised the similarity to her own mother. Not in looks, though they could have passed for sisters easily enough. It was in the stoic expression – the bracing, the wincing. They were woman who took masochistic pride in their ability to take raw emotion, wrap it into a ball, and then swallow it whole. She wore an old-fashioned pinafore and was fussing with the ties as she took it off.

Natalya spoke above the noise of a television cartoon playing inside. 'Does Elizaveta Dmitrievna Kalinina live here?'

The pinafore was pulled off and held in a bunched fist. 'I'm her mother.'

'Mrs Kalinina, may I come in please?'

'Of course.'

Natalya followed her into a spotless kitchen that smelled of detergent. Liza's mother had been waiting in the apartment for her daughter to return with nothing else to occupy her mind. There was an anti-bacterial spray on a surface. Mrs Kalinina picked it up, then a moment later stared at it, wondering what it was doing in her hands.

'What happened to Liza?'

'I've got some—'

Natalya stopped. The jazzy theme music to *Masha and the Bear* filled the kitchen as a door opened. A boy of no more than two years old waddled in.

He glared at Mrs Kalinina. 'Baba… *Medved*,' he said.

'Who's this?' Natalya knelt in front of him.

'Artem… Elizaveta's son.'

The boy grabbed his grandmother's shin and tried to drag the woman towards the living room. The next few minutes would change the course of his life and yet he was oblivious to anything except the next episode of his cartoon. Natalya fought against the desire to ruffle his hair or put a comforting hand on his shoulder. She realised the instinct to protect was for her own sake, not his. The guilt at bringing pain to their door.

'Artem, go and play,' his grandmother said.

'*Medved,*' he repeated.

'You want the bear? All right, I'm coming.'

Artem returned to the room he had come from. Elizaveta's mother followed him. The theme music started again and Mrs Kalinina returned.

'You need to prepare yourself, Mrs Kalinina.'

Elizaveta's mother gripped the pine kitchen top and tensed like a prize-fighter expecting a punch.

'The police found your daughter this morning on the Toksovo highway.'

Mrs Kalinina was silent for a few seconds. 'Liza – she's called Liza.'

'Liza is dead.'

She put a hand on Mrs Kalinina's shoulder and the woman leant into her. She felt shudders as the woman sobbed silently.

Elizaveta's mother stepped back as if embarrassed by the outburst of emotion. Her body heaved as she let out a massive breath.

'A car accident?'

'No,' Natalya said.

The hand gripped the pine top. 'How?'

'We found Liza by the roadside. The pathologist will be called; until then we won't know how she died.'

'Mrs Kalinina,' she added, 'I need to ask you some questions. I can do it another time but it would help if I could speak to you now.'

Elizaveta's mother turned to the open door where *Masha and the Bear* was playing. 'I guess he's mine now. I thought I'd finished with all that.' She spoke as if motherhood had been a chore she was glad to leave behind. Her brown eyes told a different story; they stared ahead, sucking up the pain.

'Who is Artem's father?'

'Alexei… Alexei Stotsko. Liza met him on her first job after graduating. He ran away like a scared little lamb when he got her pregnant.'

'Does he visit?'

'Not in two years, and Liza never asked him for anything either.'

'When did you last see her?'

Mrs Kalinina stared ahead, unable to meet her gaze. 'Yesterday morning. She left at one and told me to expect her home in the evening.'

'Where was she going?'

Liza's mother shrugged her shoulders. 'She said she was having lunch with Katya, a friend from her old antenatal class.'

'Have you got her address?'

'No, but Liza left her VKontakte account open on the computer. I messaged Katya after putting Artem to bed. She told me they had no plans to meet.'

'Did Liza take her phone with her?'

'No. When I called her it started ringing in her bedroom.'

The intercom in the apartment let out a long buzz. Natalya turned to a small screen fixed to the wall and saw two faces: a man and a woman. They looked official and she wondered for a second if Dostoynov had forgotten that she had agreed to inform Elizaveta's next of kin. The man didn't look familiar, but the woman did. She was blonde, pretty, no more than thirty. His shoulder partially obscured her face. Still, there was something there that triggered a memory.

An ID card covered the screen and Mrs Kalinina squinted to read it.

'Yes?'

When the man spoke, his voice sounded waspish. 'Investigator Ilya Yelin, *Sledkom.*'

And there it was – the only words that needed to be said. *Sledkom*, the shortened name for *Sledstvennyi Komitet*, the Investigative Committee.

CHAPTER 6

They imagined themselves to be the Russian FBI, a well-funded elite who only dealt with the most serious cases. She disliked *Sledkom* on principle. They often went after the blameless on behalf of the guilty. On the Kremlin's orders they had once prosecuted an innocent man. Not only had he been innocent – his funeral had taken place in Preobrazhenska three years before the court case began. Even Stalin hadn't sunk to the absurdity of putting the dead on trial.

At the door, Ilya Yelin was wearing a red, all-weather jacket over his suit, and his sandy hair had been trimmed and feathered to perfection. He was slim and a good twenty centimetres taller than Natalya. The woman he was with hadn't surfaced.

Yelin's eyes narrowed, lending him a waspish air to match his voice. 'Are you *menti*?'

'Criminal Investigations Directorate.'

'Which unit?'

She felt in her pockets for her purse and removed her ID card. 'Senior Detective Ivanova, Serious Crimes.'

Yelin's identification card flashed between his fingers to show that he was following protocol if nothing else. 'Main Investigations Directorate.'

Natalya turned to Liza's mother. 'Do you mind if my colleague and I take a look in Liza's bedroom?'

'It's the second room on the left. Don't make a mess, I want it left the way she had it.'

Yelin followed her to the bedroom. Inside, the colours were neutral and there was little of Elizaveta's to suggest it was anything other than a guest room. She supposed Elizaveta had moved back in with her mother when she fell pregnant.

There was a laptop on a dresser. Yelin jerked the attached mouse and the screen came to life, showing the massive painted penis on Liteyny Bridge.

'Nice girl,' he said.

She closed the door behind Yelin. '*Sledkom* on Christmas Eve,' she said, 'this is a real honour.'

'Yeah, Happy Holidays.' Yelin unzipped his all-weather coat. 'At least you saved me the unpleasant part.'

Natalya stepped up to him. 'So you're an Investigator in the Investigations Directorate of the Investigative Committee. Anyone would think you were trying too hard to be taken seriously.'

He sighed in response, as if she was barely amusing.

'So what's your interest?' she asked.

Yelin lowered his head to hers. 'We're taking the case. That's all you need to know.'

Natalya dropped her voice to a whisper. 'Isn't it beneath you? As far as I can tell, she wasn't a terrorist or rich.' She paused. 'She is dead though. Perhaps you were thinking of arresting her.'

Yelin gave her a thin-lipped smile, little more than a sneer. 'Like I said, it's ours now. Let's keep this civilised.'

Natalya held up her hands, 'OK, it's your case and I'm going home. I'll send my notes and evidence when I'm back in the office.'

Yelin was pulling on latex gloves. 'Why don't you tell me what you've got now and save us some time?'

'With her mother and son in the apartment? Have you no shame?'

'Apparently not. In any case, I thought you wanted to go home. A call from my colonel to yours and—'

'—All right, no need to get heavy. A traffic *ment* found Elizaveta in a drainage ditch behind a snow bank on the Toksovo road. No visible signs of injury or sexual assault. Whoever dumped her left tyre prints and boot marks. Send a request and I'll have our expert criminalist forward the casts he took. The pattern of *livor mortis* indicates she was left in a sitting or standing position for some hours after death, then moved. There were signs of *rigor mortis* in the facial muscles, suggesting her death occurred early evening.'

'You're a pathologist now?'

'Just trying to help. Timing coincides with Liza telling her mother she was meeting her friend Katya for lunch and would be back in the evening. Katya denied them having any plans – you can find her on Liza's VKontakte friends list.'

'What about the kid's father?'

'Alexei Stotsko – they split a while ago...unlikely to be involved.'

'What about the traffic *ment*?'

'Sergeant Taniashvili, based at Toksovo. She'd been in the ditch for an hour when he found her.'

Yelin arched an eyebrow. 'How do you know that?'

'It snowed in Piter from approximately seven till nine. There was no snow on the body, so she must have been dumped later.'

Yelin ran the sole of his shoe over the bedroom's tiled floor; it left a dark mark from the rubber. 'The girl's in the morgue now – I'll have to take your word that there was no snow on her.'

'You don't need to. I took pictures on my phone.'

'You'll send them?'

'Anything for *Sledkom*.'

He ignored her sarcasm. 'So what do you think happened to her?'

'No idea. Perhaps she went to a party at one of the *dachas* nearby and had an aneurism or overdosed. The owner found her and panicked. Perhaps she was poisoned or suffocated.'

'That's it?'

'That's all I have.'

'Then you can go now.'

She bristled at being dismissed like a servant, but reacting badly wouldn't get her the answers she wanted. 'This case should be with the local *menti*, but here you are on Christmas Eve. What got *Sledkom* so excited?'

Yelin stared at her and his thin lips barely moved when he spoke.

'As if I'd tell you,' he said.

7

Artem had left his episode of *Masha and the Bear* to watch her leave – a puppy seeing off a stranger on its territory. He gripped his grandmother's leg in the hallway.

'*Sledkom*, that's good, isn't it?' Mrs Kalinina asked.

'Yes,' Natalya said, trying to put some conviction in her answer.

The truth was that everyone lied to the bereaved. Cheating husbands and wives became loyal in death; sociopaths became driven, complex characters. Her attempt at self-justification didn't make her feel better, and anyway, it hadn't worked. Mrs Kalinina's face had crumpled as if registering physical pain.

Natalya returned to the Hunter. She paused. Next to her was a navy-blue Lexus saloon. Ilya Yelin's partner was in the passenger seat applying lipstick using the sun visor's mirror. She rapped on the window. The investigator moved slowly, already aware of her presence. She tapped again on the window and pressed her ID card to the glass.

The investigator lowered the window. 'Yes?' she said, her face half-turned.

'Senior Detective Ivanova… I saw you on Mrs Kalinina's intercom monitor.'

It was the lips. Her make-up wasn't for vanity. Natalya remembered hearing about a *ment* two or three years ago. Her brain scrambled to come up with a name: Dubnik… Sergeant Tatyana Dubnik, whose face had taken twenty stitches after a jealous ex-boyfriend got physical. He had used whatever organ he used for thinking to reach the conclusion that if he ruined her looks no one would want her again.

'Tatyana?'

The head turned fully now. One cheek was slightly larger than the other and the teeth were too perfect – most likely implants. Otherwise, the boyfriend had failed. Tatyana Dubnik was stunning.

'Captain?'

'So you're *Sledkom* now?'

Dubnik looked at her warily. 'Yes.'

The ability of *Sledkom* to scoop up anyone with investigative experience was impressive. In the last few years they had been busy poaching detectives from all the state-level police departments across the republics. They'd never approached her, though. She assumed the sticking point had been her reputation for honesty. A constant rumour ran that *Sledkom* would eventually control all the serious investigative work in the country. Then again, she'd also heard *Sledkom* was going to be disbanded. The country ran on oil and rumours.

As far as she could remember, Dubnik had only been assigned to the Criminal Investigations Directorate for six months.

'And still under thirty. I can't fault your ambition.'

Dubnik's eyes creased, acknowledging the compliment. 'How's it going up there?' She glanced towards the apartment block.

'The mother?' Natalya put her elbows on the sill and leaned into the open window. 'Tough. She'll be OK, though, and it's a good thing the boy's too young to remember.'

'So, what can I do for you, Captain?'

'Investigator Yelin. He's your mentor, I take it?'

'Yes.'

CHAPTER 7

'He didn't want any boiler-room talk in front of Elizaveta's mother. He asked me to tell you what I know. Unfortunately there's not much, but I'll help if I can. What questions have you got?'

She saw indecision in Dubnik's face and raised the stakes. 'Don't worry, I need to get home. Ask Yelin to call me after Christmas. I'm based at Suvorovsky.'

Dubnik flicked up the Lexus's sun visor. 'No, that's fine. He probably wanted to ask you about her friends.'

'You think one of them dumped her in the ditch?'

'No,' Dubnik paused, uncertain if she should continue.

Natalya knew better than to push her to keep talking. She let the silence build.

'Well, it's too cold to stand here. It was good to see you again.'

'He wants their names,' Dubnik said.

Natalya nonchalantly blew on the fingertips of her gloves. A studied impression of indifference. 'Why?' she said finally.

Dubnik stuffed her lipstick in a handbag. 'Political.'

Natalya leaned in until her head was fully inside the Lexus's interior. 'You mean Elizaveta was connected?'

'Connected?' Dubnik looked momentarily confused. 'No, not political that way. You mean you don't know?'

'Maybe I do if I'm asked the right question.'

'Our FSB liaison told Ilya – Investigator Yelin – that Elizaveta Kalinina was a Decembrist.'

Natalya looked thoughtful, as if she had suspected as much. Now she'd got what she wanted, there was no need to play footsie with Dubnik. 'That's bad news for the family then.'

'What do you mean?'

'You tell me the last time *Sledkom* investigated an activist's death properly?'

Dubnik's reply was acid. 'She brought it on herself.'

It looked like Yelin's subordinate was in the right place after all. No wonder they had fast-tracked her.

Dubnik read her reaction. 'I've heard of you too.' She aimed an immaculately manicured red fingernail at her face, 'You're the *ment* who doesn't know when to stop.'

Natalya stepped back and smiled to herself. Apart from riling Dubnik, she had picked up something useful from the exchange: Elizaveta Kalinina had been a Decembrist, the latest group of disaffected citizens targeting the crooks and thieves running the country. The investigation into Elizaveta's murder was over, she was sure of that. *Sledkom* would charge some unfortunate with dumping her body or her murder, or perhaps do nothing at all.

During the drive home, she thought of her own dear mama. After returning to St Petersburg, she had been a resentful daughter until her mother's early heart attack. In the years that followed, her bitterness was replaced by a crushing guilt. They were two of a kind, her mother and Mrs Kalinina. In her head, a crossed wire was already linking both women. The weight of her guilt would be eased by helping Mrs Kalinina get justice for Elizaveta. There was Artem too. If Yelin and Dubnik had their way, those *korruptsioners* would let him grow up without knowing what happened to his mother. She wasn't going to let that happen.

Back in her apartment, she changed out of her suit and began cleaning in preparation for Anton and Dinara arriving the next day. The place was a mess and she was glad Mikhail wasn't there to get in the way.

When they lived in Germany, her father had decided they would celebrate their Christmas on the Gregorian calendar, the same day as Western Europe and America. After her parents separated she continued the tradition as an act of rebellion. Now that she was married and had a stepson, the two traditions merged. They opened presents at Western Christmas, then again on New Year's Day to match the Russian custom, then finally had a dinner the following Sunday to celebrate the Orthodox Christmas on the traditional Julian calendar.

After two weeks of celebrations, the apartment was strewn with rubbish, Mikhail had mild cirrhosis, and their Christmas tree was forced to survive as a shabby New Year's *yolka* until the end of January. She took out a vacuum cleaner and began sucking up the pine needles from the floor.

The sound of the key turning in the lock was masked by the noise of the machine and it was only when she glanced in the hallway that she saw Mikhail kicking off his shoes.

'Misha?' She jabbed the button on the hoover to kill the noise. 'What are you doing here?'

Mikhail appeared to be on the verge of tears, not that he would ever show any to her.

'What's wrong?'

'That bastard,' he began, then stopped, barely able to order his thoughts.

'Who?'

'Dostoynov, who else?'

'What's going on?'

Mikhail went to the kitchen and pulled out a bottle of Ochakovo. He yanked off the ring-pull and took a long draught of the beer.

'Don't drink them all. We've got Dinara and Anton tomorrow.'

'I've cancelled it,' Mikhail said, wiping his mouth with a palm.

He continued before she could speak. 'That bastard Dostoynov. He called me an hour ago. Do you remember a lazy pig of a detective called Leonid Laskin?'

'The *alkanaut*. Wasn't he the first to go when they introduced the breathalyser at headquarters?'

'That's right. Well, Dostoynov discovered Laskin had been getting his cases suspended due to lack of evidence when he'd done no work on them at all. Dostoynov has reopened them.'

'So?' she asked. 'Why did you need to come back from Saint Patrick's to tell me, and what does this have to do with Dinara and Anton coming for Christmas dinner?'

'You know the monastery on Konevets Island?'

She said, 'Should I?'

'It's on Lake Ladoga. Fuck, I have to pack,' Mikhail announced suddenly, handing her the Ochakovo bottle. He went into their bedroom and dragged a suitcase from the top of the wardrobe, dropping it onto their bed.

She followed him in. 'What's going on, Mikhail?'

'The monks have got a chapel there dedicated to Saint Nicholas the Wonderworker. Three years ago, one of them found a decaying body on the grass outside. It had a freshly made cross pressed into one hand. A juvenile female, according to the pathologist, and she'd been dead for at least two years. Too much decay to see how she'd died. Just before he was sacked, Laskin had been trying to close the case, but the prosecutor wouldn't let him.'

She drank his beer, unable to decide if her dominant emotion was anger or relief. 'Misha, where are you going?'

'Let me finish. Fuck, where's my underwear?'

'I don't know, it's *your* underwear, not mine. What's going on?'

Mikhail had a bundle of thick socks in his arms. He dropped them into the suitcase. 'A month ago we got a DNA match when a maternal uncle of the dead girl tried to smash up a bar. So we got a name for her: Diana Maricheva. She was from a town in Siberia called Inkino. Last record we have is her buying a train ticket to Piter in September 2012. Poor girl was only fourteen years old.'

CHAPTER 7

Natalya looked over her shoulder and surveyed the piles of torn wrapping paper strewn on the floor, the previous night's glasses, full ashtrays, and the halo of pine needles from the moulting Christmas tree.

'Misha, where the fuck are you going?'

He tossed thermal underwear into the suitcase, then woollen mittens. He stopped for a moment. 'Dostoynov has screwed me, Angel. The prosecutor wouldn't let them bury the girl so she's been in the morgue all this time. What's left of her body is now in a zinc box at Pulkovo airport. I have to take her home and update the family on the investigation.' He almost spat. 'What fucking investigation. Laskin, that lazy *khuyesos*, did nothing.'

'Why don't you change the flight? Go after Christmas.'

'Because you missed the best part. Dostoynov told the family to make the funeral arrangements – they are burying her on Monday. Dostoynov had someone in Travel book me a seat on an Aeroflot flight to Novosibirsk two weeks ago, then he kept his mouth shut until all the other flights were full.'

'What about a train?'

'You're joking, right? Iraq is closer than Inkino. Dostoynov fucked me and there's nothing I can do. If I complain, he'll lie and say he told me about it weeks ago. My plane leaves in less than three hours. I'm spending Christmas Day in an airport hotel.'

She handed him his beer and he drained it.

'Talk about revenge being served cold.' He snorted. 'It's minus thirty there, Tasha. Take a piss outside and I'll lose my dick. That's not funny.'

'So Anton isn't coming tomorrow?'

'I called Dinara on the way and told her not to bother. Don't be angry, Angel. I suggested Anton stays with her.' He continued without waiting for a response. 'Also, I saw your Hunter parked outside. Mind if I take it to the airport?'

He pressed the empty bottle in her hand. 'You can stay with Rogov and Oksana if you want. Stepan offered… he says they've got enough food to survive an apocalypse.'

'I'll be fine here. Thanks.' She shook her head slowly. 'You're in Siberia… on Christmas Day?'

'That's what I'm saying, Angel.'

She let out a sardonic laugh. Lieutenant Colonel Dostoynov's parting words came back to her. 'Try to have a happy holiday.' The bastard had been warning her.

8

Natalya picked at a piece of shrimp from the plate of appetizers balanced on her lap and sipped from a glass of Satrapezo. She had started the bottle at six. Mikhail had been gone a day. Anton, her adored stepson, was with Dinara. Her feet were propped on the coffee table. She ate a slice of pork and sipped some more. She put down the glass and switched on the TV.

It was a government advert. A clean-cut boy is sitting at a nightclub bar. A girl approaches and drags him to a secluded area.

'Are you over eighteen?' she asks breathlessly.

'Of course,' he replies, 'I'm an adult.'

She pulls at her clothes as if the place is unbearably hot. 'Did you vote?' she asks.

'Why would I?' he says.

The girl shoves him away. 'Then you're not an adult.'

The election was nearly two months away and it was hard to avoid the charade. Adverts all over the city implored people to take part. There were competitions for iPads and iPhones open to any citizen who photographed the inside of a polling booth to prove they had voted. It was the only competition in the whole circus.

Natalya cared about voting as much as she did about the room-temperature shrimp on her plate. The real leader of the opposition, Alexei Navalny, was banned from standing, and he was never mentioned on television unless it was to criticise him. Three years ago, another opposition leader, Boris Nemtsov, had been assassinated.

The election was a rigged exercise whose sole intention was to legitimise the thieves in charge.

The ennui was setting in. She rummaged through her collection of box sets to find a disc from the last series of *Spets*. This was Orthodox Christmas Day, the occasion she had mocked as a teenager for its link to an outdated calendar. She shouldn't have cared, but she was alone and it was still a day of family time. Her sister, Klavdiya, had phoned earlier from Hannover and put on her excitable nephew Oskar. She had spoken with her father too, who was becoming more cantankerous each year. The call she'd been waiting for, however, never came. She imagined Mikhail in a hire car, buried beneath a snowdrift with Diana Maricheva's skeletal remains in the boot. More likely he was buried in the nearest bar. As the evening passed, she began to wish he really was entombed in snow, suffocating with each breath. It did little to lift her spirits.

Instead of watching *Spets* – a show Mikhail hated because it starred actual gangsters – she left Channel One playing. Watching *Spets* would cause her to open another bottle of Satrapezo. She would be forty this year; time to be sensible, and besides, tomorrow was a working day.

The Channel One news began. It started with footage of a Christmas Eve mass the president had attended, followed by a live greeting from Patriarch Kirill to the astronauts aboard the International Space Station. Next there was a teaser for the local news about a dead woman discovered in a drainage ditch by the Toksovo highway. She decided to stay up a little longer. The cork came out of her bottle and she poured the remainder of the Satrapezo into it.

After more adverts, she watched an enterprising reporter locate Sergeant Taniashvili and bring him back to the crime scene for a re-enactment. Taniashvili's face was flushed as he pointed out a bank of snow, standing on what should have been a sacrosanct area for the forensic technicians. Behind Taniashvili, she could see the road had been reopened. All that remained of the crime scene were the cones the two *menti* had used to fix the tape in place, and even they had been pushed against the snow bank to avoid impeding the traffic. Now her glass was empty and she couldn't recall drinking from it.

Back at the studio there was speculation – there was always speculation – about how Elizaveta had ended up in the ditch.

'A drug addict,' said one presenter with a shrug.

His colleague, a supposed intellect, wondered aloud what a young woman might have been doing in such a quiet place. The inference was clear: Elizaveta was a woman of low morals. The propaganda had started.

Feeling depressed and a little drunk, she turned off the TV and went to the study to switch on the computer. While it booted up, she went into the kitchen for a fresh bottle. After pouring herself another glass of Satrapezo, she typed 'Decembrists' into the Yandex search engine. It brought up an American indie band with a similar name, an unfinished novel by Tolstoy, and an article on the original Decembrists. She skimmed the main text about the liberal revolt whose failure ultimately led to the bloody revolution of 1917.

Below the article was a link to a YouTube video. She clicked on it and watched a figure standing outside a court, his face hidden by a scarf. He held up a cardboard sign that read in English: 'The trial of Pavel Gavrilov, film director.' It was a reaction to Gavrilov's trial for fraud because he'd had the temerity to include Tchaikovsky's homosexuality in a biopic of St Petersburg's most famous son.

Half a dozen activists approached the court. Two carried air-horns, the other four held wooden boxes using thick rubber gloves. They climbed the steps to the court entrance, put down the boxes, and slid back the lids. Rats tentatively sniffed the air, then a blast from the air-horns sent them scurrying from the boxes to the courthouse. The YouTube footage switched to the televised recording of the film director's trial, where a murmur rippled through the gallery. Spectators left their seats, orderly at first, then panic broke out. Men and women scrambled over the barrier into the courtroom, knocking down the police trying to hold them back.

After it had finished, she clicked on a button to subscribe to the Decembrists YouTube channel. The next clip was called 'Retirement Present'. Activists doused the FSB director's car in blood, and she watched the pandemonium that followed, with agents chasing protesters across the Sampsonievsky Bridge. She got ready for bed, wondering if Elizaveta had been involved.

Sometime in the night, she dreamed the phone had been ringing.

The next morning, in a swirl of fat snowflakes, she parked her ageing Volvo on Suvorovsky Prospekt and walked the rest of the way to the five-storey stone monolith of the St Petersburg headquarters of the Ministry of Internal Affairs. Inside, she cut through the main Criminal Investigations Directorate to the section set aside for the Serious Crimes Unit. She was due to appear as a prosecution witness against a wife who supposedly killed her husband with cockroach poison. She had some time to herself first, and started the day reviewing her notes on the case.

Her phone rang. A ground-floor receptionist told her someone was waiting for her. She tucked the old case notes in a drawer and went downstairs.

She scanned the reception area. A young woman was sitting in the waiting area, looking as nervous as a criminal in an interview room. She was in her mid-to-late twenties and was wearing a black padded leather jacket. The edges of her ears were dotted with studs. Natalya thought she looked a little like the actress Marina Aleksandrova – no make-up, clear skin, a beauty marred only by the dark circles around the eyes.

'Captain Ivanova?' the woman said.

'Yes,' Natalya said.

'Can we talk outside?'

No name offered. Natalya sized up the woman. 'I can spare five minutes,' she said. 'There's a Tam-Tam across the road.'

'Thank you.'

She didn't have a coat on, and shivered as they crossed to the restaurant. Inside, a big-bellied uniformed *ment* was at the counter ordering croissants and coffee. She pulled open the door and saw the young woman hesitate. The policeman looked up and scowled as the heat of the café escaped through the door.

'Don't worry,' said Natalya, 'you'd have to pull out a gun to get his attention. Nothing comes between a *ment* and his breakfast.'

The uniformed cop gave a nod of acknowledgement to Natalya then turned back to the counter.

'Why don't you sit down?' She pointed to a small, mosaic table nearest the door – a position more likely to relieve a nervous customer. 'You look like a skinny latte type of girl?'

She got a tight smile in return and ordered two coffees before pulling up a chair. 'Now, what's the problem?'

'She said you would be like this.'

'Grumpy before my first shot of caffeine?' Natalya said, not wanting to spook the girl by asking who she had been talking to.

'She said you were kind. Well, she said "soft" but I took it to mean kind.'

Natalya's awkwardness at the compliment was only relieved when the waitress brought the drinks over. They were both quiet until she had gone.

'So, how can I help?'

'I'm worried about my brother… he's missing.'

She brought out a colour picture of a slender man with sun-bleached shoulder-length hair standing in front of a marble cathedral. He wore linen trousers and a pressed shirt, old-fashioned clothes that made Natalya think of a TV presenter on a history programme.

'This was in the summer. We were on holiday in Florence with our parents.'

'Do you want to tell me your name first?'

'No… not yet.'

'I need to call you something. First name?'

'Vita.'

'Cool name.' She took a sip of the coffee. It was good, but she needed a litre of it to moderate her hangover. 'So why do you think he's missing?'

'Listen, he's gone. The three of us – me, him and our older brother – we were meant to meet up on Christmas Day. We do it every year, there's no way he would have missed it.'

'How long has he been missing?'

'Friday or Saturday, I'm not sure.'

Two days. It didn't seem urgent, but her eyes told a different story.

'Why aren't you sure?'

The uniformed *ment* walked past them to leave, and their conversation dropped to a conspiratorial silence. He frowned at them in mild amusement then left.

'Max lives with our older brother.'

'So this missing brother – he's called Max?'

Vita looked at Natalya, beseeching her not to tell anyone, then said, 'Yes.'

'And why did you ask for me?'

Vita scanned the near-empty coffee shop.

CHAPTER 8

'Valeria… Mrs Kalinina. She told me you saw her on Saturday.'

Natalya fought against her hangover to stay alert. 'You were speaking to Elizaveta Kalinina's mother?'

'Yes.'

'When?'

'Yesterday.'

'On Christmas Day?'

'Yes, on Christmas Day. That was yesterday, wasn't it?'

Natalya ran a hand over her face and massaged the flesh underneath. 'So how do you know Mrs Kalinina?'

'I've never met her before.'

'Then how?'

'Please trust me when I say I can't tell you. I saw Elizaveta and Max together a few times. Now she's dead and he's missing.'

'So you heard about Elizaveta and wanted to ask her mother if she knew anything.'

'Yes.'

'Why didn't you try the police?'

'Because I don't trust them. Next question?'

'You came to me, remember? I'm only trying to help.'

'I wouldn't be here if there was someone else I could try.'

'Thanks.'

'I told you, I don't trust the police. Please keep asking your questions.'

'How old is he?'

'Same age as me. We're twins… twenty-seven.'

'Any history of mental or physical illness?'

'None.'

'What did Elizaveta's mother say about Max?'

'She didn't know who he was. She told me Elizaveta had lied to her about where she was going on Friday.'

'Then listen to me. From what you've said, it's possible your brother's disappearance is connected to Elizaveta's death. You have to speak to *Sledkom*. It's their case now.'

Vita scowled. '*Sledkom* don't give a shit.'

'And you think I do?'

'I don't, but Valeria does – she told me to find you. She said you were different.'

'What else did she say?'

'*Sledkom* took Elizaveta's laptop. They kept asking Valeria about the Decembrists – that's all they were interested in.'

'Let's go back to Max. You said he hasn't been seen since Friday or Saturday. Which day was it?'

'I don't know. Oleg, our older brother – that's who Max lives with – he's got this ancient car that he's in love with. Max borrows it sometimes. He took it on Friday morning. I've asked around, but that was the last time anyone saw him.'

'So why did you say Friday *or* Saturday?'

'Because Oleg last saw Max on Friday, but when he woke up on Saturday morning his car was outside.'

'But Oleg didn't see Max on Saturday?'

'No.'

'What about the keys?'

'That's funny.' Fine lines creased Vita's brow.

'What is?'

'The keys. Oleg was moaning that Max had left them in the car.'

'Look, Vita, you've got to be careful.' Natalya looked around the café to make sure they couldn't be overheard. 'You've given away the fact that your brother Max is a Decembrist – don't look shocked, that's why you came to see me unofficially. It's also why you saw Elizaveta's mother before contacting the *menti*. From what I know, the Decembrists are secretive, which means if you saw Max and Elizaveta together then there's a good chance you are one too.'

'This was stupid,' Vita hissed under her breath. She was already standing, her latte untouched. She pulled the door open and was gone.

'Wait,' Natalya called out.

Vita didn't stop. She began running across the icy pavement. Natalya thought of giving chase, then decided against it.

At the junction, Vita came to a halt and looked over her shoulder.

Natalya watched the girl for a moment, and then realised she was expected to go after her. She sighed and began jogging. Soon she caught up.

'I thought you were chasing me.'

Natalya shivered and wrapped her arms around herself. 'Why should I? You're not a suspect.'

'You accused me of being a Decembrist.'

'No, I said you are one and you need to be careful.'

'So you're not on their side?'

'I'm not on anyone's side. But' – she checked her watch – 'I've got roll call in a few minutes. If you want me to help, you'd better decide quickly. Your choice.'

She started walking back to the Tam-Tam, then heard the crunch of footsteps on ice as Vita followed. Natalya held open the door. They returned to the table.

'Did you ever watch our videos on YouTube?' Vita asked.

'I've seen the one outside the courthouse with the rats, and the one where you trashed the FSB director's car.'

'Don't watch them at home, they can trace you.'

Natalya shook her head, 'Are you all this paranoid?' She regretted the word as soon as it was out of her mouth.

Vita fought to keep her voice level. 'Elizaveta is dead, my brother is missing, and you dare to call me paranoid.'

'Sorry, poor choice of words.'

Vita scanned the restaurant, nervous that her outburst had been overheard. She was quiet for a few seconds. 'What happens now?' she asked.

'I need permission from my boss to carry out an initial investigation, but if he hears your brother is mixed up with the Decembrists the case will go straight to *Sledkom*.'

'So you can't do anything?'

'I didn't say that. First, I want you to lose the earrings, dress like office plankton, then go to your nearest police station and tell them your brother is missing. Stress how unusual his disappearance is. That'll start the paperwork. What does your brother do?'

'He's a professor.'

'Perfect. Make sure you tell them that. In the meantime I'll see what I can find out. Come to my apartment tonight?'

'Where are you?'

'Near the stone lions on Lviny Bridge. Here's the address.' She took out a pen and began writing on a napkin. 'I'll be home at six.'

'Do you live alone?' Vita asked.

'At the moment. My husband's away in Siberia… Long story.'

Vita took the napkin and tucked it in a pocket of her leather jacket, then left without a backward glance.

Natalya finished her coffee and started drinking Vita's latte. This was a dangerous plan that could backfire spectacularly. If Max's disappearance was connected to Elizaveta's death, things were looking bad for him. Either he'd run away after harming her, or he was afraid for his own life, or he was already dead. Finding Max, though, would go a long way to solving the mystery of Elizaveta's death.

But there was one major problem. If Dostoynov or *Sledkom* found out what she was up to, her career would be over.

9

The morning went slowly. She took the Metro to Vyborgskaya station and walked to Kalininsky District Court, arriving in time to discover her eleven o'clock appearance had been delayed. She went for a freezing stroll around the district, finding herself outside the orange-bricked, decaying mass of the regional prison. Early on in her career, she had often felt a twinge of guilt at supporting a system where the brutal punishments of the state rarely fitted the crime – one of the reasons why she had applied to join the Serious Crimes Unit. Usually, the individuals she supplied to the Federal Service of Punishment Fulfilment were pitiless, violent individuals who deserved little compassion. She would sleep badly knowing this court case involved one of the rare exceptions.

She was called late in the afternoon. Defence lawyers were scarcer than Siberian tigers, and she found herself facing a poor one who hadn't mentioned that the near-catatonic defendant in the cage had suffered unrelenting domestic abuse. She had tried to steer his questions to hint that there was mitigating evidence, but the judge put a stop to it. At least the poor woman was lucky enough to see a jury. Before 2016, women never saw one – juries were only available for cases that carried a life sentence, and the criminal code forbade women being sentenced to life. That wasn't so bad, but a jury was fifteen times more likely to acquit than a troika of judges.

With her part as a prosecution witness over, she left the case to rumble on without her. It was gone 5 p.m. by the time she caught a packed Metro train and returned to the Suvorovsky Street headquarters. She had been hoping to avoid Lieutenant Colonel Dostoynov, but he called out to her as she attempted to slink past.

Six months ago Dostoynov had shared an office with Mikhail. Now he had his own. His most recent act had been to paint over the yellow staining on the walls from the decades of chain smoking by his predecessor, Colonel Vasiliev. The windows were open to clear the paint fumes, and there was an instant chill in the office that Dostoynov in his shirtsleeves was oblivious to. A newly installed palm plant on the grimy window ledge attempted to impress on the unwary that Dostoynov had human qualities.

'Colonel.'

There was no offer to sit down. The chair and small table perpendicular to his desk were reserved for his immediate subordinates. As the only major left, that was Mikhail's place when Dostoynov wished to speak with him. The table was tiny, and Mikhail had complained that a caster was missing from one of the chair legs, causing him to pitch forwards. She suspected it was another calculated humiliation.

'Good Christmas, Captain?' Dostoynov asked jovially.

So he'd called her in to find out about his shaming of Mikhail. Well, he wouldn't hear it from her. If Dostoynov wanted to dance, he'd discover she was an old-time punk kind of girl.

'Very pleasant, thank you, Colonel.'

He looked at her smugly, as if he had expected her to say as much. Until he spoke again, she wondered if that was all he'd intended to say. 'I was sorry to hear of the Elizaveta Kalinina case. All your efforts won't be wasted, of course – *Sledkom* have the manpower and resources to make sure the girl's family get justice.'

She did her best impersonation of a loyal underling. 'It was the natural course of action, Colonel. Elizaveta Kalinina was a Decembrist.'

CHAPTER 9

'I wondered if it was something like that.'

His face took on a new expression: a near-perfect facsimile of innocence. She turned away out of embarrassment for him. Next to the potted plant she saw a picture of the president, taken from the Sochi Winter Olympics.

He caught her looking at it. 'You like it?'

'It's a fine picture, Colonel. May I ask if you brought it from home?'

Dostoynov sighed. 'Amusing, Ivanova. Have you ever wondered why you're still here?'

'Is it my clearance rate, Colonel?'

'Partly that. Also your reputation. More pertinently, it doesn't do the unit any harm to include a few idealists. Speaking of which,' – he looked up at the picture – 'this election coming up. I suppose you're a Navalny supporter?'

'No Colonel, it's Putin all the way. Truly, I'm surprised we need elections when we already have the perfect leader.'

'Then why do you suppose he puts himself through it every six years?'

'Because it's a mask, Colonel. Take the election away and everyone will see what's underneath.' The words were out. She had spoken rashly. Inevitably Dostoynov would now probe to see how far she would incriminate herself.

'And what would that be?' he asked smoothly.

Putin? He was the same as any other third world strongman who spoke of patriotism while stuffing his pockets. 'Well, beneath the mask…' She leaned forward to scrutinise the portrait. 'You can't deny that he's had work – dermal fillers in the cheeks… Botox… I'd guess at a facelift too.'

'Captain, you really are amusing. I must share your joke with the other heads of the Directorate.'

Despite his warning, Dostoynov was amused. You could say what you like about the FSB, but they didn't employ idiots. One hundred per cent paranoid, one hundred per cent amoral, zero per cent stupidity.

She put on the timid expression of a submissive who was only eager to please the men in her life. 'Was there anything else you needed me for, Colonel?'

'Yes. Tell me, Captain, how does Major Ivanov like his new case?'

Given the amount of effort he'd invested to get Mikhail on a plane, she shouldn't have been surprised by the question.

'If I can speak candidly, Colonel?'

'Off the record, then.'

Dostoynov was smiling, but she wasn't about to tell him his scheme would never work. Mikhail loved being a *ment* and he'd endure any number of humiliations to stay. Dostoynov had to force a resignation. Sacking was too blunt a tool when the detectives in the unit looked up to Mikhail. A relatively inexperienced Lieutenant Colonel was dependent on the goodwill of his subordinates.

'To begin with, Mikhail thought you were reprimanding him with a banishment to Siberia.'

'You think so?' Dostoynov was as coy as a sex salon worker.

'At first he did,' she said. 'Until you gave him the Diana Maricheva case. It's invigorated him. Misha's happier than a hunting dog on a scent, or in this instance, a bunch of bones. You must have known Misha loves a good Agata Kristi. Thank you, Colonel, for not bearing him any ill will.'

'Thank you for the *honesty*, Captain. You'll be gratified to hear Diana Maricheva is just the beginning. If your husband is happy now, he'll be delirious when I've finished with him.'

She was dismissed. Her chance of a minor victory ruined.

10

On the way home she stopped at a *produkti* to pick up some fruit and vegetables, then stuffed them in her fridge, pausing to sniff at the remains of *selyodka pod shuboy*. The dish of 'herring under a fur coat' was left over from New Year's Day, and it didn't smell so good any more. She scraped it into a bin at arm's length, to keep the pickled beets from staining her clothes. It was then that she caught the radio playing quietly in the spare room. She hurried out of the kitchen and pushed open the door.

Her stepson, Anton, was on the floor, propped against his bed, both legs folded at an angle that would hospitalise her if she tried.

'Hey, can't you knock first? I might have been naked.'

He was scraping the dirt under his fingernails with a paring knife. For fear of being labelled uncool, she restrained herself from embracing him.

'Hey stepchild.'

'Hey stepmother. Thought I'd come see you and practise being sociable.'

White, skinny ankles protruded from a pair of cheap black trousers. A white shirt sported a tie that hung loosely around his neck like a noose. She frowned. 'Aren't you supposed to be at college?'

'I'm there now, can't you tell? A star pupil too – best grades in class.'

'That's because your father overpaid the bribe to the admissions tutor. Do you even attend lectures?'

He shook his head. 'Only when an inspection is called.'

She noticed a pack of half-smoked Sobranies – Mikhail's own brand. One of the many packets he'd 'lost' in recent months.

'You got me.' Anton held out his hands for some imaginary cuffs. 'You want one?'

'Stopped in September.'

'You smoked at your New Year's party.'

'I was drunk.'

He tapped the packet. 'Mind if I do?'

'If it's outside.'

While he got to his feet she took a parka from the back of the hall door.

Outside, he blew on his hands. 'Fuck me, it's colder than a nun's—'

'Habit?'

'Yeah,' he grinned, 'a habit.'

She looked down to *Lviny Most*, the Lions Bridge, where snow billowed around the pedestrians shuffling over the frozen Griboyedov Canal.

Anton puffed on his cigarette. A few months ago he coughed when he smoked. Now he sucked on the Sobranie like a drinking straw.

'You know why I stopped?' she said.

'Because it's bad?'

'Hmm,' she said.

'Natasha, why don't we have more words for snow?'

She was amused by the clumsy attempt to change the subject. 'Because we don't care about snow.'

Another suck on the Sobranie. 'What do we care about?'

'Drinking,' she said. 'Plenty of words for that. I bet there's even one for drinking while thinking up words for snow.'

He grinned his crooked smile. 'I'm sure.'

'So what's with the shirt and tie?'

She was inhaling his second-hand smoke and finding it more pleasant than she'd hoped.

CHAPTER 10

'Mama thought, as I'm not really a student, I ought to be bringing in some *zelenye*.'

'Good idea.'

'You think so? I was hoping you would talk her out of it.'

'No, I'm in favour. Your papa will be glad too.'

Anton sniffed the sleeves of his shirt. 'I stink of oil.' He held up the paring knife. 'I haven't figured out how it gets under my fingernails when I don't go near a car.

'You work in a garage?'

'Yeah. Bogdan – the owner – he's an ex-boyfriend of Mama's or something.'

'Do you know anything about cars?'

'*Grand Theft Auto* without the shooting?' He shrugged. 'Shit, I'm not a mechanic, Bogdan tells me to do the invoices and answer the phone.' He rubbed his fingers together and sniffed them. 'Must be some oil on a door handle. It's cash-in-hand, though.'

'So the tax office won't question why someone with a student exemption is working full-time.'

'Hey, you're a detective.'

'And you're a smart arse. Are you staying tonight?'

'If that's OK. Mama bought herself a puppy. There's shit everywhere and she expects me to clean it up… She'll give it to an animal shelter when she gets bored.'

The buzzer sounded.

'Papa?'

'No, he'll be away for a few more days.'

She left Anton finishing his cigarette and she pressed an intercom button on the door.

'Delivery.'

'OK, come up.'

She heard the main door buzz as she pressed a button. A minute later there was a knock. Natalya looked through the spyhole and saw the back of a head and a cobalt blue suit. Unless the driver was delivering for Swarovski, the woman was overdressed. She turned. It was Vita. The leather jacket had been replaced by a suit, her natural beauty covered by a layer of expertly applied make-up.

'You look smart,' she said as she opened the door, ignoring the ridiculous subterfuge of Vita posing as a delivery driver.

'I was at work.'

'You reported Max missing?'

'I went to the station in Admiralty… Have you heard anything?'

'No, but I've been in court all day. Come in.'

She held open the door while Vita took off her shoes in the hallway.

Vita stopped. Lines creased her forehead. 'Who's that?' Her voice echoed suspicion. She stared through the glass door to Anton stubbing out his Sobranie on the balcony railing.

'My stepson. He's a student.'

On cue, Anton opened the glass door to the balcony.

'Anton, meet Vita,' Natalya said.

He leaned over to shake her hand in an act of effortless cool. Natalya observed Anton's noose-like tie had been quietly transferred to his pocket. His trademark slouch had gone.

'You're a student?' Vita asked. 'Where?'

'Nowhere. It's a fake to keep me out of the army. My father bought me a place.'

'Vita is helping me with a case,' Natalya said quickly, before Anton incriminated Mikhail any further.

'Oh,' Anton nodded conspiratorially. 'You're a *ment* too?'

'Interesting.' Vita gave out an amused expression. 'You think I look like one?'

CHAPTER 10

Anton was deflated momentarily then attempted to resume his aura of cool. 'No, I just thought, if you're helping then—'

'It's confidential,' Natalya interrupted. 'Would you like a coffee, Vita?'

'Thank you.'

She looked pointedly at Anton, who raised his hands in surrender. 'All right, I'm going.'

Natalya waited until he was out of the room, then took a seat at the dining table. Vita followed suit.

'Now tell me about your brother.'

'His name's Maksim Nikolayevich Timchenko. He's an associate professor at the Repin Institute.'

'So "Vita" makes you Vitalya Nikolayevna Timchenko?'

'Dr Timchenko, to be accurate. I'm an associate professor too. I run a course on twentieth-century history – "Revolution to Evolution" – at the university.'

'Sounds fascinating.'

'It would be if we weren't living in a country with selective amnesia. Want to guess what'll happen to me if I give a lecture on how Hitler and Stalin arranged to split Europe in two like a pair of evil giants playing knucklebones? We started that war we're so proud of. I suppose you've never heard of the Molotov-Ribbentrop Pact.'

'You'd be wrong. I grew up in Germany.'

She'd seen it earlier in the café. Vita was passionate. One of the many overrated virtues that got people killed.

Vita took a deep breath. 'Sorry. One of my students was arrested last year. He got eighteen months for re-posting an article on Ukraine.' She snorted. 'Another war we didn't start.'

'Let's get back to Max. Where are your parents?'

'They live in Belgium… retired academics. Max, Oleg and I visit them every year.'

'Have you told them he's missing?'

'Not yet. I'm hoping I won't have to.'

Anton returned with a tray of empty cups and milk and began laying them on the table. He seemed desperate to catch Vita's eye. 'Who's missing?' he asked.

'Anton,' Natalya hissed, 'this isn't appropriate.'

'It's OK… it's my brother. Your stepmother has agreed to help find him, unofficially.'

'Natalya's brilliant,' Anton began, 'there was this Swedish girl kidnapped last year—'

'I agreed to help *unofficially*,' Natalya said, stopping him. 'That means you die before you breathe a word about it.'

'Do you want me to swear some sort of oath?' he asked, turning to Vita.

'With blood,' the young woman suggested.

Oh God, thought Natalya, now the girl was flirting back.

'Blood?' Anton mock gulped.

'An oath written in blood with a few words to Satan asking him to claim your immortal soul if you fail. Nothing else will do… unless you can just keep quiet.'

'I might do that one then. How can we help?' he asked.

'*We* can help by leaving,' said Natalya.

'Right.'

Natalya waited until they were alone again. 'Vita, I need all the information you can find. All the places Max might have gone, bank account details, phone number… social media. The names of anyone who might want to harm him.'

'I'll get it.'

'Good.' Natalya lowered her voice. 'The Decembrists… do you know what he was doing?'

CHAPTER 10

'Max wouldn't talk about the stuff I wasn't involved in.' She raised her eyebrows ironically. 'He did it to protect me.'

'Then find someone for me to talk to.'

'I can't do that. They'll never trust me again.'

'You have to. Explain the situation. I promise you, they'll be safe with me.'

'OK, I'll try. Is there anything else?'

'Not for now. I'll try some contacts of my own.' She left the rest unsaid, and with good reason. Had Vita known who she was about to approach, she would have left the apartment immediately, gone home and packed her bags.

His smile was perfect – charming, but not overdoing it.

'Something for the cold?' Anton asked, returning with a bottle of Stolichnaya and a smaller tray with shot glasses.

It was a frivolous gesture considering Vita's nerves and the fact that her brother was missing.

'No… I have to go,' Vita said, pulling on her boots.

The door closed, and Anton hastily made an excuse to leave. Despite Natalya's objections, thirty seconds later he was gone too.

She found his pack of stolen Sobranies on the table and lit one off the stove, then returned to the balcony. Five metres above, illuminated by the streetlamps, she watched Anton, his footsteps silenced by the snow as he hurried after Vita. He caught up with her by the broken pavement skirting the Griboyedov Canal. Anton and Vita were in step now. They reached a small white Fiat. He got his phone was out and tapped on the screen to get her number. This was a complication she didn't need.

11

Despite the freezing air, she kept the balcony door open to stop the apartment stinking of their cigarettes, and sought out a bottle of single malt from the kitchen. She poured a glass and the smoke-infused liquid burned as she swallowed, mapping out the contours of her stomach in fire. It was apposite. The last time she had drunk whisky had been on her last big case, in the presence of the FSB agent she was about to call.

Half hoping the number wouldn't be there, she scrolled through the address book on her iPhone. Her finger stopped on a name: Major Belikova. She topped up her glass then made the call.

It was answered immediately. In the background Natalya could hear traffic.

'Belikova.'

She recognised the voice, one she'd thought of as sharp enough to pickle a salted cucumber. Now it sounded weary.

'It's Natalya Ivanova.'

'Who?'

'The annoying *ment* you tried to kill six months ago.'

'Pffft. Six months and you're still breathing. Are you calling to complain? I can fix the situation for you.'

'Maybe I missed hearing your voice.'

'No need to get fresh, Captain.'

'Are you still in the Economic Crimes Directorate?'

'Hey, don't get away from the small talk yet. I want to hear about your life. Are you still screwing that major?'

CHAPTER 11

'We're married.'

'So that's a no, then.' Natalya caught a high-pitched cackle. 'What about your stepson? Anton, wasn't it?'

'The one you threatened to send to the Donbass People's Militia?'

'Don't be sore, I was just doing my job.'

'Some job… Anton's fine.'

'So, what do you want, Ivanova? I mentioned you to a Colonel I know in a certain department. I told him you speak English and German, and everyone thinks you're so pure you have an intact hymen – mine went long ago, I can tell you that much. He told me he'd shave his balls to have an idealist like you inside Europol. If you ever want to talk, I can do things for your career you wouldn't believe.'

'Thanks for the offer, but he can keep his balls hairy. I need a favour.'

'You don't even know my first name.'

'What is it?'

'If I told you I'd have to kill you.'

'You tried that already.'

'Are you still brooding over that? All right, it's Margarita. Now I'll have to send someone round. Expect it when you least expect it.'

The shrieking returned. A door closed.

'Is Margarita really your name?' she asked.

'Am I really going to have to shoot you?' Belikova sighed. 'My father was a Bulgakov fan. He named me after the famous witch in his book – that's fathers for you. We rebel against them our own way. Mine is a snowflake, so you can imagine how happy he is about my career choice.'

There was a long blast of a car horn, then intense traffic noise as Belikova lowered her window. Natalya heard, "Do that again, *piz'da*, I dare you… I'll shit on you if you do that again."

The traffic noise disappeared and she caught a world-weary sigh. 'Moscow is full of fools, Ivanova. Tell me what you want. Make it quick.'

'The Decembrists—'

'Shh, don't say that over the phone.'

'I'm sorry, I—'

There was a cackle. 'I'm teasing, but seriously don't say that shit on an open line. What do you want?'

'I've got a dead body. Elizaveta Dmitrievna Kalinina. *Sledkom* have just taken her off my hands.'

'And you want her back?'

'No,' she lied, 'but I'm curious.'

'Curiosity, you know what it did to the cat?'

'Was it tossed in a mass grave near Toksovo?'

'Funny.'

'*Sledkom* took my case because someone in your *organisation*' – despite Belikova's relaxed attitude Natalya found it hard to speak on an open line – 'told them Elizaveta belonged to that group of activists.'

'So what do you want?'

'I want to know how your organisation knew.'

'I'll do you a favour. Then you can do one for me another time.'

'Thank you.'

'Don't thank me yet. I'll ask around, so long as it doesn't get me in the shit with my colonel.'

There was another long blast of a car horn. 'Another fool… I've got to go.'

The call ended abruptly.

Natalya tuned her radio to the BBC World Service. A programme had already begun on the life of Eva Perón. The whisky had made her dopey, and she dozed off listening to the story of Evita's embalmed body and how it had gone missing for sixteen years. Evita, Elizaveta Kalinina, and Diana Maricheva: in her half-sleep she believed the universe was trying to tell her something about women whose souls never rested if their earthly bodies had been moved.

There was a ringing noise in the apartment. She jerked awake on the sofa, then scrambled to locate her cordless phone.

'Angel?' Mikhail's voice.

She didn't reply.

'Can you hear me?'

More silence, then, 'How did you get out of the snow drift?'

'What?'

'You were buried alive for two days,' she said.

'Angel, what are you talking about?'

'It's the only excuse I can think of that's good enough. Why haven't you called?'

'Ah.'

The moment she heard him speak she'd promised herself she would be unpleasant, but his voice was already feeling like a hot shower after a long day. Marriage was like that – a voltmeter needle flickering between love and irritation.

'Ah,' she copied.

'Angel, listen to me. Novosibirsk wasn't the nearest airport. Dostoynov sent me six hundred kilometres away, then the *mudilo* made sure I had no time to arrange a transfer. I've been driving for a day with a dead girl's bones in the boot, a shovel, and two sleeping bags… on roads that would put Antarctica to shame.'

'Where are you now?'

'Inkino – where Diana Maricheva's family live. I'm with Marat, the town's police chief. I tried calling, Angel, I did. I even called you on Christmas Day but my battery died… I forgot to pack a charger.'

She frowned at the vague memory of a phone ringing in the night, and experienced a pang of guilt.

'How long are you going to be there?'

'Thursday at the earliest. The funeral was today, but the gravediggers weren't expecting her. The ground was so tough they had to crack the topsoil with a pneumatic drill while the family were waiting with the coffin – not the ceremony you might hope for when burying a child. Maricheva's mother wants to speak to me tomorrow. How do I explain the only reason I'm here is because my boss is trying to fuck me?'

'Maybe you can solve the case. I told Dostoynov you love a good Agata Kristi.'

'Seriously?' he said. 'In what way do you think that was helping me? Dostoynov will use it to ruin me if I fail.'

Mikhail sounded so exhausted he was slurring.

'Misha, I did it because the arsehole wanted to gloat and I wouldn't give him the satisfaction. I told him you were invigorated by the challenge.'

He let out a sigh of pure weariness. 'OK, I get that, Angel, but I'm so tired of the whole thing. I wonder if I should resign and do something else.'

'Right.'

'I'm not kidding, I can barely get myself out of the chair. I'll think better in the morning. I'll have to. Diana's mother has got all the relatives lined up to meet the great detective from the big city. What the hell am I going to say?'

'Tell them you'll do whatever you can. Mean it.'

'Whatever I can to find a girl who has been rotting for six years? They need a clairvoyant, not a detective. Maybe I can do something useful by arranging a séance.'

'Have you found out anything?'

'Yeah. Marat… the chief, he's been filling me in. The girl got dressed for school but never arrived. Marat took a hard look at

Shugaley, Diana's stepfather. After she'd gone, some of her school friends came forward to claim he'd propositioned them. The mother defended him, of course. Anyway, whatever happened to the girl happened in Piter. There's nothing here.'

'Come home soon then.'

'I will. How are things?'

'The woman in the ditch, Elizaveta Kalinina? *Sledkom* took it from me.'

She waited a few seconds until the silence was awkward. 'Only, I think I've found a way.' She stopped. How could she tell him on an open line that another Decembrist had gone missing and she was hoping to solve both cases, and embarrass *Sledkom* as a bonus prize?

'That sounds dangerous. What are you talking about, Angel?'

'Nothing. Dostoynov has got me clearing paperwork on old cases.'

'That means he likes you. If he didn't, you'd be in Siberia keeping me warm… Marat's just come back, I'd better go.'

'OK. I love you.'

'I love you too, Angel.'

She put the phone down. It was the first time she'd considered the full extent of her deceit. By going behind Dostoynov's back, she was risking her job. That was a chance she was prepared to take, but Mikhail's job was in danger too. If they were both kicked out, they would be screwed.

12

It had taken four days for the case to make its way to the Criminal Investigations Directorate, and that had only been with the attendant publicity that Max brought. He was an associate professor working for a prestigious institute, not a Decembrist like Elizaveta, whose reputation could be so easily destroyed. She had read some of the articles written by paid trolls and hacks claiming Elizaveta had a drug problem, she sold her body, or else, the old Soviet catch-all: she was a foreign agent. Natalya hoped that Valeria – Elizaveta's mother – hadn't read them.

She had dreaded trying to persuade Dostoynov that Max's disappearance was important enough for the Directorate. And even then, there was no guarantee he would assign it to her. The reality had been far easier. She had simply presented herself at morning roll call where, over the heads of the seated detectives, Dostoynov had given it to her as the next available senior officer with 'a little time on her hands'.

Back at her desk, she spent the first ten minutes familiarising herself with the thorough work already conducted by a local Admiralty District *ment,* Sergeant Smolin.

Rogov turned up a few minutes later. 'Boss, Dostoynov told me to help you with this missing professor. Promise you won't try to get us killed this time.'

She ignored him and finished reading the file. 'This Sergeant Smolin's good,' she said, passing it to Rogov. She knew her words would sting.

He studied the photograph of Max Timchenko, the same one Vita had shown her, and began thumbing through the pages of the report.

CHAPTER 12

The flicking accelerating as he grew agitated. Finally, he reached into his pocket, withdrew one of the new, Crimea-themed bank notes from his wallet, and slapped it on her desk.

'Here's two hundred, Boss.'

'What for?'

'I'm betting we'll see a transfer application from this Smolin soon. He's after a promotion, I know his sort.'

'Put your money away,' she said, quietly satisfied that her words had hit home. 'Besides, is it so wrong to be ambitious? You should be grateful he saved you some shoe leather.'

She took the file from Rogov. 'I'll give you the highlights: "No hospital admissions or fatalities reported within Leningrad Oblast administrative district for Professor Maksim Nikolayevich Timchenko".'

'So? I reckon this professor is on a sabbatical with one of his students.' Rogov wet his lips and she felt sullied to guess his thoughts. 'I don't blame him either,' he continued. 'I saw one of them on Rossiya-24. A bony *telka* with tits like baked apples and eyes like a rabbit's. I'd happily crush her.'

She rolled her eyes deliberately, 'Not according to A.K. Zharinov.'

'Who's he?'

'An administrator at the Sberbank main office in Severo-Zapadny. Sergeant Smolin went to see him. Max Timchenko's last account transaction was on the fourth of January. Our helpful Sergeant even copied his recent statements.'

Rogov grunted, 'So? That just means one of the Little Miss Apple-Tits can afford to look after him.'

She flicked to a sheet in the file, not wanting to encourage his fantasies. 'No Miss Apple-Tits: "Preliminary search of apartment registered to brother, Oleg Timchenko – address attached – no indication of planned absence. Luggage intact. Car – a one-year-old black BMW mini – parked on the street"… etcetera.'

'OK, I get it. You're saying the egghead is really missing. Where do we start, Boss?'

'The brother.'

She raised an eyebrow as Rogov joined her at the queue for the breathalyser. He was often over the alcohol limit in the morning.

'Yeah, well, Boss. I've been ordered to cut down.'

'By Oksana?'

'Nah, she's hoping I'll have a coronary so she can find someone better looking.'

'An impossibility, surely.'

'Yeah… Anyway, it was him.' Rogov jerked a thumb upwards.

'Dostoynov?' she whispered.

'He told me I'm out if I don't quit.'

'Quit what… drinking?'

'Everything.' The muscles tightened in Rogov's jaw. 'Smoking, drinking, eating shit, sitting on my *zad*… he said even my attitude needs to go on a diet. You don't think it's about Mikhail? Getting rid of me to punish him?'

'Could be,' she said to ease the pained expression on Rogov's face. The truth was, Dostoynov was physically fit and rarely drank alcohol. Like any puritan, he took a dim view of anyone who wasn't as iron-willed. Still, it wouldn't do Rogov any harm.

'Better do what he says,' she said.

Rogov blew into the breathalyser and signed for a Makarov; she did the same, and picked up a set of keys for a departmental car. They zipped up their padded jackets and she pulled on her black Cossack's hat made of 'fish fur' – the artificial kind – while Rogov fixed his *ushanka* in place. Outside, he methodically worked the car park, pointing the fob on an extended arm and clicking the button until he saw the indicators flashing on a saloon car-shaped block of snow.

Oleg Timchenko's apartment on Podolskaya Ulitsa was in a block halfway between the Art-Nouveau-styled Vitebsk Station and the Technological Institute. Like any other grand street in St Petersburg, it had suffered from decades of neglect, with uneven stucco and rusting ironwork over the ground-floor windows. Spaced at every ten metres or so, massive grey-painted steel pipes were fixed to the exterior to direct the deluges in the spring thaw.

Without looking inside the building, she knew the communal hallway and courtyard to the rear would be squalid, with bare concrete and decomposing cigarette butts hidden by layers of dirty snow. Step inside an apartment, though, and it was a different story; each home was a proud display of individuality. It amazed her that Russia's experiment with communism had lasted for so long.

Parked neatly by the pavement was a black Mini. She pulled out the notes and checked the registration – it belonged to Max Timchenko. She pressed a button and waited for the buzzer to sound. Rogov wheezed alongside her as they climbed to the third floor. A door was already open, the frame blocked by a *kachok*, an iron-pumper, wearing a sports vest and latex shorts. He smelled of liniment and sweat.

'Oleg Timchenko?' she asked.

'Yes.'

Max's brother's legs were normal-sized, making them look skinny compared to his inflated torso – a body-builder who spent too much time doing bench presses at the expense of other exercises. Up close, she also noticed facial acne – a sign of illegal steroid use.

She felt in her jacket pocket for her purse and took out her ID card. 'I'm Senior Detective Ivanova… this is Detective Rogov. We'd like to speak to you.'

'Is this about Max?' There was no trace of emotion in the eyes.

'Yes.'

The body-builder stepped aside. The apartment was immaculately clean. Clearly a man's place, judging by the charcoal drawing of a rhino on the wall and the two black-leather recliners trained with laser accuracy on a large television. Between the chairs, a litre container of a thick brown liquid rested on a small table. The apartment was chilly from the open window, letting in street noise as well as freezing air.

An image on the television screen had been paused, capturing a topless muscle-man midway through a one-handed press-up. She wondered briefly how it was possible for Oleg to be so closely related to an arts professor, and if their shared childhood had been difficult as a result – that might explain his lack of empathy.

'Have you heard anything?' Oleg asked.

'No,' she said. 'Do you mind switching that thing off? It's distracting.'

'Sure.' Oleg flicked a switch on a remote to kill the muscle man on the television.

'Is this your apartment or his?' Rogov asked, making it clear to her that he hadn't read the notes prepared by Sergeant Smolin.

'Mine,' Oleg replied. 'Max finished his studies in Moscow two years ago. He's saving up for his own place. I gave him my spare room, and he never left.'

'You didn't mind?' she asked.

His massive shoulders heaved in a shrug. 'Why would I? He's my brother… he pays half the bills.'

'What's this?' asked Rogov, picking up the container on the small table and sniffing at it.

CHAPTER 12

'Protein shake.'

'Do they work?'

Oleg glanced at Rogov's shirt, pulled taut by his overhanging belly. 'With a lifestyle change.'

Rogov grunted and put the container down. 'When did you last see Max?' he asked.

'I'll deal with that,' Natalya said. 'Why don't you take a look at his room?'

Sooner or later she would have to decide what to do with Rogov. He would buckle if Dostoynov applied the slightest pressure. With Mikhail's job on the line, as well as her own, she couldn't risk telling him Max was a Decembrist.

'Boss.' Rogov frowned, unhappy that he was being shut out.

'In there.' Oleg pointed at an ancient wooden door next to a framed picture of Nataliya Kuznetsova, the power lifter, posing in a competition with her extraordinary, chemically enhanced muscles.

She waited until Rogov had gone. 'Tell me about Max. When did you last see him?'

Oleg dabbed at an inflamed area of acne on his cheek. 'Friday, the day before Christmas Eve. He went out for lunch.'

'What time was he due back?'

'Early evening.' He slumped in one of the leather chairs, picked up the protein shake container and sipped from it.

'And when did you last see him?'

'Around eleven that morning.'

The timing matched the excuse Elizaveta had given her mother about meeting someone for lunch. 'Who was he going to see?'

'I didn't ask.' Oleg gave her a quizzical look.

She wondered if he knew about Max's political activities and disapproved of them. There was no way to ask without betraying Vita's trust.

'Who do you think he was going to see?'

'Dunno. His friends are arseholes.' Oleg drank some more of his shake. 'Always wanting to discuss stupid shit.'

'Do you have any names?'

He heaved his shoulders again in a shrug. 'They cleared off a few weeks after he moved in with me.'

Because he made them as welcome as an investigative reporter in Grozny. 'So what happened then?'

'I stayed up until one o'clock, wondering where he was.'

'What else?' she asked.

'Nothing else. I was pissed off because he hadn't come home and he had my car.'

It was coming back to her. Something that had got lost in the hangover. 'Your car?'

'I didn't mind – usually I take the Metro anyway – but I needed it on Christmas Eve to get a few things. Max and Vita had done the shopping but they always buy shit I don't like.'

'But then you found it?'

'Yeah, he'd left it outside. Was it you who spoke to Vita?'

She flicked her eyes in the direction Rogov had gone, then back to Oleg as a warning for him to be careful. 'Yes.'

'I saw the car on the street,' Oleg said. 'We have this dish by the TV where we always leave the keys, but they weren't there. I searched the apartment before I found them.'

'Where?'

'Still in the ignition. I wasn't happy.'

If Max's disappearance was the result of a brotherly argument turned violent, then claiming to find the keys in the car was a nice touch – an attempt to place Max's last movements away from the apartment.

'And you never heard him come in?'

CHAPTER 12

'I use ear plugs at night… the traffic keeps me awake.'

'So Max might have got home after one o'clock, then left before you got up.'

Oleg rubbed his cheek again. 'Or maybe he never came in.'

Now he was distancing himself even more from Max's movements. In her experience, it was the guilty who often thought up helpful explanations for the police. If Elizaveta's death was also related to Max's disappearance then Oleg was unlikely to be a suspect, but he wasn't doing himself any favours.

'Have you used your car since?'

Rogov emerged from the bedroom. He was wearing latex gloves and shook his head slightly – he'd found nothing obvious.

'Only for a supermarket run on Wednesday.'

'What's going on?' asked Rogov.

'Mr Timchenko is explaining that Max borrowed his car on the day he was last seen.'

Oleg's chest expanded a little. 'It's a 1989 Audi Quattro.'

'What's it like to drive?' Rogov asked, then looked at her. 'Sorry, Boss, the Quattro is a legend.'

'No, let's stay on the subject of cars,' she said. 'I have an ancient Volvo, so excuse me if I don't understand why you men love these old models.'

'Was Max into classic cars too?' she added.

Oleg gulped down some more of his protein shake. 'Nah, he was like you.'

'Captain,' she reminded him.

'Yeah, sorry.'

'Then this raises an interesting question. Why did Max borrow your car when he already has one registered in his name?'

'The black Mini,' added Rogov. 'It's parked outside.'

'Yeah, that's his. He borrowed my Quattro maybe once a month. He offered to pay half the insurance – obligatory and comprehensive – so I wasn't going to argue.'

She frowned. 'Why would he do that if he wasn't into cars?'

'You should know,' began Oleg, 'You're the one who spoke to Vita.'

'Who's Vita?' asked Rogov.

Oleg was silent.

'Look, Boss, if you—'

She cut him off. 'I'll explain later,' she said.

'No, I'd like to hear now.'

As subordinates went, Rogov was strictly of the insubordinate variety. She conceded he had a right to know though. 'Vita is Max's twin sister. She came to see me on Monday.'

'And that's the big secret?'

'Yes.' She ran her hands over her face, aping tiredness to disguise the lie.

'You spoke to her?' asked Rogov.

'I saw her for maybe five minutes and told her to report Max missing.'

Rogov frowned, 'But that's nothing. Why didn't you tell me?'

'Just drop it Rogov, I didn't think it was important.'

She dreaded going home with him now. The sulking was going to last for the rest of the day. Except this time it wasn't. His hands were on his hips. After the indignities he'd suffered from Dostoynov, she could see he'd had enough.

'So, Boss, why are you so keen on knowing why Max used the Quattro?'

She sighed. 'Because I'm guessing he was the careful type.' She avoided using the word paranoid in front of Oleg. 'The Mini was only a year old.'

'So that would make it safer. It would have airbags and shit.'

CHAPTER 12

'Look, Rogov, can't we talk about this another time?'

'Boss, can't you just tell me?'

'Did he always use the Mini for work?' she asked Oleg.

'Yeah.'

'And he was cagey when he borrowed your car?'

Oleg rubbed his chin. 'Not cagey. He used it when he fancied a drive out of the city.'

'I still don't understand,' said Rogov. 'Why are you saying it's safer for him to use the Quattro?'

She exhaled heavily. It sounded like a groan. 'Because, as an imported vehicle, the Mini has an emergency response system and satellite navigation.'

'So the Mini's even safer,' he said.

Suddenly it occurred to her that Rogov's unusual petulance and anger was nicotine withdrawal – he hadn't had a cigarette all morning. She thought of going to the nearest *produkti* and buying him a packet of Winstons to end his misery.

'My theory is Max borrowed the Audi when he didn't want to be found. He was worried someone could use the response system in the Mini to track his movements, or if he was arrested we would check his sat nav to find all the places he'd visited.'

'Boss.' Rogov had an earnest look now. His eyebrows had lifted in the centre like one of the city's famous drawbridges. 'Boss,' he repeated. 'We can't do this shit. Not again. You're talking FSB, aren't you?'

Well, at least it was out in the open.

Oleg scratched an area of inflamed skin. 'Max used to go on demonstrations until an OMON riot cop gave him a tap on the head at the March of the Millions… left him with a few stitches. After that, he told me he'd stopped playing politics. He never stopped worrying about the *menti* though. When he borrowed my Quattro he took the dash cam out.'

So Oleg didn't know Max was a Decembrist. Presumably he didn't know about Vita either. Well, she wasn't going to be the one to tell.

'That's all I'm saying about the car.' She raised a placating hand to Rogov. 'Max was probably worried that he was being bugged or followed, not that anyone was actually doing it. I don't even know if it's possible for the FSB to bug a car's safety system.'

Rogov snorted. 'So he only borrowed Oleg's car when he was feeling paranoid. With respect, Captain, that's bullshit. Also, don't you see? Max went missing the same day we found Elizaveta Kalinina. If he was into politics and so was she—'

She cut him off. 'As Oleg said, Max hasn't been involved in politics for a long time. The March of the Millions was six years ago. Let's not complicate matters.'

Oleg was watching them both. 'If you're both finished, I need to take a shower.'

Unlike a murder or kidnapping that left a body or ransom note, a disappearance left a question mark, and everyone reacted differently. Vita's reaction was bordering on hysteria – though she was evidently closer to Max. Oleg, on the other hand, was disturbingly blasé.

She asked, 'Was there anything else you noticed? Was Max depressed or worried, or frightened of anyone?'

Oleg rubbed his cheek, scraping his acne. 'Nothing I can think of.'

'We'll be in touch.' She turned for the door.

'I was angry with him,' Oleg said after a moment, his eyes not meeting hers.

She stopped. 'Why?'

'My Audi, he always kept it clean. This time he left it in a real state. There was ice and mud all over the seats.'

13

The flatbed truck had been spewing thick white diesel fumes into Podolskaya Ulitsa for the last twenty minutes while it manoeuvred into position to raise the Audi Quattro. In his padded tracksuit and hoodie, Oleg had been calm until then. He had even signed off the paperwork authorising Natalya to remove the vehicle without a warrant – though she had insinuated his refusal would be viewed with suspicion.

The driver in his blue overalls returned to his cab after ratcheting the nylon straps to the car's frame. As the Audi was lifted, it pitched, rubbing the rear bumper against the accumulated snow by the road's edge.

Oleg wailed, waving his inflated arms. He hammered his fists on the window. 'Stop, you're scraping it.'

The driver's hearing had become selective. The Audi tilted again.

'What the fuck are you doing?' yelled Oleg. He yanked open the door. 'You incompetent bastard.'

'Stop him.' She tapped Rogov lightly on the shoulder – his hearing had become selective too.

'Me?' Rogov whined. 'He's the size of a fucking gorilla.'

'Shit, I'll do it myself.'

Oleg's head was inside the driver's cab. His fingers had curled into fists.

'Mr Timchenko,' she called, 'step away or I'll arrest you.'

A sneer passed across Oleg's lips. 'For what?'

'Interfering with the duties of an investigator. If you hit that man it's prison, I can't make it simpler than that. How will you help Max from a jail cell?'

'I think we should bring him in, Boss.' Rogov had decided belatedly to back her up by standing behind her. 'I've seen it before. When I was in the militia it took four of us to stop a skinhead ripping up a bar... steroids.'

Rogov spoke low, next to her ear. 'With a temper like that...'

He left the rest unsaid but it was easy to guess the rest. With a temper like that, he could have killed his brother.

'Maybe,' she said. Perhaps Oleg had found the mud in his beloved car after Elizaveta and Max had returned from a trip in the Audi. He'd been unable to contain his rage and killed Max, then was forced to dispose of the witness.

She felt the weight of the handcuffs pulling on her jeans, and was tempted to unhook them. Instead, she touched Oleg on the waist. 'Come on, go inside. If they damage your car I'll help you file for compensation. It's not helping Max.'

She reached up to his shoulder and turned him around.

His eyes were pink, and she was surprised to see tears. 'I miss him,' he said.

'I know. Go inside. I'll take care of this.'

'Will you bring him home?' His lip trembled. A man unused to his emotions, now unable to keep them in check.

'I'll do my best. I promise.'

She watched him waddle uncertainly to the apartment block door.

Once he was out of hearing-range she turned to Rogov. 'I want to know where Max took that car, and I want to know what Oleg has done with it since.'

He looked horrified. 'How do I do that?'

'I don't care,' she said, annoyed by his lack of support. 'You're supposed to be a detective, aren't you?'

14

There was a genius behind the upright piano. Dark, swept-back hair and an expression of manic joy on his face. Madman or drug addict, she couldn't decide and she didn't care. He looked Korean, and in his crow-like voice spoke fluent Russian, English, German and, as far as she could tell, French. He impersonated Vysotsky, Viktor Tsoi, even Radiohead. He knew everything and could play anything, striking the keys with abandonment and precision. A genius.

'What about "In Piter we drink"?' Natalya yelled.

'Leningrad,' the pianist growled back. 'Best band in *Rodina*.'

The singer started a passable imitation of Sergey Shnurov, the lead singer of Leningrad, making up for the absence of brass by pounding on the piano.

'"In Rostov they have amazing hash brownies",' Natalya half-sang, half-shouted. At least a dozen others joined in.

Opposite Natalya, Rogov's wife sipped a Coke Zero – she had come to take her husband home an hour ago. Rogov was leaning over the table, huddled conspiratorially with Mikhail.

Natalya pointed in the air and shouted along to the chorus.

Oksana was waiting patiently for the music to finish. Finally, she asked, 'Is Stepan in trouble?'

'Rogov? Nah,' Natalya shouted back, caught out by the drop in volume. 'He's an arsehole but he's OK.'

Natalya put an arm on Rogov's shoulder, 'You're an arsehole.'

'Yeah, I'm an arsehole.'

'See' – she turned back to Oksana – 'but he's our arsehole.' She jabbed her chest with a finger.

Oksana winced.

Diagonally across the table, Mikhail's face was luminous.

'Natashenka, what's all this noise for?'

'You're an arsehole too.'

He laughed. 'Why me?'

'Because' – she fought for a reason – 'You left me.'

Oksana sipped her Coke. 'You're drunk, Natasha.' There was no smile, only a bitter edge to the words.

'Misha.' She held up her glass of wine. 'To Rostov!' He clinked her glass.

He tapped her glass half-heartedly. 'Sure.'

'Misha, have you got any fucking cigarettes? I need one.'

'Angel.' He stood, holding up the packet.

She saw Mikhail slip a Sobranie to Rogov. If she saw it, then so did Oksana.

'You smoke that, I'm leaving you here,' Oksana hissed.

'Oh, baby, don't be like that. I'll see you at home, my *kroshka*.' Rogov tried to pass it off as an endearing goodbye.

'You can fucking walk then. Don't lose your keys like last time.' Oksana pushed the table against Natalya to get up.

She left.

'In Piter we drink… in Piter we drink!' the three of them sang to themselves.

Rogov had the expression of a naughty child. 'It's safe. She's gone. I can hear the exhaust.'

Outside, they puffed greedily on the cigarettes.

'Are you angry with me, Natashenka?' Mikhail asked.

'No,' she pulled herself into the open folds of his overcoat, 'Only Dostoynov. Hey, what was it in Rostov… apart from amazing hash brownies? I can't remember.'

CHAPTER 14

'I'm going to see an ex-bank robber.'

'Yeah, bad man.'

'Another of Leonid Laskin's cases.' Mikhail added.

'Laskin the *alkanaut*?' Rogov giggled. 'I used to drink with him.'

'I told you Dostoynov gave me his old cases? Well, this one is ancient – a seven-year-old robbery.' Mikhail exhaled a cloud of bluish smoke. 'I've got to see a thief to see if he remembers doing it. Laskin never bothered to check his alibi. What's the betting the thief has amnesia?'

Natalya scuffed her boot on some ice crystals. The celebration was meant to be a welcome, but it had become a farewell – Mikhail had only been back a day, and now he was leaving again. 'How long this time?'

'Two to three days.'

'Then he'll have another one ready for you.' She crunched the ice and twisted her boot to grind it.

'Hey, maybe he'll send you to Paris next time.' Rogov chuckled at his own joke.

'You're funny.' The nicotine was fighting through a fog of booze. 'What happened to the other case… that girl?'

'Diana Maricheva?' Mikhail spoke smoothly. He wasn't as drunk as her – neither of them were. If she had any more booze they'd have to pour her into a taxi.

'They were all there,' he said, smoking quietly. 'Mother, the stepfather – Shugaley, aunts, uncles, even the local *menti*, all crowded in a House of Culture and expecting me to be the one to catch the bastard who turned Diana into fertiliser.' His eyes had become moist. 'It's like looking for wind in a fucking field.'

She pressed against Mikhail's body and he wrapped his arms around her. She'd missed the stupid idiot. 'What about the place where they found her?'

He spoke over her head. 'It was Konevets Island in August, when it was crawling with tourists – people hiring boats, tour buses, cruises even… Laskin took a few statements, but I wouldn't wipe Rogov's arse on them.'

'Hey,' complained Rogov, who hadn't been listening.

'What were the bones in? Plastic?'

'No, white cloth… no good for fingerprints.'

Rogov asked, 'What happened to this girl?'

'Her body was left outside the Chapel of Saint Nicholas three years ago, and it was already decaying. The pathologist said she'd been buried somewhere else for a few years before being brought to Konevets.'

'So the killer grew a conscience,' suggested Rogov.

'How many times have you known that to happen?' Mikhail blew a plume of smoke over her head. 'Also, he had to get across the lake with what was left of her body. Why risk being caught when you're already free?'

She asked, 'Before you left, you said something about a cross?'

Mikhail extended the thumb and forefinger of his left hand in front of her. 'It was this big. Made from olive wood. Nicely done, but not professional. My guess is someone made it for the girl.'

Her legs were aching and she'd need to wash her hair in the morning. Still, it was worth it to celebrate his brief return before Dostoynov despatched him again. She was becoming a believer in *Lada* – the old pagan god of love and marriage – or else she had forgotten just how good Mikhail smelled: a perfect balance of savoury and sweet.

'And the cloth?' she asked. 'Had the girl been buried in it?'

'No, it was new. What are you getting at, Angel?'

She wasn't sure herself. The cigarette was making her feel sick now. She sucked in the freezing air and tasted bile at the back of her throat. 'Maybe it wasn't the killer who found the girl.'

'Then why didn't they call us?' asked Rogov.

CHAPTER 14

'I'm not sure, but there must be a reason. Why dig her up, wrap her in a sheet, then take her to Konevets for a monk to find?'

Mikhail squeezed his arms together, pulling her tighter against him. She could feel his belly filling the concave arch of her back. 'You think they had something to hide?'

'Maybe.' She puffed on the cigarette again. 'What about a building contractor who dug up her body by accident and didn't need the *menti* wrecking a tight schedule? What if he's religious and handy enough with wood to make the cross?'

'That's still wind in the field,' complained Mikhail. 'What am I supposed to do – track down every contractor who worked in Leningrad Oblast in 2015? Most won't even be on the books.'

'No,' she said, pulling away from Mikhail's grip. 'Unless he was working on Krestovsky Stadium, his building project will be long finished. And he'll have been paid too, which means he won't care so much about keeping quiet. He's probably more worried we'll think he killed the girl if he comes forward.'

'I've got an idea,' she said. 'Do you know a journalist?'

'We're not supposed to speak to the press,' sniffed Rogov. 'They hang around headquarters like dogs by a butcher's shop.'

Mikhail was silent for a moment. 'I use a freelancer – Pyotr Revich. We haven't spoken in a long time.'

She could feel the nicotine working on her brain. 'Misha, if Diana's family got to a cynical *ment* like you, imagine what a journalist could do with the right words. Ask Revich if he'll write about a girl who ran away to the big city and the heroic detective who won't let her death be just another statistic.'

'Sorry, Boss, what's this got to do with the case?' Rogov asked.

Mikhail was nodding. 'No, I get it, Angel. Revich will lay on the guilt and I'll ask Dostoynov – when he's not being an insufferable prig

– to see if he'll go on the record to say we're not interested in who dug up Diana's body.'

Rogov's forehead creased. 'But if you find this builder, all he'll tell you is where the girl was buried. It won't get you very far.'

She was appalled by Rogov's lack of vision. 'Of course it will help. There could be forensic evidence, maybe even witnesses.'

Mikhail joined in. 'And it will get Dostoynov off my back for a few weeks. That is, until the trail goes cold. Then he'll tell the commanders I can't deliver.'

Rogov had left his coat inside. He stretched his denim shirt-cuffs over his hands. 'And when that happens, Misha, you're fucked.'

15

Tuesday had passed in an alcohol-induced blur. All day her head had felt like an overripe melon. Now it was Wednesday evening and Mikhail still hadn't returned. Rather than waiting around for him at home, she risked an icy drive in her Volvo.

On either side of the Toksovo highway, pine branches drooped, their branches buckling under the weight of fresh snow. The scene looked the same, except the pollution-stained banks lining the road had gained an extra twenty centimetres in height. She slowed down, anticipating the sharp bend where she had almost crashed the Hunter nearly two weeks before. At 6 p.m. it was as dark as the sky she had seen that night. The sign for Kuzmolovsky Cemetery was there, almost obliterated by frost. She slowed to a crawl and turned off the main road.

In the cemetery car park she left her Volvo next to a little Japanese jeep of the patronising kind designed for women that was never meant to be used off-road. If there had been a streetlamp to see, she imagined it would be painted a pastel shade. In her glove compartment she found a torch and swept it over the vehicle, seeing a car seat in the back, before turning the beam to the cemetery – an enclave of the dead surrounded by the vaster numbers of Stalin's victims in the forests beyond.

The light caught picture frames propped at the base of each gravestone. Occasionally her torch illuminated rectangular troughs in the earth – plots for the people still alive. In the summer, when the ground was soft, gravediggers guessed at the number of deaths over the coming winter.

Back on the main road she kept close to the snow bank, sweeping the torchlight behind her to alert approaching cars. The wind picked up and a gust blew a dusting of snow off the pines, enveloping her in a miniature blizzard. She folded up her collar to meet her Cossack's hat and tucked her gloves under the sleeves of her coat to hide her exposed wrists. Ahead, tatty police tape flapped in the wind, half-absorbed by the compacted snow wall.

There were lights twinkling at the area where Elizaveta's body had been discovered. She switched off her torch as she saw another beam of light slashing against the bank to the forest floor, and stepped inside the broken snow wall. Inside the ditch was a runway of candles in glass jars lining the interior of the bank and the rise to the forest. A figure in a hooded suede coat with a woman's shape was positioning a glass portrait on top of the frozen mud wall. The feminine jeep. The child seat. She fought to remember her first name.

'Valeria?' she called out.

Elizaveta's mother was too engrossed in her task, or else was simply indifferent. She was fixing string to the glass portrait. Once it was in place, she stood on tiptoes to tie the string to a rock at the edge of the forest. Valeria stepped back and lifted a candle in a glass jar to check her work. A red balaclava covered her face, decorative white circles accentuating the holes around the eyes and mouth. On a middle-aged woman it was grotesque – the face of a nightmare clown.

Natalya stumbled against the snow bank.

'Can you take that thing off?' she said.

Valeria peeled up the bottom half of the balaclava. She gave a cheerless smile that was no less sinister. 'Weren't expecting that, were you?'

'Why are you…?' She stopped because she knew why. She'd seen pictures of the Decembrists in their garish balaclavas and surgical masks.

'Where was it?' she asked.

Valeria was nonchalant. 'Hidden in a box of Artem's baby clothes.'

CHAPTER 15

'Elizaveta's?'

'Of course.'

'Did you find anything else?'

'Just this. I wanted to wear it, I don't know if you'd understand. I suppose the police will claim she was in Pussy Riot now.'

'Did you tell *Sledkom*?' Natalya asked.

Liza's mother opened her mouth a fraction, as if she intended to spit. 'No.'

'Why did Elizaveta hide it?'

Valeria pursed her lips as if she disapproved. 'Maybe she was in Pussy Riot after all… will you tell *Sledkom*?'

'Not if you don't.'

'You are a strange *ment*.' Valeria turned her attention back to the frame. 'I could see it wasn't a surprise to you, that Liza was political?'

'She was in a group of activists called the Decembrists… that's why *Sledkom* took over.'

'What do you think?' Valeria asked.

Natalya inspected the frame. It held a photograph taken from a maternity ward. Elizaveta was cradling Artem, her face pink with the exertion of labour.

'I put it up high so people would see her when they drive past.'

She felt Valeria Kalinina scrutinising her, checking her reactions to see if they were genuine. 'It's beautiful.'

'And what are you doing here?' Her voice was like granite. Natalya knew Elizaveta's son would survive. The country had been built by women like Valeria.

'I was driving past,' she said. It was a weak reason.

Valeria shrugged, sensing the truth behind the lie. She tapped the glass on the picture with a gloved hand. 'I want people to see who she really was. Liza came home every night… she wasn't a drug addict.'

'I'm sure she wasn't. Those journalists are evil.'

'It wasn't a journalist… it was that man from *Sledkom*.'

'Investigator Yelin?'

'Him. He said Liza had fallen in with bad company… one of them had given her some drugs. That's why he needed to know their names. He's a liar, you can see it in his eyes. Besides, the only friends of Liza's I know are from her antenatal class.' There was the cheerless smile again. 'So that's what I did. I gave him all their names so he can chase his tail.' Valeria straightened her back. 'So have you given up on Liza too? Shall I tell Artem his mother was a drug addict who deserved to die in a ditch?'

Natalya felt claustrophobic, caught between the snow bank, the wall of frozen mud, and a grieving mother. 'It's *Sledkom*'s case. If I help you, I'll lose my job.'

Liza's mother snorted. 'It must be very important, that job of yours.'

'I haven't given up on your daughter.'

'But are you going to do anything?'

'I promise I'll do my best.'

'You said that before. You stood in my kitchen and said, "I'll do my best".' Valeria shook her head. 'There, I'm finished for today. Next time, don't make promises you can't keep.'

Valeria picked up a ball of string and tucked it in her pocket.

'I'm sorry.'

'If you want to be sorry, find out how she died. Tell everyone she didn't die from drugs.'

'I…' the excuse was frozen on her lips. She had thought to say something about waiting for *Sledkom* to get the results of toxicology tests. It was all bullshit, though. The regime didn't admit to making mistakes. There would be no toxicology report.

CHAPTER 15

Valeria sensed her indecision. 'See? You can't even do that. I hope the girl looking for her brother has more luck with you.'

'I'm sorry.'

Valeria scythed the air with her hand. 'There you go again with the sympathy.' She started walking in the direction of the cemetery, then she turned, unable to control herself. 'I don't want to see you here next time.'

Natalya stayed among the candles flickering in the breeze. A minute or two later an engine rattled in the night – the Japanese jeep, she assumed – and the twin beams of headlights lit up the highway. Natalya cut through the gap in the snow bank and began walking. The wind had dropped and the road was eerily quiet. She felt in her pocket for her iPhone, flicked its address book and tapped the circular image of a tanned man wearing a running vest.

It was answered after two rings. 'Captain?'

'Wait a moment.'

A car approached and she crossed the road to give it space.

'Leo, I've got a job for you,' she said, hurrying across the road to the cemetery side. 'It might get you into trouble.'

Primakov paused. 'Of course, Captain, whatever you want.'

'You don't owe me anything, Leo.'

Except she knew Primakov wouldn't see it that way. He'd betrayed her on her last case, and no matter what she said, the guilt would weigh on him.

'It might be dangerous,' she said. 'Dostoynov won't approve.'

'It doesn't matter.'

She was exploiting his need to make it up to her. Calling him had been a mistake. If anything bad happened to him it would be on her conscience.

'Leo, just forget I asked.'

'Captain, I'm not doing it for you. I want to be on the right side.'

'It's always the losing side, Leo.'

'It doesn't matter. When I'm old, I want to look back without feeling shame. Tell me what you need, Captain.'

'You know that case we were looking at not so long ago?'

'When you spent the night with Rogov?'

'Don't remind me.' She cut off the main road for the cemetery. Her Volvo was the only vehicle in the car park. 'How do you feel about doing some digging? Just you and me.'

'Nervous, Captain.'

'Same here, Leo. And there's one more thing: no more Monsoon Malabar. After this we're even.'

She had been asleep when Mikhail's arm scooped her waist and pulled her back to his chest.

'You smell,' she said.

'You get used to it after a while... I did.'

He lifted her hair and kissed the nape of her neck. A shiver ran along her spine.

'How do you feel about having sex with your husband?'

'I'm not sure... what time is it?'

'Does that make a difference? It never used to.'

She stretched her arm behind her back and patted the side of his hip. 'Misha, you're naked.'

'And you're wearing a T-shirt.'

'Ramones, 1978.'

His hand slipped beneath Joey Ramone's white plimsolls. It briefly cupped her belly before heading south.

'I'm not awake yet.'

'Sorry, Babe.'

She felt something brush against her foot. 'Misha? Are you wearing socks?'

CHAPTER 15

'It's cold, baby.'

'We're married, not dead. Take them off now.'

'OK.' He lay on his back and fumbled. 'Socks off.'

She grabbed the bottom of her T-shirt and pulled it over her head. 'And now I'm out of excuses.'

16

Five concrete steps down to the basement of Clinical Hospital No. 31, she saw the pathologist standing in front of a door propped open by a fire extinguisher.

Natalya held up a box of candied pralines. 'Anjelika!'

The pathologist groaned and Natalya caught something about '*menti* bearing gifts'.

She kept going with her exaggerated cheerfulness. 'Anjelika, how are you?'

'My psoriasis is flaring up again. This damned weather makes me itch, and look what I have to wear… plastic. It's torture.' Anjelika Fedyushina sucked on an apple-scented e-cigarette.

Natalya held out the offering. 'I got these for you.'

The pathologist barely glanced at the pralines. 'My physician tells me to lose weight or I can look forward to type-two. And you've got competition. A handsome lieutenant offered to buy me breakfast.' She puffed on the e-cigarette. 'I'm old enough to be his mother, and no doubt his mother's in better shape than me.'

Anjelika took the box of pralines from her. 'So, what do you need?'

'The woman on the Toksovo highway two weeks ago.'

'The political?'

Natalya inhaled sweet apple along with the faintest hit of nicotine. 'Yes.'

The pathologist's face was unreadable. 'Drugs.'

'Really?'

CHAPTER 16

'*Sledkom* said she was a user. I told them all the standard toxicology tests were negative and she had no needle marks. Yelin – the tall, skinny one – told me Kalinina had taken a synthetic drug, maybe salts or some other shit we can't test for. Who am I to argue with the mighty *Sledkom*?'

'So you didn't… argue?'

Dr Fedyushina rocked her head from side to side. It seemed an awkward gesture. 'You go against these people and they destroy you. Haven't you learned that one yet?'

'I missed my self-preservation lessons. So, the post-mortem report… was it just for them?'

'You mean is there anything useful in it?' Dr Fedyushina let out a puff of steam. 'I wouldn't wipe my backside on it. A few tests are outstanding but it won't affect the conclusion. It says what everyone wants to hear. Yelin is coming today to pick it up. Stick around and you might meet him.'

'I've already had the pleasure. Did Elizaveta get the full autopsy or was it an "external only"?'

'External.' The pathologist shrugged. 'They had already decided. There was no point wasting my morning on her.'

'Time of death?' Natalya asked.

'Sometime between the fourth and fifth of January? By the time she came to me she had *rigor mortis* and was half frozen. The cold screws up everything, so your guess is as good as mine – most likely better.'

'Anjelika,' Natalya began, 'I found her lying in a ditch but she had *livor mortis* on the lower half of her body.'

'So someone moved her.'

'They dumped her in a ditch. Elizaveta had a boy, Artem. He's two years old.'

The pathologist raised an arm as if waving her away, 'I know what you're doing. Don't you think I'm sympathetic? I saw the stretch marks.'

'Anjelika, I need to know how she died, so I can tell her mother.'

She didn't blame her any more than she blamed Leo or Mikhail. Officials didn't have to take a bribe: there were a hundred other ways to be compromised.

Anjelika sucked on the e-cigarette and was quiet for a moment. 'I'll tell you something. I've got kids.'

'I think I knew that.'

'Then listen, I don't want that boy growing up thinking some monster forced himself on his mother. I checked for defensive wounds and tested for sperm and seminal fluid. There were none. If that helps you or not, I can't say.'

'As a human being it does… thank you.'

'Now you'll have to find out the rest yourself.'

The pathologist returned to her e-cigarette.

'We should play badminton again. I liked our games.'

'I'm too old and fat. You always beat me. I'll take your candies though.'

'What about your diabetes?'

'I'll give them to the technicians – it keeps them sweet.' Anjelika tucked the e-cigarette inside her gown. 'I'm going in now,' she said. 'And I'm getting so absent-minded I keep forgetting to shut the door.'

Natalya waited a few seconds. Then she stepped into the basement and nudged the fire extinguisher with her foot. The door closed behind her. The paint in the corridor was oatmeal-coloured and old-fashioned radiators belched out heat. It smelled unpleasantly of artificial apple-scented disinfectant too, and she was surprised Anjelika added the same flavour to her nicotine.

Dr Fedyushina had stopped ahead; Natalya caught up.

CHAPTER 16

'So why are you sniffing around a *Sledkom* investigation?' Anjelika asked. 'Are you looking for a terminal career break?'

'I don't trust *Sledkom*. Elizaveta Kalinina was my case.'

'Well, I hope your conscience keeps you warm. *Sledkom* are due at ten, it's best if they don't see you.'

'Why are you helping me?'

'Helping?' The pathologist narrowed her eyes. 'Didn't you know? I'm not here. You're talking to yourself.'

Anjelika swiped a magnetic card through a slot by a set of stainless-steel doors. 'Here's another example of lax security,' she said. 'Someone could just walk in behind me and pick through the papers in my office. I expect they won't bother with the report on the desk because they'll discover my filing cabinet is more interesting.'

She let go of the door and Natalya slipped her foot in the gap before it closed. 'I'm off to the morgue. My assistants are in there too, clearing a backlog. This will help' – she held up the box of candied pralines.

Beyond the double doors the apple disinfectant smell intensified, but it did little to hide the vinegary sting of formaldehyde that burned her sinuses and brought tears to her eyes. On her right, frosted glass windows showed blurred figures in white. Beneath Anjelika's grumpy exterior was a fully functioning conscience. Five years ago, Natalya had been in the pathology lab when black, putrefied liquid oozed out of a corpse she'd help fish out of the Moika. She had gagged on the stench and vomited. Instead of laughing at her expense, Anjelika had taken her outside and offered her a napkin and a cigarette.

Further along the corridor she found rows of offices with name plaques. She hurried past them, conscious that the individuals inside could see her through their windows. She continued past four and checked the plaque to confirm she had reached Anjelika's.

The office door was unlocked. She closed it behind her. The room was untidy, with boxes of the in-house journal from the Russian Union of Pathologists piled up against one wall. She took Anjelika's chair with its beaded seat cover and flicked through the papers on her desk. She located a manila folder containing a single sheet with official stamps and Anjelika's signature. On it the cause of Elizaveta Kalinina's death was listed as 'Overdose by narcotic analogue.'

That was no surprise. Anjelika had said as much. The only relief was that Elizaveta's mother would never see it – relatives were not permitted to view autopsy reports. She was about to check the filing cabinet when she heard a murmur of conversation and the tapping of shoe leather on the hospital tiles.

'That's her office,' she heard a man say.

There was a murmur of thanks, followed by receding footsteps. A new conversation started. A man's voice – snide, superior. The woman, his subordinate, barely spoke. Ilya Yelin and Tatyana Dubnik. The beaded seat cover rattled as Natalya sprang out of the chair.

There was a sharp knock and Yelin called out, "Dr Fedyushina?"

Natalya held her breath and pressed her ear to the door. It was hot in the office. Pinpricks of sweat broke out on her forehead.

The door handle jerked and she thought to grab it. Instead, she jammed the toe of her boot against the door and held her breath.

The door jerked on its hinges. 'It's locked,' Dubnik said. 'I'll call her.'

Natalya let out a slow breath. She heard Anjelika's phone ringing on the receiver of Dubnik's mobile. It was replaced by a tinny voice.

'We'll be there,' Dubnik said, hanging up. She addressed Yelin. 'Fedyushina's on her break. We're to meet her at the canteen now.'

Natalya waited for the footsteps to recede and pushed herself away from the door. The filing cabinet was locked. She pulled open the desk drawers until she found a key. She worked quickly, knowing that anyone walking past would see her. The first drawer was packed with folder dividers. She flicked through them, looking for Elizaveta's name. All she found was administration documents, brochures and invoices. She went to try the second drawer, then noticed a taped message on the last: *Autopsiya*. She knelt to the floor and pulled it open. The drawer was crammed with dividers splitting files chronologically. Her fingers skipped to the most recent folder and she pulled out all the papers, before closing the drawers to the cabinet and ducking behind Anjelika's desk.

There seemed to be little order to them. She found a scrap of paper, a computer printout, with E.D. Kalinina listed under *Subjekt*, then another, and put them aside. From experience, she knew the full range of toxicology tests would take months and Anjelika's work was already compromised. Some tests would be cancelled, others discarded because they didn't agree with the official cause of death.

In the pile, a stamped and signed sheet confirmed there were no traces of opioids, amphetamines, cocaine or marijuana in Elizaveta's blood. Another sheet confirming a blood-alcohol reading of 0.000 mg/g. She finished flicking through the papers and then retrieved the tiny digital printouts she had set aside. Several were chits confirming tissue samples had been submitted for the brain, liver, kidneys, heart and lungs, along with the stomach contents and vitreous – eye jelly.

Anjelika had hinted there was something important in the cabinet, but she had missed it. She sorted through the papers again and found a printout no bigger than a shop till receipt. It read, "*Subjekt: E.D. Kalinina.*" and had several numbers printed against chemical formulae. One of them had been circled in blue pen: "CO_3^{2-}".

Outside, there were fresh footsteps. She went to brace herself against the door but was too slow.

Anjelika entered and instantly recoiled. 'Detective Ivanova,' she said as a warning.

Natalya held up the printout. 'I found it, thank you, Anjelika.' She brushed past the pathologist, nodding at Yelin and Dubnik on the way.

She kept walking, her boots echoing on the corridor, her heart beating twice normal speed. The image of Ilya Yelin's agitated face fixed in her mind. His dark eyes observing her with cold interest.

17

Her mobile rang on the way to her Volvo. It was a reminder that she'd received a voicemail message. She cursed the hospital basement's lack of signal and tapped the screen.

"Boss," the voicemail began. "We got the bodybuilder's Audi on the ANPR. Call me, it's urgent."

The message ended. She checked the time: he'd called over an hour ago.

She knew what it was about. She'd asked – no, ordered – Rogov to find where Oleg Timchenko's beloved Audi Quattro had gone the day Max disappeared. And he'd found it on one of the automatic number plate recognition cameras monitoring the main highways. But what was so urgent?

Ice crunched as she jogged to her car, calling Rogov on the way. His phone was ringing. She unlocked the car, wedging the mobile between her right ear and shoulder.

'*Privyet*—' he said.

'Rogov, wait for me.'

'Shit,' she hissed as his voicemail message continued talking over her.

There was a beep for the caller to leave a message. 'It's Natalya,' she said, 'I'll be at headquarters in ten minutes. Don't do anything stupid.'

It took an eternity to cover half the city. By the time she found a parking spot on Suvorovsky Prospekt it was nearly eleven o'clock. Rogov wasn't at his desk. She checked all the meeting rooms and eventually found him in Dostoynov's office. He was seated in the broken chair normally reserved for Mikhail. Opposite them both was the hulking frame of Oleg.

She lingered, waiting for Dostoynov to gaze in her direction. When he did, he offered no encouragement to join them. Rogov's cheeks were flushed, even with the fierce air-conditioning. She went to her desk and checked her emails, but couldn't concentrate.

After half an hour, she took a call. The sharp voice at the other end belonged to Major Belikova.

'Margarita, what a pleasure,' she said.

'Likewise, Ivanova. If you still care, I've got some news about that favour you asked for.'

'I care.'

'Then meet me this evening. You can be my date. I'll see you at the trampoline centre.'

'Where are you?'

'The cultural capital. Didn't I tell you I'm from Piter? I'll see you at the Razgon on Stachek, 6 p.m.'

Time passed slowly. Shortly after noon a dejected Rogov walked past her, escorting Oleg. Vita's brother scowled at her, rubbing his wrists.

'Captain, a moment please.'

Dostoynov's voice was unambiguous. How much harm had Rogov managed to do by acting on his own initiative?

In the office, she wasn't offered Mikhail's chair, or any other – a clear message she was in trouble. She closed the door behind her.

'Where have you been, Captain?'

Had Ilya Yelin realised she had been sniffing around the pathology department to find out about Elizaveta's autopsy? If he had, he would surely have told Dostoynov.

CHAPTER 17

She decided to lie. As an ex-FSB officer, Dostoynov ought to appreciate the gesture. 'I visited Max Timchenko's sister, Vita. They were quite close, apparently.'

'Anything useful?'

She recognised the same expression of feigned interest she saw on Mikhail's face when he asked her about her day. 'She gave me a few names to follow up but no one held a grudge against her brother.'

'No matter. Your sergeant has been busy this morning. I understand you asked him to look for the whereabouts of Oleg Timchenko's car.'

'Yes, Colonel.'

Dostoynov was quiet for a moment.

'Rogov told me your interesting theory that Max Timchenko borrowed his brother's car because it couldn't be tracked.'

She despaired at Rogov's inability to keep his mouth shut. 'It was only a theory,' she said.

'A theory confirmed when Oleg told you Max routinely removed the dashboard camera from his car when he borrowed it. I may only be a Lieutenant Colonel, but that tells me Max Timchenko is involved in criminal or political activities. I'm inclined to think that, as an arts professor, he's political.'

Dostoynov's tone was friendly. It made her more alert.

'According to Oleg,' he continued, 'Max returned the Quattro a matter of hours after Elizaveta Kalinina's body was discovered. I have to ask the question, Captain, are your liberal sensibilities stopping you from seeing an obvious connection? One that even Sergeant Rogov was able to make?'

Dostoynov looked up without raising his head; the effect was menacing. 'Anything to say, Captain?'

'I don't agree, Colonel. *Sledkom* believe Elizaveta Kalinina died from a drug overdose and Max Timchenko doesn't match the profile of a dealer.'

'Let's cut out the shit, shall we? *Sledkom* don't care. They labelled Kalinina a drug addict to discredit the Decembrists and round up her contacts. As far as they are concerned she's one less traitor to worry about.' He held up his hand as if to say he didn't agree with it. 'While you were busy making house calls this morning, Sergeant Rogov found an ANPR camera. Less than an hour before that traffic *ment* found the girl's body, it captured Oleg Timchenko's Quattro in Toksovo, barely six kilometres from her. The bodybuilder has no alibi. Maybe it was him, or the missing brother, or both.'

Christ, Rogov had been using a snow shovel to dig a hole for her. 'It could be a coincidence, Colonel… the car driving by.'

'I don't have your experience, but it looks to me like these Timchenko brothers are the missing piece of the puzzle in a *Sledkom* case. A piece you are reluctant to give them.'

'You said yourself, Colonel, *Sledkom* aren't interested in Elizaveta's death.'

'And you are?' he asked pointedly.

'No, Colonel. I just want to find Max Timchenko. Sledkom have already taken one case from me. I don't want to lose this one too.'

'That's not your decision, it's mine… and anyway, it's pure fiction. If Sergeant Rogov noticed—'

She opened her mouth to protest.

'Don't look so innocent, Ivanova. If *Sledkom* hadn't stolen some of my best detectives, I'd serve them your head on a spike.'

He ran a hand over his smooth cheek. 'This whole thing is a fucking mess, Ivanova, and it's your fault… did you know Rogov arrested Oleg Timchenko this morning?'

'For what?' Her voice sounded shrill.

'So you didn't.' Dostoynov blew out an exasperated breath. 'Elizaveta Kalinina's murder, what else?'

CHAPTER 17

'Is he still under arrest?'

'No, I let him go. I told him Rogov had an attack of overenthusiasm. He's pissed off. Maybe he killed the girl, maybe he didn't, but that's *Sledkom*'s job, not ours. Yours was to find this missing professor.' Dostoynov half-rose in his chair and planted his palms on the desk. 'Despite what you say, it's clear that Max Timchenko's disappearance is connected to Elizaveta Kalinina's death. *Sledkom* have it now and if I hear you're investigating, I'll fire you on the spot. Is that understood?'

'Yes, Colonel.'

'Good. Now get out.'

18

After work, she went home for a change of clothes, but then got trapped by rush-hour traffic on the way to Kirovsky District. It was 6.30 p.m. when she parked her Volvo in front of the Kontinent shopping mall on Prospekt Stachek.

Margarita Belikova – if that was her name – was waiting outside, looking uncomfortable in a long-sleeved dress, a wool hat and thick tights.

'Ivanova, you're late,' she snapped. 'I've been freezing my ovaries off.' The major pulled on an emergency door, letting out a blast of high-pitched shrieks into the evening air.

She followed Belikova along a corridor that became increasingly noisy. At another door the FSB major took time to appraise Natalya's jogging bottoms and trainers. 'Ivanova, did you think you were going to join in the family fun?'

'I was playing safe,' she said.

In reality she was glad – she was more likely to turn an ankle than perform a somersault.

There was more shrieking as the door opened. It was an ideal place to have a conversation without being overheard, though she suspected the major had chosen it for convenience: there was a taller version of Belikova looking anxiously around. The woman's eyes settled on them. 'Margo? I've been looking for you.'

So her name really was Margarita.

'I'll be in soon, Roza. It's work.'

CHAPTER 18

Natalya was scrutinised by the taller woman. 'Don't be long, I'm cutting the cake.' The door closed.

'Damned sisters, eh, Natashenka?' Belikova called out above the cacophony. 'It's my niece's birthday today. Fifteen eleven-year-old girls screaming and jumping on trampolines – my ideal of hell. There isn't a headache pill big enough for this shit. I need two minutes with a Kalashnikov and a sympathetic prosecutor.'

'You said you had something on Elizaveta Kalinina?'

'I do.'

Belikova pushed on a door adjacent to the one behind which her sister had disappeared. Inside, there were balloons and candles, and food boxes piled up for a party yet to start. 'We'll talk in here. Those little bastards have given me a migraine.'

The major waited for the door to close before speaking. 'Do you remember the president's birthday?'

Natalya frowned. 'Didn't he get my gift?'

'You're funny, Ivanova. I'll add that to your file: 'good sense of humour'. On the president's birthday the Decembrists poured fake blood over the FSB director's car.'

'I saw it. I prefer the one where they released rats into the courthouse.'

'Well, the blood wasn't real anyway,' Belikova sniffed. 'But this is the interesting part. The director's security men ran after all the little agitators on the bridge. One was caught.'

Her eyes widened. 'Elizaveta?'

'You win the star prize. She was the spotter for the group.'

'What did you do to her?'

Belikova shrugged. 'That's all I got. Perhaps she was given a fright, then sent home to think about her son. Maybe she was recruited as an informer. Do you know how she died?'

'*Sledkom* say she overdosed on a designer drug. Something that conveniently doesn't show up on toxicology tests.'

'An undetectable poison, you say? We've got the patent on all of those. I've solved the mystery for you – the FSB killed her. It was our patriotic duty.'

'I doubt it. Elizaveta wasn't significant enough for an FSB assassination.'

'Well, I was surmising.'

'Did she really inform on the group?'

'You're straining our relationship, now, Ivanova. You want me to ask the dead woman's case officer?'

The door opened. In the gap, Roza scowled at her and Belikova. Above the roar of children shrieking, a smaller number were singing: "It's a pity that my birthday is only once a year."

'Oh fuck,' said the FSB major. 'I've got to go.'

'Don't tell anyone,' she called out to Belikova's back. 'I'm already in the shit with my Lieutenant Colonel.'

At home, Natalya took off her boots in the hallway and saw Mikhail and Anton's shoes already there. She went into the kitchen and found them nursing empty beer glasses; they smelled of cigarette smoke. When Anton hugged her she also caught an oily odour from his garage job. Mikhail gave her a perfunctory kiss on the lips.

'Good day?' she asked.

'Better than good for him.' Mikhail jerked a thumb at his son. 'The sister of your missing academic… he's been on a date with her.'

She frowned, and remembered watching Anton running out of the apartment after Vita. 'Is this true?'

Anton gave a bashful nod.

'You can't see her. She's involved in a *Sledkom* case.'

CHAPTER 18

'Come on, Natasha,' said Anton. 'She's Max's sister. It's not like she's killed him.'

Mikhail, always the more morally flexible, was smiling. 'You have to admit, Vita's better than his usual drop-outs.' He ran a hand over Anton's buzz-cut to show his put-down had been a joke.

'Anton, can you leave us a moment… I need to talk to your papa. It's confidential.'

'If it's about Vita I want to stay.'

'He's old enough to hear it,' said Mikhail.

Not so long ago, Mikhail would have ushered his son into another room. Perhaps it was the feeling that he wasn't going to be a *ment* for much longer and there would be no reputation to protect.

She eyed Mikhail. 'Well, it's on your head… this morning Rogov arrested Oleg – Vita's older brother. Now do you see why it's a bad idea?'

Mikhail reached into the fridge door and twisted the ring-pull off a fresh bottle of Ochakovo. 'For killing Max?'

He filled his glass and passed the remainder of the bottle to Anton.

She wished she'd never started it now. 'Dostoynov ordered Rogov to release Oleg. It was a mistake… my point is that' – she took a breath – 'Actually, I'd much rather discuss this in private.'

Anton glanced up as he poured the Ochakovo into his glass. 'I deserve to know.'

'Will you swear not to repeat anything?' Mikhail said

Anton held up his hand imitating a court witness. 'I swear.'

'You see, Natashenka, you can't win.'

She scowled. 'If you promise… Do you remember the woman in the ditch on the Toksovo road?'

Anton gulped his beer. 'The Decembrist? Vita told me about her.'

'I was working on the case. This morning, Uncle Stepan found out that Oleg's car was caught by a camera six kilometres from her body.

Oleg told us Max borrowed his car that day, but we only have his word for it. And obviously Max is still missing.'

'But it was a mistake. You said your boss told Uncle Stepan to release him.'

'Only because politics are involved. It's too early to say if Max or Oleg are implicated. You need to keep away from Vita until it's over. How would it look to Elizaveta's mother if she hears the police let Oleg go and then she finds out you are going out with his sister?'

'Not good, I guess.'

'No, not good.'

Mikhail patted his pockets for his cigarettes.

'Outside,' she said.

He pulled out a Sobranie and held it between his fingers.

'So you're still looking into the girl's death?'

'Elizaveta left behind a boy still wearing nappies. *Sledkom* don't care. If you think they are so great why don't you apply to join them?'

'Because they don't give a damn about anyone except themselves,' Mikhail said. 'Maybe it's you who should apply.'

Mikhail's words had stung. She was about to retaliate when a memory stopped her. 'There's something I don't understand.'

'What?' he said, more accusation than question.

'I went to Anjelika this morning… the pathologist. I was asking her about Elizaveta's death.'

Mikhail shook his head. 'I don't fucking believe this. Dostoynov wants me out and you're playing these games. If we both lose our jobs how will we survive?'

She felt in her pockets for the machine printout from Anjelika's filing cabinet. At the top were the printed letters: "*Subjekt: E.D. Kalinina.*" The numbers underneath corresponded to chemical formulae. 'Anjelika wanted me to find this.'

CHAPTER 18

'What do you mean *find*? Didn't she give it to you?' Mikhail ran his fingers through his hair. 'Angel—' he began.

'Save the speech, Misha. I took it from her filing cabinet, all right? I'm not looking for absolution. I want to know what it means.'

Mikhail snatched the paper from her and squinted at the figures.

'It's a formula,' she said. 'I know "C" is carbon and "O" is oxygen, but it's not carbon dioxide or carbon monoxide. You've seen more autopsies than me. Why did Anjelika circle it?'

'Carbonate,' said Mikhail matter-of-factly. 'Did Anjelika let you steal anything else?'

'Some *Sledkom* goons interrupted me before I had the chance to find out.'

Mikhail gave out a mirthless laugh. 'They did? Well, at least it can't get any worse for you.'

'So what's this carbonate?' asked Anton.

'Why don't you ask Anjelika next time you're rifling through her office?' said Mikhail.

'I might do that.'

'Seeing how we're all being open, do you know what I heard?'

Mikhail's tone had changed. She wondered if it had something to do with his lack of affection. Normally he grabbed her by the waist and kissed her full on the lips; today she got a peck more deserving of an ageing relative.

'What?'

'I heard Dostoynov ordered you to drop the case of the missing professor now it's linked to Elizaveta Kalinina's death. He told you to keep out of *Sledkom's* business or he'll fire you.' Mikhail scowled at his son. 'You need to go away now, this is private.'

'I'm not going anywhere. Are you saying no one is looking for Vita's brother?'

'*Sledkom* are,' said Mikhail.

'But you said they won't do anything,' complained Anton.

'They'll be fine,' he said.

'Don't lie to him, Misha.'

Anton was outraged. 'What the fuck do I say to Vita? Max is her twin brother. She deserves to hear this.'

'Nothing. You promised, remember?' Mikhail waved a hand, dismissing his son. 'And watch your fucking language.'

19

Predictably, she had barely arrived at headquarters when her phone began ringing. She pulled off her scarf and coat, discarding them on her chair.

'It's Vita. I need to talk to you.' In the background she could hear a hubbub of conversation: students at Vita's university.

'No pleasantries?' Natalya asked.

Vita stopped. 'What? You arrested my brother, what do you expect?'

'I'm cold and grumpy,' Natalya said. 'How are you?'

'Angry.'

'See, it feels better already.' She looked around the office to make sure she couldn't be overheard. 'Anton said you're seeing each other.'

'What's that got to do with anything?' said Vita.

As much as she hated to think badly of Anton, Vita was stunning and super-smart. She wasn't so much out of his league as playing a different game entirely: her chess to his Cossacks and Thieves.

'It's got a lot to do with me. He's the closest I've got to a child of my own.'

Vita's voice rose in pitch. 'You think I'm using him to stay close to the investigation?'

'Well, are you?'

'Don't be ridiculous… I like him, but we've had one date.'

Rogov walked past, and she rolled her eyes to imply the call wasn't important. He carried on to the refreshments area, but she knew he wasn't so easily fooled.

'Why did you call, Vita?'

'I want to talk to you… in person.'

'Change the tone or we're going nowhere… it's up to you.'

'I've got one brother missing and instead of finding him you arrest the other one. You want me to be nice?'

Natalya exhaled heavily to convey her weariness. 'Meet me at midday, somewhere in the centre.'

'That works. I'm teaching until eleven thirty. What about Ulitsa Gorokhovaya 2? The entrance on Admiralteysky Prospekt?'

'OK.'

She hung up. The entrance to what? She tapped the address into Yandex. It brought up details for the History of Political Police Museum. At least Vita hadn't lost her sense of humour.

She left a message with a sullen Rogov, telling him she was going to check out one of her old domestic violence cases, then she drove to Clinical Hospital No. 31. She shivered inside her Volvo for twenty minutes until Anjelika opened the basement door and propped it in place with the fire extinguisher.

'Anjelika.' She crossed the distance to the fire exit.

'What do you want?'

'To apologise.'

Anjelika took out her e-cigarette. 'They questioned me… *Sledkom*, like I was a naughty child.'

'Did you say anything?'

'No, I lied for you. I told them you were retrieving a report for Mikhail. It's that case of his – the Siberian girl – you'd better get your story straight in case they check.'

'Thanks… you did Diana Maricheva's autopsy?' Natalya asked.

The pathologist blew a cloud of vapour. 'You know about it?'

'He's my husband… we even talk to each other occasionally.'

CHAPTER 19

'Like that, is it?' Dr Fedyushina asked.

'Right now it is,' she said.

The pathologist drew on the e-cigarette again. 'So what do you want this time?'

'The carbonate levels on the printout… what do they mean?'

Dr Fedyushina sighed; the query was too easy. 'Carbon dioxide dissolves in the blood as carbonate. The body regulates it to balance acid levels and energy.'

'That doesn't tell me anything,' she said.

Dr Fedyushina blew out steam. 'Without oxygen, carbonate levels increase… how about that?'

'So she was starved of oxygen?'

The pathologist nodded. 'Didn't you see her eyes?'

Anjelika, a kindly type, often tried to help improve the knowledge of the *menti* who visited her. It was patronising, if well meant.

'It was dark,' Natalya said. 'Wait' – she rooted through her pockets for her iPhone – 'I took some pictures.' She pulled out her mobile and tapped on the image of Elizaveta's lifeless pupils. 'What am I looking for?'

'Red specks… petechiae,' the pathologist said. 'Don't you ever watch *Sled*, Natalya?'

'I'm more of a *Spets* kind of girl.'

She enlarged the picture with her fingers and studied the eye, then she checked the other images from the photo burst. 'I can't see any red spots.'

'It's not always obvious,' Anjelika said. 'What about the neck?'

'Nothing that I noticed.'

'Good… I concur. So not strangulation, hanging, or killed with a ligature.'

'What about a pillow over the face?' asked Natalya.

'Pressure on the face often leaves marks too, and it's hard to pinch the nostrils and force the mouth closed without leaving bruises or defence marks.'

'So what do you think killed her, Anjelika?'

'A plastic bag over her head… something like that.'

'Homicide?'

'Suicide is unlikely, given she was moved after death.'

'I concur,' said Natalya, earning her a sharp glance from the pathologist.

Anjelika sent out a plume of steam. 'Did you find anything else while burgling my office?'

'Just that.'

'You should have looked harder.'

Now she was beginning to tire of the games. 'What else, Anjelika?'

'I couldn't do an internal examination so I used biopsy needles to take samples of the liver, lungs and heart. There was something in the lungs… like hairs, but much smaller.'

'Animal?'

'Smaller. I carried out more biopsies. There was no calcification on the pleura, so the exposure was limited and unlikely to have contributed to her death. The highest concentration was in the upper areas of the lung. I'm not an expert' – a cloud of nicotine infused vapour enveloped the pathologist – 'but I'd say it was recent. Perhaps your victim had been on a building site or went to Asbest.'

'Anjelika, what—'

'I'll give you a bigger clue. Asbest is thousands of kilometres away in Sverdlovsk Oblast. The town is named after the mineral they mine. I checked the fibres under an electron microscope.'

The pathologist examined her blank face. 'For Christ's sake, Natalya, I'm talking about asbestos. Your victim was exposed to asbestos.'

20

She parked on the allocated pavement spaces on Admiralteysky Prospekt, passing a fresh election poster of Vladimir Putin resembling an aggressive bank manager. There was no sign of Vita outside the History of Political Police Museum and it was too cold to stay on the street. She paid the 150-rouble admission and went inside. Above the wide staircase she turned into the first room. She left it, skimmed through the second, and then stopped at the third, dedicated to the *Okhrana*, the Tsar's secret police. While she waited, she found herself studying a restored version of the office used by Felix Dzerzhinsky, the head of the Cheka during the Red Terror. She wondered how many thousands he had condemned to death between its buttercream walls and icing-sugar woodwork.

Approaching footsteps made her turn. Vita was wearing her cobalt blue suit underneath an all-weather jacket. She was wearing make-up, but there were bags under her eyes that were harder to disguise. Two young men in office clothes began a conversation between themselves, exchanging furtive looks in Vita's direction.

'Why meet here?'

'I thought you might be amused. And here we are at old Iron Felix's room.' She stepped back. '"We stand for organized terror!" That's what he's famous for saying.'

The two men looked amused by her outburst; they leaned in, keen to join their conversation. Natalya returned a stare colder than the temperature outside. The men turned away, seeming to find a more interesting exhibit.

'You didn't invite me here to discuss politics.'

Vita took off her gloves and stuffed them in her jeans. 'Everything is political. Do you want to tell me about Oleg?'

'Have you spoken to him?' Natalya asked.

'So you can tell me his car was seen near Elizaveta Kalinina's body?'

She smiled bitterly at the younger woman. 'I'll pretend you didn't hear that from Anton.'

'I've got no idea what you're talking about,' said Vita. 'Oleg is an oaf sometimes, but he won't have been involved in Elizaveta's death.'

'All right, I'll tell you this. I didn't order his arrest – that was thanks to an overenthusiastic sergeant. Because of him, my boss joined the dots between Elizaveta and Max. *Sledkom* have been given the job of finding Max.'

Vita's head did a little jolt. Perhaps Anton hadn't been the source of her information after all.

'You're off the case?' Vita asked.

'Yes.'

'But *Sledkom* won't be interested in finding him.'

'I know,' she said, not unkindly. 'They want to discredit the Decembrists. If they find out Max was one too, God knows what they'll come up with. Maybe they'll say he sold the drugs that supposedly killed Elizaveta.'

'He's not a drug dealer,' Vita hissed.

'I'm not *Sledkom*.' She studied Vita, wondering if she could be trusted. Vita had taken a leap of faith with her and that hadn't got her very far. 'Elizaveta didn't die from a drugs overdose,' she said quietly. 'She was suffocated… murdered.'

Vita's hands moved involuntarily to her mouth. 'That's awful… I only met her a few times. She always noticed me on demonstrations when I was speaking with Max. I think she liked him.'

CHAPTER 20

'Maybe they were seeing each other secretly.'

'Max? No. Even if we don't look alike, we're twins… we never kept personal stuff from each other. Besides, it meant breaking the group's stupid rules. Will you keep looking for him… and Elizaveta's killer?'

Natalya felt tired and it was only midday. 'I'll do what I can, but I'll lose my job if my boss finds out.'

'Your job,' Vita snorted.

'Don't be asinine. If I'm sacked it means no access to databases, no money, no resources, no powers of arrest.'

'What do you need?'

'I need to be able to do my job.'

'I can help.'

'Vita, there's nothing you can do.'

'Yes there is. I'll speak to the others.'

'You mean the Decembrists? You'll attract *Sledkom*. They'll come after you.'

'I'm not scared.'

'I don't believe that – you're too smart not to be.'

Vita took her hand. The sudden physical contact was disarming. 'Let's change the subject. Which room shall we try next? We've done Cheka, what about OGPU or KGB?' she said, making the secret police sound like a wine choice.

Natalya squeezed the hand to acknowledge the gesture, then let it go. 'Let's go to the first room. I saw something on the FSB. Maybe we can learn from the bastards.'

The museum was filling up and she pretended to flick through a folder on the secret police in the Chechen wars. 'Can I ask you a question? Do you know if Max or Elizaveta went to any building sites?'

'I don't know.'

'What about Asbest?' Natalya asked. 'Did she ever visit the town?'

'Like I told you, we didn't socialise. Why?'

'I'm not sure yet.'

'Want to know why I asked to meet you?' Vita asked.

'I thought you were angry about Oleg's arrest.'

'I am, but there's another reason. Last time we met you asked to meet someone in the group. Adelina, one of the founders, has agreed. I was surprised, but people are scared. After Elizaveta was killed and Max disappeared… well, they are convinced someone is after them.'

'Thank you.'

'Don't thank me yet. They see all *menti* the same way: municipal, state, OMON, *Sledkom*. To them, you are werewolves in uniform. You have no idea how much they despise you.'

'I'll remind myself to bring flowers. Vita… there's something I want to say too. We need to talk about Anton.'

'Don't worry. He won't say anything.'

'That's not what I meant,' Natalya began. 'I don't feel comfortable with you seeing him.'

'Because you believe Oleg is involved.'

'Not just that. The truth is, I admire you for being an activist, but if *Sledkom* catch you, they'll connect you to Anton. I can't let that happen.'

Vita zipped up her padded jacket. 'I'll be careful.'

'I'm serious. You need to stop seeing him.'

Natalya made a move to grab the sleeve of Vita's jacket, but the woman shifted out of range.

'I'll be careful,' Vita said.

21

Outside the museum, her phone rang. It was Rogov.

'Boss, where are you?'

'I'm in Admiralty. You?'

'Just finished lunch at Saint Patrick's. I'll come to you. Where's good?'

'The Bronze Horseman,' she said.

'I'll be there.'

She passed the time shivering and watching naval cadets pose for photographs against the snow-blanketed statue of Peter the Great on its stone plinth.

Rogov arrived, holding out a paper cup. 'Coffee?'

'Thanks.' She took a sip. It was cold, but he was trying. 'So, why all this secrecy?'

'Boss…' he paused, tilting his head to one side – a suggestion they should walk in case the naval cadets overheard them.

They crossed the road to the embankment. The Bolshaya Neva River was frozen. A wedding party stood on the ice, waiting in a stilted pose for the photographer. A couple skated nearby. Further on, a group were playing a frisbee game with elaborate rules. She could have sold postcards of the picture and made a fortune.

'Is this better?'

'Yeah.' He rubbed a mittened hand against his jawline. 'Misha says you're still looking into the dead Decembrist.'

'Misha should keep his mouth shut, and her name was Elizaveta.'

'Well, if you are looking, I'm in.'

She stopped. First coffee, and now Rogov – a man who embodied Darwinian self-preservation – was offering to help on a case that would turn his career into radioactive ruins. Had Mikhail put him up to it? That was likely, more so than the idea that Dostoynov had ordered Rogov to watch her – he would surely have sent someone more loyal.

Politeness stopped her from pouring the cold coffee over the embankment railings. 'Dostoynov will fire me… Misha might file for divorce.'

'Dostoynov,' he spat, fishing in his pockets for a packet of Winstons. He tapped out a cigarette, then lit it.

'How's your health drive?'

He grunted something incomprehensible. 'Between us, we know Misha is fucked… it's a matter of time.' He sucked on the Winston. 'And I'm never going to be what Dostoynov wants: some gym-bothering *zhoposnik* with the liver of a newborn child. That's not me. In Piter we drink.' He saluted her with his cigarette. 'In Piter we drink,' he repeated. 'The man is a *robotnik*, so I'm fucked, and you, well, I reckon you're—'

'Fucked?'

'Yeah. Fucked.'

She caught a breath of sour, sweet beer that explained his lively behaviour. 'So you want to help?'

'As long as it isn't… you know?'

'Dangerous?'

'You nearly got me killed last time… I have to think of Oksana,' he added.

'Thanks for the offer. I accept. There are a few things you need to know. For one, Elizaveta was suffocated. There were asbestos particles in her lungs too, so maybe she was visiting a building site. Here's another: Max Timchenko was a Decembrist.'

CHAPTER 21

Rogov gripped the railing, his cigarette poking between his knuckles. 'Shit... how long have you known?'

'A while. I didn't want to put you in a compromising position with Dostoynov.'

'But you knew all along they were connected,' Rogov snorted. 'The professor didn't use his *ksiva* or external passport for travel by rail or air, no credit card or bank activity. Nothing in hospital admissions, deaths, or detention... the bastard returns his brother's car then disappears. Oleg has to know where he's hiding. Give me some time alone with him and I'll get the truth.'

'We're not doing it that way,' she said. In truth, Rogov was more than likely to come off worse in any physical encounter with Oleg. 'Anyway, I'm not sure Max harmed Elizaveta. In Russia, political activists are usually the ones having the killing done to them.'

'You think these arty types can't get dirty? What about that ballet dancer who got six years for an acid attack?'

'I'm only saying we need to keep an open mind. We'll know more when we get the forensics on Oleg's car. I'm hoping Leo can find out without alerting *Sledkom* or Dostoynov.'

'Primakov? Is he in on this too?'

'He offered to help.'

'So what do you want me to do?'

'The Decembrists have made a lot of enemies, and just the type who don't worry too much about morals.'

'With respect, Boss, this is liberal bullshit. You're looking for a conspiracy because you don't want to think badly of the professor.'

'Nevertheless, I want you to go back to your traffic cameras and see if anyone else was there. Maybe Max was following whoever killed Elizaveta.'

Rogov smoked his Winston, his face betraying nervousness. 'Like who?'

'Judges, prosecutors, politicians.' She enjoyed seeing the spread of alarm on his face.

'It's almost the weekend, Rogov. When you get home, take a look on YouTube at the Decembrists' political stunts. Compile a list of their targets. On Sunday, go to headquarters when it's quiet, track down any vehicles the targets had access to – including any registered to family members. Once you've done that, run them against the number plates from the ANPR cameras. Let's see if anyone else was on the road. Whatever you do, don't declare overtime. If you start logging extra hours Dostoynov is bound to be suspicious.'

She took a sip of the cold coffee and supressed a shudder, 'And thanks for this.'

22

Saturday. With Anton staying at Dinara's after working at the garage, she decided to stay in and have a quiet evening with Mikhail. As she cleared the dishes, the living room was filled with the sounds of a recorded hockey match. By the time she came out, Mikhail was absorbed by the game, and she migrated to the study. She examined the roads around Kuzmolovsky Cemetery on Yandex Maps. Elizaveta's body had been found on the road heading towards Toksovo, but the killer could have doubled back from one of the *dacha* communities. She wanted to call Rogov and ask for a progress update, but it was late, and she didn't want to speak to Oksana, who was being as pleasant to her as permafrost.

She poured out a glass of Satrapezo. Out of four cases given to her by an old Georgian boyfriend, there were only two bottles left. Soon she would have to start buying red wine or take a Georgian lover. Listening to the shrill whistles and crowd-calls coming from the television, she wasn't entirely averse to the idea.

After carrying the glass back to the study, she used Yandex's satellite image option to zoom in on the building complexes in the area. One of them alone, Okhtinsky Park, contained dozens of *dachas*. She opened up a new tab and looked up the properties on a real estate site. The first place she found would take her a hundred years to buy on a captain's salary.

The TV went quiet. Mikhail entered, pouring an Ochakovo into a glass. He held out a Sobranie to her. 'I won't tell anybody.'

She took the cigarette and stood. 'You're a terrible influence.'

'I pride myself on it.' He looked at the screen. 'What are you looking at?'

'I was wondering if Elizaveta died in one of the *dachas*.'

'Maybe we should get one.' He took the mouse from her and clicked on a link to a real estate company. 'Fuck… there's one here for five hundred million roubles.'

'How much of your soul would that buy?'

'I'm not sure how much is left.'

'That money you took…'

'Tasha, let's not go there again.'

'What does that mean, let's not go there? Let's pretend it didn't happen or let's pretend it's not still in your secret bank account?'

'I'm going to the balcony to smoke.'

'Wait, I want to talk to you.'

'And I don't. The mafia threatened to kill me unless I got one of their pricks off a murder charge. End of story.'

'And yet you took the money.'

'What was I meant to do? Tell an *avtoritet* in the Tambovski mafia to fuck off? This is old ground, Tasha. Why do you want to argue? I thought we were having a pleasant evening.'

'With you there and me here? You're shutting me out because you're shutting yourself out. You've been doing this for weeks. I don't want an argument, but we need to talk about it. I know you're honest – I worked with you for long enough. If you don't fix this, it will eat away at everything we have.'

She could feel the words forming in her brain, but didn't know if she had the courage to release them. But they came out before she could stop them. 'Your dishonesty will destroy this marriage.'

'And your honesty will destroy us all.' He shook his head in disbelief. 'What do you expect me to do? Sell our apartment and live on the streets?'

CHAPTER 22

Beer slopped over the glass and ran down his fingers. She wondered how many Ochakovos he'd had. 'If I stop paying for Anton's fake university, let's see how long it takes before the army comes for him.'

'Christ, Misha. We'll survive without the money, you know we will.'

'That was before that bastard Dostoynov began forcing me out.'

'You're better than this.'

'Save me the holy bullshit.' He tapped the computer screen. 'If I was a real crook we'd have one of these for the weekends. I did it once, Tasha. I'm ashamed of it. Now that's the end.'

'Is that your final decision?' she asked, but he had already left for the balcony.

'I'm away next week,' he called out, 'interviewing the monks on Konevets to see if they remember anything. I was going to rush back. Now I'm not so sure.'

She turned back to the *dacha* on the screen with its sauna and landscaped gardens. The image distorted as tears blurred her vision.

23

She took the Metro to avoid the bad-tempered Monday-morning traffic, and found Rogov waiting for her in the office, his ample backside crushing the papers and computer keyboard on her desk.

'Morning, Boss.' His breath smelled of mint – it wasn't masking alcohol, for a change. He scanned the immediate area and lowered his voice. Had anyone been in the vicinity, they would automatically have been suspicious.

'I found thirty-two Decembrist targets from their YouTube videos.'

'Good work,' she said.

Her mobile rang and she pushed Rogov off her desk. She didn't recognise the number, but took it anyway.

'You wanted to speak to me.'

A woman's clear voice, no discernible accent.

'Who is this?'

'One of the many who ran across the bridge that day.'

So it was the Decembrist Vita had found for her: Adelina. 'I understand,' she said, nodding at Rogov, who sensed intrigue and retreated reluctantly.

'You wanted to meet?' Adelina asked.

'Yes.'

'Tauride Palace Gardens, the entrance on Potemkinskaya. Come alone. I'll recognise you. If you're not there in fifteen minutes you can forget it.' Adelina hung up.

CHAPTER 23

Natalya jogged down the stairs and out of the building. Hunched against the chill, she set off along the icy pavement running alongside the massive Tauride Palace, which had served as the State *Duma* until the revolution. She arrived with a few minutes to spare. No one was at the entrance. She scanned the pale trees bent by snow inside the gardens. The place was empty, save a few wandering visitors. Above the sound of traffic, a buzzing noise made her glance upwards. A drone hovered overhead, its white belly visible against the grey sky. Nearby, a municipal employee was shoveling snow off the path. He was chewing sunflower seeds and spitting out the shells as he worked.

He stopped when he saw her. 'Is your name Ivanova?'

'Yes.'

'I'm to give you this.'

He held out a sealed envelope. She opened it to read the slip of paper inside: "Go to the Monument to the Victims of Political Repression."

She began jogging. The whine of the drone picked up. Now she wondered if the Decembrists were playing one of their pranks, filming the idiot *ment* on a paper chase through the city. The drone, she was sure, was trailing her, monitoring the space behind as she jogged unsteadily on the pavement.

At the embankment she turned left, then slowed down when she saw there was no one waiting by the two bronze sphinxes. On one side of the sculptures they appeared normal; on the other, facing Kresty Prison on the far bank, they were grotesque: the flesh stripped to half-skulls, the ribs jutting out, like emaciated cows. It had been commissioned over twenty years ago when the country had a stronger stomach about confronting its past.

She stopped to read the inscriptions on the monument while the drone took up a stationary position overhead. She could make out a tiny lens focusing on her, and she turned her face from it. A *ment* examining a monument to political oppression was certain to be amusing to a few radicals, but if Adelina met her, they would have damaging footage – *kompromat* – that could be used against her. Ten metres away, a woman walked towards her, a mobile phone pressed to her ear, although she wasn't speaking. She was tall, her head covered by the hood of her long coat, a scarf over her mouth.

Natalya fought to keep her eyes level, not to acknowledge the drone or woman. 'Make that fucking thing disappear before I walk away,' she said, as if talking to herself.

'I don't know what you're talking about,' Adelina replied, speaking quietly into her mobile. A few seconds later, the drone lowered to the embankment. A squat, heavily bearded man intercepted it and began packing it into a black case.

'So what was the idea?' she asked. 'To put me on YouTube?'

Adelina kept the scarf over her mouth, disguising her face and muffling her voice. 'I don't know what you mean. I was asked to meet you, so this is what I'm doing.'

'You've got one activist dead and another missing. Maybe you should try being helpful.'

'And maybe we got off on the wrong foot. What do you want to know?'

'Were Max and Elizaveta working on something together?'

'I don't know.'

'What do you mean, you don't know?'

Adelina adjusted the scarf to talk. 'State media call us terrorists, so we take security seriously. If Max or Elizaveta were working on an action I wouldn't know.'

'Is there anything you can say?'

Adelina shrugged. 'About Elizaveta? She joined last year – a buildings surveyor. As for Max, I can't tell you anything.'

'Because you don't know?'

CHAPTER 23

'No, because he might be alive. If he returns I don't want his safety compromised. Nevertheless, I doubt I can tell you anything you don't already know.'

So the meeting was a waste of time. Not only that, they had film footage which could cause her serious trouble. 'Well, thanks for nothing.'

'Remind me who wanted the meeting?' Adelina said, acidly.

There was a commotion further along the embankment. A man shouted, '*Politsiya*!' The bearded drone operator began running towards her, clutching his case. Adelina craned her neck to see past her. 'You bitch. You set us up.'

A car braked as Adelina ran across the road. The bearded man stopped when he saw Natalya. Behind him, Rogov was waving furiously. Natalya tried to block the man's path. He swung the case holding the drone, knocking her off her feet. Her arms flailed, making contact with one of his ankles. She locked both hands. He continued, limping, dragging her across the road. A Toyota van swerved, its tyres missing her legs by centimetres. She let go. There was no point dying. He hadn't killed anyone.

She scrambled to stand. Her hands stung, the knuckles bleeding where they had scraped the road. The man hobbled to the centre of the four-lane highway. She felt for the clip to release her Makarov.

'Rogov,' she yelled. Where the hell was he?

There was a pistol shot. She heard a dull crack against the bodywork of a passing car.

'Shit,' she heard Rogov curse. She saw him on the embankment path fiddling with a tiny gun.

'Rogov,' she yelled. 'What are you doing?'

Rogov fired again. The drone operator staggered, dropping his case. A lorry in the nearside lane clipped the case into the path of an oncoming car. The car caught it with a glancing blow, cracking it open. The drone spilled out. Seconds later an SUV went past, tearing it to pieces. The man hesitated, then ran for a gap in the traffic. Natalya went after him. She dived for his legs again, but he shook her off. He took another step and she caught the trouser leg of his jeans, holding onto it with one hand while she drove her fist into his crotch. He tottered into the traffic, then Rogov was on him too, the three wrestling until she managed to grab one of his arms. Rogov took the other arm and they forced him to stand, then returned to the safety of the embankment path.

Rogov had the drone operator against the river railings and handcuffed his wrists behind his back.

'You shot me, you bastard *musor,*' the man shouted.

'Who, me?' asked Rogov. The tiny pistol was gone.

'I need medical attention.'

'You got hit by a stone chip from a car…' Rogov saw her and looked for approval. She grunted non-committally.

'Bullshit, you shot me.'

'You're mistaken,' said Rogov amiably as if they might have been having a mild disagreement.

There was a circular bruise on the man's neck. Already it was turning black. She glanced at the tell-tale bulge on Rogov's ankle.

She could taste rubber and diesel exhaust on her breath.

'What the hell were you doing?' she hissed.

'Looking out for you.'

'You messed everything up… and you nearly got me killed.'

'Nataly—'

'Captain.'

A shadow of pain crossed Rogov's face. 'Captain, these people can't be trusted. They were filming you.'

She took a pointed look at Rogov's ankle where he was hiding the Wasp pistol that fired the steel-core rubber bullets. Next to them, the angry, battered drone operator glared pointedly at the Monument to the Victims of Political Repression.

'Go back to headquarters, Rogov.'

'But what about her?'

Natalya followed the direction of his gaze to see Adelina on the other side of the highway. She was filming them on a mobile phone. 'Just go, Rogov. Leave them to me.'

Rogov left huffily, shoulders hunched, as he strode in the direction of Tauride Palace.

'I'm sorry,' she said.

The man stared at the monument for a full second, then spat on the pavement.

'And that's a fair reply.' She squatted on the pavement next to him. 'Got any cigarettes?'

'You fucking shot me.'

'My sergeant can be a little overzealous... About those cigarettes?' She arched an eyebrow.

'Left pocket,' he said after another silence.

She felt for the packet in his wool coat and took out a pack of Marlboro.

'And don't think of taking anything else.'

'She patted his pockets. Just your *ksiva*... so I know what to call you.' She withdrew his internal passport and glanced at the name before tucking it back. 'Gregor Bortsov, it's so very nice to meet you. My name is Captain Ivanova of the Criminal Investigations Directorate.'

'Is this where you offer me the chance to walk if I pay an administration fee?'

She found a lighter stuffed in his packet of Marlboro and lit one. She inhaled deeply. 'Taking bribes isn't my style.'

He stared at the remains of his drone on the road, before looking up at Adelina. He repeated the gesture, willing the other Decembrist to notice something. Natalya had seen his curious signal; Adelina hadn't.

'You want a cigarette too?' she asked.

'That's very generous. Why don't you take the handcuffs off so I can smoke?'

'And let you run again? I don't think so.' She lit another Marlboro and pushed it between his lips. 'You didn't mention your drone. How much was it? Fifty thousand?'

She waited for him to inhale, then withdrew the cigarette.

'Eighty-five.'

'I'd be pretty mad if I were you, seeing it smeared on the road like that.'

'That's not my style,' he said, aping her.

She shoved the cigarette between his lips and glanced at the debris scattered on the highway – the destroyed case, the smashed casing and torn rotors. The area he'd been staring at held the main body.

'Why were you filming me?' she asked.

'I wasn't. I was just taking it out for a practice-run along the Neva when your man came at me.'

'Nice try. I saw the lens. It's been following me since the Tauride Palace Gardens.'

'Am I under arrest?'

That wasn't an option when *Sledkom* would be only too happy to relieve her of a Decembrist and take him into custody. On top of that, she'd need a new job once Dostoynov discovered she was still looking into her old case.

'No. I'd prefer not to take you to headquarters, if it's all the same to you.'

'Then take the bracelets off. Don't you have a barrel?' he said, dropping his eyes to her Makarov.

CHAPTER 23

'Odd as it may seem, unless you present a danger to the public I'm not allowed to shoot you.'

He sniffed. 'There's enough *menti* that would.'

'You're right though. I can't take you in and, regrettably, I can't shoot you. That leaves only one option.' She brought out a key and unlocked the handcuffs. Gregor rubbed his neck.

'Now, I don't know what Adelina told you but I'm not looking to round up any Decembrists – that's *Sledkom*, not me. I need to find who killed Elizaveta Kalinina and what happened to Max Timchenko.' She took a puff on the cigarette. 'Did you know them?'

'I know Max.'

'Any idea where he might be?'

Gregor pressed his lips together and shook his head slightly. 'You think we haven't been looking for him too?'

'How did you meet him?' she asked.

'Why?'

'Just curious.'

'I suppose it doesn't matter – it's old history,' Gregor said. 'We met a few years ago when I was in *Voina*. He wanted to set up a new group that was harder for the authorities to break up.'

'Were you there when *Voina* painted that huge penis on Liteyny Bridge?'

'Maybe I was.'

'Then it's a real honour to meet you.' She stuffed the cigarette in her mouth to shake his hand.

'You're an odd *ment*.'

'Just the old-fashioned type who hasn't forgotten who the criminals are. What about Elizaveta?'

'Liza? I didn't like her at first. She was too straight, I thought maybe she was an undercover *ment* – no offence. Anyway, she was OK in the end. We did stuff together.'

'What stuff?'

He leaned against the railings. 'You know, actions… situations… stunts, whatever you want to call them.'

'Did you ever work on a project with just Max and Liza?'

'Max was planning something on his own, something big. He wanted me to film it and Elizaveta—'

'Because she was straight?'

'Yeah. Most of us are ex-art school or social science drop-outs but she was different. Like I said, straight. No one was suspicious of Liza.'

She watched Adelina cross the road, her mobile on an outstretched arm, still recording.

'What were Max and Liza working on, Gregor?' Natalya asked.

Adelina took hold of his arm. 'Shut your mouth and don't say a word. We're leaving.'

Natalya pointed to one of the bronze sphinxes. 'Hey, why don't you go stand over there and read a few inspirational quotes?'

'I filmed your colleague shooting him,' Adelina said. 'If I post it online he'll lose his job… you too.'

'If you want to treat me as the enemy, try remembering that I'm doing this for Max and Elizaveta's families. I'm already in a world of shit for it too. *Sledkom* are in charge of the case, not me.'

'You were the one who arrested Max's brother. Why should I trust you?'

'Because I'm one of you. We're fighting the same people.'

'You think you're one of us?' Adelina snorted. She tightened her grip on Gregor's arm. 'Come on, let's leave this *vatnik*.'

The two Decembrists crossed the embankment carriageway and went down a side street, disappearing from view. Once they were gone, she removed her police ID card and stepped onto the road. At the last lane she held out her hand at an oncoming pick-up truck and let the driver get a glimpse of her gun. The truck grunted as he braked; something heavy shifted in the cargo bed.

She went to his side window. 'Police. Stay here and block this lane.'

The driver switched on his hazard lights and she scanned the tarmac, picking up the pieces of the drone and its case. When finished, she crossed to the pavement and waved at the truck driver with a shattered rotor disk. She found a waste bin and dumped the smaller pieces of drone along with the broken case. That left the main body. She leant against the bin and turned the mangled part over in her hands. Finally, she found a tiny slot above the lens. She pushed a button and the drone's micro-SD memory card was ejected into her palm.

24

At headquarters, Rogov was at his desk completing an expenses form.

'Where's Dostoynov?' she asked.

'Promotion board.'

'For full colonel? Already?'

'The FSB look after their own,' he said without looking up.

'Not like me, you mean?'

'What? No, Boss, I didn't mean it like that… and I'm sorry I fucked up earlier.'

She waited to catch his eye. 'Did Misha put you up to it?'

He looked away. 'He was worried about you, that's all. Did I fuck up?'

'No, I got what I needed. Is your computer on?'

He wiggled the mouse and the screen came to life.

'Good. The group's targets.' She hesitated to use the word 'Decembrists' in an open office. How many of their targets did you say you found on YouTube?'

'Thirty-two.'

'Including family.'

'Yeah, and I've already put their number plates through State Vehicle Registration.'

'Anything?'

'Have you seen their videos, Boss?'

'A few.'

'Well, there's this one they did last year – a tax inspector had bought his own emergency light so his new S-Class could cut through the Moscow traffic. The group decided to make a point by turning his Mercedes into a police car. They broke into his garage at night, spray-painted it white and added a blue stripe. They did it blindfolded,' Rogov added with glee.

'And this tax inspector was picked up by the ANPR camera near Elizaveta's body?'

'Half an hour before the traffic *ment* found her.'

'Good work, Rogov. Submit a request for his phone and credit card records. If Dostoynov asks, tell him you're helping Misha with the Diana Maricheva case.'

'Boss.'

'Before you do that, log onto the police property database. I want to know if any of their targets had a place near Toksovo – most likely a *dacha*.'

He swallowed. 'Can't I do it at home through the official register? What if Dostoynov comes back?'

'We have no choice. VIPs won't be on *Rosreestr*, and they are the ones the Decembrists go after. The only way is to use our database.'

'OK, Boss.'

She felt her phone buzz and patted him on the shoulder as a parting.

The number was withheld. '*Da*?'

'It's Vita. Have you heard anything?'

'Not yet. I'm still looking'.

'Well, I've got something that might help, it's going out tonight.'

'Vita, what have you done?'

'What you asked for.' She hung up.

25

Ominous, grey clouds hung over a city that was already turning to dusk. She left the office for a coffee at the Tam-Tam on Kavalergardskaya Ulitsa where she had first met Vita. On the way, her phone rang again. It was Primakov.

'Captain, I'm at the centre. We've got the forensics back on the Audi Quattro.'

'I'll be there.'

Despite the gloom she needed the exercise and walked the two kilometres to the centre. On the way she pondered why she continued to live in a country with such bleak weather. A good summer could never make up for the bone-shattering cold of a black winter, and that was without *Rasputitsa* – the spring and autumn seasons of mud that brought fresh misery.

At the side entrance to the North-Western Regional Forensic Centre on Nekrasova Ulitsa she found Primakov waiting for her. Also with him was a good-looking man in a lab coat with curly black hair who looked Mediterranean. She found the two chatting amiably and wondered if they were in a relationship. As much as she was fond of her expert criminalist, and she was sure he was equally fond of her, Leo Primakov was a deeply private individual. They could be illicitly married for all she knew.

The Mediterranean in the lab coat had a laptop pressed under his left arm, and held out his free hand to her. 'Luka Hernandez.' He grinned conspiratorially, showing perfect teeth that would put a dentist out of business. 'Leo tells me you want some inside knowledge.'

CHAPTER 25

'You're a forensic technician?'

'Newly qualified. Leo asked me to take a look as a favour. I never could say no to Leo.'

Primakov, she noticed, wasn't grinning.

'Luka, would you show the captain what you found?' Primakov said.

'Sure, hold this.' He handed his laptop to Primakov and went towards a sheltered car park, where he tapped numbers into a keypad before pulling open a pair of metal gates.

They entered a cavern of vehicles covered in blue plastic, allocated to individually numbered bays. Luka stopped at the fourth and handed a pair of latex gloves to her and Primakov. They pulled them on while Luka tugged on the plastic sheet to reveal Oleg Timchenko's Audi Quattro.

'This is a conversation.' Luka retrieved his laptop and set it on the roof of the car. 'No paper trail, Captain. No reports to superiors. My name must not be used.'

'I already told you Luka, the Captain won't say anything.'

'I won't, you have nothing to worry about,' she added.

'Then let's begin here.'

He opened the laptop and she saw he'd planned for this. He might have just qualified, but he had the confidence and demeanour of an expert. Primakov had chosen well.

A photograph of an orange tyre-print filled the laptop screen. 'This is the cast Leo took using liquid sulphur,' Luka began. He double-clicked the image to enlarge it. 'The detail isn't as clear as dental stone but you can make out the tread pattern and sipes if you look closely.'

While she peered at the tiny jagged lines used for winter tyres, Luka opened a new image and put it side-by-side with the photograph. 'This is a dental cast I took from one of the Quattro's tyres.'

The forensic technician knelt by a wheel arch where the tyre and rim had been removed, exposing the axle.

'The Audi has four-wheel drive – it works best when all the tyres have the same tread pattern.' He straightened and tilted the screen for her. 'These are Continental TS-80s, a very close match for the cast. With help from the department I might narrow them down to this car, but without resources it's the best I could do… and it's good enough for you.'

'Why?' she asked.

'Because that was the warm-up act.'

Luka pulled on the passenger door. She peered inside to see large rectangles of fabric cut out of the seats. The *ment* tasked with returning the car to Oleg would be wise to make a swift exit.

Luka rested the laptop on the bonnet and tapped the keyboard to reveal an image of blue-tinted fibres that had been enlarged until they were almost transparent.

'These are consistent with samples we took from Elizaveta Kalinina's coat,' he said. 'She was in the passenger seat. Another warm-up act.'

She was beginning to tire of the way he revealed Elizaveta's final hours with the flourishes of an amateur magician. 'What about DNA and fingerprints?'

'DNA on a hair follicle on the passenger seat is an exact match for your victim. No fingerprints detected; the victim was wearing gloves.'

'Oleg's brother, Max, knew her,' she said. 'It's possible the DNA came from a previous journey in the car. What about the driver?'

'The car is twenty-nine years old and has four previous owners. A thorough search would find more – a lot more, in my limited experience – but I identified Oleg Timchenko's DNA and three unknowns.'

'Did you check the unknowns against the DNA database?'

'No hits, but the database has only been operating for eight years and is restricted to serious criminals.'

'What else?'

CHAPTER 25

'Plenty.' He stepped around the Quattro to open the boot. 'Take a look for yourself.'

She noticed Primakov was standing clear too; presumably he already knew the results.

Inside the boot was a grey carpet, which was worn but clean. There was no obvious forensic evidence she could see. A large rectangle had been cut through the thick material of the floor.

'You found something?'

'Yes,' said Luka.

Now he was waiting. For what, she didn't know. For applause?

'There was a body in there, wrapped in plastic.' Luka grinned with his perfect teeth and she wanted to punch him.

'How can you tell?'

He traced a finger along the edge of the carpet. She saw a narrow, brown discoloration of the material.

'Someone washed it,' Luka said, 'but you can see the original mark. There's a straight line you could put a ruler against. The blood seeped out and ran along the edge of the plastic, creating the line. Once I saw that, I took an interest in the recess.' His finger glided over a point in the boot. 'The Audi had been customised to include a subwoofer.'

'That's a speaker, right?' she said.

Luka nodded. 'I took it apart. The blood had got inside. Whoever cleaned the carpet didn't notice.'

'So the DNA you found on the seat was from an earlier trip and Elizaveta's body was transported in the boot?'

'No.'

'No?'

She caught Leo raise his eyebrows, signalling to her that he was unamused by the theatrical games.

'I did find a match, though,' said Luka. 'Using a DNA sample from the Audi's owner, Oleg Timchenko. For one thing, there was no Y chromosome, which means we can rule out the sister and the mother. In any event, Leo tells me both parents live in Belgium. A body wrapped in plastic and hidden in a car boot won't be auditioning for *Dancing with the Stars*—'

'Meaning our missing professor didn't run away,' said Primakov, who'd had enough of Luka's theatrics. 'Max Timchenko is dead.'

They waited while Luka locked up the garage.

'Can I have a lift home?' she asked Primakov.

'I walked too. My car is being steam-cleaned,' he said. 'It's the only way to get the stink out. If that doesn't work, I'll set fire to it.'

'There's a lesson in there, Leo: don't buy an ex-patrol car. That reminds me of something,' she said. 'Let's wait for Luka.'

The forensic technician finished locking the garage. 'Was there anything else?' he asked.

'Yes,' she said. 'When I spoke with Oleg Timchenko, he told me his car was returned in the early hours, when he was asleep. He complained that ice and mud had been left on the car's interior. Did you see any?'

Luka shook his head. 'No. I guess the brother cleaned up.'

26

Her feet crunched on the ice and pavement grit as she walked with Primakov along Nekrasova Ulitsa.

'Captain, do you think Oleg is responsible?'

She shook her head, more out of tiredness than to answer his question. 'Max and Elizaveta were Decembrists. It's more likely to be connected to their political activities.'

'But you can't rule out Oleg.'

'No,' she said, 'but I know Elizaveta and Max were working on something together.'

Primakov said, 'So she visits Max but finds Oleg there. He assaults her—'

'Her body had no defensive wounds and there were no signs of sexual assault,' she said.

'Then what if Max returned his prized Quattro covered in mud and Oleg lost his temper. I heard he tried to attack the pick-up driver who took his car to the forensic centre.'

'Then what about Elizaveta?' she said.

'Suppose she witnessed him killing his brother.'

'Then Oleg would have kept quiet about Max getting his precious car dirty. Also, how did he carry two bodies out of his Admiralty apartment without being seen? And how did he kill them without a sound?'

'That's true,' said Primakov. 'My neighbours bang on the wall if I use my dishwasher at night.'

'From what we know, Elizaveta died sometime between lunchtime and evening. I can't see Oleg being involved, but we need to account for his movements earlier in the day.'

'I agree, Captain. What about someone on our side – the FSB? I heard the Decembrists embarrassed their director.'

'I asked one of their agents.'

Natalya decided not to mention it was Margarita Belikova; she had forced Leo to cooperate with them on her last major case.

'They thought the FSB killed her or might have contracted the job to those thugs they use when they want to keep their hands clean.'

'Then maybe it was them. That would explain why *Sledkom* aren't interested in finding who killed Elizaveta.'

'I just don't think they care. The Moscow Mint would create a new medal if the government heard someone was going around killing political activists.'

'What about Max?' asked Primakov. 'Why didn't the killer dump their bodies in the same place?'

'Who knows? Maybe he wanted to confuse us by making Max look responsible for her murder.'

'It was badly executed, though,' said Primakov. 'That's a clue in itself. The blood in the speaker, the tyre and boot prints… if you believe Oleg, the killer also left mud and ice in the Quattro.'

'Here's a theory then: Max and Elizaveta saw something they weren't supposed to, forcing the killer to act spontaneously. It takes planning to dispose of bodies in winter. The ground is too hard for grave digging.'

'So not the FSB, then,' said Primakov sounding relieved. 'They have their faults, but they don't leave a mess like this behind.'

'No, and not those so-called patriotic groups the FSB use for their dirty work. Elizaveta would be hidden under layers of snow if

CHAPTER 26

Taniashvili hadn't found her, and we still don't know where Max is. Those thugs would have left both bodies in the open to encourage the others to stay out of politics.'

'So it was someone the Decembrists upset?' asked Primakov.

'I think so.'

'And we can rule out Oleg?'

'I didn't think he was your type anyway.'

Primakov winced.

'I'm sorry, that was flippant.'

'That's OK. I'm not used to talking about it. Maybe I need some practice.'

She warmed to the theme immediately. 'OK, let's start with who your type is.'

'Dark hair, slim build,' Primakov said, almost instantly.

'Luka, then. You both seemed friendly, and he's gay, isn't he?'

'Him?' Primakov let out a short laugh. 'His father's a Cuban communist who brought up his son on cigars and machismo. If Luka is gay, he'll be the last to know.'

She looked at Primakov – the silver parka framing his black hair. Beneath the tan that seemed to resist the UV famine of winter, he was actually blushing like a schoolboy.

'The thing is…' He stopped and shook his head. 'No, it doesn't matter.'

'I've never told a soul,' she said.

'I know, but it doesn't matter. Let's go back to our career-ending case.'

They crossed the Fontanka by Belinskogo Bridge and she was forced to shout to compete with the wind and traffic. 'No, let's finish for the day. Come to ours and have a beer.'

'You sure?'

'You're helping me reduce Misha's stock of Ochakovo.'

'How is the Major?'

'Worried about his future.'

She felt her phone vibrate and answered it, pushing a hand against her ear to blot out the noise.

'Yes?'

'Captain Ivanova, this is Pyotr Revich.'

'Who?'

'Pyotr Revich. I'm a journalist. Your husband asked me to do a story about the Siberian runaway.'

'Diana Maricheva,' she said.

'She was meant to go in Thursday's paper but it went in the Saturday edition. That's good news for you – the circulation is better. The problem is I can't get hold of your husband.'

'He's talking to monks on Konevets Island.'

'That explains why he left your number. He told me to call if I hear anything. Well, I have. Misha asked me to share whatever I found out. If it's not a problem, I'm expecting the same courtesy.'

'That's fine.'

'Good, can you take down an address?'

She signalled to Primakov and mimed writing on a piece of paper. He shook his head and tapped his temple to signify he would remember. She relayed the address to him. 'OK, I've got it.'

'A woman called me on Saturday evening,' Revich said. 'You need to speak to her. She says she knows who buried the girl.'

27

Primakov glided up the concrete steps of the Primorsky apartment block as if pulled by an invisible string. She, on the other hand, was out of breath after seven flights. At the woman's apartment on the tenth floor she found him waiting for her, and forced her breathing to calm. They were both forty this year, but her occasional trips to the gym were no match for his clean lifestyle and an almost religious attitude to running. At least it was a modern block by Piter standards, and the smell of tobacco on the landing was merely unpleasant – not like the accumulated stench of the older buildings.

The apartment was opened by a stringy woman wearing a smock with the logo of a steam iron. Natalya presumed she worked for a laundry or dry cleaners.

'Vera Morozova?'

'*Da.*'

Natalya took out her identification card. 'Captain Ivanova. Criminal Investigations Directorate. This is Expert Criminalist Primakov. May we come in?'

'No, my boyfriend works nights. It's better we don't disturb him… wait a moment.'

Vera Morozova returned with a quilted coat. 'Let's go to the roof.'

Primakov shrugged and began jogging up the remaining steps.

'I bet he has no problem chasing criminals.' Morozova pointed out Primakov's retreating backside.

'Unfortunately he looks after crime scenes. I do the chasing.'

'Still,' Morozova said, 'he doesn't hurt the eyes.'

At the roof, Primakov held out his identification card to a group of sullen teenagers who were smoking, their feet dangling over the edge of the block. They got to their feet and scowled, unhappy at relinquishing territory to the *menti*.

Vera Morozova pulled a packet of cigarettes from a pocket in her coat and cupped her hands against the wind to light it.

Natalya knew better than to harry a witness, and she scanned the dark horizon for the nearly complete Gazprom headquarters – the eighty-seven storey skyscraper looked like a giant rocket ship and was already the tallest building in Europe.

'My sister saw the article in the Saturday Supplement,' Morozova said. 'It was my ex-husband, he found the body – Dmitry Nikolayevich Morozov.'

Natalya took out her notepad.

Vera sucked on the cigarette, her upper lip showing vertical smokers' lines. 'He made me swear I'd never tell a soul, but that was when we were married. I don't owe that *zadnitsa* anything now.'

'What is his job?' she asked.

'He's a gamekeeper,' Morozova said.

So not a building contractor, as she and Mikhail had thought.

'Where?'

Morozova flicked ash onto the roof. 'A hunting lodge in Karelia.'

She wrote down the address.

'Tell me, is Dmitry Nikolayevich religious?'

'Dmitry?' Morozova seemed amused. 'Dogs and guns, that's all he ever cared about. Wives not so much. God even less.'

It didn't fit. Diana Maricheva's remains had been taken across Lake Ladoga to one of the country's holiest sites and they had made a handmade cross for her. Whoever discovered her took their religion seriously. The gamekeeper's hunting lodge and Lake Ladoga were both in Karelia. That would be an unlikely coincidence, if Karelia wasn't the size of the average European country. She took out her phone and glanced at the time: 5.38 p.m. She wondered if Mikhail would be back – and if she cared.

'Why don't you start at the beginning?' she said.

Morozova tapped her cigarette. 'I looked up the date because I knew you would come. It was Tuesday the eleventh of August, 2015.'

'How can you be so accurate?'

'Dmitry was due home for our silver wedding anniversary. I had to cancel the restaurant when he didn't come back from work. The next I saw him I could see he hadn't slept. I accused him of seeing someone. He denied it and said he couldn't remember what he'd been doing. I threw a few plates until his memory improved, then he said he'd been hunting sika deer when one of his dogs came running back with a bone. It didn't belong to any animal he knew so he took it off the dog and followed it when it went to get another. That's when he found her.'

'What did he find?'

'A body halfway to a skeleton. Black skin, no teeth.'

'What about clothes?'

'I can't remember… I think she was naked.'

'How did he know she was female?'

She shrugged. 'I didn't ask.'

'What did he do with her?'

She sucked on the cigarette. 'Once Dmitry started talking about it, he wouldn't stop. We'd always wanted to have children. He said he'd gone away to make sure the girl got a Christian burial. At least I knew he wasn't screwing around. People don't make up those kind of stories.'

'You said Dmitry wasn't religious?'

'No, he wasn't. And he never told me he took her to Konevets Island. I only found that out when I read the article. I called the paper. It must have been him. Was I wrong?'

Natalya avoided the question. 'Why didn't he report the body to the police?'

'You'll have to ask him that. I told him he had to speak to the *menti* but he refused – he said he couldn't.'

'Because he was worried we might think he'd killed the girl?'

'Maybe.' The lines above her lip folded as she pulled on the cigarette. 'Whatever the reason, he didn't want to tell me.'

Morozova's attention wavered as Primakov joined them. 'Who owned the estate when the body was found?' he asked.

'A state prosecutor… a woman.'

So that was the most likely explanation for Morozov keeping quiet. A hunting lodge with its extensive grounds would be well beyond the means of an honest prosecutor on a state salary.

'What was she called?'

Morozova raised her head to the dark sky. 'I'm not supposed to say.'

Natalya looked around. She could see why the kids came here. The wind blowing off the roof was icy – it would be hard to tolerate it for long, and yet it had one of the best views of the city.

'Shulgin,' Morozova said, breaking the silence. 'He said her name was Kira Shulgin.'

They took the stairs. 'Wait, Leo,' she called.

He stopped a flight below her.

'Are you hungry?'

'A little.'

'Come to mine. I've got frozen pizza and beer.'

'Captain, have you got anything that isn't—'

CHAPTER 27

'Carbohydrate?'

He nodded.

'I don't think so. You can have the salad I bought for the pizza, but if you call me "Captain" while we're off duty I'll make you drink beer.'

'I'd like to, but I have to feed my cat.'

'Another time then.'

They walked some more. 'Natalya?'

Now that he was using her name it felt strange. She almost wanted him to stop.

'Yes?'

'You looked surprised when she mentioned the owner of the lodge. Who is Kira Shulgin?'

'You know Misha picked up some cold cases from Leonid Laskin the *Alkanaut*? This Diana Maricheva case was one of them. He said Laskin had been trying to get rid of it, but a pain-in-the-*zhopa* prosecutor wouldn't let him.'

Primakov said, 'Let me guess. Kira Shulgin?'

'Exactly. Now, what's the betting she's religious?'

28

There was something soft and jazzy playing in her living room. The music sounded decent, not that awful rap metal Anton liked to play. There was an odour of spices too, that she was sure weren't hers.

She removed her boots in the hallway and put them next to a black studded pair.

'Hello?' she called out.

She knew it couldn't be Anton. His idea of cuisine was crisps. They had been his snack of choice ever since the Moscow Patriarchate had declared them sinful.

In the kitchen she found Vita stirring a pot of something that smelled better than anything she had made before. Anton stood by her side, nursing one of Mikhail's Ochakovos.

'Hey Natasha.' Anton kissed her on the cheek. 'We were going to surprise you.'

Vita smiled and kissed her too. For once the girl seemed happy and it was about to be the worst day of her life. Her brother was dead. Max was her twin, which made it worse. She caught Vita's eye. She should tell her now. Waiting was crass.

'Is Papa coming home?' Anton asked.

'Not as far as I know,' she said. 'The last I heard he was on Konevets Island talking to monks.'

His voice dropped. 'Have you heard anything about Max?'

'Let's not talk about it,' she said. 'What are you cooking? It smells amazing.'

CHAPTER 28

'A massaman curry,' Anton said, as if he made it all the time. 'Hey, have you seen YouTube?'

'What are you talking about?'

He turned to a laptop propped on their small breakfast table. 'There's this group called the Decembrists,' Anton began. 'Vita told me they do stunts like *Voina* used to.'

'Elizaveta Kalinina,' she said. 'The dead woman I saw on the Toksovo road. She was one.'

'That was your old case, wasn't it?' The evangelical gleam in his eyes set off an alarm bell.

Anton tapped Vita's laptop.

She tried to focus on the screen but her attention kept being drawn away to Vita, who had lifted a pan lid, releasing coconut-infused steam. She'd never broken bad news to anyone like this before. A knock on an apartment door with a pair of sombre looking *menti* and half the job was done. This was far messier. Not too close to home so much as at home.

'Natasha, you're not looking.'

Vita caught her gaze. She frowned uncertainly at the girl: a warning that she had bad news. It was ridiculous now to think Vita had deliberately seduced Anton to get inside information on the case, or at least to make sure her unofficial investigation stayed on track.

'Sorry, Anton.'

She tilted the screen to cut out the reflection. It took her a moment to work out what she was seeing. A small group of passers-by were standing near a granite slab of a building onto which images were projected: a child playing with a dog in a park, then a girl of about sixteen in a white dress standing before a priest, a graduation picture, and finally one she recognised: the photograph of Elizaveta cradling Artem in the maternity hospital.

The building looked familiar too, despite the images distorting its façade. She felt nauseous. It was the *Sledkom* regional headquarters in St Petersburg. The projected image changed from the maternity hospital to block writing, each line taking up a storey of the building:

ELIZAVETA D. KALININA
28 JUNE 1992 – 05 JANUARY 2018
MURDERED.
CAPTAIN IVANOVA, N. N.
MUST INVESTIGATE.

Christ, what had they done?

'That's you, Natasha,' said Anton. 'You're famous now.'

She felt suddenly exhausted, the day's events catching up with her. This was a godawful mess.

Vita set glasses on the table and she caught the girl's eye again. 'Let's go outside.'

Anton picked up a packet of Mikhail's cigarettes from the table.

'You need to watch the curry,' Natalya said to him.

Anton looked disturbed. 'What do you mean?'

Vita had sensed something. 'Just stir the fucking thing,' she snapped. 'I don't care.'

Below the balcony, the city was alive. A group of students were posing on the pedestrian bridge between the pairs of stone lions. The bridge had been built in the same year as the Decembrists' failed revolt: 1825. Now a new breed of idealists with the same name were dying. Karl Marx had written that history repeated itself, first as tragedy and then as farce. If it was true, she wasn't laughing.

CHAPTER 28

Vita folded her arms. 'Before you blame me, I told you we were planning something. You really messed things up with Adelina though. She wanted nothing to do with you.'

'What are you talking about?'

'The thing we did outside *Sledkom* headquarters.'

'Vita, that's not why I want to talk to you. Did you know we took Oleg's car?'

'Do I? He talks of nothing else except his stupid Quattro and what you might be doing to it. He behaves like it's all he cares about and we haven't got a missing brother. I wish to God Oleg was missing instead.' She put a hand to her mouth at the blasphemy.

'A friend of mine had a forensic technician take a look at his car.'

The mood had shifted. Vita was silent, staring down at the students taking their silly pictures.

'Vita, I've got some bad news. The worst.' She searched for the young woman's eyes and held her gaze for a second. 'There was blood in the boot.'

Natalya went to put a hand on her shoulder and Vita shrugged it off.

'Whose blood?'

'Max's.'

'What does it mean?' Vita asked. 'Has someone kidnapped him?'

Until Oleg was clear of suspicion she had to be cautious. 'There are some things I can't tell you, but I believe Max was murdered by the same person who killed Elizaveta.'

Vita thrust her against the railings.

'I don't believe you.' Angry tears were in her eyes.

She thought of Max's battered body wrapped in plastic.

'I didn't mean to push you,' Vita said.

'It's all right.'

Vita threw open the doors to the living room. 'Anton, I have to go,' she called, then turned to Natalya. 'I'm sorry. I need to tell my parents a detective who isn't on the case believes Max is dead. What does that mean? Max is dead? Max might be dead? Is he even dead? How do you know from a little blood?' Vita ran a hand through her hair. 'Really, what the hell do I say to them? And what the hell do I tell them about Oleg?'

What could she say? Oleg had no alibi to speak of and he was the last person to see Max alive. It was highly probable, too, that his car had been used to transport both bodies. Then there was the clincher: the killer hadn't destroyed the Audi afterwards; it had been driven home and left outside Oleg's apartment, where he had cleaned it the next day.

'Max won't be coming home… tell them that,' Natalya said. 'It's enough for now.'

Anton left soon after Vita, finding some excuse about needing fresh work clothes from his mother's apartment. Sometimes she wondered if she was kidding herself that they were close. When Mikhail was away, Anton always returned to Dinara's. When Mikhail was there, Anton invariably found an excuse to stay. She knew it wasn't fair to blame him. Dinara was his mother, and a possessive one at that. No, it might not have been fair, but she was tired of being abandoned.

She finished a portion of the massaman curry and slumped on the sofa with one of Mikhail's beers to save her dwindling supply of wine. She'd had little time to process the YouTube video Anton had shown her. For one thing, she doubted *Sledkom* were going to surrender their case to her after such a tame protest. For another, they would suspect she had been feeding information to the group that wasn't in the public domain – especially the knowledge that Elizaveta had been murdered.

Her house phone rang. Out of habit, she glanced at the time. It was after ten. Only Mikhail would call now.

CHAPTER 28

'*Da*?'

'Ivanova?' It was Dostoynov. 'Why haven't you been answering your mobile? I had to get this number from Rogov.'

'I'm sorry, Colonel. My battery must have died.'

'At cadet school, did they ever teach you about the hierarchy of police groups?'

She knew better than to question him. 'Yes, Sir.'

'Good. Tell me about it.'

She paused, wondering what it was leading to. 'Local police are at the bottom. Then there's OMON when a little muscle is needed, after them there's us at state level.'

'Continue,' he said.

'Then there's *Sledkom*, the FSB, and the Federal Guards Service.'

'Good, you do know the hierarchy. So when this terrorist group attacked a convoy belonging to the FSB director, and one of the activists was found dead three months later—'

'Two,' she said.

'What?'

'There are two dead: Elizaveta Kalinina and Max Timchenko.'

'That's odd,' he said, 'because I haven't heard of another body being reported. Don't interrupt me next time, Ivanova. If you're too naïve to guess what's going on I'll spell it out for you. *Sledkom* are using this woman's death to break up the Decembrists before the idiots get someone killed. You are not part of this plan.'

'What about Elizaveta, Colonel? Doesn't she deserve justice?'

'A drug addict who sought the destruction of the republics? Hasn't she seen justice already?'

The answer chilled her.

'If you think we're monsters, Ivanova, take a good look at Ukraine or Libya. Do you believe all those people protesting for change wanted civil war and anarchy? Still nothing to say? I'll say it for you, then. A Colonel General of Justice has requested a meeting with me first thing tomorrow morning. That's a Deputy Vice Chairman of *Sledkom* to you. Don't leave the office until I get back. You might want to clear your desk in preparation. Sleep well, Captain.'

She put the phone down. In her handbag she found her mobile and plugged it in. While waiting for it to charge, she opened another of Mikhail's Ochakovos. If tomorrow was going to be her last day, a hangover would be the least of her problems.

By the time her mobile came to life, showing twelve missed calls, half the beer was gone. Apart from increasingly irate messages from Dostoynov, she found one from shortly after nine from Mikhail.

'Hi Babe,' he said.

The message ended after he realised he was speaking to her voicemail. Mikhail had been gone for two days and she had received precisely two words from him. Two more, she realised, than she had left for Mikhail.

The next message was from the journalist, Pyotr Revich, asking about the gamekeeper's ex-wife and if there was anything useful he could use "as per our agreement". After Revich she listened to a recording from Rogov warning her that Dostoynov had "grabbed me by the eggs" and forced him to give up her home number.

She left the phone charging. In the kitchen she found a pack of Mikhail's Sobranies that Anton had forgotten to steal. She lit one off the gas stove and stepped onto the balcony. Above her apartment she could hear her neighbour Sergei singing something morose and melodic in his fine baritone. She recognised it as "Black Raven", a folk song about a dying Cossack singing to the bird circling over his body. The vans that brought Stalin's victims – alive and dead – to the forests around Toksovo were Black Ravens too. At moments like this she wondered if the universe was warning her of an impending catastrophe. She listened to the song until her cigarette had finished, then went to bed.

29

In preparation for her last day, she pressed a blouse to go with her blue suit, polished her best winter boots, and even spent some time applying a little make-up. By ten thirty Dostoynov still hadn't appeared in the office, and his absence was making her increasingly nervous. She found Rogov at his desk, his wastepaper bin piled up with printouts.

His hand jerked to shield the papers on his desk. He relaxed when he saw her.

'Hey, Rogov.'

'You want tea, Boss?'

'Sure.'

They went to the refreshments area and loitered there until it was empty. She swilled out her mug and then placed it under the tap of a stainless-steel samovar. Rogov scanned the buttons on the drinks machine before choosing a Coke Zero. He took a gulp and let out a burp. 'Boss, I've found something. Well, lots of things.'

He belched again. 'Remember the tax inspector who showed up on the ANPR cameras?'

'The one who got his Mercedes repainted by the Decembrists?'

'Him. I discovered he's got a *dacha* in the Pushkin Cooperative, eight kilometres from the girl's body.'

'Good work,' she said. 'I've got some news too. The forensics on Oleg's Quattro put Max in the boot and Elizaveta in the passenger seat. We need to find out what Oleg was up to that day.'

'You want me to do that?' asked Rogov.

CHAPTER 29

'Yes, but we can't go there. Oleg will complain and Dostoynov won't be amused. What else do you have?'

Rogov swilled his Coke. 'I've been finding addresses for the thirty-two people targeted by the Decembrists.'

'And?'

'And there are better ways to commit suicide.'

'Why?'

'Because I found *dachas* belonging to five gangsters who used to run with the Malyshev mafia as well as a mansion belonging to the daughter-in-law of the Governor – she used to work in a club, so I can guarantee it's not hers. I also matched two judges and a state prosecutor.'

'Kira Shulgin?' she asked.

'No, it was the old fart who was nailing the film director for making that Tchaikovsky movie.' He wrinkled his nose as if he didn't entirely disagree with the prosecution. 'Why mention Shulgin?' he asked.

'A bad guess,' she said, tossing a tea bag into a waste bin. 'Shulgin was the one who wouldn't let Leonid Laskin bury his Siberian girl case.'

'No, it's not her. Before I narrowed the search to Leningrad, the register came up with properties all over the country for these crooks – the Black Sea, Moscow, Kursk, Sochi… enough to shame an oligarch.'

She paused. 'Want to hear something exciting? Dostoynov called last night to say he's going to fire me.'

She heard crisp footsteps approaching.

'Captain, don't let me interrupt your gossip.' Lieutenant-Colonel Dostoynov was in his dark-blue dress uniform and looked as if he'd spent longer getting ready than she had. 'Actually, Sergeant Rogov, why don't you come along too?'

They followed Dostoynov to his corner office. Inside, the potted plant he'd bought was dying; its leaves hung limply over the pot, much like Rogov's arms in his huge shirt – he was exuding misery.

'Let's deal with you first, Sergeant.' Dostoynov glared at him. 'In this unit, you're cow shit when I need steak. Yesterday our network administrator came to see me. He said you've been nosing at restricted properties on the register. I've wanted to get rid of you – I make no secret of that – and now you've done me a favour. Pack your things, Sergeant, you're suspended pending a formal meeting with the union. Leave your identification card and Makarov.'

Rogov was staring, unfocused. 'Please,' he begged. 'My wife…' His voice trailed off.

'Colonel, I must protest,' she said. 'I gave him that assignment.'

'I'll deal with you next, Captain.'

Dostoynov turned to Rogov with a menace she hadn't heard before. 'Are you still here?'

'Shut the door behind him.' He waited for her to close it.

'Good, that's one down. And now Captain, you'll soon look at Sergeant Rogov with envy.'

'You're going to fire me too?'

'This election coming up? You once told me it was a mask. If it was taken away, people would see a dictator.'

'I didn't use that word, Colonel.'

'But don't bother pretending it's not what you meant. Let me ask you a question. How do you suppose *Novaya Gazeta* survives? Six journalists from a liberal newspaper assassinated, yet no one administers the *coup de grâce* to save us all a few trees?'

'Because former Premier Gorbachev was its founder?'

'No, it's because with *Novaya Gazeta* operating we can say we have a free press. With elections we can say we live in a democracy. My predecessor, Colonel Vasiliev, told me a pain-in-the-arse liberal like you is worth ten detectives. Want to make a guess why?'

'Colonel, I only want to do my job. Nothing more.'

CHAPTER 29

'And that's it.' He slapped his desk. 'When opposition politicians and busybodies slandered the department he pointed to a *ment* like you and said, "but here's a virtuous one, so you must be mistaken. In fact, please go ahead and fuck yourself on the way out." That was Vasiliev's way. His methods aren't mine. When I was getting my backside warmed this morning I thought of nothing except firing you and heaping more misery on your husband.'

'Col—' She stopped, then frowned. She wasn't being fired. Someone had protected her. What possible motive could they have?

'That little YouTube video the Decembrists made? Since yesterday it's had eight hundred thousand views, and it'll be four million by March. The government are trying to get it removed.'

'You mean it's because of the election, Colonel?'

'Of course it's because of the fucking election, it's got more choreographers than the Bolshoi. The government doesn't need a scandal.'

'So, you're not firing me?'

'Not only do you stay, but *Sledkom* have been ordered to return your case. Frankly, they made no progress. The Decembrists are still active and their attempt to discredit them failed. No one believed their story that Elizaveta Kalinina was a drug addict. Your job is to find who killed the girl and what's going on with this professor. If you discover the names of these traitors playing student politics, your orders are to hand them to me.'

'Yes, Colonel.'

'Before you go, you need to know this: *Sledkom* want revenge for that little stunt. They think you're in league with the Decembrists.'

'I didn't know anything about—'

He held up a hand. 'And when they come for you, I'll be there holding the door open for them. Now get out.'

In the unit's open-plan area she found Rogov. Two detectives were consoling him as he stuffed items from his desk drawers into his coat pockets.

'I'm sorry, Stepan. I didn't think he would do that,' she said.

'Don't be sorry. I volunteered.' He scowled in the direction of Dostoynov's office. 'This place is going downhill anyway.'

'What will you do?'

He paused for a moment as if considering it. 'The World Cup? I'll make a fortune on security.'

She doubted it. Dostoynov was unlikely to provide a good reference. 'Well, good luck. Don't forget he still has to get your dismissal past the union.'

She waited for the two detectives to finish their goodbyes to Rogov.

'What about you, Boss?' he asked.

'I'm staying. *Sledkom* have given me my case back... more like they've thrown it in my face.'

'You're staying?' He crumpled a little, as if the thought of leaving alongside her would have earnt him respect.

'You might be better off out. *Sledkom* want revenge.'

'Shit, Natalya.' Rogov ran his fingers through his hair. 'I've lost my job.' He stared ahead for a moment, unfocused. 'What the hell do I say to Oksana?'

'It was my fault... Tell her that. She'll blame me anyway.'

'Maybe I will.' He forced a smile. 'Listen, Boss, I've got something for you.' He pulled out his bottom drawer to reveal a sheaf of papers. 'These are the properties I matched. I printed them off real estate sites.'

She took them from him. 'Thanks.'

'And I've got the Audi's documentation. Oleg told me his car had been repaired before the holidays – a problem with the fuel injectors. They serviced it too.'

'Thanks,' she said, not knowing what else to say.

'You don't get it, do you, Boss?'

'What are you saying?'

'They log the mileage on a service. It was in the garage a week before Max borrowed the car. If Oleg can tell you how many trips he made, you can work out where Max went – assuming the steroid-injecting *kachok* isn't lying.'

'You did well, Rogov.'

'Thanks, Boss.' He locked the desk drawers and deposited the key under an encrusted coffee mug. 'Maybe my last act as a detective.' He took his ID card out of his wallet and dropped it on the desk.

He looked up as if he'd remembered something. 'No, *this* is my last act. I'm leaving you with a question. I went through everything the Decembrists put on the internet. Some of their shit went back a few years. Most had a pack of idiots running around in balaclavas. So the question is this: if the girl and the professor were up to something, why didn't I see it on YouTube?'

30

Rogov left after a lot of back-slapping and murmurs of discontent directed at the closed door of Dostoynov's office. Everyone knew he wasn't the greatest of detectives, but he'd been there for fifteen years; many of the old-timers were fearful that he might not be the last to go.

Natalya felt in her handbag for the memory card from Gregor's wrecked drone. After a few minutes she gave up and upended her bag onto her desk to sift through the contents.

Dostoynov came out of his office. 'Captain, what are you doing?'

'Some old photos,' she said, finding that lying to him was becoming second nature. She held up the memory card and tucked it in her jeans pocket.

'After you've finished with your personal affairs, perhaps you would tell me the next steps in your investigation.'

She thought for a moment. 'I'd like to question Oleg Timchenko.'

'I'll save you the exercise and bring him in. What else do you need?'

That *Sledkom* general had really warmed his backside. She'd never known Dostoynov to be so helpful.

'I want a team to search for Max Timchenko.'

'The Directorate is being squeezed by the World Cup and the election. I can't give you that.'

'I'll settle for Expert Criminalist Primakov.'

'I'll request his assistance. Is that all?'

'No, I also want the cause of Elizaveta Kalinina's death reviewed. Her son shouldn't grow up thinking his mother was a drug addict.'

CHAPTER 30

'You ask a lot.'

'You asked me, Colonel.'

'Don't be insolent.' His eyes narrowed a fraction. 'And now a favour for a favour. Those properties Rogov was looking at… You said it was on your orders?'

'Yes, Colonel. I believe Elizaveta Kalinina and Max Timchenko were both Decembrists.'

'Max Timchenko was one too?' He glared at her for a fraction of a second. 'You know, Ivanova, there's a lot you don't tell me.'

'Well, Colonel, one theory I have is that they were both killed by someone who had been targeted by the group. I asked Sergeant Rogov to check if any of them lived in the vicinity of Toksovo.'

'In that case, how did the brother get his car back? Did your missing professor rise from the dead to take it home for him?'

'No, Colonel. I think the killer returned the car after hiding Max Timchenko's body.'

'Why?' he asked.

'So we would think Max killed Elizaveta, then ran away.'

Dostoynov stretched in his chair. 'Or perhaps their killer lives in the city and needed to get home. Have you considered that? The brother, for example. Maybe the woman and the professor had something going on – Oleg got jealous and killed them. He brought his car home because he couldn't bear to abandon it.'

'Yes, Colonel. I have considered that theory.'

'Then we are of the same mind. Now, these people Rogov was looking up on the property register? Do you intend to waste police resources on them?'

She cursed Dostoynov, knowing what was coming.

'No, Colonel.'

'Good, then we can close that line of enquiry. Focus on the brother. He's the obvious suspect. Find out the names of the Decembrists too, while you're at it. That is an order, in case you claim to have misunderstood later.'

'Yes, Colonel.'

In the afternoon she was called by a custody sergeant. She found Oleg in an interview room seated on one of the four bolted chairs fixed around a Formica table. He was visibly shivering – they had brought him outside in only his gym shorts and vest. His thick arms were stretched back by handcuffs, forcing out his enormous chest. A raised weal ran along one cheekbone. He stared down at the table. Two tear-tracks lined his face. All his bravado had been erased by a few slashes of a police baton.

'Oleg,' she said.

He looked up. There was pain in his eyes.

'I'm sorry about your brother.'

He twisted his neck one way, then the other, wiping fresh tears against his shoulders. 'Vita told me. Are you sure he's dead?'

'Not one hundred percent, but I wouldn't hold out hope. Do you need a lawyer?' she asked. 'We can provide free legal assistance.'

'I didn't do anything.' He sounded defeated.

'You resisted the police when they brought you in.'

He shook his head slightly. 'Four cosmonauts came at me in riot gear. I had my hands in the air but the bastards kept hitting me.'

At least that explained Dostoynov's helpful offer to fetch him. He wanted Oleg bruised so he'd look guilty and be too cowed to argue himself out of trouble.

'Do you want to register a complaint?' she asked.

'I've been told they won't press charges.'

'Who told you that?'

'Him.' He jerked his head as Lieutenant Colonel Dostoynov's face passed the frosted window.

CHAPTER 30

Despite the assurance, she'd place money on a judge hearing of Oleg's scuffle with the *menti*.

'Officially,' she said, 'I have to tell you it's within your rights to refuse to answer any questions and your silence won't be interpreted as guilt. Unofficially, if you're innocent don't even think of being silent, and don't sign anything you don't agree with. If my boss decides to charge you, you're screwed. Judges convict over ninety-nine per cent of defendants. This is your trial. Right now. Do you understand?'

Oleg drew a breath. 'Yes.'

Dostoynov entered and took the chair next to her.

'Can you take the bracelets off… please?' Oleg asked.

'That wouldn't be wise,' said Dostoynov. 'Oleg created quite a scene earlier. We don't want to see it repeated.' He brought out a notepad and snapped down the top of his pen decisively. 'Shall we start at the beginning?'

Natalya took out her notepad on cue.

Police interviews were a double-act, with the two *menti* befriending, bewildering, or threatening a suspect, working off each other with an almost supernatural sense of timing. The goal was to get a signed confession: the Queen of Evidence. Dostoynov, being straight out of the FSB, would have a different style. Looking at Oleg's battered face, she had more than an idea what that involved.

Dostoynov leaned back in his seat to affect an air of disinterest. The bolted chair allowed for little movement and he abandoned the effort, choosing to hunch over the Formica table instead. He looped his fingers together in a thoughtful pose.

'Oleg, when did you *say* you last saw your brother?' Dostoynov asked.

'I already told that sergeant before.'

Yes, thought Natalya, but now your words will be twisted.

'With your permission, Colonel, I'd like to take Mr Timchenko back to the previous week.'

Dostoynov looked out to the frosted glass of the window as if he was bored by the proceedings. 'Go ahead.'

'Oleg,' she said, 'your Audi Quattro underwent a repair recently.'

She watched him frown as he wondered what his car had to do with anything. She nodded, encouraging him to talk.

'It had a problem with the injectors,' Oleg said.

'Is this going somewhere?' asked Dostoynov.

'Yes, Colonel. If you'll permit me to continue, I'll explain in a moment.'

'Oleg, after your car was repaired, where did you drive it? I need to hear about every trip you made.'

Oleg twisted in his seat, straining to create some space for his arms. 'I picked it up from the garage in Kalininsky District – they specialise in German classics. After that I went to see a friend in Aleksandrovskaya to test the new injectors.'

'What's that, sixty kilometres?' she asked.

'Sixty-four. I take the same route every month.'

She wrote the number down.

Dostoynov shifted as if something of mild interest had attracted his attention. 'You see this friend once a month. You're a *kachok* – if we did a drug test what would we find… hmm?'

Oleg rubbed his paper-thin skin. 'I don't take steroids.' His eyes caught Dostoynov's and he looked away sharply.

'Then who is this friend?' Dostoynov asked.

'I get arthritis in my fingers. There's a guy Max recommended, he does acupuncture. If you take the bracelets off I'll show you.'

She looked to Dostoynov.

'Any trouble in here,' he said, 'and it'll be worse than an OMON's baton. Are we clear?'

CHAPTER 30

'Yes, Colonel.'

'All right.' She took out a key and removed his handcuffs, looping them through her belt.

Oleg rubbed his wrists. She could see purple lines on the skin – whichever OMON prick had put on the handcuffs had done them up deliberately tight. He held out his hands, the fingers splayed. Even Dostoynov could see that the joints were swollen.

'Thank you, Oleg. If we can get back to the car,' she said, trying to take control of the interview. 'Did you use it on any other occasions before Max borrowed it?'

'I didn't go anywhere else in the Quattro,' Oleg said. 'Just that one trip. It's too much hassle in Piter, easier to use the Metro.'

She made another note. 'That's all I needed. Now, if you would answer the Colonel's question – what were you doing that day?'

'Nothing much.' He twisted in his seat and rubbed his wrists again.

Dostoynov's eyes narrowed – a dog catching a scent. 'So there's no one to corroborate your story?'

'It's the truth. Max was my brother. Why would I hurt him?'

Dostoynov affected a yawn. 'You have my sympathies.'

Oleg twisted his body towards her in a conscious effort to shut out Dostoynov. 'What do you want to know?'

'Where were you on the day Max borrowed your car?' she asked.

'Shopping.'

'What for?'

'Boots – my old ones were letting in water. I went to the Galeria on Ligovsky Prospekt.'

She made another note. 'Then how did you get there?'

'By Metro. I left around eleven thirty and was back by three o'clock.'

Dostoynov interrupted. 'If you did go to the Galeria you'll be on half the cameras in the city.' He turned to her. 'Captain, can you verify that?'

She scribbled a note.

'Now what did you buy?' asked Dostoynov.

'I bought the boots on my credit card. I'll get you an online statement.'

'Thank you, Oleg.' Natalya made another note. 'What did you do after three o'clock?'

'I went home. I watched TV and did some weights.'

She nodded again, to encourage him to keep talking.

'Well, after a while I began to wonder about Max. I thought maybe the injectors on the Quattro had been playing up again. He'd left his phone, so I couldn't call him.'

'What were you watching on television?' Dostoynov asked.

'*Vladenie 18*, and an American series about kids fighting something upside down. I can't remember the name.'

'Until what time?' Dostoynov asked.

'Nine.'

Dostoynov frowned. 'Six hours of TV? I find that improbable. Why don't you tell us the truth? Did you meet Max and Elizaveta?'

'No, I was home, the TV was just playing in the background.'

'So you have no alibi after three o'clock. Then you woke up the next day and—'

'Colonel, if I may. Can we go back to the television?'

'I don't know what this has got to do with—'

'Colonel. I don't think we've finished establishing if he has an alibi.'

'I believe we have, Captain. No one can verify his story.'

'It's not a person who can substantiate his alibi, it's a thing,' she said, turning to Oleg. 'Mr Timchenko – how were you watching *Vladenie 18* and this American series?'

'Television, I told you.'

No you idiot, she thought. 'How were you watching it?'

CHAPTER 30

'Oh,' he said, scratching acne on his nose, 'I was streaming *Kino*.'

'We can check that,' she said.

'Anyone can admit to watching a film, Captain. A few minutes on Yandex and I could find the programme guides for a few channels. If you ask Mr Timchenko I'm sure he'll be able to tell you all about what he supposedly saw.'

Oleg said, 'Mostly I was doing weights. I stopped following the programmes. I prefer hardcore horror.'

She groaned inwardly at Oleg's inability to help himself. 'So you can't even describe what you were watching?'

'One was something to do with vampires.'

Dostoynov abandoned any pretence of being disinterested. 'You have no alibi for the time in question.' He was louder, flecks of spit flying from his mouth. He was a cliché of a TV cop. 'Why did you kill Elizaveta?' he demanded. 'Did she reject you? Did you kill Max when he tried to save her? Tell me the truth, Oleg. Tell me now and it'll be better for you.'

'I am telling you the truth. I didn't do anything.'

'It's really no good arguing,' said Dostoynov. 'You should have tried harder to establish an alibi.'

'That's not correct, Colonel.' She chose her words carefully, a soldier stepping through a minefield. 'If he was streaming *Kino*, his television will have stored the activity. We'll need to check it, and his phone too.'

'If,' said Dostoynov. In his imagination she suspected the interview was a battle where his iron will would break his opponent. Now it had turned procedural he was losing interest.

'Oleg,' she said, 'do you give me permission to check your television, mobile phone and credit card records? A warrant will waste time.'

'Yes.'

'Thank you. Now, I've got a few more questions,' she said.

Oleg wiped away some fresh tears with a palm. 'How could I refuse?'

Easy now, she thought, you're not out of trouble yet. 'When we spoke last time, you said the keys for your Audi had been left in the ignition when it was returned. Has Max ever done that before?'

'Never.'

'And he left the car in a mess?'

'Yeah. I cleaned up. Except I should have left it… after what Vita said—'

She glared at him, willing him not to incriminate his sister. He took the hint and stopped talking.

'Because you realise,' she said, 'you were washing away forensic evidence?'

'Yeah, that's what I meant.'

'Tell me about the mess.'

'Muddy footprints.'

'Where?'

'In the driver's footwell.'

'Nowhere else?

'The tyres were muddy too.'

'And you cleaned them?'

'Yeah, cursing Max for it. I feel like a louse now.'

'Anything else?'

Oleg stretched in the chair and she feared the bolt-heads might shear with the strain. 'The driver's seat,' he said. 'There was ice, and mud in the folds of the leather. Fine stuff. It stank.'

'What of?'

He shrugged. 'Dunno. It just smelled really bad.'

CHAPTER 30

They were outside the interview room. 'What was all that about?' Dostoynov demanded.

'I thought you asked me to focus on Oleg, Colonel.'

'Don't be smart.'

'If he's innocent he could get twenty years for a double murder – maybe life.'

'Maybe one day you'll learn when to keep your mouth shut. Take a look at this electronic evidence of yours, Ivanova, but I'm not convinced. Maybe his sister was the one watching television.'

So she provides an alibi after he murdered her twin brother? 'I'll look into it, Colonel,' she said, acting as if his ridiculous idea had some merit.

31

Leo Primakov sat on his toilet seat with a yellow towel tied around his waist. He stared at the tiny water heater, willing it to boil for the fourth time. There was a thermometer in his medicine cabinet and he thought of checking if the bath water in his freezing apartment was cooling faster than the boiler and two saucepans on his stove could heat it.

The State Pathologist used similar methods to estimate the time of death. It turned his mind to the effect of temperature on Elizaveta Kalinina's corpse. Had she remained undiscovered in the concrete ditch for another day or two, her body would have frozen solid.

All the apartments in his block had been out of hot water for over a month and there was still no word as to when it would be restored. Steam hissed from the electric boiler. He placed a bucket underneath it, before turning the tap at its base. He collected the water and poured it into the bathtub. At the stove, he dipped his index finger into the dedicated saucepans. The temperature was just bearable – that meant around sixty degrees Celsius. He gripped the handles using the corners of his towel, briefly lifting the flaps and exposing himself to the neighbouring apartments. A layer of steam curled over the water as he emptied the pans into the bath. He dipped in a hand to check the temperature, then discarded his towel and lowered himself in.

He preferred showers – the thought of wallowing in the same water that held his dirt and body waste made him feel queasy – but the shower was dependent on the hot water that fed the block, and he'd take queasy over cold any day. Over the last month he'd become a slow convert to bathing, and felt his muscles relax in the warm water. He closed his eyes and saw the dead woman's face, knowing in a minute or two she would fade. There was something about a bath that cleansed the soul, working deeper than any shower nozzle.

He leaned over to pick up the bottle of Georgian brandy on the bath's edge and poured a large measure into a glass. He felt the water temperature drop a notch and took a sip. There was a double knock on the door. He ignored it. By the time he threw on some clothes the bath would be cold and the visitor gone. Besides, he rarely had visitors. It was more likely to be some drunk calling for a neighbour.

His phone rang and he held the glass of *chacha* on the edge of the bath while he lowered his head and submerged his ears. Under water, the ringtone of his phone was distorted. It sounded like a doorbell in a distant apartment.

'For Christ's sake, Leo!' Natalya yelled from the corridor outside.

He pulled his head out, splashing soapy water into his brandy.

'Just a minute, Captain,' he called.

It was freezing in Primakov's apartment and Natalya kept her coat on while waiting for him to dress. A single room served as a kitchen, diner and living space, and in one corner she observed a tortoiseshell cat studiously ignoring her from its position on a heated blanket. Elsewhere, the apartment was basically furnished. It wasn't a surprise. Primakov was honest and relied on his salary. In Piter that got him a modest apartment in a Primorsky high-rise.

He returned to see her looking at a series of prints from Natalia Goncharova, which added colour to the otherwise lifeless room.

'My mother's,' Primakov said, towel-drying his hair. 'How can I help, Captain?'

'I wanted to tell you in person. *Sledkom* returned my case.'

'They have?'

'The Decembrists caused a stir and the government doesn't want any aggravation this close to the election. Any other time and they'd be cracking skulls. Dostoynov has given the case to me on condition I put Oleg's head in the frame and feed a few Decembrists to the wolves. I'm more inclined to make myself a pain in his *zhopa*.'

'I wouldn't expect any less of you, Captain.' Primakov looked longingly at his closed bathroom door. 'Is that all you wanted to see me about?'

'No, Leo. That photography business of yours. I loved the pictures you took of Anton and Misha.'

'It's not working out. July was the last time a client paid me.'

'But you still have the equipment?'

'Yes, Captain.'

'Then I don't suppose you can see what's on this?' She felt in her pocket for the micro-SD card. 'And can you keep it here when we've finished? I don't want *Sledkom* getting hold of it.'

'Sure.' He took it from her and switched on his computer. 'What is it?'

'Drone footage. There were three Decembrists working together on something: Elizaveta, Max, and the group's cameraman, Gregor Bortsov – I got it from him. I'm hoping it will show me what they were up to.'

He plugged the card into a USB adapter and attached it to his computer. After the machine had finished booting, Primakov clicked his mouse to open the contents of the SD card. A directory of twelve files appeared. She quickly scanned the list, looking for the most recent.

'Delete that one,' she said.

'Captain, this is evidence.'

'Gregor secretly filmed me. The last thing I need is Dostoynov or *Sledkom* finding me on a Decembrist recording.'

CHAPTER 31

Primakov hit the delete key and the file disappeared. 'I'll scrub it properly later,' he said. 'What about the others?'

'All the files are dated June to September last year. Are there any more? I was hoping to find one from the day Elizaveta died.'

'No, that's all the files… Captain, would you like something to drink?'

'Natalya.'

'Then, Natalya, you can have water, tea or *chacha*.'

'I'll risk the *chacha*.'

While Primakov fetched the Georgian brandy, she clicked on the drone's first recording. It had been taken in the pale glow of a white night and there was no accompanying audio. In the colourless light, Gregor turned his face away from the drone's camera as it soared above woodland and edged around the circumference of a brick wall.

She took the brandy from Primakov. 'Thanks.'

'What are we looking at?'

'God knows, but it's fucking huge,' she said.

'I can see a lake and a launch,' Primakov added. 'It looks like Gregor is being cautious, slowly working the drone inside.'

'Over-cautious. The place looks deserted,' she added.

Three motionless bulldozers were parked on an expanse of brown where the property's grounds were being extended into nearby woodland. Further on, trees had been stripped of their branches and the trunks were stacked lengthways on a logging truck. The drone continued over a glass-covered swimming pool, tennis courts and landscaped greens.

'What are those things?' Primakov asked. 'Sheep?'

She froze the video. 'No, they have long necks… llamas or alpacas.'

'Wow.' He shook his head in amazement.

Gregor lowered the drone to a height of five metres. It swept past an aircraft hangar, then a helipad, and tracked a newly tarmacked road leading to the centrepiece of the estate: a pseudo-gothic mansion complete with marble columns. He brought the drone to each window, attempting to capture the décor inside. Most were shuttered, and he continued until he found an uncovered window revealing a gymnasium with a pair of treadmills and cross-trainers. Behind them, in chrome and black, was a weights station facing a wall-length TV screen. The drone pulled away and they followed the video to the end.

The file from mid-July showed the drone taking off from a woodland less cultivated than the first property. The drone rose to trace the circumference of an Italianate palace, then edged over a metal fence.

Natalya sipped the *chacha*. It was a cheap brand and she felt it catch her throat like a pepper sauce.

A uniformed figure emerged briefly from a guardhouse; the drone lost height and retreated to the safety of the woodland. In his haste to leave, Gregor's camera caught two figures standing near an old car.

She tapped the screen to freeze the image.

Primakov leant forward. 'Is that—'

'Yes,' she said, interrupting. 'Elizaveta and Max, and the Audi Quattro.'

A second later, the footage ended and she opened the next file. A sprawl of cranes, tracked vehicles and workers in hard hats were assembled seemingly haphazardly around a construction the size of a school gymnasium. A group of men with pneumatic drills were digging up the concrete from an earlier site.

'The pathologist found traces of asbestos in Elizaveta's lungs,' she said. 'Maybe she got it there.'

'Asbestos is used in a lot of things besides buildings.'

'Like what?' she asked.

Primakov shrugged. 'Insulation, filters, vehicle brakes… clutches.'

'You're no help.'

CHAPTER 31

The drone skirted around the building site's chain-link perimeter, and withdrew before the workers heard its rotors.

The next file had the same start as the others, Gregor releasing the drone, then turning away – she assumed it was to limit his exposure and allow more of the footage to be used. It was another grotesque estate owned by individuals whose wealth – had it been shared – would have made the inhabitants of an entire town prosperous. She saw manicured lawns, followed by the centrepiece: a baroque mansion with a tiled sage-green roof.

She yawned – it was getting late.

'Did you see that?' he asked.

'What?'

'Look at the top,' he said. 'I'll take it back.'

Primakov tapped on the progress bar to rewind the video, then let it play again.

'There.' He paused the screen. 'You see that?'

She stared at a peach-coloured blur of pixels. 'Is that someone naked?'

He nudged the video's progress bar. 'Shit, it's gone…'

He moved the mouse a millimetre to the left and clicked the button again. The figure was visible for a second, but the drone was climbing as it continued to trace the perimeter – she assumed Gregor hadn't spotted the figure.

'I've got an idea.' Primakov said.

He closed the image then selected a new application. The Adobe icon flashed on the screen as new software loaded. He reopened the last file and tapped out a series of commands.

'I bought this for wedding videos.'

This time the video opened with the individual frames running underneath. Primakov stopped the progress bar when the naked figure reappeared; he selected individual frames until he had the clearest image. She watched him focus on the figure, enlarging it until the legs were frozen in mid-stride. Raised forearms were rectangles. It had blocks for its short, dark hair, and a Lego brick face.

There was a flash of peach-coloured pixels on the chest.

'Female?' she asked.

'I think so.'

'Any chance we can improve the image?'

'A little, but not nearly enough,' Primakov said.

'We should keep watching… maybe she appears later.'

Primakov closed the image and Gregor's drone continued its tour of the perimeter: it flew over a brick wall that blocked the view from an external road and reached thick woodland to the rear. Once it had covered the circumference, the drone dipped inside the property, passing an empty guardhouse and another building with a green-tiled roof, and a plunge pool to the rear.

The drone continued on its fly-past, weaving between the buildings. The place was deserted – even the small guardhouse by the main gates was unoccupied.

'Where are the cars?' she asked.

Primakov shrugged with his mouth. 'There'll be a garage somewhere to keep their Porsches and Ferraris dry.'

The video finished. Primakov clicked on the remaining files. One was of a luxury apartment complex in the centre of Piter, another of a shopping mall under construction, swarming with workers. Finally, she watched the drone survey an old estate with a boating lake.

'That's everything. I'm surprised most of them were empty,' Primakov said.

'I'm not,' she said. 'These people travel with their entourages, shuffling from the ancestral home to the town house – one for Piter, one for Moscow – to the country *dacha*, the winter sports *dacha*, the resort on the Black Sea…'

'Captain. Why were they killed?' Primakov asked.

'They were Decembrists – what else?'

'Yes, Captain, but the motive?'

'Revenge. They exposed a corrupt official who had wanted to stay under his rock.'

'Then talk me through it… I'm missing something.'

'Max and Elizaveta went out for a drive—'

'But how did the killer know where they were going?'

'They were followed?'

Primakov shook his head gently, not wanting to contradict her. 'But until recently even we didn't know Max and Elizaveta were Decembrists.'

'The FSB knew. They told me Elizaveta was caught after one of the stunts. Maybe she wasn't cooperating, so they gave her name to someone looking to take revenge.'

Primakov frowned.

'What is it, Leo?'

He sipped his *chacha*, wincing as it burned. 'I don't think the motive is revenge.'

'Interesting theory.'

'You said it yourself, Captain. The footprints in the snow, the tyre marks, the blood and mud. If the murders were planned then it was the work of an amateur, and I don't think someone with that kind of money hires amateurs. The killings were spontaneous.'

'I think you're right.' She swirled the *chacha* in her glass and sniffed at it without drinking. 'Rogov went through everything the Decembrists put on YouTube. He didn't find the project Max and Elizaveta had worked on. What if they were murdered so the owner could keep hiding in the shadows? These drone videos might have captured where they were killed.'

'But the most recent one was in September,' Primakov said. 'That was months before Max and Elizaveta's last drive. Perhaps there is more footage somewhere – can you contact Gregor?'

'I'm not sure... We didn't get off to a great start last time. I smashed his drone – that's how I got the micro-SD card.'

'How do you know Gregor wasn't with them when they were killed?'

'I don't know, Leo. Maybe he'd moved on after the filming. He did all the Decembrists' videos, not just Max's little project.'

'Or he killed them. Say they had an argument on the way and Gregor lost his temper. He returned the Quattro because he had no way of getting home.'

Primakov finished off the glass and grimaced as the *chacha* went down.

32

Her apartment wasn't freezing. At this time of year she always kept her coat on while fumbling for the heating switch; now the warmth forced her to remove her hat and gloves, and to drape her padded jacket over her mother's throne chair. Apart from the heat in the apartment, the dining table had been cleared of the mess she'd left at breakfast. Along with the remains of the meal from the previous evening too.

'Misha?' she called out.

She listened intently for sound, but there was silence. In the gloom, her apartment's phone handset was flashing to alert her to a new message. She pressed the play button.

She recognised the voice of Misha's journalist. He was tetchy. 'Captain Ivanova, this is Pyotr Revich. Have you spoken to the witness in the Diana Maricheva case? Please call tomorrow. Don't forget our arrangement.'

He left a phone number; she didn't write it down. She flicked through the address book on her mobile phone and selected Mikhail's name. The call took an age to connect.

'Babe?'

'Misha, where are you?'

'The apartment was messy, Natashenka.'

'You were home?'

'I was. Now I'm in Pulkovo.'

'The airport?'

'Where else?'

'Why?'

'Because Dostoynov is an arsehole. You remember Marat, the police chief I stayed with in Inkino? He called to say Shugaley, Diana Maricheva's stepfather, has been accused of having sex with her. The mother went to see Marat a few days ago.'

'She went missing in 2012. Why has she come forward now?'

'Apparently the mother thought Diana was lying because she didn't like her new papa – you know how it goes. After my last visit she's been chewing on it and thinks there might be something to the accusations.'

'Sounds like bullshit.'

'I smelled that too. Marat reckons she's only talking now because she's divorcing him. Marat went round and found underage porn on Shugaley's computer. Dostoynov wants to see if I can squeeze a confession out of him.'

'A confession to her murder? Diana ran away from home.'

'Who knows? It makes sense if she got desperate for money and blackmailed Shugaley to get herself out of a fix. He could have found her in Piter.'

'That's going to be hard to prove.'

'We'll see.' She heard the distorted sound of an intercom. 'Listen Babe, we're boarding, I've got to go.'

OK, darling. I miss you.'

'You do?'

'Of course.'

'So you didn't call for a reason.'

'I thought we'd been burgled by an obsessive cleaner. I was just checking it was you.'

'Well, you are a messy bitch.'

It had been meant as a joke, but she still felt herself prickle at the word. 'Misha, before you go, I heard from your journalist. A woman named Vera Morozova came forward to point the finger at her ex-husband.'

CHAPTER 32

'Must be contagious. I'd better watch my step.'

She let out a laugh; it was louder than she had expected. 'I went to see her. She told me her ex is a gamekeeper at a hunting lodge. He'd confessed to her about finding a body in the woods and taking it away for reburial. He's not that far from Lake Ladoga and Konevets Island either. If you want I'll have a word with him.'

'Thanks, Babe. I'll be back in two or three days… Christ, I don't even know what day it is.'

'Tuesday.' She glanced at the time on her TV's digital box. 'At least for another half an hour. Misha, there's something else. I think this woman is telling the truth. You know the prosecutor who wouldn't let Laskin the *alkanaut* close the case?'

'Kira Shulgin?'

'Her. Guess who owns the lodge where the gamekeeper works.'

She heard him chuckle. 'Fuck… that is interesting.'

'There's something else.'

'There's something else?' He was laughing now – it sounded a little manic. 'What else is there?'

'You may have heard. Stepan… Rogov. Dostoynov suspended him today. He'll be fired once it's cleared with the union.'

'He told me. He said you defended him in front of Dostoynov. You have a good heart, Natashenka. Too good for the rest of us.'

'What does that mean?'

'Nothing. I'll see you when I'm home – that's if Dostoynov ever lets me sleep in my own bed again. Stay safe, Babe.'

'You too, Misha.'

She slept fitfully. Sometime in the night she was woken by the buzzing of her intercom. She ignored it for as long as she could, tried to incorporate it into a dream, even tried the earplugs she used when

Mikhail's snoring became unbearable. But eventually she made the mistake of wrapping her quilt around her and padding across the cold tiles to press the intercom button.

'*Da*?'

'Major Dmitrichenko, St Petersburg Anti-Corruption. I have a warrant to search your apartment.'

So this was the revenge Dostoynov had spoken of. Investigations into police corruption were handled by *Sledkom*. Well, they wouldn't find anything. After she'd discovered Mikhail's secret account she made him remove any trace of his dirty money from the apartment. She'd even used specialised software to clean up the deleted data on their computer.

'Who is named on the warrant?'

'Captain Natalya Nikolayevich Ivanova. Is that you?'

'Yes, I'll let you in.'

She checked the temperature on Yandex: it was minus twelve Celsius outside. A padded jacket and *ushanka* only did so much before the fingers numbed, the nose pinched and the cheeks froze. She made herself a coffee and lit a cigarette off the stove. Fresh out of cadet training, she'd faced enough metal doors and knew stalling tactics only worked for so long. Soon they would wake up every apartment in the building until someone let them in.

Hidden by the darkness, she opened the curtains covering the balcony and peered down at three clouds of condensing breaths and cigarette smoke.

She went to the hall and pressed the button. 'Why are you still there?'

'Captain Ivanova, you're making it worse for yourself.'

'Wait, I'll try again.'

She opened the glass door and gasped at the cold as she stepped onto the balcony.

'What about now?' she called down.

CHAPTER 32

The three amorphous shapes shuffled. None of them spoke.

'No good?' she yelled.

She went inside and finished her coffee. When activists and opposition politicians were arrested they treated it like a tiresome interruption to their routine. How they did that without showing fear, she didn't know. Her hand was shaking as she smoked the cigarette to the filter. She pressed the intercom button to let the three inside, then left her apartment door on the latch.

There was a slow padding of boots up towards her apartment. Major Dmitrichenko was as solid as she imagined. Behind him were the *Sledkom* investigators Ilya Yelin and Tatyana Dubnik, in case she hadn't understood the real reason for the visit. All three were grey and world-weary. Was it the late hour or the shame of pursuing fabricated cases? She figured the former. *Sledkom* were beyond embarrassment.

The papers the major thrust in her hand gave little away. They contained the name of a judge, a seal and a statement authorising them to search for the relevant evidence to pursue a corruption charge.

'Yelin,' she said, 'unless you want to feature in your own investigation, I would advise you stick to the criminal procedural code.' The Sledkom investigator went to object, and she held up a hand to stop him. 'The only jewellery belongs to my mother and I would be grateful if it's still here when I return.'

She left, expecting one of them to apprehend her. Perhaps they were grateful for the warmth of the apartment. More likely the raid had been intended to intimidate her. She hoped she'd convinced them it had failed. She went upstairs and rang the bell of Sergei, her old neighbour. The retired violin teacher was wearing a dressing gown wrapped around his skinny frame and an amused expression, as if he'd been expecting her.

'Drink?' she asked.

He stroked his goatee. 'Always, darling.'

33

She shivered and felt for her quilt. Her hand returned with a fur blanket. She twisted it round her body and felt sleep draw her in. Her eyes opened. There was a noise: the whistle of a kettle on a stove. Her mouth was dry, her throat raw. She closed her eyes. She opened her eyes again. A second had gone past. Or an hour. She groped in the pocket of her jeans on the floor. Her phone displayed the time: 7:10 a.m.

'Drink.'

Sergei held out a cup of black tea and a pair of white pills. She noticed he had already shaved around the edges of his beard.

'*Spasibo*.'

The tea burnt her tongue and she dry-swallowed the pills.

She was on a chaise longue. The fur blanket smelled prehistoric; it might have belonged to a mastodon.

Sergei turned his face away while she pulled on her jeans. 'You told me to wake you at seven. I heard you talking in your sleep.'

'I was?'

'Yes.' Sergei's grey goatee bobbed. 'Profanities. Colourful ones. Who are you angry with?'

'No one in particular.'

'The world, then.'

'You might be right.'

'You know the poet Marina Tsvetaeva?' he asked.

She shook her head. 'Not well.'

'Tsvetaeva said the heart isn't a physical organ, it is musical.'

CHAPTER 33

'I sing like a crow, Sergei. I'm sure my heart does too. What does that mean?'

He shrugged. 'It means poetry can only take you so far.'

She stood. Her head span. Lights flashed.

'Are you ready?' he asked.

They took the steps down. No one to her knowledge smoked in the corridor any more, but it still reeked, thick as bitumen.

'Are you sure?' he asked.

She took a deep breath and pushed her key into the lock.

The apartment was tidy, just as Mikhail had left it.

'No floorboards ripped out.' Sergei said. 'Nothing stolen?'

'Not that I can see.'

He raised his eyebrows. 'And you're sure they were *Sledkom*?'

Natalya inspected her glass ashtray. The investigators had even extinguished their cigarettes carefully. 'Maybe they just wanted to get out of the cold.'

She opened the door to the study. The drawers containing her paperwork were empty. There was a space on the table where the computer had been. In its place was a receipt under a paperweight.

'It doesn't look so bad,' Sergei said.

'It's worse. If *Sledkom* wanted to scare me they would have ripped the place apart. This was a surgical strike.'

'Have you done anything?'

She thought of the bribe to get Anton into his fake university and the mafia money Mikhail had pocketed.

'Nothing.'

'Then you'll be fine.'

Sergei tightened the belt on his dressing gown and looked away, unconvinced by his own answer.

34

After Sergei left, she showered, found a change of clothes, and then went looking for Leo Primakov. An hour later her Volvo was skipping and bouncing over the ice on the Toksovo Highway.

'Is your heater working? It's freezing,' Primakov complained.

'Barely.'

She slowed at Kuzmolovsky Cemetery and pulled over at the spot where she had spent the restless night in the Hunter with Rogov. Primakov zipped up the hood of his silver parka. They followed the snow wall running alongside the road.

'What are we doing here, Captain?'

'Humouring me.'

'Are you all right?' he asked.

'Not really. *Sledkom* are trying to build a corruption case against me. They came to visit last night.'

'You?' he said.

'Don't look so shocked. There's always something. I'm trying hard to pretend it doesn't bother me. So hard in fact that I want to talk about something else.' She studied his earnest expression. 'Are you OK, Leo?'

'No, not really.'

'This case?'

There was no sound except for their footsteps crunching on ice crystals.

'It's nothing to do with work,' he said finally. 'It's about the one who sends me coffee. His name is Jaap. I met him on holiday in Amsterdam two years ago.'

CHAPTER 34

Finally he was opening up – not that it was any of her damned business. 'Do you have a picture?' she asked.

He scrolled through the images on his phone and passed it to her. She saw a picture of Primakov and another man sitting astride mountain bikes, their legs and Lycra shorts spattered with mud. Leo had a glow about him that she'd never seen before. Apart from Jaap's charming smile, he had a V-shaped upper body and the angular face of a model.

'He's an ugly bastard, isn't he?' she said.

'Completely… he's grotesque.' Primakov's grin matched Jaap's, then faded. 'I can't stay here, Captain. In Amsterdam I don't feel like a circus freak… he wants me to move in with him.'

'You can't leave.' She tried to laugh off her instant reaction. Without Primakov she would have no allies once Dostoynov got rid of Rogov and Mikhail. Then again, she was hardly going to survive in the Directorate much longer.

'Eventually I will,' he said. 'If they'll let me in.'

'You're so secretive, Leo. Why are you telling me now?'

'My English teacher at school, I swear he made up half the words he taught us. Jaap says I can get by without Dutch, but my English needs to improve.'

He was so morose she wanted to laugh. 'You need English lessons?'

He nodded. 'No one can find out. I don't want anyone to suspect I'm leaving.'

'I won't tell anyone.'

'What can I trade?'

'Yourself.'

'Me?'

'Yes, and I've already got you. Dostoynov is having you assigned to the investigation… now it's official.'

'I'm flattered.'

'Don't be. When he realises I'm not planning to round up any Decembrists he won't be happy. *Sledkom* might get interested in you too.'

'How long do you think you have left, Captain… before the colonel decides you're too much trouble?'

She let out a sigh. 'I don't know, Leo.'

'Perhaps you need an escape plan too.'

'I was thinking of Germany, but Mikhail won't move and I won't leave Anton behind. Anyway, this place is addictive, we've got the best criminals in the world.'

Primakov punted the toe of his boot into the snow wall to shake off fresh flakes. 'Well, here's to another suicide mission,' he said.

Her father had told her there was no god or devil. People brought order to the world and decay returned it to its natural state. Now that she saw the roadside shrine, she realised the devil *was* decay. The police tape marking the crime scene had gone, absorbed by the snow or else blown into the forests beyond. She leaned over the bank to find the picture of Elizaveta cradling Artem in the maternity hospital. It was half buried.

She clambered over the bank to the drainage ditch and reclaimed the picture. She wiped it clean, then found the string Valeria had used to secure it to the forest's edge. Her fingers were stiff as she retied it using a Cossack knot that was unlikely to fall apart so easily. At the edge of the ditch she found a pack of spare candles. She patted down the snow and fixed half a dozen of them in place, hoping they would still be there when Elizaveta's mother returned.

After accepting an arm from Leo, she climbed over the bank.

'Now I can think clearly,' she said. 'From the *livor mortis*, we know Elizaveta was already dead, propped up in the passenger seat. Max was in the boot, but his blood was found nowhere else.'

CHAPTER 34

'And the mud, Captain? If we believe Oleg – and I'm not certain that I do – he said there were muddy footprints on the driver's side but nowhere else. The boot prints I found here were clean. If he's telling the truth, then the killer dumped Elizaveta first.'

Without her realising it, a cigarette had passed gracefully from her pocket to her lips. A lighter was in her hand, her thumb sparking the wheel against flint. She hesitated for a second, knowing she would regret it, then abandoned herself to her latent addiction.

She puffed on Mikhail's Sobranie. 'What about the blood?'

'He washed it off when he dumped Max.'

'That makes sense. Oleg said there was ice, and the mud he found smelled bad. We need to find a river or a lake.'

Primakov moved fractionally away from her cigarette smoke. 'Maybe he carried him into the forest and found a stream.'

'No,' she said. 'The soil is as hard as iron here, he'd need earthmoving equipment.'

'So why didn't he dump both bodies in the ditch?' he asked.

'To throw sand in our eyes.'

She puffed on the cigarette. The nicotine was making her nauseous. Her internal organs had been requisitioned as a vodka processing factory and were resenting the extra load.

'What were they doing out here… Max and Elizaveta?' he asked.

'Isn't it obvious?' she said. 'They were making one of their YouTube films. Max was the director of the operation, Gregor did the filming.'

'And Elizaveta?'

'She had trained to be a building surveyor. Maybe it was something to do with the properties on the drone footage. She knew which laws had been broken to build the places, the value of the materials and land, and how many billions they cost on the open market – all the facts for a great exposé.'

'And that's why they were killed?'

'It's my favourite theory so far.'

'Captain,' Primakov hissed, 'this is serious.'

'We're not here to sit around and play *durak*. The Decembrists put their lives at risk to expose crooks and two of them were killed for it. You once told me you liked things to be black and white? There's no grey here.'

He scuffed his boot on the snow. 'I'm still in, Captain. I'm just nervous, that's all.'

'Me too.' She stubbed the cigarette out then picked up the butt. 'We'd be damned fools not to be. Let's find where the killer took Max.'

35

They returned to the Volvo. The late morning, then afternoon, disappeared in snow-bordered lanes that led to *dachas* or dead-ends. Of the properties they found with a water source, all were lit, and after making several enquiries at each place, she heard they were fully occupied in the hours between Elizaveta being killed and Oleg finding his Audi the next day. At each property it would have been impossible for the killer to bring Max's body in without being seen – assuming Oleg hadn't lied.

She took her foot off the accelerator and let the car coast. 'We're approaching Toksovo,' she said. 'The killer didn't drive to a populated area, not with a dead woman in the passenger seat.'

She pulled over and turned the car around. They were silent for a while. It began snowing as they passed the shrine to Elizaveta. A month ago, she recalled how the snow had held off long enough for Taniashvili to find her body. Now it was burying all traces of the roadside shrine as if her body had never been there. She guessed black ravens weren't the only omens around.

Beyond the cemetery, Primakov pointed out a rough track. Her Volvo rocked as she turned, steering around craters of frozen mud. She stopped at a closed gate, orange with rust. Through a three-metre chain-link fence a portable concrete mixer had spewed its solidified contents out onto its drum.

She pressed the horn and climbed out of the car to wait for the owner. Primakov joined her, tugging at the hood on his parka.

'No one's coming,' she said after a minute, her breath condensing in the freezing air. 'And it looks like the building work was abandoned.'

'More likely they stopped for winter,' he said.

She got out and tugged on the gates. The chain securing them rattled. 'So if you were driving around with a body you needed to get rid of…'

'Yes, it's an obvious place.'

She wiped snow off the gate's chain. 'This padlock is new. Shall we take a closer look?'

Primakov shifted uneasily. 'To break in?'

'Of course. Can you pull the gates apart? I might be able to squeeze through.'

He shook his head slightly; was it out of disagreement or weariness? 'Yes, Captain.'

He put his back against one of the gates and forced his arms against the other. The gap was barely ten centimetres wide. She tried to squeeze through the opening. Metal stabbed at her chest.

She retreated. 'No good… any ideas?'

Primakov scanned the track and dragged out a half-buried plank. 'I'll try this.'

He jammed it against a fence post, tested it with his weight, and ran at it. His foot landed square in the middle. Using the extra height and momentum he propelled himself upwards. His hands grasped at a rod securing the top of the fence. She watched, impressed, as he strained to raise his body to the bar, wondering how many in the Directorate were capable of a similar feat. He twisted his legs over the bar, then dropped cat-like to the ground inside the building site. The only thing she thought lacking from his display of acrobatics was a gymnast's dismount.

'You'd make a decent *ment*, Leo.'

CHAPTER 35

He grinned and raised a single hand in what she thought was acknowledgement, before she noticed the nylon overshoes in his fist. He stopped to pull them over his boots, then took out some latex gloves. While Primakov was strolling around the site, she blew onto her hands to warm her stiff fingers. Her breath sparkled with the effort.

After a few minutes, Primakov returned with the mischievous glint of a child given permission to be bad. He passed her a steel bar through the gap in the gate. She inserted it into the shackle of the padlock and leant on it. Nothing happened at first. She threw her weight on it and fell to the ground. The lock had snapped open.

Inside the building site she saw a prefabricated hut half hidden by trees. A paving slab lay against the door, forcing it closed. The wood around the lock-housing had been torn away.

'Looks like they did have an unwelcome guest,' she said.

'But why didn't the owner call us?' he asked. 'There were *menti* all over the place when we found Elizaveta.'

'The holidays,' she suggested. 'Perhaps they missed the news too.'

'Perhaps.'

She replaced her woollen gloves with latex ones and pulled aside the paving slab to enter the hut. She switched on her phone's torch. Opposite the damaged door was a makeshift kitchen with a sink and stainless steel urn. Beyond it was a storeroom; its door had been dented by a boot heel and the lock ripped from its housing. She opened it to see empty shelves, and hooks on the walls and ceiling.

'It looks like tools were stored here,' she called out.

'Someone stole them?' Primakov said from the doorway outside.

'Or the owner emptied them after the site was burgled.'

Primakov knelt and scooped snow away from the space beneath the hut. After clearing the drift he shone his light inside. 'Nothing down here.'

'OK, let's walk around. You go left, I'll go right.'

She passed a mound of gravel frozen into a solid mass like peanut brittle. Further along, topsoil had been removed in preparation for the foundations. A trench ran along the boundary. She shone her light into its depths and saw flat, reflected snow.

'Captain, over here.'

She put a hand to her forehead and scanned the site to see Primakov's silhouette against undergrowth. She jogged to catch up with him.

'What is it?'

'A water source… or at least, ice.' He ran his light over a frozen, ten-metre diameter lake.

She knelt at its edge and wiped snow from the surface to find solid ice.

'Captain… evidence.' Primakov complained.

'What choice do I have?' she said. 'Dostoynov won't help unless we find a body, and we can't do that—'

'It's all right, I understand… rules were made to be broken,' he said without conviction.

She cleared some more of the lake surface. 'I can't see anything underneath.'

'Perhaps the killer used a chainsaw from the hut to break the ice?'

'Maybe,' she said. 'There's nothing we can do here, not without the tools.'

'What about headquarters?'

She thought of Dostoynov's refusal, or worse, a full-scale assault on the lake that would yield nothing except a rebuke. 'We need to be certain before we can call for help.'

She tried to peer through the lake but sleet had mixed with the surface water and refrozen. It was like looking at the surface of an ice rink after a skating session.

'What shall we do?'

CHAPTER 35

She traded her latex gloves for her woollen ones and felt instant relief from the cold. 'Stay here and clear the snow off the ice. I've got an idea.'

Half an hour later, she dragged the tea urn over the frozen ground.

'Oy, blyat!' she cursed as boiling water splashed her hands. Seconds later the wool of her gloves stiffened as the water froze.

'Are you all right?' Primakov called out.

'I'm fine,' she shouted, thought she wasn't. Even over ice, the full urn was half her body weight and felt as much. Her arms ached with the effort and the skin on her wrists was blistering. She passed a mound of sand turned to cement by ice.

'Or I might not be,' she called.

Primakov joined her; he took the urn and carried it the rest of the way.

'Ready?' he asked.

'Yes.'

He kicked over the samovar. Boiling water spread across the opaque surface of the lake. Steam rose above the surface. The water froze, as smooth as glass. She shone her torch over the ice and saw inky blackness.

'Shit, it's too dark.'

Primakov was walking around the lake's circumference. He stopped by a bench. 'I can fix that.'

He bent down by the bench and the lake lit up with a dozen blue spotlights embedded in its floor.

She stepped gingerly onto the ice. There was no need – it was solid enough underfoot to take her Volvo across. She worked methodically over the lake. On the opposite side to Primakov she felt the ice grind beneath her where it had broken and refrozen. She squatted over an area white with frost that the water from the urn hadn't reached.

'Can you see anything?' Primakov called.

A mass of pondweed pressed against the ice. Then a sliver of pale blue, a reflection from a spotlight. She shone her torch on the area. Underneath was a still shape, a dark bulk in the opaque ice. She traced an outline of shoulders then a leg – it had been in the clear area all along, pressing against the ice. She returned to the pond weeds. No, not weeds, hair. The frozen water on her hands had grown stiff, the burns numb.

'Primakov,' she shouted. 'Call Dostoynov.'

Cones of light criss-crossed the building site. One was fixed on the two *politsiya* cutting a square in the frozen lake with ice saws. They called out to another officer, who joined them. Between the three men, they brought out the body and laid it on a plastic sheet. A duty doctor in fur hat and mountaineering jacket was already kneeling by the corpse. She approached him, tuning out the complaints of a nylon-clad forensic technician.

The doctor spoke without looking up; he'd heard her approach. 'His head's twisted to one side,' he said. 'You don't get that with drowning victims.' He turned on a penlight torch and swept it over the swollen head. 'Wound near the right temple.' He focused the light for her to see.

'A bullet?' she asked.

'No, a hammer perhaps… too blunt for a knife.'

'Fatal?'

'That's for the pathologist to say.'

The penlight swept over the hands. 'Not much bacterial decomposition. How long's he been in?'

'Nearly a month,' she said.

'Lucky it's cold. I bet this one doesn't look so far off his last photograph… if you ignore the colour.'

'No,' she said, staring at the unseeing eyes of Max Timchenko.

CHAPTER 35

She leant against her Volvo, tiredness forcing her eyes closed.

'That's a good trick... falling asleep on your feet.'

She jerked awake on hearing Dostoynov's voice. In all the years she'd worked on violent crimes, it was unusual for a Lieutenant Colonel to attend a crime scene. She wondered if he was too green to know any better, or if he was there to monitor her.

'Sorry, Colonel. It's been a long day.'

'And rewarding, too.'

His tone was friendly; she took it as a warning and blinked, trying to stay alert.

'You found the missing professor. That'll embarrass *Sledkom* – they won't thank you for it. Have you checked the brother's alibi?'

She stifled a yawn. 'Not yet, Colonel.'

'Then don't bother. I'll assign it to Popovich. He can take it up with forensics.'

She didn't need another complication. Like Leonid Laskin, Pavel Popovich was another *alkanaut* whose career got in the way of his drinking. Along with Primakov, he was one of the two expert criminalists assigned to her unit. Popovich was more than capable of screwing up Oleg's alibi without any direction from Dostoynov.

She scanned the Lieutenant Colonel's face, looking for an ulterior motive. He was close enough to kiss the top of her forehead, forcing her to look up. 'Accept help,' he said. 'You'll have to trust someone eventually.'

If she needed support, Dostoynov would be at the bottom of the list. 'Yes, Colonel.'

'And I've seen corpses look more animated than you, Ivanova. Take tomorrow off. I'll take care of things until you return.'

'Is that all, Colonel?'

'No... I was hoping to find you here. I heard *Sledkom* paid you a visit last night.'

'Yes, Colonel.'

'You took their case' – Dostoynov was momentarily distracted by two *politsiya* lifting Max Timchenko to a body bag – 'and now you've made them look incompetent. You'd better throw them a bone before they eat you alive, if you know what I'm saying.'

She knew.

He returned his gaze to her. 'I don't suppose *Sledkom* discovered anything incriminating?'

In any other country the question would be outrageous. 'No, Colonel.'

'Well don't take too much comfort from that. They will. They'll find something even if there's nothing there to find.'

36

Back at her apartment she rubbed cream into the blistered skin on her hands and thought of calling Mikhail. It was four in the morning but Inkino was in Novosibirsk Standard Time. She imagined Mikhail enjoying breakfast with Marat, the town's police chief. She reached for her phone on the sofa. The distant ringtone echoed the four thousand kilometres between them. It was picked up and she caught the distorted chatter of a police radio in the background.

'Wait a second,' Mikhail said, then, 'Hey, Babe.'

'Misha.'

'You sound tired.'

'I spent the night on a building site. My missing academic turned up.'

'Dead?'

'Yes. Primakov and I found him under an ornamental lake on the site. Did Diana Maricheva's stepfather confess?'

'Shugaley? No, and it's going nowhere. Diana's mother was still in mourning when they got married. It caused a scandal in the town. One of Diana's friends told me Shugaley was more interested in the daughter than the wife. He's denying everything, of course. On top of that, there's nothing to show he's been anywhere near Piter.'

'Are you treating him with respect?'

'You mean, did we squeeze the squirrel's balls?' She heard another man laugh and guessed he was in a police car with Marat. 'That's not a bad idea, Babe. There I was, wasting time trying to gain his trust.'

'How long will you be there?'

'A day or two, unless he starts talking. Did you check out Morozov?'

She ran a hand over her creased face. The gamekeeper who found the girl's body. She'd offered to speak to him.

'Not yet.'

'Can you do it? I heard from my friendly journalist. Revich isn't happy, especially after that article he wrote about Diana. His editor was holding space.'

'I'll see him tomorrow. Dostoynov has given me the day off.'

Be careful what you tell Morozov – I don't want to piss off his boss. I've seen Prosecutor Shulgin when she's angry. She gets ugly.'

'Another thing, Angel.' He sighed; it sounded like a hiss. 'I got a call from Dinara last night… well, the middle of the night.'

Mikhail's ex-wife was usually after only one thing. 'She wanted money, I suppose.'

'No, for a change. She came home to find three officials outside her apartment. I think you know who they are.'

It was a consolation he was stuck in a car with Marat, or else he wouldn't have been so friendly – but why had *Sledkom* gone to Dinara's?

'They came to our place yesterday too,' she told him. 'It's me they want.'

'Then they went to the wrong house. Natalya' – he paused – 'to me it sounds as if they want to collect a debt. Make sure you pay them.'

He hung up, leaving the unspoken threat turning in her mind.

She showered and put on the dark-blue trouser suit she had last worn to visit Elizaveta's mother. The city was quiet, eerily so. Her breath sparkled as she took the pedestrian bridge over the misty Griboyedov Canal, the suspension cables disappearing inside the lions' mouths, sinister in the gloom. In the black morning, it was easy to think the worst of Piter – of revolution and the siege, of black ravens and mafia wars – and yet she couldn't imagine waking up to a different cityscape. She meandered through the streets, her boots catching broken slabs, as she crossed the Moika Canal.

At a five-storey block in Admiralty District she pressed the buzzer and let it ring.

'*Da*?' said a man's voice after a minute. *Anton's voice.*

She was surprised, but then, why not? They had been avoiding her, so she hadn't seen how close they had become. Hadn't wanted to, she supposed.

'Anton, it's Natasha. Is Vita there?'

'Um… yeah.'

'Are you going to let me in?'

The door lock clicked.

Outside the fourth-floor apartment she found Anton standing in the doorway wearing a pair of jeans and a T-shirt.

'It's five thirty, Natasha. Don't you ever sleep?'

She ran a gloved hand over the stubble of his freshly shaved hair. 'It's nice to see you.'

'I need to speak with Vita.' She took off her boots in the hallway.

'Wait here, I'll wake her.'

With Anton gone, she examined Vita's home – a lifetime's habit as a detective. Instinctively she began to wonder how much of the décor was a reflection of the young woman's personality. One wall was decorated with black-and-white photographs of the punk queens Yanka and Patti Smith; another had the whale skeleton poster from the film *Leviathan* next to a print from the cult vampire movie *Night Watch*. They seemed to match Vita's three personas: the serious academic, emo, and political activist.

The furniture was pure IKEA – a good choice for an anti-corruption campaigner. IKEA had fought a near-impossible battle to do business in the country without paying bribes.

'She's here.' Anton had his arm over her shoulders and was guiding Vita out of the room. She was wearing a pink dressing gown and a nightdress with pictures of little bears, childish emblems that gave her an added vulnerability.

Vita shrugged off his arm and sat down. Her movements were slow. 'You've come to tell me my brother is dead.'

Natalya found a chair and faced her. 'Yes.'

She continued speaking to cover the silence that followed: 'We found him at a building site three kilometres from Elizaveta's body.'

'Did he suffer?' Vita asked, her voice almost a whisper.

Natalya noticed how small the younger woman's hands were. 'He took a blow to the head – he wouldn't have felt anything after that.'

'And that's it?' Vita mouthed.

She frowned, uncertain what Vita meant. And that's Max's life over with? And that's all she was to be told?

'I'm sorry.'

'You said that already.' The voice was stronger now, bitter.

'Do you want a drink or something, Natashenka?' Anton asked.

She shook her head.

He turned to Vita. 'You want something?'

Vita stared ahead, not hearing the question.

'So what happens now?' Anton asked.

Vita fidgeted with her hands. 'She says something sympathetic, then leaves.'

'I can stay if you want, Vita,' Natalya said.

'No, I want you to fuck off.'

Vita was quiet for a moment, shocked by the violence of her own words. 'I didn't mean that. Please forgive me. I was hoping Max had run away. I knew he wasn't the type, though – he was always putting himself in danger.'

CHAPTER 36

Anton pulled out a packet of Mikhail's Sobranies and Vita glared at him.

'Do I have to go to a morgue or something?' Vita asked.

'No,' Natalya said, 'that only happens in movies. Someone will show you a photograph of Max's body.'

Vita shivered and pulled on the hem of her nightdress to cover her bare legs. 'Do you know who did it?'

'Not yet. I need to ask you some more questions. I'd like you to arrange an interview when you're ready.'

'Ask me now.'

She glanced from Vita to Anton in what she hoped was an obvious manner. 'We'll need to talk about Max's political activities.'

'Anton, maybe I'll have that coffee?' Vita asked.

'Sure.' He went to the kitchen, taking to his subservient role.

Left alone, Vita began crying softly. After a while, a quiet fury evaporated the tears. 'What do you want to know?'

'Max was working on a project with Elizaveta and Gregor Bortsov.'

'With Gregor?'

'I retrieved the footage from his drone. It showed them visiting various large buildings: country estates, an apartment complex, a shopping mall… I wonder if someone didn't like what they were doing and tried to stop them.'

'I'd like to see that.'

'Maybe you can. It's on an SD card. You can have it when I've finished.'

'Don't you need it as evidence?' asked Vita.

'It'll disappear if I log it at headquarters. It's safer with me… and I can always make a copy.'

'What do you want for it?'

'Nothing. That video was the last thing they were working on. Maybe the other Decembrists can help you finish it. When he grows up, Elizaveta's son will hear a lot of shit about his mother. I'd like him to know who she really was.'

'There is something you want, though.'

'You're right, Natalya said. 'I need to know about Gregor Bortsov.'

Vita reached for a blanket and pulled it over her legs. 'He was in *Voina* before us. You know those OMON trucks they park outside their office on the Griboyedov Canal?'

'Sure.'

'Then you'll remember someone setting fire to one a year or two ago. The police found Gregor's prints on the crate carrying the Molotov cocktails. He's been couch-surfing ever since, waiting for the OMON to forget. He only joins us on our actions when he wants to.'

'I need to speak to him again.'

'You suspect Gregor?' Vita asked.

'I just need to ask him some questions.'

'No you don't. If he was working with Elizaveta and Max then he's a suspect. Isn't that right?'

'Vita' – she held out a comforting hand; it was swatted away – 'just arrange for me to speak to him. If he won't talk to me I'll have to raise it with my superiors and that's going to cause him a world of trouble.'

'Because he's one of us?'

'Yes, when they realise he's a Decembrist my boss will hand him over to *Sledkom*.'

37

The small analogue clock showed 7:05 a.m. Natalya felt for the Volvo's heater grill and let her fingers linger over it. After leaving Vita's apartment she'd gone to find Primakov.

'Your car is still cold,' he complained in the passenger seat.

His parka rustled as he shuffled. 'Are you safe to drive, Captain?'

'No. Are you?' she asked.

His eyelids strained to open. 'I slept for an hour.'

'An hour more than me,' she said. 'Sometimes that makes it worse, it reminds your body what it's missing. I'll let you drive if I crash.'

'Your eyes are closing. Drink some more, Captain.'

She gulped some of his exotic coffee and handed back the thermos cup before it spilled. The caffeine did little for her creeping tiredness, though.

'Better?'

'Yes,' she lied.

He glanced at the atlas – the mobile signal had disappeared thirty minutes before.

'Where are we?'

'Karelian Isthmus… halfway to Finland,' he added, glumly. 'You need to take a left turn in half a kilometre.'

She eased her foot off the accelerator and let the Volvo slow naturally. On the icy road, braking sharply would earn them a guest appearance on one of those horrific 'Last seconds of life' dash-cam videos that Anton liked to watch.

She took the turn. A few minutes later Primakov looked up from his atlas. 'I think this is it.'

Beyond a stone wall was a three-storey A-frame building with accommodation blocks to one side.

'And Shulgin's a state prosecutor too,' she added. 'Makes you wonder how many lives paid for its upkeep.'

'Captain, you never told me she was a prosecutor. I thought we were going to see a gamekeeper.'

'Don't get nervous, Leo. You'll miss this when you have a boring life in Amsterdam.'

'I'm looking forward to it,' he sniffed. 'Besides, I need to be alive to enjoy my new, boring life.'

She followed a lane skirting the stone wall and stopped at a gate, where a camera tracked them.

An intercom was built into the brick. She got out and pressed the button.

'Captain Ivanova, Criminal Investigations Directorate. I'm here to speak to State Prosecutor Kira Shulgin.' She held up her ID card to the camera.

'Do you have an appointment?' An old man's voice rasped. The rasp started a cough.

Natalya waited for the hawking to stop. 'You've got a hearing problem,' she said finally. 'I don't need one.'

'Then nobody's here,' he said.

'What about your gamekeeper, Dmitry Nikolayevich Morozov?' she asked.

He coughed again, less heavily this time. 'What's it about?'

She turned to Primakov in the passenger seat and rolled her eyes at him. 'What's your name?' she asked.

'I just work here.'

CHAPTER 37

'OK, "I just work here", this is police business. Be a good little doggy and fetch Dmitry Morozov before I take you away for puppy training.'

The guard coughed again. 'Wait.'

She got behind the wheel and closed the door. Sleep overtook her instantly. When Primakov woke her she had been having an unhappy dream about Anton drowning. A white-haired, white-bearded man wearing padded camouflage fatigues was standing by the gate, gripping the barrel of an upright hunting rifle.

'Morozov?' she slurred.

'I think so, Captain,' said Primakov. 'Did you bring your gun?'

She ran a hand over her face. 'No, it's at headquarters. I'm not meant to be working today.'

Primakov stared through the windscreen at Morozov. 'Well, I'm sure he'll respect that.'

'Leo, did you ever hear the story of Comrade Wolf?' she asked.

'Yes, I've heard it before.'

'A goat falls into a pit,' she began before he could stop her, 'then a fox falls in. After a while a wolf joins them. The three animals are all staring at each other then suddenly the goat panics and starts bleating, Maa! Maa! Maa! Maa! The fox looks at the goat and says, "What's all this bleating about? Comrade Wolf knows whom to eat."'

'I've never understood what it meant,' said Primakov.

'It means there's no point moaning. Morozov will either shoot us or he won't, and there's nothing we can do about it.'

Primakov zipped up his parka. 'Thanks, Captain. That was reassuring.'

'Any time.'

She pulled on her Cossack's hat and climbed out. Primakov reluctantly followed.

'Dmitry Nikolayevich,' she called.

The gamekeeper grunted and spat, then kicked snow over the phlegm. She guessed he'd been the one talking to her over the intercom, and had made them wait on purpose.

'Can we talk?' she asked.

'We're talking.'

'What about his gun?' whispered Primakov.

'I'll deal with it.'

She spotted a pouch of tobacco protruding from the breast pocket of Morozov's jacket. 'Can I have a smoke?' she called out. 'I stopped over Christmas and it's killing me.'

She watched as Morozov propped the rifle against a gatepost to reach inside his pocket. While he was distracted she gave a thumbs-up sign to Primakov.

'I suppose I'll have to roll it for you?' the gamekeeper said.

'Unless you want me to lose half your tobacco in the snow.'

He dropped a wad expertly onto the paper and shaped it into a cone. She leaned in to take it from him and accepted the offer of a light. Morozov rolled one for himself and lit it.

'So what's this about?'

She puffed on the cigarette she hadn't wanted. The coarse tobacco made her cough.

'Maybe you shouldn't be smoking,' Morozov said.

She held up a hand while waiting for her coughing fit to subside. 'We're here to look at the gravesite. I brought an expert criminalist along.' Primakov raised a hand in greeting.

Morozov returned a neutral expression.

'Diana Maricheva,' she said. 'That's the name of the girl you found.'

'I've never heard of her.'

CHAPTER 37

'I was expecting you to say that. Diana ran away from home when she was fourteen. She had her whole life to look forward to, but some evil bastard ripped it from her.'

Morozov spat another globule of yellow phlegm onto the snow. 'I'd like to help, but as I said—'

'On the eleventh of August 2015, a few years after Diana was murdered, you came across her body. My guess is your boss, Shulgin, told you to get rid of the girl. It's a sensible move if you're a state prosecutor with unexplained wealth and you don't want pictures of your fancy hunting lodge appearing on the evening news. Shulgin is religious, though: she worried about Diana's immortal soul, if not her own. She tells you to take the girl to Konevets Island and leave her with a cross so the holy fathers will know she belonged to the One True Church.'

'I still don't—'

She held up an index finger. 'You can lie when I've finished.'

Morozov grunted.

She continued, 'After a few months, Diana's remains go into cold storage and an alcoholic excuse for a detective puts the investigation in the freezer. Feeling guilty that her need for self-preservation brought no justice for the girl, Shulgin refuses to close the case. But that's all she can do without bringing reporters to her door.'

'I wish that bitch kept her mouth shut.'

'Prosecutor Shulgin?' she asked.

'My ex-wife. She's the only one I spoke to about the girl.'

'I can't confirm—'

'I know it was her. Kira – Prosecutor Shulgin – told me about the article. I knew then the bitch would start talking. Does it still stand?'

'Does what?'

'The paper said the *menti* won't arrest me. I'm retiring soon and I don't need that shit.'

'And I'm not looking to upset a state prosecutor either,' she said. 'As long as you didn't kill the girl I don't care what you did.' She took another tentative puff on the roll-up and coughed.

'You should give them up, Captain,' Primakov said.

She tossed the cigarette to the ground. 'I think they've given up on me.'

Morozov picked up his rifle; Primakov stiffened.

'Hey, what are you doing?' said Natalya.

'Showing you where I found the body. I can tell you like wasting your time… there's nothing but snow and trees.'

'And what about that?' she nodded to the rifle in his hands.

Morozov glanced at the gun and frowned, puzzled that she would consider it an issue. 'Be my guest.' He passed the rifle to her, then slapped a ten-round stripper clip in her palm. 'Can you handle wolves? Best to kill one on your first shot, else it makes them bolder.' He twisted his head towards her Volvo. 'There's an entrance to the woods at the back. We'll drive there.'

Morozov and Primakov climbed in her Volvo. She propped the rifle in the passenger footwell and followed an ancient stone road circumventing the fence.

'What is this place?'

Morozov leaned forward from the back seat; he smelled of smoke and pine needles. 'Catherine the Great had it built for some aristocrat she was screwing. His family was here until the revolution. After that, the place was strictly for Communist Party high-ups. By the 1980s it was a wreck, then it passed from one oligarch to another.'

'How long has Prosecutor Shulgin lived here?' she asked.

'Since April 2015, but she's only here on the occasional weekend.'

'When did you start?' asked Primakov.

'Twenty-four years ago,' said Morozov.

The car jolted as it caught a rut.

CHAPTER 37

Her eyes flashed to the mirror to catch his expression. 'So you were here between 2012 and 2013?'

'Did I kill the girl, you mean? I was working then, sure, but there's no staff, so I have to be everywhere. I'm more handyman than gamekeeper. Since the last owner left I've been doing security too. The only time I go in the forest is to check for poachers and keep an eye on wolves. Sika deer attract the greys.'

'When did you find her?' Primakov asked.

She smelled the smoke and pine needles again as he sat forward. 'Like you said, August the eleventh, 2015. My wife gave me shit because I missed our anniversary to take the girl to Konevets Island. We got divorced soon after; I can't say I'm sad about it.'

The path continued past the ancient brick wall and she continued, trailing impenetrable-looking brush.

'Pull in here,' said Morozov.

The Volvo slid on icy stones and came to a halt by a small wooden gate. Morozov left the car and opened the gate with a key attached to his belt.

She caught up to him. 'Dmitry Nikolayevich,' she asked, 'who owned the lodge before Prosecutor Shulgin?'

'Roman Agrashov. A chancer who pissed off a bigger chancer.'

'Where's he now?'

'Italy, somewhere on the outskirts of Rome… a Roman in Rome. He took his money away before it was taken from him. You know how it goes.'

'How long was he living here.'

'Six years.'

'2009 to 2015?'

'Yes.'

'I'll need a list of everyone, including staff and visitors, between 2012 and 2013.'

'You won't get it from me. I used to get nights and weekends off when it was quiet – like now – or else I kept out of the way unless Agrashov needed me.'

'What type of people came here?'

'Agrashov tried to attract the Maserati and Hummer types, but the lodge wasn't flash enough for their tastes. Most of the time it was quiet unless he brought friends from Moscow, then they partied all weekend. You'd have to get their names from him.'

With the rifle strapped to her back, she began wading through the snow; it was knee-high and spilled over the tops of her boots. The cold seeped through her thin suit trousers. In the grey light, she saw Morozov squint at the trees, change direction, then trudge along a new path. A log cabin appeared in the gloom. He walked up to it, unlocked the door with a key from his pocket, and then went inside.

'What's he doing?' Primakov asked.

She lowered the rifle and passed it to him, then placed her hands on her thighs and bent over.

'Are you all right, Captain?'

'I'm tired, that's all… and cold.'

'Your trousers are wet, you'll freeze out here.'

She looked at the material stained indigo by melted snow.

'Don't worry about me… Keep an eye on Morozov.'

'I don't know how to use a rifle.' Primakov's right hand slid along the butt. He kept it at hip height.

'Don't you have a police background?'

His mouth creased. 'Natural sciences.'

The latch on the hut door creaked. She looked up to see Morozov with a snow shovel in each hand. Primakov's finger had slipped inside the trigger guard.

CHAPTER 37

'He's not going to kill us with those.' She straightened. 'I'd better have it back.'

Primakov handed her the rifle as Morozov reached them.

The two men began walking along a new trail. She followed, dragging her feet through the churned snow in their wake. They stopped at a clearing fifty metres away. Her legs felt as if they had been submerged in icy water.

Above a tree was an overhanging branch with a red ribbon bleached pink by exposure. She guessed Morozov – or the girl's killer – had put it there to mark the grave. She watched Primakov take one of the shovels. He and Morozov began clearing the snow beneath the branch.

She leant against the tree and rubbed her gloves vigorously against her thighs, trying to draw some heat to them. Occasionally she looked up as the men twisted and threw shovelfuls of snow over their shoulders, steam ejecting from their mouths at regular intervals. Finally, they stopped and leant on their tools.

She pushed herself off the tree and joined them. An area three metres by two had been cleared, revealing a blue tarpaulin.

'Careful, Captain.'

She looked at her feet; there was a rectangular depression in the centre of the plastic sheet.

'Kira wanted it laid in case anybody ever came asking questions,' Morozov said, when his breathing had settled.

'But she never called us,' she said.

'That too… she's a complicated woman.'

'More like a trapped woman,' she said.

Morozov twisted his mouth in a lopsided gesture; grin or sarcasm she couldn't tell. 'Well, that's all in the past… you know about it now.'

The gamekeeper removed his gloves and rolled another cigarette. He studied her soaked trousers. 'You need to get in soon.'

The flesh on her thighs was numb. She felt the creeping cold on the bones within, turning them to stone. 'I know.'

'Then what are you waiting for?' said Morozov.

Primakov took the cue, and they stepped clear while he pulled the tarpaulin away. Natalya felt in her pockets for her mobile and switched on the torch.

Morozov had been right: there wasn't much to see. The hole was wide enough to take a man. The edges straight. A well-made grave.

'What happened to the earth?' asked Primakov.

'Behind the tree. Whoever buried her didn't pack it down. I'm surprised the wolves didn't find her.'

She angled her torch at the frozen mud walls of the grave. The beam shook. She shivered. Her teeth chattered. She put a hand to her jaw to stop it moving.

'Told you it's not much,' Morozov said. 'Just a hole in the ground. I dug out everything of her I could find.'

'What about clothes?' Primakov asked.

The gamekeeper shook his head. 'She was naked.'

'What about the ribbon?' she asked. Nobody replied and she wondered if she'd spoken the words at all.

'Captain?' Primakov was saying. 'Captain?' He walked towards her, his brow folding in concern.

'I'm fine,' she said. She sat down in the snow. Her words came out slowly.

She tried to shake off Primakov's hand. He ignored her and put an arm under her knees. He lifted her off her feet and into blackness.

She was wrapped in a blanket on a camp bed in Morozov's hut. The gamekeeper was feeding kindling into a fire grate, Primakov folding her suit trousers over the back of a chair. For a second she worried about being undressed by one of the two men, and then decided she didn't care.

Primakov was saying something about the grave. She tried to stir and felt a weight pushing her down. She was gone again.

38

Someone shook her.

'Captain?' said Primakov.

Her eyelids were shuttered. She forced them open.

'Captain, we were due back hours ago.'

She pushed herself to sitting. The hut was warm; it smelled of smoke and pine, just like Morozov. In her half-sleep the gamekeeper had become a wood spirit, an indivisible part of the forest. There was a mug of black tea on a three-legged stool beside her. It was almost scalding, but she sipped it anyway, feeling the heat radiating from her stomach.

Her wool trousers were dry and laid out on the camp bed. They were wrinkled and had shrunk. She swung her feet over the edge to pull them on. She saw Morozov and caught his narrowed eyes as he studied her with a greedy look. She wondered what he took away from a leer. Power, perhaps? It certainly had nothing to do with the amount of flesh on display – her winter underwear was about as sexy as her annual tax *deklaratsiya*. She examined her suit trousers. They were tight at the waist, short in the legs – ruined.

'What were you both talking about?' she asked.

'When?' said Morozov with a wink at Primakov. 'You've been asleep all morning.'

'I heard something about Diana's grave.'

'If I may, Dmitry Nikolayevich?' Primakov sat on the edge of the wooden chair that had held her trousers. She could imagine he'd been perched like that for the last three hours, nervous in the presence of the gruff woodsman.

'Dmitry Nikolayevich was telling me digging is hard work.'

'Have you ever made a deep hole?' Morozov said, sounding irked, as if he'd been short-changed by Primakov's answer. 'I laid a sewage pipe last year. It's back-breaking work. I'll tell you, the girl's grave took hours to dig. Somebody knew I don't come out here often in the summer. It's in winter when the wolves get bolder.'

The gamekeeper's cigarette had gone out. He bent down to push a pine log on the fire. As the flames caught, he brought the end of his cigarette to it.

'And it was just like the other grave I found,' he said.

39

In the hut, Morozov and Primakov had cut and shaped plastic sheets to fit over her ruined trousers. They had wanted to leave her near the warmth of the fire, but she had refused. The sheets were stiff, but they were keeping her dry for the moment, even if they didn't do much for the biting cold. It was snowing now, the pale sun the brightest they could expect all day. Morozov was in front, Primakov behind him, both men wading through a fresh snowdrift that reached their hips. Wind whipped up a flurry around her, turning the two men into blurred shapes.

'Over here,' Morozov called.

She followed his voice to find them standing at the edge of another copse.

'Now watch.' Morozov took another step and disappeared.

At first she thought he had fallen in the drift. Then Primakov extended a hand. She drew closer and realised Morozov had jumped into a ditch. He ignored the hand and climbed out.

The gamekeeper brushed snow off his legs. 'I fell into the bastard last summer. The hole was covered over with twigs, so I didn't see it. I thought I was dealing with a poacher. Then I remembered the girl's grave. It was the same size as hers, except there's no body in this one.'

Primakov's voice was urgent. 'Captain, we need a forensic team out here.'

'Wait a minute, Leo.' She turned to the gamekeeper. 'Any idea how long this grave has been here?'

CHAPTER 39

In the weak light, Morozov's white hair and beard had merged with the snow, creating the illusion of a disembodied face. 'I can tell you that,' he said. 'The old sewage pipe runs near here.' His finger traced a line across the snow. 'When I was digging it out, I used to stop here for lunch – it's a pleasant spot in June. I swear there was no hole then. I slipped a disc laying that damned pipe and couldn't work for a month. When I came back in July… well, that's when I fell into the bastard and landed flat on my back.'

Morozov tilted his head. 'And then I looked up.'

Natalya followed his gaze. Above their heads, tied to a branch, was a faded red ribbon, fluttering in the breeze.

40

She slept after dropping off Primakov at his office, and woke up with a fierce hunger at 4 p.m. Without Misha and Anton to justify a shopping trip to the Dixy, she fried two eggs and ate them with stale bread. After her depressing meal, she showered and sat down on the sofa. Primakov was right to request a forensic team in the woods, but there was no way Dostoynov would sign off the additional resources. Diana Maricheva's murder was the case meant to bury Mikhail's career, not revive it.

She plugged in her mobile to check for messages. There had been one from Dostoynov asking where she was, and another from Vita telling her Gregor would meet her at 5 p.m. "at the place where you destroyed his drone".

By the time she reached the embankment with its two grotesque sphinxes, she was fifteen minutes late. Gregor was a figure hurrying away in the distance.

'Wait,' she called out.

He stopped, raising a hand to acknowledge he'd heard her.

She caught up with him. Gregor was wearing an unflattering padded jacket that accentuated his round belly, a grey *ushanka*, and an FC Zenit scarf to obscure his face. He was carrying a backpack.

He pulled the scarf off his mouth. 'You're late.'

'I wasn't in the office, I was home.'

'*Lviny Most,* I hear… nice place.'

So Vita had told him where she lived. She wasn't impressed.

CHAPTER 40

Gregor shuffled on the pavement, crunching salt and ice under his boots. 'Keep moving, *ment*. Any sign of trouble and you'll never hear from me again.'

'If I wanted trouble I'd have brought a few friends along. OMON want to talk to you about that riot truck of theirs you burned. Then there's *Sledkom* – they want to destroy the Decembrists. If I bring you in there's a good chance my boss will fancy you for the murders of Elizaveta and Max.'

He stuffed his hands in his jacket pockets. 'Don't try and set me up. I didn't do anything.'

'I'm not,' she said. 'I only want to find who killed two of your friends.'

'Then let's make a deal. I hear you have something of mine.'

She felt another flash of annoyance that Vita had told him about the drone's micro-SD card. It seemed being Anton's stepmother, as well as the detective investigating her brother's death, wasn't enough.

'I promised Vita I'd give it to her when I finished the investigation.'

'Then we've got nothing to talk about.'

Or maybe she had misjudged the girl. Had Vita used the lure of the footage to persuade Gregor to meet her?

'That's what Adelina would say, not you. Did you film that stunt outside *Sledkom* headquarters?'

'I might have done.'

'Then you helped Vita get the case reassigned to me, so let's stop pissing in the snow.'

Gregor stared ahead as if weighing up his options. 'You'll give the footage to Vita?'

'When the investigation is over… I promise.'

'What do you want to know?'

'What was Max's project? The one he was working on with you and Elizaveta.'

'Haven't you worked it out?'

'I haven't got time for games. I'm tired, I was up all night looking for the body of one of your friends.'

Gregor slid an arm out of his rucksack and unzipped the main compartment. 'Max put this together.' He held out a ring binder stuffed with paper. 'You don't need me.'

She brushed it away. 'No, I need to talk to you.'

'Like you did last time? That *musor* shot me with a rubber bullet.'

'I'm sorry. That was a mistake. Tell me, what were you doing with Max and Elizaveta the day they were killed?'

'What?' The scarf was up, hiding his face. 'You're talking shit, *ment*. The last filming I did for Max was back in September. He didn't think we had enough to go public – he never did – so he started revisiting the places. You ask me, he wanted it to be perfect so he could use the documentary for his own ego… to drop the Decembrists and become famous like Alexei Navalny.'

'You're saying you weren't with them?'

'For Christ's sake, *ment*, I've just told you that, haven't I? After September we took a break, then we had that little stunt with the FSB director's car. Around December, Max and Liza started going back to the places we'd filmed. I wasn't there. Is that clear enough?'

'I can't go on your word, Gregor. You need to prove it.'

'I... was… not… there. Fuck this! If you want to know who killed them, look in there.' He tossed the ring binder to the floor.

'On your drone footage, I saw a naked woman…' she began, but Gregor was already walking away.

She stooped to pick up the ring binder and watched Gregor pace towards Liteyny Bridge. Against the darkening sky, she thought she could make out an aura of self-righteousness around him.

41

Thanks to the trio from *Sledkom* she was missing a computer, and using the one on her desk at headquarters wasn't an option – not for what she had in mind. She took the Metro to Komendantsky Prospekt, then began walking. On the way, she passed a walled area next to a car park where a group of ten or so boys stood around a fire of broken pallet boxes. They were smoking and passing a bottle of spirits between them, happy in their misery. One of them called out to her and she increased her pace, closing the distance to Primakov's block.

Her phone rang. She tucked Gregor's ring binder under her arm to answer it.

'Hi Babe, just checking you're still alive.'

'Wait a minute' – she saw the green cross of a pharmacy and hurried to the well-lit shop front – 'I'm fine, except I nearly froze to death this morning.'

'Shit, Babe. Are you OK?'

'I am now. I went to see Morozov, your gamekeeper. It was definitely him – the one who found Diana's body. He even took me to her grave.'

'That's great news – are you going to solve my case for me too?'

'Misha, I haven't finished. Morozov told me an oligarch was living there between 2012 and 2013, when we think she was killed. His name is Roman Agrashov.'

'Where is he now?' he asked.

'Rome.'

'Fuck.'

'Maybe Revich could try to interview him,' she said.

'Maybe.'

'What happened to Diana's stepfather? Did you beat a confession out of him?'

'Shugaley? No, he stuck to his story. Marat started getting heavy with him… it made me uncomfortable, but it's his town.'

'Listen, Misha. You can tell Marat that Shugaley didn't kill her.'

'What?'

'Morozov took me to an empty grave he'd found. This one had the same dimensions as Diana's and was well made. You don't go to that amount of effort unless you intend to put a body in it. Both graves had a ribbon tied to an overhanging tree branch so the killer could find them when he returned with a victim.'

'Perhaps the killer spotted Morozov and decided to abandon the second grave,' Mikhail said.

'Maybe. The oligarch and his entourage cleared off when Shulgin bought the place, so it's not him or Shugaley.'

'Why not?' Mikhail asked.

'If Morozov is to be believed, this one was made last July. He was working in the area last June and he's certain it wasn't there before.'

'Thanks Babe, I'll tell Marat to release the pervert.'

'But you said there were underage images on his computer.'

'There were, but Shugaley wasn't distributing them. Possession of child pornography isn't illegal.'

'It fucking should be. Think of those poor kids.'

'I know, Babe. I felt dirty after ten minutes in Shugaley's company but the law's the law.'

'At least you can come home now… there's nothing left for you there.'

CHAPTER 41

'I'm tired of all this, Angel. Dostoynov has let me make a hole in his budget with nothing to show for it. Now it'll be easy to have his friends in the Directorate back him up.'

'You'll find something else. The World Cup will need additional security; they'll pay a fortune for a major from a serious crimes unit.'

'An *ex*-major.'

'Just come home, Misha. I'm starting to miss you.'

'Only starting?' he said.

'Well, you know it takes me a while to get warmed up.'

'Hey,' Mikhail said, 'I nearly forgot the reason I called. I spoke with Rogov today.'

'How is he?' she asked.

'Miserable. Dostoynov told him his sacking has been delayed. He thinks the union intervened.'

'Or with you half out the door, Dostoynov thought Rogov was one too many to lose. Still, it'll be good to have him back,' she added, knowing she wasn't convincing Mikhail.

'I wouldn't be too hasty, Babe. He was insufferable. He kept moaning about being unfairly persecuted. I mean…' Mikhail trailed off and she felt his exasperation that his own career was over and yet he had to listen to Rogov whining.

'Misha, do me a favour. Ask Rogov to go into the office and gather all the information he has on Oleg's car. Tell him to bring it to Primakov's apartment.'

'Sure, I'm just about to go for a drink with Marat, I'll call him first. Did you say you're in Primakov's apartment? Should I be worried?'

As far as she knew, no one else in the Directorate knew Leo was gay. There was a lightness in his tone, though, that told her he wasn't serious.

'I'm using him for sex, I hope you don't mind. That's why I asked you to send Rogov over.'

He let out a laugh. 'Now I know you're joking.'

She watched Primakov walking from the Metro station and gripped the ring binder to raise her hand in greeting. 'I'd better go, Misha. I've got work to do.'

'I thought you were off today?'

'I am. This way it's harder for Dostoynov to know what I'm up to.'

'Be careful, Babe… I've only got one of you.'

'You too.'

She hung up. Primakov was waiting for her, his hands stuffed deep in the pockets of his parka.

'I was updating Misha.' She put her mobile away. 'Thanks for coming along this morning.'

'Any time.'

'Any news, Leo?'

'Some… do you want to come in?'

Without waiting for an answer, he tapped a magnetic key against the lock and pulled on the metal block door. In his hallway she removed her boots. The tortoiseshell cat watched her from its position on a heated blanket. It didn't move and she didn't blame it – Primakov's apartment was barely warmer than the temperature outside.

'Any news on the hot water?' she asked.

He changed his mittens for a pair of fingerless gloves. 'They've been saying it'll be fixed in a couple of days.'

'That's good, isn't it?' she asked.

'They've been saying it since January.' He put down fresh food for the cat; it refused to move off its blanket.

'How was your afternoon?' she asked.

'I spoke with Pavel,' he said. 'He was bragging that Dostoynov requested his services personally to look into Oleg's alibi.'

CHAPTER 41

Primakov washed the saucer and put it away; nothing was out of place in his apartment.

'Pavel's hopeless,' he continued. 'He doesn't know a thing about gathering electronic evidence. Also, it's a job for a forensic technician, not an expert criminalist.'

She shook her head in disdain. 'It's because he is hopeless. Dostoynov is worried I'll connect Max and Elizaveta's deaths to one of the people the Decembrists were targeting. For the sake of his career, he'd rather Oleg was charged.'

'But that's cynical.'

'It's why I can't interview Gregor. If Dostoynov hears he was working on a project with Elizaveta and Max, he'll prefer him to Oleg. Nailing a Decembrist for the double murder will warm Dostoynov's cold black heart.' She rubbed her hands together. 'Did you find out anything else today?'

Primakov blew on the fingertips of his gloves. 'Luka took a look at a footprint in the building-site hut – there was one on the door that had been kicked in. He's certain the tread pattern matches the mould I made by the drainage ditch.'

'So the same person took part in the killings of Elizaveta and Max... we already suspected as much.'

'So what brings you here, Captain?'

'This does.' She laid the ring binder on his circular glass table. 'I got it from Gregor.'

'What is it?' he asked.

'Some notes on costs and buildings, and the 2015 Property Register.'

'And only three years out of date,' he said.

'It belonged to Max – it's what they were working on.' She opened the file. 'Some of the properties have been highlighted. I think they were the ones he was interested in – I'm guessing they were owned by government cronies and had disappeared off the public register.'

She pointed to a handwritten annotation. 'On some of them he's updated the ownership records. There are a few sketches of buildings too; I think Elizaveta might have drawn them.'

'There must be hundreds in there,' Primakov said. 'You didn't come here just to show me this, did you?'

'No,' she said, awkwardly, 'those *Sledkom* bastards have taken my computer away and I can't do it at headquarters. I need to borrow yours.'

'So you didn't want me at all,' said Primakov, deadpan.

'I could do with your help.' She tapped the ring binder. 'We need to find which of these appeared on the drone footage. Do you still have the SD card?'

'Yes, but Captain, this will take all night.'

'No, it won't. I've brought a secret weapon… Rogov.'

Primakov's eyebrows creased as if to say "Please, God. No."

From her call to Mikhail, it had taken Rogov less than an hour to arrive at Primakov's apartment. He joined them at the glass table and Primakov found him the remains of his *chacha*.

'I still don't get why I'm here, Boss.'

'Did you bring what I asked for?' she said

He pulled a sheet of paper from a briefcase. 'Everything on the muscle-man's Quattro.'

'What's your feeling on him?' she asked.

Rogov's mouth twitched. Flattered to be asked, she thought, not that he would ever admit it. 'Like I said before, he's a steroid-injecting *kachok*.'

'But a murderer?' she asked.

'Why not? He didn't get on with his brother, and looking at his place I don't think he was one for the ladies.'

'And the steroids might make him lash out,' added Primakov.

CHAPTER 41

'I can't see him getting their bodies out of his apartment,' she said, 'not in Admiralty District.'

Rogov tipped the *chacha* into his mouth. 'So the three of them went for a drive together and the *kachok* lost his temper. Maybe he tried to squeeze the girl and she didn't appreciate it.'

'All right,' she said. 'Rogov, I need you to help us out with his alibi. I need you to drink tonight.'

'Is this a trick, Boss?'

She said, 'Oleg's alibi depends on electronic evidence. Dostoynov asked Pavel Popovich to check if it stands up.'

'He asked Pavel, not me,' said Primakov indignantly, 'because he's a lazy swine.'

'We need to keep Oleg away from harm,' she said, 'until a competent authority in the forensic department can check his alibi thoroughly… That means we need to keep Popovich off our case.'

'You want me to get Pavel drunk?' asked Rogov.

'Yes, and I'll sign it off as overtime.'

Rogov ran a hand along a freshly shaved chin. He had been given a last-minute reprieve and she felt a twinge of guilt that she was dragging him back to his old habits.

'I'll cover for you with Dostoynov too,' she said, 'and you can sleep on our sofa tonight so Oksana won't give you trouble. Tell her you have to work all night on a stakeout.'

'And it's good, right? I'm doing it to save an innocent man?'

'He might be guilty,' said Primakov.

'Don't let Popovich outdrink you,' she said. 'I don't want him guessing what's going on and running to Dostoynov.'

Rogov went to leave. Primakov called after him, 'Make sure he's completely wasted… and I mean *fucked*.'

42

'What was the mileage on the Quattro's last service?' she asked.

Primakov checked Rogov's paperwork: '76,132 on the twenty-ninth of December.'

'And now?'

'76,344.'

'What's the difference?'

'212 kilometres,' he said without seeming to pause.

'When I interviewed Oleg, he told me he used the Quattro for one trip, to visit an alternative health practitioner in Aleksandrovskaya. He said it was sixty-four kilometres each way. That leaves—'

'Eighty-four kilometres,' said Primakov.

'You're a machine, Leo.'

'Thanks… I think.'

'So if Oleg is telling the truth,' she continued, 'in those eighty-four kilometres, Max and Elizaveta drove somewhere, their bodies were dumped in the vicinity of Kuzmolovsky Cemetery, and then the car was returned. But that number could be wrong if Oleg forgot a journey, or the killer drove around… or if Oleg lied about the whole thing.'

She leant on the table with her elbows and propped her head in her hands. 'How do we even work out how far the car went?'

'It's not so bad,' said Primakov. 'The minimum is he killed them in Piter, dumped their bodies, and then drove around for an hour or so to confuse us. The maximum is forty-two kilometres from the city – and that assumes he was driving in a straight line, so it's unlikely to be that high.

CHAPTER 42

'Thanks, Leo.' She took out the papers from Gregor's ring binder and gave half to Primakov. 'Now let's see which properties fall in range.'

She worked through the addresses Max had highlighted in the property register, occasionally stopping to use the Yandex search engine on her phone to check areas she was unfamiliar with.

Outside, it had turned black, the windows reflecting the scene in his apartment. While he waited for her to finish, Primakov drew the blinds.

She checked her notes. 'How many did you get?' she asked.

'Four.'

'I had three. Now let's take a look at them on Yandex and see if we can reduce the number.'

'The nearest one I found to Piter is postal code 194044.'

Primakov brought out a laptop and entered the number into the search engine. It brought up a street in central St Petersburg. 'Bolshoy Sampsonievsky Prospekt,' he said. 'I'll try the satellite image.'

He clicked the mouse and zoomed in on a property until the angle switched to street level. 'It's an apartment complex.'

'That was on the drone footage,' she said. 'The apartments have got lights on and cars parked outside. Even if Max and Elizaveta got past the *konsierzhka* at the entrance, then what? They would have seen nothing except locked doors. What's next?'

She thumbed through the papers and gave him a fresh postcode. He selected satellite view, and a shopping mall under construction appeared. 'We saw that on the drone footage. It's in the city centre. There would be too many witnesses two days before Orthodox Christmas. Also, too many workers for Max and Elizaveta to get inside without being stopped. Let's discount it for the moment.'

The next was a *dacha* complex north-west of the city. 'I didn't see this on the drone footage.'

'No,' she said, 'for whatever reason they weren't interested in it. Maybe the owner wasn't well known.'

The remaining four were the same – none of them had appeared on Gregor's drone videos.

She pinched the bridge of her nose with her thumb and forefinger. 'We're missing something, Leo.'

'Then we've made an assumption that's incorrect.' He began tapping his finger on the table. She glared at him irritably, but he didn't appear to notice. He picked up his phone and tapped the screen. Tap. Tap. Tap.

'Leo, I wish you would stop—'

He looked up. 'Oleg said it was sixty-four kilometres to the acupuncturist in Aleksandrovskaya. I've just checked. The shortest route is fifty-four from his apartment – I guess he was nervous.'

'And ten fewer for him is ten more for us?' she said.

'Exactly. We're looking at a fifty-two-kilometre trip each way.' Primakov stifled a yawn and she realised he'd barely slept.

'We have to go through the whole file again.' She glanced at the time on her phone. It was after nine. 'Do you want a break?'

'I'm fine, Captain.'

They studied the addresses in silence.

'Zero,' he said after a while.

'Two,' she said a few minutes later. 'The first is a mansion owned by Semion Yablonev, the son-in-law of the presidential advisor.'

Primakov clicked on Yandex and looked up the property details on a real estate site. 'It was sold in 2016 to an oligarch who made his money on wholesale vegetables.' He entered the postcode and checked the satellite view. 'I'm sure this one wasn't recorded by the drone.'

'Then Max left it alone because of the ownership change,' she said.

She gave him the address of the second property. 'And this one belongs to Anna Alexseyeva Chubarova.'

CHAPTER 42

'Who's she?'

'The wife of the Minister of Emergency Situations – Vasily Ilyich Chubarov.'

Primakov typed in the address. It brought up a map.

She leant over Primakov and kissed him on the crown of his head.

'Captain?'

'Look at the map.'

'It's to the east of Oselki.'

She looked at the screen and grinned. 'And you have to drive past Kuzmolovsky Cemetery to get there.'

'Let's see what it looks like.'

Primakov clicked on the button to change the map to satellite view. He zoomed in on the address and a massive estate filled the screen. At its centre was a mansion with a green-tile roof. Without speaking, he attached the USB adapter to his laptop and inserted the drone's SD card. He opened the files and selected the fifth. Natalya glanced at its timestamp: Tuesday 19 September 2017.

A few seconds later the video started, and Natalya watched the blurred pixels of a naked woman running for cover before she disappeared from view.

43

After her freezing morning at Morozov's hunting lodge, she needed to be better prepared for her next journey out of the city. At home, she put on a layer of thermal underwear, then woollens, and grabbed Mikhail's enormous blue raincoat from the back of the door. She drove to the five-storey block in Admiralty District, and after picking up the plastic bag from the passenger seat, she pressed the buzzer by the block door.

'It's Natalya,' she said.

The lock clicked and she took the stairs to the fourth floor. Vita opened the door. She was in pyjamas and judging by the state of her eyes had been crying all evening. Berlioz's 'Great Mass of the Dead' was playing on a stereo. Natalya remembered something about it commemorating the fallen from one of the French revolutions – apt music for her brother.

'Come in,' said Vita. 'I'm being miserable.'

'You're mourning, that's different. I won't disturb you, I came to give you something.' She took out the plastic bag and gave it to her.

'What is it?'

'The ownership records,' Natalya said. 'It's a list of all the places Max and Elizaveta were planning to expose. There's this too' – she took out the tiny micro-SD card – 'it's from Gregor's drone. You can finish what they started.'

'Thank you,' said Vita.

'Don't thank me, just make sure you get the bastards.'

CHAPTER 43

She left the city behind. The Volvo's heater seemed to be working now and she was feeling drowsy. Her phone rang as she passed the roadside shrine to Elizaveta. She saw the glow from flickering candles before her Volvo's headlights caught the picture frame. Natalya groped for her mobile on the passenger seat. It was late for anyone to call – nearly eleven. She glanced at the phone while trying to focus on the road ahead. The number started with the St Petersburg area code but it wasn't stored in her phone's address book.

She answered the call.

There was a howling rage at the other end of the line. 'You stupid bitch, you were meant to fix it.'

She recognised the voice of Mikhail's ex. They had not spoken since the divorce; she didn't realise Dinara had her number.

'What's wrong?' she asked. 'Is it Anton?'

'Of course it's not fucking Anton – it's Misha. And it's your fault, you stupid bitch. Misha told me it would be OK. Well, it's not.' Dinara let out an exaggerated laugh; it sounded demented.

'Just tell me what happened,' she said.

'They had a search warrant.'

'*Sledkom*?' she asked.

'Who else?' Dinara snapped. 'They asked about a bank account. I told them I had no idea but they still took my computer away, and Misha's old papers.'

'But you don't know anything.'

'For a *ment* you can be damned stupid. Did you forget he was married to me? I haven't.'

At least Dinara was being careful not to spill the details over the phone. At home, she'd used specialist software to clear their computer of any traces of Mikhail's secret account, but she hadn't thought what incriminating evidence might be in his ex-wife's apartment.

'How long have you had that computer?' Natalya asked.

'Why? Has Misha offered to buy me a replacement? That's kind. Tell him I want a Dell XPS.'

'I'll ask him,' she said to avoid an argument.

Dinara said, 'You do that.'

'How old is your computer?' Natalya tried again.

'That piece of junk? He bought it for me seven years ago – it's slow and the hard disk is full.'

That was long enough. He'd used Dinara's computer to access his account for two years before he moved out in 2013. Dinara was a hoarder too; it was unlikely she would delete old files, old bank statements or emails. For all her rage, she had to agree with her – she had been damned stupid.

'Did *Sledkom* say anything?' she asked.

'No, they just put it in a box and carried it away. This has got to stop,' Dinara said. 'Did you want Misha or not? We were happy before you turned his head. He would have been better off with me. Now we'll all end up alone.'

She let Dinara talk until there was only a heavy silence left.

Beyond the town of Toksovo, she continued on the road. The traffic was light and a snowplough had passed recently, scraping the road clear. She propped her phone on the dashboard to follow the map. After Oselki she took a right turn. The road had been sprayed with yellow salt and where the surface had been worn and pitted before, it was now sleek, black tarmac. The minister's ownership of the mansion may have been kept off the books, but his wealth and power extended beyond the property.

She recognised the high stone wall from the drone footage and pulled over. Primakov had joked about the case being a suicide mission; he was right, though. It was late; she was alone and unarmed, and looking for the suspect in a double murder. She promised herself she would take a look and see if there was anything to prove Max and Elizaveta had been there. If she was lucky, she might find a trace of the naked woman too. Once she found something, she would get out.

The gates to the mansion were attached to brick piers. They were bronze and ornate with a double eagle motif; they were also solid enough to make a tank driver pause for thought. She got out and zipped up her coat. A camera fixed to a post inside the grounds turned with her movements. She found an intercom buried in one of the piers and held her ID card to its tiny lens.

'Ivanova, Captain. Criminal Investigations Directorate.'

A nasal voice projected through the tiny speaker. 'How can I help, Captain?'

'I'd like to speak to someone inside.'

'Do you have an appointment?'

'Do I need one?'

'You do, and stars on your shoulders if you're thinking of coming back.'

'Thanks for the advice.'

'No problem.'

She took her finger off the buzzer.

She drove quietly back the way she had come, looking for hidden cameras monitoring the road, but the Red Army Choir might be lurking in the shadows for all she could see. Away from the highway, the trees were in darkness between the quarter-moon sky and the barely luminous snow.

Vasily Chubarov was a government minister. Entering his property without cause wasn't only illegal – it was against the Russian constitution. Chubarov would have to open fire in a market square with a

Kalashnikov before he could be searched, because he had immunity from that too. There was one thing she clung to: a ready-made excuse – the deeds for the property were in his wife's name. That was as far as she'd got. She had no justifiable reason to enter the estate.

She parked the Volvo, drawn by a break in the trees to the left, and got out. In the drone video, Gregor had been near the main entrance just out of sight of the cameras. If Max and Elizaveta had returned in January, this was a likely place.

Outside of the warm car, the cold shocked her lungs. She pulled the hood of Mikhail's jacket over her hat and withdrew her hands into its sleeves. Snow reached the tops of her boots as she waded through the break in the trees. The path – if there was one underfoot – climbed and her breathing became laboured. At the top, the path dipped, exposing raw earth and gravel where cars had skidded and clawed their way over the brow. To the right was a narrow parking space, hidden from the road below. She wondered if Max had stopped there, using the Quattro's four-wheel drive.

A corner of the mortar wall she had seen at the entrance was untended. It was crumbling and covered in frozen vines as thick as cables. She thought of using them to climb over, then saw twisted loops of razor wire submerged in the snow on top. She kept walking, tracing the perimeter of the property. After ten minutes, she came across a solid oak door. A camera was fixed above it, focused on the immediate area in front; the security detail inside hadn't seen her.

She heard the low growl of a diesel engine and thought it had come from the road below. Then it cut, and she smelled its exhaust in the air. Another sound – the groan of a bolt lock shifting in the gate. A guard in a blue-grey uniform stepped out. He was solidly built, like a boxer, and had a flattened nose.

'You're a determined *ment*, aren't you?' he said.

CHAPTER 43

By the nasal drawl, she guessed he'd been the one on the front gate. 'I was just taking a look around.'

'Of course you were. Lucky the owner's away or you'd be facing people who don't fuck around. Why don't you come into my kennel and warm up.'

'I should get back.'

'Are you sure? You can have the grand tour for free. I used to be a *ment* too… Petersburg OMON.' He held out a thick hand to her. 'Viktor Aksarin.'

She glanced at his security belt. It held a pistol – a P-96, she thought, judging by its striated grip.

He saw her looking at it. 'I'll put my barrel in the glove box if it makes you feel any easier.'

She had to admit it was better than climbing the wall. 'I'd like that,' she said.

Aksarin took her through the gate to a black Land Cruiser parked on a cleared path; it had 'Frontline' stencilled on the side. She didn't hesitate to climb in. Even with her layers of clothing, her face was still exposed.

Aksarin started the engine and turned off the path, following his tyre tracks across a vast, snow-blanketed lawn with muffled shapes hiding sculptures or topiaries. Ahead, fixed spotlights illuminated a neo-gothic mansion with towers at the corners and its distinctive green roof.

'It's like something out of a fairy tale at night,' said Aksarin.

'One where all the princes are billionaires,' she said. 'And the castles are owned by one of their relatives.'

'Better than leaving them to decay,' Aksarin said. 'And these old places cost a small fortune to run.'

'Stop, I'm starting to feel sympathy for them.'

'No you're not,' he grunted. 'But they're not all bad.'

The Land Cruiser skirted the massive house, passing a white-painted wooden church, and stables that had been opened up to serve as a garage. There were no cars inside.

'What are all these buildings?' she asked. It was where she had seen the naked woman running.

Aksarin stared ahead as the path twisted. 'Recreation facilities: all-purpose gymnasium, swimming pool, *banya*... and here we are: my kennel.'

He parked in a space to the right of the main gate and they walked to a narrow guardhouse made from the same stone as the mansion. It had a single room with windows built all the way around for visibility. She followed him inside to a small office with four TV screens – Aksarin took up much of the space and she lingered by the doorway. From her position, she looked at one of the displays and recognised the path she'd taken at the back; Aksarin had seen her long before she reached the gate.

The security guard sat on the edge of his desk and offered her the chair; she took it.

'I thought I wouldn't get in without an official invitation.'

'To be honest, I'm glad of the company,' Aksarin said. 'It's quiet here... too quiet at night, especially in winter. You said you were from the Criminal Investigations Directorate? What brings a detective out here?'

'I'm investigating the deaths of two anti-government activists.'

Aksarin let out a low whistle. 'That's going to lose you some friends.'

'Sanctions are more popular than me right now. In fact, I'd appreciate it if you kept my visit to yourself.'

'Sure. All *menti* together, right?'

She nodded. 'Do you work here all the time?'

'Is this an interview?'

'If you like.'

CHAPTER 43

'And to think I let you in… I'm here maybe two days a month. My company – Frontline – rotates us.'

'So someone from your company is here all the time, then?'

'No, not always. When the owner comes they bring their own security.'

'It's OK, you can mention his name – Chubarov, right? And he's a minister, so the security you're talking about will be Federal Guards.'

'You ever seen them?' he said. 'Tough bastards who don't mess around. They make *Spetsnaz* look like the Young Pioneers. You don't ever want to get on their bad side.'

'Then maybe you can help me so I won't have to come back. Can you tell me who was here on Friday the fifth of January?'

'Two days before Christmas?' Aksarin mused, glancing upwards in thought. 'Not me, I had the week off.'

'You can prove that?'

'Sure.'

She thought of the naked woman caught by the drone and the timestamp on the file. 'Another date I'm interested in is last year: Tuesday the nineteenth of September.'

'I'll need to check my calendar at home.'

She wondered how to approach the next question. 'This company you work for – Frontline – how do I find who was working on those days?'

He raised one eyebrow. 'With their client list, I wouldn't advise you calling them to find out.'

'What about you?' she asked. 'What made you leave OMON?'

'Chechnya. It's where I got this' – he tapped his nose. 'My sergeant smashed it in with a rifle butt for not having his breakfast ready when he woke up.'

'My husband was conscripted in the first war. He won't talk about it.'

'That's for the best. After what I saw, I like the quiet life.'

'My husband joined the state police afterwards. I think he wanted to do something positive, to make up for whatever happened out there.'

Aksarin smiled wryly. 'Like I said, best not to talk about it. So that's what this conversation was about. Spreading a little butter on me so I'll help you?'

'You said yourself, if I approach Frontline, your director will speak to my superiors and I'll be in the shit. I need to know about those two days, though. Can you get a printout of the staff rota?'

'It might incur some expenses.'

She felt in her pockets for her purse and removed two 1,000-rouble notes, along with her card. 'Will a pair of *shtuki* cover them?'

Aksarin pocketed the notes as smoothly as a traffic *ment*. 'All right, Captain Ivanova, I'll be in touch.'

44

After lunch the next day, Natalya left headquarters on Suvorovsky Prospekt and went to the car park for her Volvo. She found Rogov waiting outside. He had no Makarov pistol – she assumed it was to avoid being breathalysed.

'Hey Boss.' His eyes were red-rimmed and his breath was sour.

'You survived your night with Popovich?'

'Just.' He rubbed his chin, producing a rasping sound. 'Yeah, I mean, I felt bad. Pavel's OK when you get to know him.'

'I just don't need him in the way. Nothing personal,' she added – though it was. 'Did he make it in?'

'No, as ordered.' Rogov performed a weak salute. 'I stayed at Pavel's last night. When I left this morning he was asleep in his bathtub.'

She thought to ask why, then decided against it. 'What about Dostoynov?'

'I signed in early so he wouldn't see me.'

'Then well done, Sergeant. It was a tough mission, but you succeeded admirably.'

Rogov grinned. 'So where to, Boss?'

'Autopsy.'

His grin faded. 'You mind if I go home for a few hours and get some sleep?'

'No,' she said. 'I don't mind at all.' Anjelika was hardly going to be impressed by a drunk *ment*.

After dropping off Rogov at his apartment, she drove to Clinical Hospital No. 31 and called Anjelika on her mobile. Five minutes later, the door to the basement opened and the pathologist manoeuvred the fire extinguisher into place.

'I brought these.' She waved a box of chocolates left over from Christmas.

Anjelika refilled her e-cigarette with nicotine solution. 'Thanks. Now you've got the case back you don't need to skulk around. You can use reception like everyone else.'

'I like it this way,' said Natalya. 'More personal.' She pulled out a pack of Sobranies.

'You're smoking?' Anjelika asked.

'Thinking about it. *Sledkom* are making me unhappy. They're sniff-ing around, seeing if they can pin something on me.'

'What for?'

'Corruption?'

Anjelika stopped pouring the solution. 'You?'

'There's always something to be found, Anjelika… even if there isn't, they'll find it.'

'I told you not to upset them… still, it's no reason to smoke again.'

'Maybe you're right.' Natalya tucked the packet into her coat pocket.

'So what do you want this time?'

'Max Timchenko… have you seen him?'

'I've taken receipt of him and had a quick look… that's all.'

'Water in his lungs?' Natalya asked.

'You mean did he drown?' The pathologist sucked on the e-cigarette. 'Timchenko had a traumatic brain injury. You're correct in that he likely survived the initial blow – a hospital could have saved him. In his case, a haemorrhagic progression – a chain reaction of brain injuries

– finished him. I doubt he regained consciousness. If it helps, you can tell that to the relatives.'

'No defence wounds?'

'None that I saw. A bag of his fingernail clippings has gone to the lab – I'll give you a call if they find anything.'

'What about the asbestos particles in Elizaveta's lungs? Did he have them too?'

Anjelika sucked on the e-cigarette. 'You'll have to wait for the post-mortem.'

'What caused the injury?'

'A right-handed blow to the sphenoid bone.' Anjelika hooked her index and middle fingers into a two-pronged claw. 'Parallel injuries from a bifurcated object… a claw hammer or crowbar. That's what I'll write in the report unless *Sledkom* tell me he died of old age.'

'Thank you.'

Anjelika stuffed the e-cigarette in her pocket, then kicked the extinguisher to let the fire door close behind her.

Back in the office, Natalya received the response from *MegaFon*, Oleg's network provider, listing the activity on his mobile. There was little of interest in the report: a few calls to Oleg's immediate family and his acupuncturist in Aleksandrovskaya. Of more importance was his credit card bill of 3,230 roubles from Sofia Shoes at 13.07 on 5 January. That supported his earlier alibi, but not the time she was interested in.

She called Primakov.

'Captain, how can I help?'

'Where are we with Oleg's alibi?'

'Unfortunately Pavel called in sick this morning. My supervisor has asked me to continue his work.' His tone was serious, and she guessed his supervisor wasn't far away. 'Some forensic technicians are analysing the television and the location data on his phone.'

'Thanks, Leo. After I left you last night I went on an excursion – that mansion with the green roof. I thought it best you didn't know.'

'Captain, that's—'

'Against the constitution?'

'A terrible idea, I was going to say.'

'Well, it wasn't so bad. At the back of the estate there's something you might be interested in: a small layby that might have captured the Quattro's tyre tracks. I would have parked there myself if I'd had winter tyres and four-wheel drive.'

'You want me to go there?'

She could feel his panic over the phone. 'We'll go together. I need to connect Max and Elizaveta to the place without using the drone footage. Think about it,' she said. 'I don't need an answer now.'

In the early afternoon Rogov appeared, looking less shabby after going home to shower and catch up on his sleep. Even a close inspection from Dostoynov would have failed to detect the signs of a wild evening.

'Boss, what's the plan?' he asked.

'A coffee at Tam-Tam?'

They huddled against an icy wind and crossed over to Kavalergardskaya Ulitsa. The place was quiet after the lunchtime rush. She ordered a latte and a black tea, and found a secluded booth.

A waiter brought their drinks to the table. 'It's good to have you back,' she said.

'Where are we, Boss?' He ripped open two packets of sugar.

'I've been going through Oleg's alibi with Primakov. You remember Gregor?'

CHAPTER 44

He tipped the sugar in his tea and stirred it. 'The hobbit I shot with my Wasp.'

'Yes, and he hasn't forgiven you for it.'

Rogov shrugged. He didn't care.

'Gregor gave me a list of all the addresses Max and Elizaveta were interested in. Leo and I used your mileage figures to work out how far the Quattro went that day. There was only one place that matched – it's to the east of Oselki. The distance is right, and you drive past the locations of both bodies on the way.'

'I don't trust Gregor, Boss.'

'The feeling is mutual.'

Rogov stirred more sugar into the tea. 'But what if the hobbit killed them and is throwing us off the scent?'

'It's a good point. He's not the easiest person to speak to either. But if I bring Gregor in for questioning—'

'Dostoynov will get a hard-on.'

'I couldn't have put it better,' she said.

'So who else is in the frame?' he asked, sipping his sugar solution.

'Apart from Oleg, that place near Oselki I mentioned? It's a mansion owned by Anna Chubarova, the wife of the Minister of Emergency Situations – Vasily Chubarov.'

'Boss, mind if I put in for a transfer before you get me killed?'

The grin to show it had been a joke remained frozen on his face.

'I went there last night,' she continued. 'I spoke to a security guard, Viktor Aksarin – he's ex-OMON. He said the Chubarovs don't use the mansion very often. I slipped a couple of *shtuki* his way and he told me he'd check his company's duty roster to see which of his colleagues was on duty on the fifth of January.'

'If Gregor is to be believed.'

'If Gregor *and* Oleg are to be believed.'

'It's flimsy, Boss… relying on two suspects.'

'There's also the possibility the FSB got someone to do their dirty work after the Decembrists embarrassed their director. That's as far as I've got.'

'You missed something. Misha.'

Her latte stopped midway on its journey to her mouth.

'What do you mean?'

'*Sledkom* asked him to come in for a formal interview.'

Her world twisted on its axis. She felt dizzy. 'Why the fuck didn't you tell me this straight away?'

She had spoken too loudly and scanned the café. There was only the waiter cleaning tables.

'He called me on the way to the airport. He was ordered to get the next flight back. You know what it's about?'

'*Sledkom* want revenge because I took their case away.'

Rogov said, 'No, it's not always about you,' and she wanted to hit him.

'They want to charge Misha with owning a foreign bank account,' he said. Rogov stared at her as if she hadn't got the punchline.

'Christ,' she hissed. 'How long have you known about the money?'

'He asked my advice at the time.' He raised his brows as if to say *some people do that.*

'But that was nine years ago.' She shook her head in disbelief.

'Misha's my friend… he asked me to keep quiet. What else could I do?'

'All right, let's think about this.' She twisted her fingers through the handle of her cup. 'They must have found something on Dinara's computer.' Nausea spread from her stomach as she thought of the consequences. 'Now once they get the account details they'll ask Mikhail to prove he bought our apartment with his own money – he won't be able to do that.'

CHAPTER 44

'It won't come to that, Natalya.'

'Of course it will. They'll seize the apartment if he can't prove he bought it legitimately. And you're wrong about something else.' She felt angry now. 'It is about me. The only reason they are doing it is because I got in their way.'

'Then maybe it's time to give up the hobbit. If *Sledkom* wire his balls to Radio Moscow he'll give up his comrades. He's a good fit for the murders too. You can't tell me he's innocent.'

'Rogov?' she stared at him and waited until his eyes met hers. 'We're not the fucking Gestapo. What's more, if I hear *Sledkom* have suddenly taken an interest in Gregor, I'll know who told them.'

'Boss, I was just joking.'

'I'm not. We'll get Misha out, I don't know how, but we won't do it that way.'

45

What passed for daylight had gone. She stopped at a Georgian restaurant and ate a lamb and pepper soup served by a waiter of indeterminate age with suspiciously black hair. She was the only customer and it suited her mood. After paying the bill, she went home. Alone in her apartment, she left a message on Mikhail's phone to accompany the seven previous ones. She found an old pullover of his and put it on to remind herself of his smell.

Around nine she took a call.

'Hey Babe.' She heard a tannoy in the background.

'Misha, where are you?'

'Pulkovo. I've just got off the plane.'

'You want me to pick you up?'

'No, I've got a ride… *Sledkom.* At least I won't have to pay the taxi fare.'

She stifled a tear. 'I'll find a lawyer.'

'Don't bother, it won't make any difference, save your money. I have to go, Babe, they are waiting for me.'

'A bull of a major, an arsehole in a red all-weather coat, and a blonde woman?'

'That's them.'

'If you get the chance, tell them from me that they're all small-minded pricks.'

'With pleasure, Babe.'

'When will you be home?'

CHAPTER 45

'I spoke to Dostoynov before I left,' – she felt a twist in her guts knowing more bad news was coming – 'the bastard called to gloat. He said a judge has already issued a custody order. I'm booked straight into pre-trial detention.'

'Where?'

'SIZO 4.'

The facility was on the far bank of the Neva, two kilometres from her office.

'They want me to know I'm responsible for this.'

'I guess they do, Babe. Better than Irkutsk, I suppose, and you can wave at me during your lunch break.'

'Hey, wait, I'm talking to my wife,' she heard him shout.

'Misha, I'm so sorry.'

'What's done can't be undone. And I don't blame you, anyway. It's why I love you.'

'I love you too.'

'They are taking my phone… I've got to go.'

After a sleepless night, she faced the humiliation of queuing outside the SIZO for two hours in the snow, paranoid she would bump into a relative of someone she had put away. Once inside, a DVD on a permanent loop showed a matronly woman instructing visitors how to behave and which items were banned. She was sent to a featureless room by a stern male guard in camouflage uniform and left there all morning. Around twelve o'clock, the guard returned to inform her she had failed to visit her husband during the allotted time and would need to make another appointment in two weeks.

She returned to work and found Dostoynov standing in the doorway of his office.

'Captain?' he beckoned her with a curled index finger. 'Close the door,' he said.

Dostoynov sat down. She stood, returning the same facial expression she'd presented to the prison authorities – the same look she'd seen on her mother's and Valeria Kalinina's faces. She was impervious to pain. He could do anything, say anything, and her demeanour would be the same.

'Colonel, you wished to see me.'

'First, let me extend my sympathies about Major Ivanov's predicament. Until I hear otherwise, I don't consider the sins of the husband to be that of the wife.'

'Thank you, Colonel.' The words almost stuck in her throat. 'Was that what you wanted to see me about?'

'No, Captain. I wanted to talk about you. Please take a seat.'

She sat opposite him.

'Now, to business,' he said. 'Last week, I asked my former colleagues to pull your file. By your expression I can see that doesn't surprise you. It shouldn't; the FSB has a file on anyone who piques their curiosity – for good or bad.'

'I wasn't allowed to take it away, so let me see if I remember it all.' His eyes flicked to the ceiling. 'Your family moved to Hannover after the Berlin Wall fell, then you returned with your mother five years later. Your father and sister chose to stay behind in Germany.'

'That must have been a wrench,' he said. 'It's tough to take rejection at sixteen, but when it comes from your own family…'

'It was over half a lifetime ago, Colonel.'

'And yet we repeat these family dramas until our dying breath. After settling in with your mother, you attended gatherings of punk musicians and were sexually promiscuous – their words not mine. Despite this rebellious streak, you were accepted into the Leningrad Oblast Pedagogical Institute, then you dropped out to join the University of the Ministry of Internal Affairs. In your reports, three professors described you as "disagreeable", "argumentative", and "destined for high command".'

'I slept with that last one, Colonel.'

Dostoynov chuckled. 'Now I don't know whether to believe you or not… Let me ask you a question. Have you ever heard of a black wolf, Ivanova?'

'No, Colonel.'

'It's a mutation caused by wolves mating with dogs in the distant past. Black wolves are outcasts, destined to be neither one thing nor the other. The wolves in their pack attack them for being different and they are shot for their trouble when seeking human company. That's you, Ivanova. The Decembrists don't trust you, and neither do we.'

She thought of the prison guard who had made her wait all morning for Mikhail just to be told she had failed to attend at the allotted time. Dostoynov had nothing on that sadist; she could put up with his wittering all day.

'Yes, Colonel.'

'The interesting point though, Ivanova, is that despite outward appearances there is little difference between a black wolf and a grey – merely a few genes for the colour of the pelt. As for you, there is no record of you attending anti-government demonstrations or joining political groups. You rail against corruption, while married to an officer under investigation, and you live in an apartment beyond both of your means. Do you know what I think?'

'Yes, Sir.'

'There you are again with your little quips. I'll tell you though, because it's clear to anyone who looks at your file. Your rebellion started when your parents divorced. You were a resentful teenager who listened to punk long after it was fashionable. You hated your mother for bringing you back to Piter, and your father and sister for letting her do it. You think you're fighting the Russian state, but you're fighting your own family.'

A single tear betrayed her. She affected a cough to bring a hand to her cheek and wipe it away. Dostoynov's face bore the constipated look of pained satisfaction.

'We're not wolves here, Ivanova. You can rejoin the pack. Bring in the Decembrists before they start bombing innocents and preaching revolution. *Sledkom* will be reasonable, your husband's disgrace isn't public yet. There's still a chance for you to make amends.'

Another tear. Her body was a fucking disgrace. She wiped it away with an angry palm.

'This case of Major Ivanov's,' Dostoynov said. 'The girl from Siberia – Diana Maricheva. Are you familiar with it?'

'Yes, Colonel.'

'Good. In view of Major Ivanov's absence, it's yours.'

'Thank you, Colonel.'

'And Ivanova, never again forget which side you're on.'

She went to the toilets, locked herself in a cubicle, and cried. After a while she wasn't sure why. Had she been crying for Misha, locked up in the SIZO, her dead mother, or even her sixteen-year-old self? At that moment, as much as she'd wanted to be like her mother or even Valeria Kalinina, she knew she wasn't built like them. She pulled the flush, examined her face in the mirror, and then quietly returned to her desk.

On her computer she found a report Leo had sent via email. It detailed the activity on Oleg Timchenko's television and streaming service, *Kino*. He confirmed the *kachok* had watched *Stranger Things 2* and *Vladenie 18*. The electronic evidence on his mobile phone supported his alibi too. It had been unlocked regularly using the phone's touch ID that required his fingerprint, and established he had remained in range of the Admiralty District cell towers, covering the Galeria mall and his apartment, until the following day. She typed a formal response and copied the email to Dostoynov, knowing it would irk him.

Her phone was buzzing on silent mode. She took the call, noting it was a number she didn't recognise.

'Captain Ivanova.'

She recognised the nasal twang before he introduced himself. 'It's Viktor… Viktor Aksarin. I'm calling to warn you, I've dropped you in the shit.'

'It's impossible to make my day worse.'

'You might want to rethink that. I'm in the car park of my firm. That information you wanted? When I went to check the staff rota my supervisor got suspicious—'

'You were caught?'

'Yeah,' he said. 'I hope you don't want those two *shtuki* back?'

'Just tell me what happened.'

'I said it was police business for a murder case and showed my boss the money. He wasn't happy that I hadn't spoken to him first. I played innocent and told him it was only to see the rota and I didn't think it was a big deal.'

'You gave him my name.'

'I had to… sorry.'

'When was this?'

'About forty minutes ago. I've just left.'

She looked over to Dostoynov in the office. He was speaking to someone on the phone. He put the phone down and glared at her.

'I was wrong,' she said.

'When?'

'When I said you couldn't make my day any worse.'

'At least they can't shoot you, right? That's what we used to say in OMON. Sometimes the Chechens did of course… they shot us.'

She hung up. The door to Dostoynov's office was open now. The finger bent, summoning her back. This time she was offered no chair, not even the broken one.

'Captain,' Dostoynov said, 'I gave you a clear order to leave the properties alone and focus on the brother.'

'Colonel, you've seen the electronic evidence… we know Oleg wasn't involved.'

'No matter. My order still stands.' He closed his door behind her. 'Now explain.'

'I have reason to believe Max Timchenko and Elizaveta Kalinina visited a mansion near Oselki the day they died.'

'What's your evidence?'

She couldn't involve Gregor – not unless she was certain he'd killed the two activists.

'Colonel, the evidence is based on the mileage of the Audi Quattro, the location of the bodies, and the fact the Decembrists were interested in properties that had been removed from the national register.'

'So, you've got nothing except a vendetta against the *elitny*. I warned you about that explicitly. I told you not to make an example of these people.'

There was a knock on the door, two more uniforms: Major Zubacheva, a smart, athletic woman and Major Kalugin, a solid, jovial man within six months of retirement. She knew them slightly from official functions.

Dostoynov waved them in while he addressed her: 'Captain Ivanova, these Majors represent the Department of Civil Service and Personnel, and the Police Union.'

'Majors, this is Captain Ivanova. As I explained five minutes ago, after disobeying a direct order, Captain Ivanova attempted to bribe a retired OMON officer to uncover the security arrangements of a high-ranking minister. In recognition of the Captain's previous exemplary service, I propose no legal action is taken. Do you agree?'

CHAPTER 45

The two majors spoke simultaneously: 'Yes, Colonel.'

Natalya let out an audible sigh of relief.

'Then we are in agreement. Now to the matter at hand, Majors, are you satisfied that the captain is in breach of article twenty-seven, on the basic duties of a police officer? Namely, she wilfully refused an instruction from her superior.'

Major Zubacheva's head bobbed. 'Yes, Colonel.'

'And you, Major Kalugin?'

A man that close to retirement was never going to object. 'Yes, Colonel,' he said.

'Then Captain Ivanova, I hereby confirm you are summarily dismissed from the Ministry of Internal Affairs of the City of St Petersburg and Leningrad Oblast.'

46

She didn't want to cry any more – tears were an indulgence – but still they came. At the Metro station, she checked the news on her phone. An entrepreneur had committed suicide in Mikhail's SIZO. Already rumours were circulating that he'd been tortured and raped on the orders of an investigator trying to force a confession. She prayed the same wouldn't happen to Misha, clinging on to the fact that *Sledkom* had no reason to seek revenge now she was out of a job. Also, Misha was a major, which would count for something – she hoped.

She stepped over a mound of decaying snow to reach her apartment block. In her mailbox she found an envelope. She read it climbing the stairs. It was a letter from *Sledkom* informing her there was a suspicion her apartment had been purchased with illegal earnings and under Federal Law she was forbidden to dispose of it until the matter was settled. She ripped the letter into pieces, sat down on her sofa and started crying again. Misha was in pre-trial detention, Anton had gone to ground, and she was out of work. Despite the darkness outside, her thick winter curtains were open. The noises from outside drifted in: the car horns and ship foghorns, the shouts and chatter, the tinny music from bars: all the sounds of the city making her feel more alone than ever.

She heard her buzzer and wiped her face clear of tears. By the time Primakov had climbed the stairs to her apartment she had splashed water on her face and hastily applied make-up to hide the blotches around her eyes.

CHAPTER 46

She let him in. 'I lost my job today, Leo.'

'That's why I came,' he said. 'Well, that and your central heating.' He unzipped his parka and draped it over a radiator.

'It's all I ever wanted to do, Leo… to be a detective and catch bad people.'

She hugged him and felt his customary awkward response.

'How did you find out?' she asked.

'Sergeant Rogov. I spoke to him on the phone. He was upset.' Primakov shook his head. 'So what's going to happen now?'

'The World Cup?' she said.

'I didn't mean that, Captain.'

She wanted to correct him – she no longer held any rank. 'What did you mean?'

'The case.'

She said, 'Now Oleg's in the clear, Dostoynov will hold someone else accountable for the killings. Gregor used to travel with Max and Elizaveta … maybe your friend Luka will find his DNA in the Quattro, and Dostoynov will connect him. Who knows?'

'It can't be left like that.'

'What do you suggest?' she said.

'We keep going.'

'Leo, we'll end up in jail… or worse. We're both civilians, which means no back-up, no gun. If we find the killer, what do we do? Ask them nicely if they'll accompany us to a police station?'

'I know, Captain, but there has to be a better way than letting them win. Whatever you plan to do, I'm in.'

She put her hand over his and squeezed it. 'Thank you.'

'And for the record, you didn't talk me into this,' he added.

Mikhail's words came back to her: 'It's why I love you.'

'So you're in?' she asked.

'That's what I've been saying, Captain.'

'Then let's stop at your office on the way,' she said. 'We'll need some things from your van.'

She was driving to Toksovo again. A block of snow broke off the truck in front and exploded onto her Volvo's windscreen. The wipers screeched to clear it.

'You need to replace your blades, Captain.'

'Thanks, I'll add that to my list. Are you sure about this, Leo?'

'No.'

The Volvo aquaplaned on the highway's icy sludge. 'Captain, please tell me you have winter tyres.'

'I have winter tyres.'

'You told me before that you didn't have any… did you buy some?'

'No, I lied. The airbag warning light is on too – in case you missed it.'

The lorry peeled away with a final spray. She drove through the town and on towards Oselki. She slowed as the road turned to newly-laid tarmac.

'Are you sure you want to do this?' she asked.

'You've already asked me, and I brought the kit… and coffee – I keep a thermos in the office. Jaap sent Ethiopian Harrar this time.'

'I won't be able to tell the difference.'

'If you promise not to tell him, I can't tell either.'

She nearly missed the turning and braked sharply. The Volvo slid, then caught grit and stopped. She reversed the car and took the turn before the traffic behind caught up. Her mind was anywhere but on the job. What job? She'd given up her career to pursue a killer who would never be caught. How many activists, politicians and journalists had been murdered since Putin came to power? Boris Nemtsov, Anna Politkovskaya, Natalya Estemirova, Stanislav

CHAPTER 46

Markelov, Anastasia Baburova, Paul Klebnikov… they were the most famous, but the list ran into the hundreds. In a fraction of the cases there were arrests, but it was even rarer to find the schemers behind the killings.

No one would criticise her for giving up. She could find a new job and a shitty apartment while waiting for Mikhail's trial and inevitable conviction. She would visit him in jail and bring toilet rolls, and learn to make cakes for him to share with the other prisoners. He'd be out before he was 50 – there was still a life for him.

'How is the major?' Primakov asked after a while.

'They won't let me see him.'

Another tear. She'd cried more today than at her mother's funeral.

He nodded again, as much to himself as to her. 'You want to change the subject?'

'Yes… tell me about Jaap.'

She lowered the window a fraction to feel the sting of freezing air on her face.

'I'm worried he'll get tired of waiting and find someone else.'

'If he does, he's a fool.'

'We'll stop here before someone sees us.' She pulled over on the snow-covered verge where she had parked before.

Primakov lifted a rucksack from the backseat, the metal in his pack rattling as they walked along the road. After a few minutes she heard the distant rumble of a car. They took cover behind a pair of birch trees as a Bentley sped past, interior lights on, the thrum of dance music cutting into the still night.

In the distance she saw the mortar wall, then the sage-green roof of the minister's mansion. Floodlights lit up the façade; inside, windows glowed red behind enormous curtains.

'They've got visitors,' she said.

He followed as she took the steep lane to the rear of the property. The cold was biting now. She rearranged her scarf until there was only a slit for her eyes. Primakov's pace never slowed. He overtook her, marching through the snow she had churned up on her last visit. At the brow of the hill he paused, and she was glad to stop and catch her breath.

'This is where I want you to search. There's no gravel,' she said, 'and the mud has frozen underneath. There's a good chance Max parked the Quattro here on the right to keep it out of sight.'

He took out the thermos from his rucksack and poured some coffee into a plastic cup. He passed it to her. 'Why did they come back here?'

She drank some of the coffee, grateful for its heat. 'Gregor thought Max was outgrowing the group. This project of his was old news – Alexei Navalny had already done something similar. A story about a corrupt minister was hardly news, but throw in a naked woman and he had a scandal. Was the minister having an affair, or even hosting sex parties? Max would be on the global news networks. He needed to find out about this woman. He brought Elizaveta because she didn't look like a radical – she had a better chance of getting them inside.'

Primakov pulled on a pair of latex gloves and his overshoes. He took out a bag of white powder and water and laid them alongside his Primus stove and two aerosol cans. He found a tyre imprint straight away and began caressing the surface with a make-up brush, gently pushing the crystals of snow aside. He sprayed compressed air from one aerosol to clear the remaining flakes. From experience she knew the other aerosol contained hairspray – he'd use that to coat the surface of the mud before taking a mould with dental stone.

'I'm going now, Leo.'

He looked up, surprised. 'I thought this was what we came for.'

'Not for me… I'm taking a look inside.'

CHAPTER 46

'You can't—'

She held up a mittened hand to cut him off. 'I left the keys in the glove compartment. If I'm not back in an hour, leave without me. Don't let anyone see you.'

'Captain?'

She kept walking, ploughing up the snow. After five minutes she slowed and scrutinised a silver birch facing the lane. At first she thought it was a trick of the light, but then she saw the unblinking red eye on the tree. She entered the forest cover to avoid it, walking in a wide circle around the camera. Through the trees she saw the oak gate Aksarin had come through. She stayed in the woods, working her way parallel to the wall.

A cold ring of metal pressed against her cheek.

'On the floor!' a male voice screamed in her ear.

She froze. He kicked her ankles away and shoved her to the ground. A boot pressed between her shoulder blades, pushing her flat into the snow. Her face burned with the cold. She squirmed, fighting to stand.

'Stay down,' he ordered – a soldier's command.

Hands grabbed her arms and forced them behind her back.

'You're hurting me, let go.'

Her wrists were zip-tied. Hands patted her pockets and pulled at the contours of her clothes. She heard a rustle of paper and guessed it was the photocopy of her *ksiva*.

'Stand her up.'

Hands under her armpits yanked her to her feet. Another gruff voice addressed her. 'You are Natalya Ivanova?'

She raised her head. 'Yes.'

The voice belonged to a man blended into the black of night. She saw a pair of eyes, disembodied by a balaclava.

'Walk.'

The red glow of a torchlight illuminated her steps. She twisted her head to see two men behind her. Each had an assault weapon dangling from a chest harness with an index finger inside the trigger guard.

'Who are you?' she demanded.

A hand gripped her shoulder and steered her through the oak gate.

One of them spoke into a microphone. 'Ulyana Tatyana 4. Trespasser to security.'

A flash illuminated the men – she saw three in black combat uniforms. One held a phone over her passport. He tapped the screen a few times to forward the image.

They approached the rear of the great house. Shadows swayed against the curtains. Outside, a huddle of men in dinner jackets smoked with purpose, keen to get inside the warmth of the house. They hushed as she was led past.

A chubby man in a thick overcoat leant against a marble pillar, a cocktail glass in one hand and a smouldering cigar between the fingers of the other. A model-tall woman in furs pulled on a cigarette next to him, her shoulders reaching the top of his head.

'Good work, boys,' the woman called to the guards escorting her.

No one responded. At the open door she caught the sound of a tuneless woman singing 'The Lady is a Tramp' to an orchestra backing.

Natalya sang along quietly to the tune. There was a madness to her now, a giddy skip to the executioner's block. Her life wasn't falling apart so much as being obliterated by an artillery barrage.

'Does anyone smoke?' she asked.

'Keep walking.'

They steered her around the side of the mansion. Steam rose from a building – the *banya* where the naked woman had been running. Now she pictured serious men inside making sweaty deals.

CHAPTER 46

She had expected to be taken to Aksarin's dog kennel, but the men stopped at the main entrance to the house. Another black uniform stood guard outside a smaller door. He opened it as they approached. In the corridor two women in tan apron dresses clattered through kitchen swing-doors carrying trays of canapés; they pretended not to notice her.

Adjoining the kitchen was an ancient larder requisitioned as a security centre. The room had been cleared, fresh carpet had been laid, but still it smelled of vinegar and spices. A well-built man in his forties wearing a black uniform was studying a bank of screens fixed to the wall. On one she recognised her Volvo. The image shook as it moved – a soldier's bodycam. The man in the security centre spoke into a microphone attached to a headpiece.

'It's registered to her,' she heard him say.

Primakov was nowhere in sight. She wondered if they had apprehended him or he was hiding in the forest.

'Did you come alone?' the major asked, turning. He wore a black beret with an insignia of a double-headed eagle and a dagger half-hidden by the Russian tricolor.

'Yes,' she said.

She remembered what Viktor Aksarin had said. The Federal Guards Service made *Spetsnaz* look like the Young Pioneers. From her work she knew something of their powers too: they had no need for warrants and could arrest with impunity – all as part of their duties to protect high-ranking individuals.

'So, Captain Ivanova, what's a *ment* from a serious crimes unit doing out here?'

The news of her firing hadn't made it onto the government databases; she saw no reason to correct the major.

'Answer my question, Captain, or things will become unpleasant for you. This is a restricted access site and you are not authorised to be here.'

'I'm investigating a double murder, Major. I believe the victims came here on the day they died.'

'Then you're on duty without a Makarov.'

'I didn't fancy getting shot by your boys.'

'You have one minute to explain yourself. Fifteen days in prison and a fine is the penalty for entering a restricted access site.'

'Major, let me talk to someone in charge.'

'You already are.' He checked his watch. 'Fifty seconds.'

She stared at him.

'Forty-five.'

'I need to know who was at this house on two specific dates.'

'We don't discuss security arrangements. Sorry, Captain, my watch was running slow, let's call it five seconds… there, your time is up.'

The two men behind clamped her shoulders again. She tried to pull away. A guard squeezed a pressure point on the inside of her elbow. Her arm turned to liquid pain. She screamed.

The door to the security office was yanked open.

'What the hell is all this noise!'

The hand released her elbow. She saw a grey-haired man with wide intelligent eyes and a deeply tanned face.

'Who is this?'

'A *ment*,' said the major, 'Captain Ivanova, Criminal Investigations Directorate.'

'What's she fucking doing here?'

'We're taking her away now, Vasily Ilyich.'

'Vasily Ilyich… you're Minister Chubarov?' she asked.

'I'm no one to you.'

'Minister Chubarov, you're the one I want to speak to. I'm investigating the murder of two people.'

'This is ludicrous. Get rid of her.'

CHAPTER 46

She spoke to his back as he withdrew. 'Minister Chubarov, were you here on the fifth of January?'

'Just get this fucking *ment* out of here,' Chubarov said without turning. The door closed behind.

'You heard the minister,' the major said.

She was in the corridor again, a thumb pushing lightly on her elbow's pressure point as a warning to behave. Ahead, a waitress was propping open a door with a champagne bucket. Natalya caught a glimpse inside the room. A singer in fifteen-centimetre heels and a gold cocktail dress was murdering 'Mack the Knife'. In front of the stage, a boy of fourteen or so was devotedly waltzing with a woman bent by age. She wore an expression of pure delight and was wearing a plastic tiara topped with pink flashing lights. The dancing couple were ringed by forty to fifty others, diamonds flashing on their wrists and necklines. The waitress returned with a tray of empty glasses, pushed the champagne bucket away, and waited for them to pass. Natalya tried to pull her arms free and felt a nerve-wrenching pain in her shoulders.

'Stop doing that, *piz'da*.' She yanked her arm free and pulled it back, feigning a punch. The guard took a half-step back and collided into the waitress. The tray of glasses crashed to the floor.

'What about the naked woman?' she yelled as a guard opened the external door. 'Nineteenth of September last year. What was she doing here?'

They frogmarched her to a waiting jeep. There were more guards in their black uniforms, like extras in a fascist movie.

'Stop!'

A very tall woman in a shimmering silver gown was pulling on boots in the hallway. She had that imperfect-perfect look that modelling agencies craved.

'Who are you?' the woman demanded.

'She's—' began one of the guards.

'I didn't ask you, I asked her.'

By the imperious attitude, Natalya assumed she was the minister's wife. She was about the right age and height: twenty years younger and a head taller than her husband.

Impersonating a police officer now was the least of her problems. 'Anna Alexseyeva, I am Captain Ivanova of the St Petersburg Criminal Investigations Directorate.'

'You know my name?'

'I want to speak to your husband.'

Anna Chubarova frowned haughtily. 'I don't give a damn about that. You said something about a naked woman.'

'Nineteenth of September last year. She was running between the main house and the *banya*.'

Chubarov had reappeared; he had thrown a heavy fur over his dinner jacket and his mood was murderous. 'I thought I told you to get rid of her.'

'Darling,' his wife said smoothly, 'a moment, please, I'm trying to find out who you've been fucking.'

'It was a Tuesday,' Natalya said. 'Two weeks before the centenary of the Revolution.'

'How should I know?' said the minister. 'That was five months ago.'

Anna Chubarova let out a cry of pain as delicate as an exhalation. 'Who was it?'

'My *solnyshka*, you have to believe me.'

'I'm not your fucking sunshine. Was it that bitch Serafina again?'

The minister took his wife's elbow to manoeuvre her indoors; she brushed it off. 'Don't touch me, you ape.'

A guard approached the couple. 'Minister, if I may speak. You were in Belarus all week at the *Zapad* exercises. You dined with the president the day before.'

CHAPTER 46

'You would lie for him,' the wife spat.

The guard took out his mobile phone. 'No, Anna Alexseyeva. It's on the internet.' He held up an image of the president with Chubarov. 'See for yourself.'

'So you're satisfied then, *ment*?' said Chubarov. 'You ruined my mother's eightieth birthday.'

'I have one more question, Minister. January the fifth.'

'No you don't.' The major was in the doorway. Chubarov turned to him. 'I want her ruined for this.'

'Yes, Minister.'

The jeep stopped next to her Volvo. She was dragged out by the collar of her coat. A guard raised the bottom half of his balaclava to show an angel's face. He unsheathed a jagged knife and pressed the flat of the blade against her neck.

'If we see you again...' he said, leaving the rest of the threat unspoken.

He slipped the knife between her wrists and sliced the cable tie.

She waited until the jeep had gone before turning on the engine. A moment later a sheepish figure emerged from the birch forest, the silver of his parka blending in with the trees. His movements were stiff and she helped him inside.

'Did you find the Quattro's tyre tracks?'

He shivered. 'I didn't have time. I covered myself in snow when I saw them coming.'

'Leo, are you OK?'

He shook his head, unable to speak for a moment. 'I've never been so scared. Next time, try harder to stop me, Captain.'

47

Despite Mikhail's absence she still woke on her own side of the bed. His pillow smelled of smoke and his own natural musk; she had slept with it between her arms but it was a poor substitute for the real thing. She stirred, hearing a noise in the apartment.

There was a sharp knock. 'Hey, Natasha, I made tea.'

Anton entered. He set a cup by her bedside, averting his eyes in case he saw exposed flesh. There was no need – she was still wearing thermal underwear.

'Thanks. How is Vita?'

'Her parents are over from Belgium. It's too soon for me to meet them so I'm keeping out of the way.'

'But how is she?'

'She's getting online abuse about Max – people calling him a traitor. Her boss at university told her to stay at home until it blows over. She's crying a lot.'

'Just be there for her… however she behaves.'

'Did you find out who killed Max?'

'Not yet,' she said.

His brows knotted in a frown. 'Aren't you supposed to be at work today?'

'They fired me.'

Anton grimaced. 'Shit, that's bad.'

'Yeah, it's pretty bad. Have you heard from Papa?'

'That's why I'm here. He asked me to see if you were OK.'

CHAPTER 47

'I am. Don't mention my job though, he's got enough to worry about.'

'Uh, OK.'

'Aren't you at the garage today?' she asked.

'I got fired too. Bogdan—'

'Your boss, right?'

'Yeah. I think he was up to something. I was talking to him yesterday and told him about you and Papa being detectives. After that he said he had to let me go because business was slow.'

'Shit, that's bad,' she said.

'Yeah, it's pretty bad.'

'Have you seen your Papa?' she asked. 'How is he?'

'I saw him yesterday. He's complaining about paying for toilet roll and he can't sleep for the noise.'

'Anything else?'

'The queue for the showers, he moaned about that too… and swearing – they get taken to a punishment cell if a guard hears them.'

'That's not what I'm saying,' she said. 'I mean, how is he?'

'Oh… they haven't charged him yet and he wasn't happy that you cancelled your visit.' Anton studied her face. In it she read an accusation.

'They refused to let me see him.'

'Papa said an investigator is threatening to transfer him to the tuberculosis ward.'

She sat up and reached for the tea. The wards were a breeding ground for drug-resistant TB; they accounted for half of all deaths in the prison system. 'It's a bluff,' she said. 'It's because he's not talking. I've never known a healthy inmate to be sent there.'

'Is it true?' he asked.

She sipped the tea. 'Is what true?'

'Why he's there. Some dick from *Sledkom* spoke to Mama. He said Papa had been helping the *mafiya*.'

She snorted. 'If that was true, he'd be in the government. He's there because *Sledkom* wanted to use Elizaveta's murder to destroy the Decembrists. I got in their way.'

'Papa said you were stubborn.'

'I am… I get it from my mother. My father called her a *lokomotiv* – not to her face, of course. Once she set her mind on something, she was unstoppable.'

'I'd like to have known her.'

'She was a difficult woman.'

'Like you, then?'

She ran a hand over the stubble of his hair.

'Are you all right, though?' he asked.

She couldn't tell him they would lose the apartment when *Sledkom* got access to Mikhail's secret account, because that meant admitting his father had pocketed a bribe. Misha was the only one who could tell him that.

'Hey, stepson, give me a minute, will you? I need to change.'

'Sure.'

After he'd closed her bedroom door she dressed and went to the bathroom. In the mirror her face looked grey. After washing and cleaning her teeth, she applied make-up; it did little to conceal the weariness she felt underneath.

She found Anton clearing her unwashed dishes.

'Don't worry about those, I was saving them up.'

'You mean like a bank? You'd be rich.'

'I'll ignore that.'

'Hey, you want to smoke?' He drew a cigarette half-out of a pack of Marlboro. 'I actually bought some. I had to give Papa the packs I stole.'

'I stopped, remember? If you're interested, Misha has a secret hoard in his bedroom cabinet. Why don't you give him half when you visit him next time… keep the rest.'

CHAPTER 47

'It's a deal.'

She put on a coat and joined Anton on the balcony.

He lit his cigarette and puffed on it. 'You sure?'

'There's nothing good about them, just don't ask me again.' She give him a thin smile. 'So, how is your father really?'

'He told me to mention a Siberian girl. He wanted to know if you found anything.'

A waft of smoke went in her face. She sucked it in. 'Nothing new. The previous owner lives in Rome. Someone needs to speak to him and find out who was on his property six years ago. Except no one will – it's a dead end; the case is finished. She was just another runaway.'

'We should go to Italy. Come on, Natasha, I'll be your assistant. It'd be like a holiday.'

'I'm not a *ment* anymore and your Papa was the one with the money.'

Anton planted a palm on his forehead. 'I've just remembered. He told me to ask you about Misha Buratino. Is he the Italian?'

She fought through her tiredness. Misha Buratino was the name on Mikhail's Cypriot bank account.

'Tell me exactly what he said.'

'Papa wanted him to go away.' He puffed on the cigarette again. 'No, that's not right, he said, "Ask Natasha to make sure Misha Buratino goes on holiday".'

She understood, at least. Mikhail wanted her to empty his secret account before *Sledkom* accessed the funds. It showed how desperate he was to think up such a bad idea. A trip to Cyprus would arouse *Sledkom's* suspicion, as would setting up another account to transfer the money.

'Tell him I can't.'

'Just that?'

'Just that.'

'What's it about, Natasha?'

'I can't tell you.'

'But it's something to do with why he's there.'

'It's best not to ask. Your father is a good man – that's all you need to know.'

'How are you going to get him out?'

'I don't know, Anton… everything's a mess. I'm open to advice.'

'Are you still looking for who killed Max?'

'And Elizaveta… yes.'

'I think that's good. Be careful, Natasha. You're my only stepmother.'

48

When Anton left, she spent her first day of unemployment shopping for groceries before continuing to the SIZO to arrange another visit. After completing the forms, she went beyond the brick perimeter and smoked a cigarette, her hands shaking. Mikhail was living in the parallel universe of the Federal Penitentiary Service with its petty rules that had barely adapted to post-Soviet times. She was tempted to scream his name out loud to see if she could reach him through the prison walls. In the end, though, she went home. Mikhail had been right, of course – he usually was. Her honesty had destroyed them.

Back in her apartment, she shrugged off her coat and put on the radio. On the two o'clock news bulletin, the announcer spoke of the election campaign approaching the finishing line – an appropriate metaphor considering the country's athletes were banned from international competition. With nine candidates in the race it was possible to believe in choice, if not democracy. Alexei Navalny, the real leader of the opposition, had a brother in prison to make sure he didn't go too far – not that it stopped him. Like the Decembrists, he continued to post online videos exposing the rot at the highest levels of government.

She took the call around three.

'Is that Captain Ivanova?'

She recognised the sound – the mouth breathing of Viktor Aksarin. 'It's just Natalya Ivanova now. You got me fired, remember?'

'Sorry about that… I heard you made an impression on the minister yesterday.'

She wondered if Aksarin had called to gossip. 'Is there a reason you called?'

'You're still interested, right? In those dead protesters?'

'Yes.'

'Then I've got something.'

'Wait a second.' She turned off the radio to concentrate. 'What?'

'One of the cleaners found a bag of women's clothes buried in the log pile that serves the *banya*. She told me there's a stain on the shirt. I took a look. It's blood, all right. I saw enough of it in Chechnya. It made me think of that woman you asked me about.'

'Thank you... Yes, I am interested. Where are you calling from?'

'My kennel at the minister's place.'

'Chubarov's gone?'

'It's safe... they all left this morning. The cleaners have gone too.'

'I'll be straight there.'

She hung up and tried Primakov. Her call went to voicemail. She tried twice before he picked up.

'It's Natalya, where are you?'

'I was in a meeting – a boring one on the new requirements for the maintenance of crime scene logs.'

She looked out of the window. There was barely an hour of daylight left.

'Do you fancy going for a drive?'

'Where to?'

'Chubarov's place. I've just been speaking with Aksarin, the security guard there. A cleaner found some bloodstained clothing in the *banya*. It could belong to that woman from the drone footage.'

'Captain, last night' – he dropped his voice to a whisper – 'I watched someone put a knife to your throat.'

'It's OK, Leo. The guards have gone with the minister. I'll pick you up outside your office if you still want to help. If it's evidence, we need to get it.'

'I'll be ready, Captain.'

49

The wipers screeched as she drove past Toksovo and took the turning after Oselki. Primakov had been quiet for the journey. He took a digital camera out of his backpack and fiddled with the buttons.

'What else did you bring?'

'An over-suit and evidence bags,' he said. 'If someone was killed there—'

'I know it's inadequate, Leo. We need forensic technicians… DNA, fingerprints. At least there won't be *politsiya* destroying your crime scene with their size forty-three winter boots.'

She saw the entrance to the green-tiled mansion and pulled up. They got out and she pressed the buzzer.

'It's me,' she said.

She heard a click, and the double-eagle gates opened with the whine of a motor. She walked inside with Primakov.

The security guard met her outside his security room. 'Who's this?' he asked, his hands buried deep in his jacket.

'Viktor Aksarin' – she turned an open palm to Leo, who was already threading his legs through his over-suit – 'this is Expert Criminalist Primakov. He's here to examine the clothes and the area where the cleaner found them.'

Aksarin held open the door to the security room. 'I'll get some torches and the keys from the stores,' he said. 'Go in my kennel to keep warm – it's colder than a Siberian outhouse tonight.'

She went inside with Primakov.

'What do you think, Captain?'

She looked out of the window. It had grown dark since they'd arrived; spotlights beyond the gates twisted the bronze double-eagles into shadows of malformed creatures.

'I think this investigation was doomed from the start,' she said, 'and it's still doomed.'

Primakov sat in Aksarin's chair. 'These clothes could be evidence, Captain. And I brought the mould kit.'

'And the minute you tell your boss where they came from, you'll be out of a job too.'

'Then we'll keep going… just the two of us.'

She puffed out her lips and blew a sigh. 'Then what? No one will be interested in the word of an ex-*ment*. Dostoynov doesn't care who killed a pair of political activists. He even exploited Diana Maricheva's murder so he could end Mikhail's career… sorry, Leo. I'm tired and depressed.'

She leaned against a radiator. 'What have you got there?' she asked.

Primakov was holding a watch connected by a USB cable to a laptop. 'A Suunto Ambit.'

'Let me rephrase the question: What's a Suunto Ambit?'

'A sports watch. I have one at home. Do you know what they do?'

She shrugged. 'Make fit people feel smug?'

'They measure heart rate and other things. This one is synchronising with his laptop.'

'And you're looking to buy another?' she asked.

'No, I've been thinking,' Primakov said. 'Imagine Aksarin is the killer. He dumped Max and Elizaveta, then left Oleg's car in Piter. How did he get back here?'

She watched him fiddle with the watch. 'So what's your theory? He ran back? In this weather he'd end up in a polyclinic.'

CHAPTER 49

'Not necessarily, Captain. I was in a race across Lake Baikal last year. My winter shoes have spikes.'

'Are you insane?'

'Sometimes I question my choices,' Primakov said.

'Anyway, it's too far,' she said. 'Oselki is over forty kilometres from the city. It's a full marathon distance.'

'But he had to get back somehow, Captain... what if he took the first bus to Toksovo, then ran here? That's only about ten kilometres.'

'Aksarin's been helpful,' she said.

'By getting you fired to stop your investigation.'

She winced.

'Sorry, Captain, that was insensitive. It's a serious question, though. How has he helped you?'

'He tried to get the rota from Frontline, and he's fetching the clothes the cleaner found.'

'But the only thing he's actually given you is the impression of helping... there's been nothing tangible.'

Primakov tapped the laptop's mousepad and the computer came to life. 'There's an easy way to rule him out... do you know what else runners do?' he added.

'Wear out their cartilage?'

'Statistics. We're obsessed with routes and lap times. That's why these watches have GPS.'

Primakov opened a screen on the laptop. 'Aksarin's already logged in. On the first entry you can see he went running today at 3:24 p.m.'

'That was just after he called me.'

'Now if I click on the link it'll show the route he took. Wait' – Primakov tapped on the entry – 'Yes... he did a loop of the minister's mansion.'

She looked at a map on the screen with its electric-blue line marking Aksarin's route on the property's perimeter path.

'He's pretty good,' said Primakov. 'Four minutes thirty-five a kilometre. That's winter conditions too.'

'Don't waste time, Leo, he'll be back soon. We need the evening of the fifth of January or the following morning.'

'Sorry.' He tapped the built-in mouse to return to the previous screen. 'He's even more obsessed than me. There are hundreds of routes.' He clicked on a tab at the bottom to open another page.

She looked out of the gatehouse windows. To her left was the *banya* building and the huge green-tiled house. She could make out the beam of a torch bobbing between them. A security light was triggered and she saw Aksarin on a snow-edged path, a canvas bag slung over his shoulder. He raised an arm in greeting.

She waved back. 'Leo, quick, he's coming.'

'I'm trying, Captain. The connection is poor.'

She heard the main door open.

'Leo,' she hissed.

'Captain, I've found something at 9:32 – the morning Oleg found his car.'

Aksarin appeared in the doorway. 'What are you doing?'

Natalya pushed herself off the radiator, suddenly uncomfortable in the confided space. Primakov clicked on the link.

'Captain.' Primakov's head jerked, his eyes imploring her to look. She glanced at the screen. An electric blue-line ran from the Toksovo bus station to the front gates of Chubarov's mansion.

'Stay there!' she yelled.

Aksarin drew an ancient, wooden-handled Nagant revolver from behind the canvas bag. He still had the P-96 pistol on his belt too. In that instant she realised he was going to kill them. Policemen knew not to fire a weapon that came with the job – bullets were accounted for – and Aksarin was an ex-*ment*.

CHAPTER 49

'Put your hands on your heads and lean over the desk,' he ordered.

They did as they were told. Aksarin patted her pockets, removing her phone, then ran his hands along the length of Primakov's nylon over-suit.

'Neither of you brought a gun – that was stupid,' Aksarin said.

Dostoynov had been right all along; she'd been blindsided into thinking the Decembrists had been killed by one of their targets.

'You lied about the clothes,' she said.

'You catch on quick, *ment*. There were no clothes… I always burn them when I'm finished. And I don't like blood, I prefer to use my hands.'

'The rota – was that a lie?' she asked.

'Guilty,' said Aksarin. 'I live here when the minister is away – fresh faces make him nervous.'

His eyes flicked to the door. 'Let's go outside. I'm ex-OMON so don't think of fucking with me.'

He pressed a button below the light switch. Outside, there was a sound of grinding metal as the main gates opened.

'You first, then her.'

Primakov shuffled in front of her, dragging his feet as if he expected a bullet any second. It was her fault for bringing him there. Most of all, though, she blamed Dostoynov – he had hindered her investigation from the start and made her take unacceptable risks. The Nagant tracked her as she stepped out of the gatehouse.

'Who was this woman on the drone video?' she asked. 'A *prostitutka*?'

'You're kidding me, right?' Aksarin said. 'Those bitches have a *svodnik* with a blade keeping watch.'

She turned to see his face. 'Who was she, then?'

His face was expressionless. 'A boring fuck by the name of Masha Gogoleva. Seventeen years old. I found her outside Obvodny Canal Bus Station. Fresh from the East with no idea where she was going. Little Masha couldn't believe her luck when I showed her a few pictures of

Chubarov's place. She was a screamer though… stupid bitch believed someone would hear her if she made enough noise.'

'Why was she running?'

'She was scared of her shadow. I prefer the ones with spirit. I let her escape, then we played chase… that got her excited all right. I'd got her to the *banya* when I heard that fucking drone. Once it had gone, I found her in there, hiding in a cupboard.'

Aksarin stepped out of the guardhouse and jerked the Nagant in the direction of her Volvo beyond the open gates. 'Those country girls get worse than me. Most of the time a *svodnik* finds them and they're hooked on salts, fucking twenty men a day in a basement.'

'So you were their knight on a white horse… I haven't heard that one before. You said you always burn their clothes. How many others are there?' She tried to keep the disgust out of her voice.

'Masha wasn't my first,' Aksarin said, 'and that woman with her *boyskaut* boyfriend won't be my last.'

'Max Timchenko and Elizaveta Kalinina?' she said.

'I mean nosey bastards thinking I was going to answer their questions. She flirted with me at the gate and said she was interested in the house. After that her boyfriend turned up and started testing me. When he asked about this naked girl he'd seen I knew they were the ones with the drone. I let them in. He thought Chubarov was having an affair with Masha, or orgies, or some shit. He had plans, he was going to make an internet film – I couldn't let that happen.'

'So you killed them.'

'I was repairing a window, so I used a hammer on him.' His eyes dropped to the Nagant. 'I wasn't expecting visitors – not like now.'

'But you didn't kill Elizaveta that way?'

'I needed her to talk. I had to know where they kept the drone film.'

CHAPTER 49

She dreaded to think of Elizaveta's terror in her final few moments of her life. The pathologist had said she'd been suffocated. 'What did you do to her?'

'All in good time, *ment*... where are your keys?'

'In the ignition.'

Aksarin put the Nagant to Primakov's temple. 'You... get in the back.'

Primakov was shaking. 'I left a note at my office saying I was coming here.'

'Right,' Aksarin said, 'and the Patriarch mentions me in his nightly prayers.'

'Were you saving girls before you came here?' she asked.

'Persistent *ment*, aren't you?' He tipped his *ushanka* to her. 'I'll give you that. I started in Chechnya. Plenty of things done to girls over there that were worse than me finding them.'

'Where else?' she said.

'You want to know how many I've killed? Frontline gave me jobs all over the Oblast. Oligarchs, ministers, *siloviki*... I've worked for them all.'

Natalya had to hand it to him. It was a brilliant move. 'And you knew you were safe because any sensible *ment* would keep well away.'

'I left a girl or two in each one... sometimes three, depending how long I was based there.'

'Who did you work for?' she asked.

Aksarin tapped his nose. 'This isn't an episode of *What? Where? When?* I'm not naming names, *ment*.' He aimed the Nagant at Primakov. 'I thought I told you to get in.'

Primakov climbed onto the back seat of the Volvo and reached for his seatbelt. He did it deliberately slowly and gave her a curious look. She guessed what it meant: between them they could crash the car and have a fighting chance of escape. The airbags might not work either – she could release the buckle on Aksarin's seatbelt at the moment of impact.

'I saw that look,' Aksarin said. 'So now I can't trust either of you. Well, I've got an announcement.'

He squeezed the trigger; the echo of the shot drowned by Primakov's shriek. Aksarin fired again. This time, after the echo there was silence.

50

An animal wail filled the night, primeval in its pain. Natalya's hands found her mouth. The noise was coming from her.

'Shut up unless you want the same.'

Blood pounded at her temples. Her mouth was dry. Primakov was still, the wounds hidden by his over-suit and the weak interior lights. She felt shame at her cowardice. If he wasn't dead already, he was dying while she did nothing.

'There's a first-aid kit in the boot. Please let me get it.'

'Why?' Aksarin said. 'He'll be dead soon enough.'

'Are you going to kill me too?'

'Not yet.'

She drew back her fist to drive it into the gristle of Aksarin's broken nose. He blocked her arm easily, as if defending himself from a child. He hesitated, then drove the hand with the Nagant into the side of her head. She was at his feet, knocked half-senseless. She tried to dispel the dizziness, the ringing in her ears. The P-96 was on his belt. If she could stretch an arm, unclip the leather stud, get the pistol— Her fingers darted for the clip. She was stopped by an explosion – a bullet blasted into the night.

Aksarin levelled the Nagant at her head. 'That was a warning, *ment*.'

'I've met selfish pricks like you before.' She imitated Aksarin's nasal whine, 'Those girls, I was saving them.'

'You want me to kill you now, is that it?'

She stood, still reeling from the blow. 'You shot my friend.'

'Do I look like I care? Get in the back with him. Try anything again and I'll put a bullet in your face – and not the kind that will kill. Understand?'

'Yes.'

Aksarin put his canvas bag on the passenger seat to start the car.

She climbed in the back. Primakov was curled on his side and she had to squeeze along the footwell. His face was shiny with sweat, his eyes open. She looked to his raised leg and the blood spreading around his right thigh, trapped under the nylon. She checked his body, looking for another tear in his flesh, then saw a neat hole in the seat – one of the bullets had missed.

His face was pale. 'Leo, can you hear me?'

His head shifted in an almost imperceptible nod that left her wondering if it had been intentional.

She leant over him to root through the discarded rubbish on the floor.

Aksarin tilted the rear-view mirror. 'What are you doing?'

She sat back and held up an empty crisp packet and an old *Podorozhnik* card for the Metro.

'First aid.'

'You're wasting your time, *ment*.'

She unzipped the over-suit and undid the fastening of his trousers, forcing the *Podorozhnik* card down his thigh to cover the entrance wound. She found the exit in the back of his jeans and pushed her hand to cover it with the crisp packet. She removed her scarf and threaded it around his leg, then pulled the ends of the scarf taut and tied them together. She kissed him on the cheek. 'We'll get through this,' she whispered.

At the tarmacked road, Aksarin took a right. They weren't going back to Oselki. He was taking them north.

'Where are we going?'

Aksarin was silent.

CHAPTER 50

The Volvo joined the main highway. It caught a chunk of ice and lurched, rocking her head against the rear of the front passenger seat.

'Where are we going?' she asked again.

'Just shut up.'

'You're taking us for a ride… like you did with Elizaveta and Max?'

'Like that.'

She caressed Primakov's pale cheek, smudging it red.

'Elizaveta had a two-year-old son. Max had a twin sister and a brother.'

Aksarin snorted. 'Then they should have thought of them first.'

'You said you weren't going to kill me yet… What do you need? I'll give it to you.'

'When I made that bitch talk, she told me she didn't have the drone film. She gave a name: Gregor Bortsov. I tried my old contacts in OMON. They all wanted to find the bastard too. No one knew where he was hiding.'

'I don't know where he is.'

'That's all right. I know Bortsov doesn't have the film any more. You do.'

She'd given it to Vita. She would die before giving the girl up. Whatever Aksarin used on Elizaveta wouldn't work on her.

'I don't have it,' she said.

His eyes narrowed at hers in the mirror. 'I know you're lying. You've seen the recording, and I don't believe for a second you gave it back to Bortsov.'

'I don't care what you believe. I don't have it.'

'I was hoping you would say that.'

How much time had passed? An hour? To her right, unseen, was the massive Lake Ladoga which ran from the east of the city almost to the Finnish border. It was snowing and Aksarin stared ahead as the wipers smeared and screeched, doing little for her nerves. Her Volvo barely held the road and she thought of throwing her body into him, except she was more likely to get shot for her trouble. And if Primakov was alive, crashing the car was hardly going to improve his chances.

He kept to the Sortavala Highway, the road bordered by snow-laden pines. It curved to the right, then he turned onto a rough track. The Volvo skidded on frozen earth.

'Where are we going?' she asked.

'Persistent little bitch. I'm going to bury you and I'll leave your fingerprints on the gun and your dead friend in your shitty car. Before that, you're going to talk.'

'You don't need to make me. I'll tell you what you want.'

'That's all right' – he patted the canvas bag – 'I brought my own lie detector.'

The Volvo skidded to a halt. He turned off the ignition. They faced a white landscape dotted with trees.

'How many have you killed, Aksarin?'

'Man is wolf to man, that's what I learnt in Chechnya. You prey on others or else you're prey. Life doesn't mean shit.'

'Women?' she asked.

'Always women. Except for the *boyskaut* and your friend.'

'Did you rape them? I hate to think their last moment of life was wasted staring at your ugly face.'

'Just for that I'll take longer. You'll beg me to kill you.' He grabbed his canvas bag from the passenger seat and climbed out. 'Come with me, *ment*.'

The scarf on Primakov's thigh had become slack; she tightened it again and took a last look at him. His face had grown pale since the journey's start. She wondered which of them would outlast the other.

Aksarin pulled open her door. 'Now.'

CHAPTER 50

She climbed out while Aksarin took out a torch from his bag. He aimed the beam at a line of churned-up snow cutting through a drift. 'Start walking.'

Despite his size, Aksarin was careful, keeping a body-length behind her. Her boots scuffed on the ground. The snow either side was at hip height – even if she tried to run, she would cover less than a metre before being shot. Her bravado was gone. She would do what she needed to survive.

In the forests beyond the field, a wolf howled a keening, lonely cry. Ten seconds later two more joined in, letting the stray know where the pack was. She thought of Dostoynov calling her a black wolf. He was full of shit.

'My friend Leo – the one you shot – there really will be a note in his desk drawer for his colleagues to find. He's the fastidious type.'

'And you think someone will ask the minister about it? No one will come.'

They had crossed to a tree line. Someone had been there recently, ploughing up the pristine covering.

'Stop here,' he said.

Aksarin inserted a hand into the canvas bag and drew it out with deliberate slowness. His fingers had curled around an olive-green cylinder attached to a corrugated rubber hose.

'We were both *menti*. You know what's coming.'

She felt sick. After the hose would come a white, tight-fitting, rubber hood. An old Soviet gas mask they called *slonik* – little elephant – because the corrugated rubber hose looked like a trunk. In her old station there had been one in the store cupboard as a reminder of the bad old days when it was brought out to extract a confession. At the start of her shifts she sometimes found the mask had moved overnight – the bad old days that never went away. She thought back to the items Primakov had listed when she'd told him about the asbestos in Elizaveta's lungs: insulation, vehicle brakes, vehicle clutches… filters.

'The filter in your mask has ruptured.'

Aksarin mouth-shrugged. 'I've never had a complaint about it… kneel before I shoot you in the legs.'

She didn't move in time. He grabbed the collar of her coat and dragged her through the snow.

'This *slonik* is from my old regiment,' he said. 'After it, people confessed to any old shit. But that was fine' – he let out a laugh – 'we never cared if they were guilty or not.'

He ripped off her hat and threw it to the ground. Another mystery solved, she thought: Elizaveta had been missing a hat too.

Natalya was twisting one way, then another. 'Stay still, bitch.'

He gripped her head between his knees and forced the mask over. The rubber – meant for army men with shaved scalps – ripped out her hair.

Then it was on.

She stared out through the thick glass eyeholes and tried not inhale; tried not to suck in the asbestos.

'Please,' she said, the sound of her breath magnified in the mask. It hissed through the green-painted filter at the end of the trunk.

He tapped his head. 'I was forgetting something.' He reached into the canvas bag and drew out a roll of duct tape. He tore off a strip then yanked her wrists behind her back and tied them together.

She exhaled the last of her breath to speak. 'What do you want from me?' It came out as muffled but Aksarin brought his head to hers – he had understood.

'In Chechnya, I was always looking for confessions. Local men collaborating with terrorists. Women hiding snipers. Old babushkas holding onto their jewellery. A girl holding onto her *kisku*. I took them to death, then brought them all the way back. I did it all night. I was a fucking expert at it. Nobody kept anything from me.'

She felt the carbon dioxide's acid burn in her blood. A piece of paper from Dr Fedyushina's office floated in her mind – the chemical formula of suffocation.

'You're keen, already holding your breath.'

She thought of Leo in the back of her car and felt a fresh surge of anger. This pathetic *piz'da* was going to take away his life if she failed. And how many more women would he go on to kill? And she would fail. There was no way out of this. Mikhail would rot in prison and she would rot in the ground.

A tremor became a shake. The shake became unstoppable. She tried to suck in a tiny portion of the dusty air, just enough to keep her alive. Her lungs disobeyed and greedily reflated. She coughed, tasting powder on her tongue. On her next breath she didn't care about the asbestos. Staying alive one minute at a time was all that mattered.

Aksarin knelt beside her, coming into view of the mask's eyeholes. He tore off a twenty-centimetre strip of the tape with his teeth then wrapped it over the filter's air inlet, sealing her breath inside her lungs. Aksarin's mouth moved. She tried to focus in case he was asking a question. Had he already asked it? The rubber of the hood dulled his voice and the glass eyeholes misted.

Another wolf howled in the night. It was closer than the last – perhaps the pack joining for a hunt. She laughed at the hopelessness of her situation.

'Where is it?' Aksarin asked.

'The wolf?' she thought. It took her a moment to remember. No, there was only one thing he wanted: the location of the micro-SD card.

'Suv…'

She had tried to speak but there was no space to exhale. Aksarin tore off the tape. The air left her. Her lungs deflated, then filled. They pumped automatically. She could breathe again. There was a swarm of bees in her oxygen-starved brain, powder on her tongue and at the back of her throat. She pulled in the air as fast as the filter would allow. It was sweet. She pretended the dust was icing sugar. The buzzing in her head subsided. She greedily drew in another breath.

'Where?' he asked again.

'Suvorovsky Prospekt,' she slurred, her brain still sluggish, 'number 55 to 57.'

'Police headquarters, I suppose.'

'Evidence room,' she said.

'You're lying. When I gave that Decembrist bitch the *slonik* treatment she told me what was on the memory card. All those fancy houses. That shit could get a *ment* in a lot of trouble. Only an idiot would log it as evidence.'

Aksarin tore off a fresh strip of tape and wrapped it around the filter. Her brain began to ache and her body burned as her blood turned to acid. Water vapour covered the glass eyeholes, obscuring her vision. The tremor was returning. She was hallucinating now. Beyond Aksarin she had seen a black shape jump above the height of the drift. It was sleek, doglike.

51

Her vision had a red aura. She made out the shape again, black as the night sky, half submerged by the snow, its tail twitching like a field radio antenna, working its way through the drift.

Natalya staggered to her feet. The movement caused the black wolf to change direction. It had been going for Aksarin. Now the tail turned to her like a shark fin in water.

'Oh fuck,' she mouthed.

Was she breathing? She wasn't sure. How long had they been there? A second? A minute? She couldn't begin to guess. She tried to exhale. Something had been on her mind just now. A black wolf – Dostoynov's imaginary creature. But this one was real: it was clear of the drift and growling a metre away. Aksarin had his gun out but he couldn't shoot it without hitting her. He didn't want to kill her – not yet. She needed to talk.

To a wolf she was a strange sight. A creature with giant glass eyes, no arms, and an elephant's trunk. She tried to breathe out. Her lungs cramped. She took a step back and felt herself fall as the ground opened beneath her. She was in a coffin-shaped hole. Above her, against the black sky, a faded red ribbon swayed in the breeze.

Aksarin fired his gun as the wolf leapt after her. She felt its weight on her chest. Pinning her down, snarling, snapping. The wolf was unharmed – his bullet had missed.

A macabre thought came to her: 'Comrade Wolf knows whom to eat.' There was no sense in bleating.

She tossed her head from side to side, flailing the rubber hose in its face. 'Come on, doggy!'

The wolf growled then lunged, clamping its teeth on the hose. She reared her head and then threw it back. The wolf shifted to improve its grip. It chewed on the rubber, centimetres from her throat.

A breath gasped out of her aching lungs. Her shoulders cramped; the arms twisted behind her. She drew in a thin, sweet stream of air – it had made a hole but it wasn't enough. She twisted her head to keep the wolf interested in the hose, then heard a man shout. The wolf dug its legs into her body and leapt out of the grave.

Her vision was speckled, a million diamonds dancing in the sky. Her brain was dying. She barely had the strength to wedge the filter between her thighs, and pull. The corrugated hose extended easily and she felt a wave of despair. She exhaled a wheeze as ancient as Solomon's last breath. She could no longer see – her vision distorted by an explosion of lights. She crouched in the grave until the metal filter dangled at her feet. She stepped on it with both boots and rolled onto her back. A second went by. She was passing out. She straightened again. The hose stretched and went taut. The mask tore at her hair. Her legs fully extended. She arched her back and the mask flew off.

Her head cleared slowly. She took a deep lungful of air and watched her breath turn to steam. The sky was black again. The red ribbon above reminded her why she was there. Aksarin had been strangely silent. She peered over the covering of snow to see him five metres away, the Nagant pressed against his right leg, his arm straightened. He was turned away from her, hiding his gun from someone to his left.

She followed the direction of his gaze. At the tree line a figure in camouflage fatigues had a rifle looped over his shoulder. Smoke from Dmitry Morozov's rough tobacco wafted in the air. She threw her body over the edge of the grave, wriggling to get clear of the stone-hard wall of frozen mud. She squirmed to get her legs over and lay panting on the surface, pulling in the icy air.

'Dmitry Nikolayevich,' she called out to the gamekeeper, then gulped down another breath. 'He has a gun.'

Morozov nodded, as if he'd suspected as much. By his side was the black wolf: a Chyornye Terrier, a mound of matted fur reaching to the gamekeeper's waist.

'How long has it been, Viktor? Three years?' Morozov called out to Aksarin. 'What are you doing here?'

'I found her sneaking around my new place,' said Aksarin.

'So you brought her here?' Morozov replied. 'That was unkind. We don't appreciate unexpected guests.'

Beyond Morozov, Natalya saw a grey fur half-hidden by a Norway spruce. A wolf, she thought – then saw a tiny orange glow. The glow floated in the air and lowered: a cigarette. A woman's flat voice came from behind the spruce. 'Dmitry Nikolayevich, who are they?'

'His name is Viktor Aksarin,' Morozov said. 'He used to work on security here. She is Captain Natalya Ivanova of the Criminal Investigations Directorate.'

The woman stepped out: severe, fifties; a sable fur with a flash of thick blue pyjamas over snow boots. She'd seen her a few times in court: Prosecutor Kira Shulgin.

'And what are you doing on my property?' Shulgin asked.

Natalya coughed, tasted powder on her tongue, and spat it onto the snow. She turned so Shulgin could see the tape binding her wrists. 'He brought me here to kill me.'

'She's talking out of her *zhopa*,' Aksarin said. 'I only meant to leave her here. I work for Minister Chubarov now. You know me, Dmitry Nikolayevich. I'm discreet. But this one' – he jerked his left hand at

Natalya – 'she's been bothering us and she's not even a *ment* anymore. Her colonel thought she was picking at garbage.'

'Is that true?' Shulgin asked.

'He's not lying,' said Morozov. 'Aksarin works for a security company called Frontline. They looked after the lodge back when Roman Agrashov was the owner.'

'If that's so, why have you brought her here?' asked Shulgin, drawing her fur coat around her.

Aksarin had no answer. He dropped into the snow for cover and fired the Nagant at Morozov. The gamekeeper twisted and fell, disappearing in the drift. Natalya waded through snow to reach him. The Nagant fired again, missing her.

A red bloom had spread through the chest of Morozov's jacket. 'I'm all right,' he said, brushing her away.

She went for his rifle, but Aksarin had already made up the distance.

'*Druzhok*… get the wolf,' Morozov said, his voice already feeble.

The Chyornye Terrier turned to her and growled.

Morozov pointed at Aksarin. '*Ne ona*.' Not her.

Aksarin levelled the Nagant as a blur of black terrier leapt for his arm. He staggered with the weight of the huge dog but he kept his grip on the revolver and fired. She thought the bullet had struck the terrier, then heard Morozov cry out.

She took the rifle while the dog tore at Aksarin. The weapon was as archaic as Aksarin's Nagant and she fiddled with it, looking for the safety. She flicked a tiny lever, saw a painted red dot, aimed it at Aksarin's head and squeezed the trigger. She was surprised when it fired. Aksarin dropped to the ground and the crack of the bullet carried long into the forest.

Dmitry Morozov had been in a bad way before the second shot. Now, the Chyornye Terrier nuzzled his face, trying to provoke a reaction.

CHAPTER 51

The dog growled when she pushed it aside to check for a pulse. It was then she saw the lake of blood underneath the old gamekeeper.

Kira Shulgin came out from behind the spruce. 'Is he dead?'

'Yes,' Natalya said, looping the rifle over her shoulder.

'*Druzhok*,' Natalya called out to the dog. The terrier looked up and she patted her thigh. 'Come on, boy.'

The dog hesitated, then lumbered towards her, its shaggy mane soaked from the snow.

52

Natalya returned to her Volvo with Shulgin. She opened the back doors to check on Primakov. He was corpse-white, lying in pooled blood.

'Not an artery,' said Shulgin. 'Or he'd be dead already.'

'Can you call an ambulance?' Natalya asked.

The prosecutor hesitated.

'If you don't, he'll die,' said Natalya. 'And I'm not going to let that happen. Call an ambulance. Now.'

Shulgin took out her phone and dialled the emergency services.

The Volvo kicked up gravel as it skidded into the grounds of the hunting lodge. Shulgin helped her to drag out Primakov, then – with each of them draping an arm over their shoulders – brought him to an ante room decorated with the heads of bears, wolves and deer. Crystal glasses and china were brushed away to make space as they laid him on an oiled wooden table.

Shulgin left while Natalya stuffed silk-embroidered cushions under Primakov's thigh. 'Stay with me, Leo,' she said. 'Think of Jaap.'

'I found this.' Shulgin returned, holding a small suitcase with a green cross. 'It came with the house… for hunting injuries.'

Natalya took it. She opened the case and took out a bottle of sterilising fluid.

'You do this sort of thing often?' Shulgin asked.

'More often than I like… guns scare the shit out of me.'

CHAPTER 52

Shulgin removed the *Podorozhnik* card from Primakov's thigh and cleaned the entry wound.

'Perhaps now you can tell me what that was all about,' said the prosecutor. 'I was fond of Dmitry,' she added, as if he'd been a favourite pet.

'The security guard – Aksarin – has been killing teenage girls. He's been doing it a long time,' Natalya said.

'Why did he bring you here?'

'To kill me.'

'But why here?' Shulgin asked. 'We're two hours from Piter.'

Natalya thought of scraping her shins on the iron-hard mud near Elizaveta's body, then of Kuzmolovsky Cemetery, where extra graves were dug in summer when the ground was soft.

'Aksarin came here last year and dug a pit. He was planning to bury some poor girl in it, then I got in his way and he decided to use it for me instead.'

'But why here?'

'Aksarin worked security for the previous owner. He knows the area. And of course he buried Diana Maricheva here six years ago.'

'Who?' Shulgin snapped.

'You don't need to pretend,' Natalya said. 'After Dmitry Nikolayevich found her body you told him move her to the Chapel of Saint Nicholas on Konevets Island.'

'How do you know this?' Shulgin asked.

'Because Dmitry's ex-wife hated him, and I'm married to Major Ivanov.'

Shulgin said, 'You're married to Major Ivanov?'

She didn't appreciate the note of disbelief in the prosecutor's voice. 'Yes.'

'The girl needed a Christian burial,' Shulgin said eventually. 'I would never have slept if I'd left her out there in the cold.'

That was the problem with corruption, thought Natalya. It put temptation in front of people who would otherwise have been decent.

'Despite being a piece of filth,' Shulgin said, 'that security guard had a point. How do I know you won't talk?'

'If you think I'm going to be quiet, you're mistaken. Aksarin has left victims all over Leningrad Oblast. When I tell the police—'

'They won't believe you.'

'Except they will, because you've got two dead men in a field and an expert criminalist with a bullet in his leg.'

'Then we are at an impasse,' Shulgin said. 'That guard said he worked for Minister Chubarov. I knew Chubarov in the 1990s – he has a colourful past. Let's say he's not the kind of man to leave his brass knuckles at home.'

'Wait,' Natalya said, 'before we start the threats, do you have a contact in the FSB, someone senior?'

'I'm owed a few favours,' said Shulgin.

'Good, give them a call. I need to track down one of their officers.'

Natalya had cleaned Primakov's wound and bandaged it when Shulgin returned. She was taken to the main hall: an apartment-block-sized mass of varnished wood and oil lanterns. Shulgin pointed to a studded leather chair with an old-fashioned dial telephone on a small table. The phone's receiver was off the cradle.

'There is a call waiting for you,' Shulgin said, then left the room.

Natalya picked up the receiver. 'Margarita, it's lovely to hear from you.'

'Ivanova, you're as funny as Ebolapox. What can I do for you?'

'My husband, Misha, is facing corruption charges and I've been fired.'

'I'm sorry to hear that, Ivanova. For once, your life is more exciting than mine. I'm watching *Interns* on TV and thinking about going to bed. Before I go, however, can you explain how you persuaded an FSB colonel to call me at home?'

CHAPTER 52

She avoided the question. 'I want to do you a favour, Margarita.'

'I wish you'd stop calling me that... and I prefer hard currency when it comes to favours.'

'I shot a man this evening.'

'Dead?'

'Very.'

'All right, now I'm mildly interested. Are you going to prison too? Maybe they'll put you and your husband together in a special cell.'

'The man I shot is a security guard called Viktor Aksarin. He has been killing girls and burying them at the places he works. Margarita, you need to contact his company, Frontline. I'm a civilian now, no one will listen to me.'

'Are you on medication? I don't need to do anything.'

'Minister Chubarov is one of their clients,' Natalya said.

'This conversation is too rich for me. For your sake I'll pretend we never spoke.'

She'd hoped Margarita would be more receptive. Now she had to betray the Decembrists – the cause Max and Elizaveta had died for.

'Contact the owners tonight,' she said, 'and you'll have a lot of grateful rich people.'

'All right, I'm pretending to listen,' said Belikova.

'The Decembrists are about to expose the real owners of the properties missing from the official register, if you get my meaning.'

'What's this got to do with the security guard?'

'A lot of them will be Frontline clients and they'll be distressed to hear Aksarin has been leaving bodies behind in the grounds of their fancy houses.'

'And how will they know that?'

'Because I'll go to the press if the police won't listen.'

'They'll kill you for it.'

'Not if we do it my way. You have the power to avert a scandal.'

'And what do you get out of this?' Margarita Belikova asked.

'I get my life back,' Natalya said.

An hour later, an ambulance arrived for Primakov. Natalya helped the crew load him onto a stretcher and watched until it was out of sight. Inside the lodge she found Kira Shulgin removing logs from a dainty silver handcart and stacking them next to a fireplace the size of her Volvo.

She stepped onto a rug with a motif of some lordling chasing a bear stuck with arrows. She imagined it cost more than her apartment.

'My grandfather lived here,' said Shulgin. 'Much like Dmitry did. He worked as a steward serving brandy and cigars to the party higher-ups in the 1960s. He used to tell me about the banned books they kept on the shelves, the movies they watched from the decadent West... the night butterflies bussed in when the wives were away. He'd got the job by being a loyal member. It sickened him to see how rotten the party was at the top. Buying the lodge was my revenge for him... I've made him the equal of all those *apparatchiks* he used to serve.'

'Do you think he would have approved of how you bought it?'

'No, it would have shamed him.'

Shulgin continued stacking logs. 'Your FSB friend – Major Belikova – called again.'

'What did she say?'

'She told me this problem of ours went all the way to the top. I've been given twenty-four hours to sign over the lodge to a man who made his money selling household cleaning products. Tomorrow the property will be in the public register, backdated to prove he's had it for years. The FSB have the list of owners from Frontline. They are all being told the same, even Minister Chubarov.'

'You've got somewhere else to go?' Natalya asked.

CHAPTER 52

'I have a place in Lomonosov,' Shulgin said. 'Don't misunderstand – the ownership change is on paper only. Once the police and press have finished, I'll return.'

'Was I mentioned in this phone call?' Natalya asked.

'Your Lieutenant Colonel has been ordered to reinstate you with all rank privileges. You will resume your investigation into Aksarin's killings.'

'And Major Ivanov?'

'Minister Chubarov has spoken with the chairman—'

'Of *Sledkom*?'

Shulgin tapped her foot irritably. 'Of course. Who did you think? Once your husband has agreed to pay restitution, all charges will be dropped.'

So Mikhail's secret bribe would line the pockets of Ilya Yelin and all the other *Sledkom* investigators who had helped to put him away. It was karma, she supposed – Mikhail had acquired it by doing much the same thing.

Shulgin glanced up from the rug as if an afterthought had occurred to her. 'Unfortunately, Major Belikova informed me your superior, Lieutenant Colonel Dostoynov – a disagreeable man, has refused to accommodate your husband. I was forced to call in some favours. I've found a new role for him.

'Where?'

'*Sledkom*.'

'He'll turn it down.'

'He has already accepted.' Shulgin flicked her eyebrows as if to say, 'How well do you know your husband?'

'Thank you for doing that.'

Shulgin looked at her with contempt. 'It's purely self-interest, I assure you. When we meet again, I won't be in your debt. And Captain, when you write that report on Aksarin's crimes, my name will not be in it.'

53

March

They left Ploshchad Lenina Metro station. The sky was grey and the pavements saturated with water from melted snow. Outside, Natalya saw a 2018 presidential election poster. It featured a picture of Peter the Great's statue on its plinth alongside the text, 'For a strong Russia, vote Putin'. Two men on ladders held a bucket of paste as they covered it with fresh paper strips for a Nissan advertisement.

'Eighteen billion roubles wasted,' Vita said, 'to persuade 110 million people that they don't live in a dictatorship.' She shook her head in disgust.

'Yeah, what a waste,' Anton said, although Natalya knew for a fact that he had voted for Ksenia Sobchak, the Civic Initiative candidate.

They stopped outside the decaying brick wall of SIZO-4. Vita and Anton were holding hands. She was surprised they were still together; surprised, but far from disappointed.

After a long wait, Mikhail shuffled through a black painted metal door, escorted by two prison guards. She was shocked by how frail he looked.

'You don't smell the same,' she said.

'I'm not the same,' he replied.

She kissed him lightly on the lips and the four of them walked towards the slate grey Neva.

'Natasha is famous,' Anton said, striking up a conversation.

'I heard,' said Mikhail. 'How many girls have you found now?'

She hadn't wanted to speak about it in front of Vita. 'Eight so far. Some of the estates are huge. We're still looking for ribbons.'

CHAPTER 53

Mikhail and Anton took out cigarettes.

'Vita,' Natalya said quietly, 'do you have a moment?'

They slowed under the pretext of avoiding the men's smoke.

'That bag I gave you with the addresses and the drone footage—'

'It was useless,' said Vita. 'Max had got some of the names wrong. Gregor and I went through them. Even the house where he was murdered didn't belong to Minister Chubarov. Some IT billionaire owned it. We couldn't trust what he'd done.' Vita sniffed, stifling a tear. 'I wanted it to be a tribute to him.'

'You can,' said Natalya.

Vita stopped. 'What?'

'The properties where Max, Elizaveta, and the girls were killed – the records were changed to protect the owners. It's a sham. I made a deal with them to get Mikhail out of prison.'

She was too ashamed to admit that getting her job back had been part of the bargain.

Vita stared at her for a while, unable to speak. Natalya could sense the anger building inside the young woman.

'You betrayed us?' Vita asked, managing to keep her emotions in check.

'Yes,' said Natalya. 'And now Mikhail is free I can tell you the truth. Max was right all along. You can still make the film.'

A storm drain flooded the pavement and they crossed the road.

'Do it for them,' she called out to Vita.

Acknowledgements

For her wise words and gentle steering, I owe a debt of gratitude – and wine – to my fine agent, Kate Hordern of KHLA. Special thanks must go to the team at Mirror Books (Paula Scott, Jo Sollis, Fergus McKenna, Simon Flavin, Cynthia Hamilton, Mel Sambells, Julie Adams & George Robarts) because these things really are a team effort. Charlie Maynard deserves a mention too for his skilful debugging of my manuscripts. I'm obliged to mention Corinne-Anne Richards, who is ready Annie Wilkes-style should I kill off her favourite characters. Last – and not least or else I'll be in trouble – I'd like to thank my wife, Jenny, for being a superb reader and critic.

Notes

In BLACK WOLF the Decembrists were not created entirely 'from the right side of my brain', as an artist friend refers to his imagination when asked for the source of his inspiration. In large part, the Decembrists' actions came from the works of the anarchist art collective Voina.

In 2010, Voina created their most famous piece, 'Dick Captured by the FSB', a 65-metre penis whitewashed on Liteyny Bridge in just 23 seconds after the barriers went up. As the drawbridge raised, a giant erect phallus filled the skyline facing the city's secret police headquarters. That same year, Voina released thousands of giant Madagascan cockroaches into Moscow's Taganskiy District Court to disrupt the trial of two men who had organised a controversial arts exhibition.

Soon Voina's artistic pranks escalated. Several police cars were overturned while officers slept inside. And it was members of Voina armed with Molotov cocktails – not Gregor – who destroyed a police riot truck in St. Petersburg's Petrograd District.

For the authorities, slow to react at first, the group had finally crossed a line. They targeted members of Voina, then Pussy Riot (Pussy Riot – a Voina splinter group – took off as Voina's activities waned). Sledkom raided apartments, fines were imposed for vandalism, there were claims of police beatings, a child taken into state care, imprisonment (the British artist, Banksy, raised £80,000 for their bail money), exile, and even a poisoning by what appears to have been a nerve agent.

Another inspiration for BLACK WOLF is Alexei Navalny, the lawyer turned opposition activist. On top of Navalny's main political activities, he hosts an entertaining YouTube channel exposing 'the crooks and thieves' at the heart of the Russian establishment. The most fascinating – to my mind at least – are the shows where he reveals the extravagant properties belonging to the nation's supposedly modestly salaried government workers.

Also by Mirror Books

Motherland

G.D. Abson

The first in a gripping series of contemporary crime novels set in St Petersburg, featuring the brilliant and principled policewoman, Captain Natalya Ivanova.

Student Zena Dahl, the daughter of a Swedish millionaire, has gone missing in St Petersburg (or Piter as the city is known locally) after a night out with a friend. Captain Natalya Ivanova is assigned to the case. It makes a change from her usual fare of domestic violence work, however, because of the family's wealth and profile, there's a lot of pressure on her for a quick result.

But as Natalya investigates, she discovers that the case is not as straightforward as it first seemed. Dark, evocative, violent and insightful, MOTHERLAND twists and turns to a satisfyingly dramatic conclusion.

Also by Mirror Books

UNREST

Jesper Stien

An unidentified man is found murdered in a Copenhagen cemetery, his hooded corpse propped up against a gravestone.

Rogue camera footage suggests police involvement, and Detective Axel Steen links the murder to the demolition of a nearby youth house teeming with militant left-wing radicals. But Axel soon discovers that many people, both inside and out of the force, have an unusual interest in the case – and in preventing its resolution.

With a rapidly worsening heart condition, an estranged ex-wife and beloved five-year-old daughter to grapple with, Axel will not stop until the killer is caught, whatever the consequences. But the consequences turn out to be greater than expected – especially for Axel himself.